The Rise of The Mad March

also by
robert espenscheid, jr.

The Jackass Alliance 2011

Shiloh Firefly 2012

Magic City 2019

The Sentinel Papers 2022

The Rise of
The Mad March

Robert Espenscheid, Jr.

Published by

Stoney Creek Publishing Group

StoneyCreekPublishing.com

Copyright © 2025 by Robert Espenscheid, Jr. All rights reserved.

ISBN: 978-1-965766-10-1
ISBN (ebook): 978-1-965766-08-8
Library of Congress Control Number: 2025900385

No part of this book may be reproduced in any form or by any electronic or mechanical means, including information storage and retrieval systems, without written permission from the author, except for the use of brief quotations in a book review.

This book is a work of fiction. Names, characters, places, and incidents are either the product of the author's imagination or are used fictitiously, and any resemblance to actual persons, living or dead, business establishments, events or locales is entirely coincidental.

Cover design by Adrienne Smith

Printed in the United States

contents

Narrator's Preface   x

part one
come together

Chapter 1   3
November 1971
Chapter 2   5
December 1971
Chapter 3   11
Jersey Moon: Tour Interview #1   13
Chapter 4   17
February 1972
Chapter 5   21
Chapter 6   27
Jersey Moon: Tour Interview #2   33
Chapter 7   34
February 1972
Chapter 8   38
Chapter 9   41
Chapter 10   46
Chapter 11   50
March 1972
Chapter 12   53
Chapter 13   58
Chapter 14   62
Chapter 15   69
March 1972
Jersey Moon: Tour Interview #3   73
Chapter 16   75
March 1972
Chapter 17   84
July 1972
Jersey Moon: Tour Interview # 4   89
Chapter 18   92
July 1972
Jersey Moon: Tour Interview #5   101

Chapter 19	103
August 1972	
Chapter 20	109
Chapter 21	116
Jersey Moon: Interview #6	119
Chapter 22	124
September 1972	
Chapter 23	129
September—November 1972	
Jersey Moon: Tour Interview #7	135
Chapter 24	141
November 1972	
Chapter 25	146
Chapter 26	148
Chapter 27	153
December 1972	
Jersey Moon: Tour Interview #8	161
Chapter 28	168
December 1972	
Chapter 29	171
January 1973	
Chapter 30	173
Chapter 31	178
February—March 1973	
Chapter 32	184
Chapter 33	188
Chapter 34	190
Chapter 35	193
Chapter 36	198
March 1973	
Chapter 37	200
Chapter 38	205
Jersey Moon: Tour Interview #9 (part one)	213
Jersey Moon: Tour Interview #9 (part two)	217
Chapter 39	220
Jersey Moon: Tour Interview #10	227
Chapter 40	232
June 1973	
Chapter 41	235
Chapter 42	241
June—July 1973	
Jersey Moon: Tour Interview #11	251

Chapter 43   255
July 1973
Chapter 44   263

part two
road songs

Chapter 45   271
July 31, Philadelphia: Bijou Café

Chapter 46   277
August 1, Camden, New Jersey: Dio's Supperclub August 3, New York, New York: Max's Kansas City

Chapter 47   282
Chapter 48   286
Chapter 49   288
August 5, Philadelphia: The Bijou Café August 7, Pittsburgh: The Spot Light Lounge August 8, Pittsburgh: The Decade August 10, Erie, Pennsylvania: The Gaslight

Chapter 50   293
Chapter 51   295
Chapter 52   297
August 15, Chicago: The Crown Theater

Jersey Moon: Tour Interview #12   305
Chapter 53   308
August 18, Madison, Wisconsin: Bunky's August 19, Madison, Wisconsin: Dewey's August 21, Minneapolis, Minnesota: The Turf Club August 23, Bismarck, North Dakota: Dakota Hinterland Music Fest

Chapter 54   312
Chapter 55   314
Chapter 56   319
August 25, Boulder, Colorado: Tulagi's August 26, Sigma Phi Epsilon, University of Colorado August 26, Tulagi's August 28, Denver, Colorado: Mammoth Gardens August 29, Golden, Colorado: Buffalo Rose

Chapter 57   322
August 31, Bakersfield, California: Mudd Jazz Lounge

Chapter 58   324
Jersey Moon: Tour Interview #13   326
Chapter 59   330
September 1, Los Angeles: Roxy Theater

Chapter 60   333
September 2

Chapter 61   336
September 2, Los Angeles: Roxy Theater

part three
snapshots and postcards

Chapter 62	355
October 1982	
Interview (abridged) with Lita Ford	359
Chapter 63	363
November 1983	
Acknowledgments	365
About the Author	367

For Hop Wechsler

the perfect summer playlist

narrator's preface

I've lived a writer's life. Making my way, I've worn a number of ink-smudged hats. English-major classes at Drake University led to a first *real* job at Global Advertising in Kansas City. Building brands, baby. A lack of purpose shifted me to journalism, rising from pressroom gofer to Sunday edition Metro and Iowa Section editor at the *Des Moines Register*.

Turning thirty, dismaying long-supportive parents, I bucked the scribes, packed my trusty Accord, headed west, and rolled the dice for an "in" at television sitcom writing. I've always made friends laugh (perhaps they were laughing *at* me).

The *starving years* followed. So many pilots, so many fingers crossed, so many hopes crushed. Yet I honed my craft. I garnered a rep for producing up against deadlines (thank you, pressroom guys). My name was passed. That's how the TV studio business worked.

Finally, a green light, a series, twelve episodes, a hit. Another followed.

Shockingly, I found myself, at forty-four, in a new millennium no less, shifting gears once again, to write and publish that long-overdue first great-American-something.

Narrator's Preface

My subject and plot line were an obvious choice. At age thirteen, I'd been handed a gift—asked to keep a journal, discovering along the way my love of the written word.

I returned to 1973, to the gift—where my writing life began.

Jersey Moon (2004)

october 1966

Port Huron, New York

Her legs were shaking, buckling at the knee. Her right eye twitched. Telltale signs, and she knew this one might be bad. They'd been partying downstairs, sinking to the usual shouting, shoving and fighting. Why the continued quiet? Why now? Gretchen cupped an ear to her bedroom door. Where was the sick, shrill laughter, the slap-around cussing?

There came a *thump*—then another; heavy, slow steps breaking the silence, each one a drunken effort, the old wooden staircase groaning under the weight. He was coming up. Bile rose in her throat.

may 1967

Central Highlands, RVN

First Platoon was pointing to the sky. A lone Huey was circling their position. Henry took note the captain on the radio, looking concerned. Worst fears realized, from above, the M-60 door gunner opened up. Rounds cascaded down through the jungle canopy. First Platoon scrambled for cover. The captain was screaming into his handset, "We're taking friendly fire!" Running to stay alive, Henry tripped and tumbled down the steep terrain. A lifetime passed. The chopper gunner ceased firing. Screams filled the mountaintop. "Medic! I'm hit!" Henry felt pain from the bloody gash on his leg. *Was I shot? No, the fall.* Lying very still, one thought raged: *If I somehow survive this insane war, I swear I'll rock the pedal to the metal—I'll live my dream.*

december 1969

Fremont, California

Blinded by the late-morning sun, Melissa squinted up at the light pole. Both the glare and the concert-poster height were a pain. She made out "SPEEDWAY" and "FREE." A shadow loomed behind. She shivered. The creepy guy, for sure. She just knew. The leering, sneering guard, making sure no one wandered off the grounds. She was off-limits, in trouble now. "*Shit. Shit. Shit.*" She turned. No, not the creepazoid; someone else who said, "Wanna go?"

october 1971

Grosse Pointe, Michigan

"Maybe something more formal."

"I look fine, Mom."

"Looking the part can't be overrated, Christine. Let's replace the sweater with your beige jacket."

A sigh was followed by an acquiescence.

"Now, I've asked Dr. Schulenberg to list his pre-med course recommendations plus his suggestions for your prepping for the MCAT. Write down everything he says, Christine. Oh, and ask about extracurriculars. He'll note your interest."

"Okay, okay."

"Your junior year, darling. Buckle-down time. Application year. We'll be ready. Such excitement."

part one
Come Together

chapter one
November 1971

Henry needed the space. The massive seven-hundred-pound Schmoller & Mueller piano was clogging up an entire corner, the proverbial bull in the proverbial piano repair shop. Big ol' uprights—the WWII Tiger tanks of the keyboard industry.

Back in '69, against his better judgment, Henry had agreed to take the circa-1925 behemoth from the Boswells' farmhouse. Frank and Helen were remodeling. The kid who took the piano lessons years past was now flying Delta Boeing 727s out from Kansas City International. Frank no longer wanted or needed the piano. Helen couldn't bear to see the treasure tossed in a ditch. Frank offered to round up his hay-baling crew to help muscle it into Henry's pickup. "Free piano, free load-up, Hollins. How can you resist such a deal?"

Henry sighed, ready to argue that he could resist *real* easy. But he took it. Hell, he still had his tie-downs in the truck from a piano move two weeks ago. He sighed again. Maybe he could clean it, repair it, lube it, tune it and find it a home—for another beginner, just like the Delta pilot way back in Ike's time. Helen was delighted. Frank grinned. They needed the space.

Yup, two years ago, the one positive result being that he'd

opted out of the moving business ("no more") and traded in his pickup for a van. As Henry's piano-repair service mushroomed, there was never enough time nor incentive to fix and pawn off the beast. A playable up-to-pitch Schmoller & Mueller might fetch a couple hundred, a price hardly worth the labor effort. Old uprights are not considered antiques. They are more like old refrigerators. Regardless, the repair work, tune-up, and sale never happened, and the Boswells' "freebie" remained a huge corner clog—until by chance, either reading the local Chronicle or hearing in passing conversation (Henry could not recall which), he became aware that Liberty, Iowa (hanging onto a population of 2,500) was now home to a state-administered halfway house. Halfway as in young perps, many recently released from confinement, making a final pit stop before being fully let free and, as they hopefully say, reintegrated back into society. Or, put another way: last chance, honcho, to get unbent and fly straight. Since Henry's hometown was situated in the middle of the Omaha-Des Moines-Kansas City triangle, where most of the rehab last-chancers either originated from or last resided, the Liberty township location was both obvious and beneficial.

The new halfway sparked an idea. There were certainly troubled souls in residence. Might music soothe the savage? Henry reasoned. Perhaps the state-run facility would agree to buy the Schmoller & Mueller or even accept the "tiger" as a generous donation from the local piano shop. Whatever worked, and why not? Free delivery, too. He'd cajole Frank Boswell to handle the transport. Frank owed him for taking the "treasure" in the first place. The state house would surely get some use out of it. Henry clapped his hands and hooted, "Perfect!" His idea smacked of Boswell payback, added shop space, and a worthy new home for the Schmo & Mule—a win-win-win.

chapter two
December 1971

William Morain, mid-fifties, slight build, pumpkin-faced, prescriptions, lots of growing-wild white hair, bicycle enthusiast, Henry's good friend, and the Liberty Halfway House director, wasn't so sure. "Probably not, Henry. Not a good fit."

"You've plenty of floor space in the dayroom, Bill."

"Having room is not a factor, Henry."

"Any keyboard players in this barracks?"

"I've no idea. What I do have here is a lot of aggression, the sources of which are not germane to this discussion. Anger is defused in a multitude of ways. Bottom line, someone, maybe more than one, will pound the piano to pulp. Now, I've got a five-hundred-pound problem."

Henry winced, "Probably closer to seven."

"There you go, sir. More fuel to the fire."

Henry was so close. He stayed positive. "I tell you what, let's give this a shot. I'll fix any keys, broken or otherwise. No charge. All I'll do is present an invoice to tune it up once or twice a year—midsummer, then again around the holidays."

Bill held an umpire's smile. "I doubt caroling will be a big deal around here."

"Hah. Well, there are times we could all use some accompaniment in our life. And I'm offering a free piano, free delivery and free maintenance." Henry was thinking ahead: *I'll call Frank, tell him I've fulfilled Helen's wish and found her piano a home; have him drop by the shop with his field truck and hay-bale crew and move the upright one more time. Frank would not be happy, but he'd git 'er done.*

"Is there a reason behind this benevolence, Henry?"

Henry grinned. "I need the space."

"If the piano becomes nothing more than a punching bag, Mr. Hollins, I'll insist you haul it out of here. I mean that."

Henry's grin was a frozen rope. "Sure."

Morain called within two weeks. "Two keys down. Three sharps missing. Strike one, my friend."

Henry arrived late afternoon. The state facility stood near empty. Bill had mentioned that many housed at the halfway worked outside jobs, either full or part time. There was activity in the kitchen. At the piano, in the dayroom, removing case parts he found two spruce keys split apart at the balance rail. Someone had indeed pounded away. He winced. There is a difference between Beethoven and a wrecking ball. Luckily, the damage was angled horizontal rather than straight vertical. Both old soldiers, E and F above middle C, were a simple wood-glue fix. Being close to home base, he decided to take the keys back to his shop and let the repair clamping sit overnight. He had plenty of old sharps on hand to replace the three missing.

The one negative was the rusted-tight fallboard lock. His standard latch keys, even a wedged screwdriver, would not pop it open. Frustration grew. Keeping the piano under locked supervision might be an answer to the halfway horde. He squirted the lock with a healthy dose of Tri-Flow to allow the lube time to work its magic overnight. Removing all the keys needed for the repair, replacing the fallboard, he was set to leave. For fun, he played a tune, fingering around the gaps. Henry was hardly Rubenstein, but with years of lessons, he prided his playing. He had pieces committed to memory, songs he liked, music he improvised. He tuned pianos. Showing off his work was a given. "Hang in there, Schmoller. You too, Mueller. I'll be back tomorrow."

"I can play better stuff than that."

Henry turned to find he had an audience of two: female, maybe late teens or early twenties. What were they doing in this place? Kitchen help? Possible. Inmates? No, that didn't equate. Equal in stature at five-foot-two or three, the salty blond had long tresses pulled back and loosely held in a ponytail, a narrow face, a pointy chin, a pinched look. She reminded Henry, at first glance, of Igor, Dr. Frankenstein's lab rat, forced to drag her one useless leg all the while intoning, "Yes, master." That was mean and terrible, but he chuckled at the instant connection. He couldn't help himself. She had a long, gently sloped nose, her best feature; the beautiful feature waiting on all the others to catch up.

And if one was Igor, the "I can play better" had to be the Germanic Visigoth storming the gates. Grim. Helmet-cut dark brown hair punctuated a leery but fearless look. Green eyes topped by black lashes and brows graced a round face, an again-best-feature soft plump nose, and generous lips that looked like they hadn't broken out a smile since Arminius wiped out the Roman legions in the Teutoberg Forest.

Quite a pair. They had Henry's attention. "Better than Neil Young? That's pretty cool."

"I meant better than you, tool man."

"Better than me? That's not hard. Here," Henry stood, waving his hand at the piano bench, "Play me a tune."

She shook her head. "Just guitar."

"You got one?"

"Yeah."

Surprise, surprise, she left, taking off at a half run. The blond stayed and stared. There was a faint shoulder shrug and a roll of the eyes. Henry smiled. Her partner soon returned, handing him a battered no-name make, missing a high E string.

Henry held the Goth fascinated as he struck E2 on the piano, held down the sustain pedal, and matched the pitch with the low E on the guitar. "Mercy. This poor baby is *so* flat." He then proceeded to tune the A, D, G and B strings using the fifth-fret method, something he'd done many times. Double-checking, he struck and pitch-matched all five guitar strings with the piano. He was now close enough. He took his time to explain the fret fingering and how to properly turn the tuning pegs. Henry handed the guitar over. "Your turn. Retune it. The strings have already lost pitch and gone flat. You need to stretch them out." Sitting together, he again struck E2, then guided her through the process.

"That's got it. Tune the guitar every day, until it becomes second nature. Ever-so-often, check your pitch with the piano." To help her remember, Henry dot-marked the keys. He grinned. "Humanity has a better shot if we're all in tune with one another." The girl then strummed with a surprised and satisfied look. "Cool."

"You're welcome."

"What were you playing?"

"Neil Young's 'Only Love Can Break Your Heart.' "

"Sounded pretty simple."

"Well, Miss ..."

She hesitated, on guard, and said, "Gretchen."

He poked his chest. "Henry. And that's the beauty of music, Gretchen. Be the score complicated, hard to play or simple and easy, the beauty is, both can sound awesome."

Gretchen pointed. "That's Mel, drummer-girl."

Mel made a face, darted to the kitchen, and returned with two wooden spoons, a whisk, a cardboard box and a pot.

With drummer Mel standing and set up at a card table, Henry plopped down on the bench and said, "Okay, let's try this. The chords are basically A, D and G."

Gretchen sighed, "Just play, tune guy."

"Henry." He grinned.

She shrugged. "Whatever you say."

Henry Hollins had a new hobby. Writing. He'd decided to take a crack at fiction, a short story. A lark perhaps, but he was serious enough to set the bedside alarm to give the typewriter at least a 90-minute workout each day. Writing was new enough to surprise him. He found that morning stumbling blocks would suddenly clear up in his head at odd times throughout the day, often while driving to piano-tuning customers. He'd exclaim to himself, "Yes, that would be perfect," only to have the perfect wording disappear from memory as quickly as it mysteriously arrived. The subconscious was tricky, always playing games. Countering, he'd bought a pocket mini-cassette tape recorder at Radio Shack and carried the portable in his shirt pocket, always at the ready. He couldn't have the world's most perfect descriptive sentence go to perfect waste. Sitting now with Mel and Gretchen, aware of his good fortune, he discreetly, just for fun, switched it on.

After a few false starts, horrendous, hilarious—take your pick—Henry kick-started "Only Love" once again, this time forging his way through both verses and the chorus. Mel banged away at her kitchen kit. Gretchen was everywhere on guitar. Henry pretty much chorded the song from memory, adding a forced vocal at times to keep the train from derailing completely. He had a serious finger problem with the missing piano keys, but given the cacophony, that hardly mattered.

Their final note resulted in a few catcalls from a small batch of wandering house residents gathered at the dayroom entrance. Gretchen was half embarrassed, half annoyed.

"We gotta go."

Robert Espenscheid, Jr.

Henry was startled, aware now the two young women were inmates.

"Wait. Gretchen. Mel. I'll be back tomorrow, same time, with the keys repaired. I might sound better with a complete middle octave. Let's do this again."

Henry watched as the two of them faced one another, shrugged noncommittally and then split. He muttered under his breath, "whatever you say," gathered his tool cases, and did the same.

chapter three

Only that evening did Henry recall the mini recorder. Had he captured anything? Rewinding, he hit play. First up were his so-called subconscious stellar descriptive sentences. Quickly, he jotted them down in his subject notebook, all the while groaning with an acknowledgment that his on-the-road revisions had not been as stellar as he first thought. Then, with a jolt, the dayroom session spat out like stray cats in heat on a backyard fence. On a second listen, surprised, he heard a few added vocals from Gretchen. He hadn't realized she'd been singing. Definitely contralto. Had to be. She was the Visigoth. Hearing the final run-through, Henry sat back, shaking his head. "Oh man, we were so laugh-out-loud bad."

He kept hitting playback. He turned inquisitive. Mel's spoon-fed beat was in and out, pounding too loud followed by a total fade, but she was hardly a first-timer. There was a drumroll on the box. Now that was funny. Henry smiled. He hit playback again. Gretchen's backing vocal intrigued. Was he imagining? He wasn't. There was something there. He couldn't put his finger on whatever it was. But amid the racket, there was a goofy something.

Robert Espenscheid, Jr.

Later, getting ready to call it a day, Henry grabbed a Falstaff from the fridge for support and played the tape to Esther.

"Hey hon, give this a listen. Tell me what you think?"

Halfway through, Esther's fingers in her ears answered his question. He smiled, nodded and offered a defense.

"This is me and a couple of add-ons down at that new halfway house in town."

"The place where you donated that old upright?"

"Yeah. Recognize the tune?"

"Sorry."

"That's no matter, but this tape is 'yours truly' historic, pretty much my first try at playing with an ensemble. I'm the forever music closet-junkie. I've never flat-out had the cojones to sit in with anyone else."

Esther smiled. "Hearing that tape, I understand the reason why perfectly."

Henry matched her mirth. Almost. "But I feel like there's an offbeat harmony here and there. We're actually out-weirding Neil Young. Let me play it one more time."

At least Esther looked sympathetic. "Please, Henry. Enough. I'm heading for bed. Don't be long."

Henry sat with his beer. Rewinding the day produced a revelation. He grinned with the realization that the dayroom session had just happened. No one had said anything like, "Let's get together sometime and jam." Mel and Gretchen had fetched the guitar and kitchen drum set, and they simply all began to play. There was barely an intro and no time for excuses, no begging off, "I'm not ready, I can't do this." They were like three kids at the ocean forgoing the how-cold tentative toe check—no wading in, no siree, just a running plunge. Henry sat in wonder. The whole shindig was so unlike him. He felt giddy, even a tad empowered, like a faded dream revived, like he'd passed some test.

jersey moon: tour interview #1

As recounted on the road,
August 1973

Jersey: What do you recall from the dayroom sessions?

Gretchen: What is this? I thought you were keeping a diary of the band tour and shit.

Jersey: I am. But what's a tour journal without writing about how the tour got started?

Gretchen: Nosy Moon.

Jersey: And I said a journal, not a diary. I'm not eight years old.

Gretchen (major sigh): Regretting this big-time already. The halfway house. Fucking A, where it all began, right? We hung with the piano guy mostly out of boredom. I mean, the halfway was all rules and restrictions. Cells without bars, and Mel and me had—what?—two more fucking months to serve in that hell on cinder blocks.

Jersey: Kind of wish you'd back off on the F thing ... and don't give me the look. Now ... shoot, I can't remember my question.

Gretchen: Thirteen, right?

Jersey (with a look of her own): Funny. Oh, Henry played you his secret tape from the first get-together, right?

Gretchen: No. He mentioned he had the thing and wanted

us to hear it. I think I told him to unwind it into spaghetti and I'd eat it.

Jersey: But the sessions kept on.

Gretchen: They did. We played whenever he showed. Neanderthals kept trashing the poor piano, and Henry had promised to keep it in one piece. So, he was at the house maybe once a week, and before you could say "Light My Fire," we began a regular practice thing.

Jersey: You guys still with the missing guitar strings and spoons?

Gretchen: Where'd you hear that?

Jersey: Nosy Moon. Remember?

Gretchen: A smart-ass, that's what you are. Henry coughed up some scratch, bought a medium gauge set and taught me to restring the guitar. Very cool. Hollins was this piano-tuning guy that traveled all over. He had all these schools he serviced, and he began picking up the odds and ends of battered drum kits. Band room stuff. A discarded floor tom, cracked crash-cymbals, glued sticks—anything he could find, even a kick drum held together with wire and tape. All junk taking up space at Iowa High, but a big improvement over a cardboard box. Odds and ends. Hah. That should be the name of the band.

Jersey: Mel still have the wooden spoons?

Gretchen: Knowing her …

Jersey: So, how long did the dayroom sessions go on?

Gretchen: Maybe six weeks. Even with Henry's doctoring, the battered piano became a frustrating problem, so he began bringing his acoustic guitar. We kept after Neil Young's stuff. Mostly "Gold Rush." He had the books of sheet music. Mel and I don't read notes. Henry had the chords. We just joined in. For fun, we tried to speed the songs up. Some of that worked for us. A lot didn't.

Jersey: Six weeks. I mean, what were you thinking the whole time?

Gretchen: That's a hell of a question, Moon. Hollins was suspect from the get-go. Mel and I hardly bought into his "this-is-cool, you-guys-are-so-talented" bullshit. Some honcho does me a favor, I step back.

Jersey: Maybe he was just being a good person.

Gretchen: You need to get out more, Moon.

Jersey: But you never …

Gretchen: Then Nellie from the kitchen staff corrals us one day and says, "You know he's married, right?" Shit. Talk about a red flag. Actually, I was surprised how pissed I got. So, we ambushed him. We ended a practice and Mel's like, "You got to get back home because your honey has a pot roast coming out of the oven, right?" Bang a gong—surprise! Henry turned pale. I'm like, "She got a name? Did you two first meet in some jailhouse?" A major confrontation followed. Hilarious.

Jersey: How *did* Henry and Esther meet?

Gretchen: He told us. She was a piano customer, and she had this weird ancient "birdcage"-type piano from England he wouldn't even try to fix. Esther says, "Well, darn, what do I owe you for taking a look?" Henry answers, "How about a cup of coffee?" And they married three months later.

Jersey: When was all this?

Gretchen: I guess the late '60s. Look, Moon, you want Henry's history, ask him. What we wanted to know was if Esther knew about us. Like, do we need guns and ammo with a psycho wife stalking our butts? And Henry says, "The three of us are nothing more than an accident," and I said, "Most shit is."

Jersey: You didn't call it quits.

Gretchen: Mel wanted to cut him some slack. We kept playing.

Jersey: Six weeks. Did you see any kind of end?

Gretchen: Are you asking, like, did Mel and me back then see us becoming a real band or something, or even care?

Jersey: Exactly.

Gretchen: No way. Henry Hollins was just this oddball guy, and we really didn't give beans about his wife, his life, his anything … and he didn't know crock about ours. But the reality was, given the monotony of the halfway house and the zombies that patrolled the rooms and hallways, the sessions were a freaking godsend. So okay, I'll admit, our dumbass playing meant something.

Jersey: And you had a captive audience, right?

Gretchen: Wrong, Miss Jersey Moon, we had a bunch of jerks screaming at us to shut the fuck up. On a positive, that was one of the first songs I wrote: "Shut the F**k Up." Well, not a song really. More like a return-fire "screw you" rant.

Jersey: That one always makes me laugh. Sorry, but I'm saying that in a good way. Okay, six weeks, then what?

Gretchen: The halfway detention felt like forever. I found this bottle of schnapps stashed in the kitchen. Drank way too much. I got shitfaced. Mel, too. We split.

chapter four
February 1972

"Goddamn, Bill, they actually ran off?"

"They bid my house-of-hope farewell, Henry. Coldest night of the year. Crazy. They didn't show up at the meal hall. Personal items in their room were missing. Coats taken. They did leave an empty bottle of peach schnapps. Not good."

"I can't believe this. I'm here for our usual get-together and they're gone? For real?"

"I'm sorry, Henry. Residents occasionally cut and run. Happens around here. We do what we can to keep tabs."

"But why, Bill? It's barely above zero out there. Snow's falling."

Bill Morain had the face lines of a half-dozen past escapes. "If I could answer your 'why,' Henry, I'd do the halfway system a world of good. Running. Chances are, that's what Melissa Minch and Gretchen Tarbat have always done—it's their go-to game plan. And brace yourself, I was just notified, there's more."

Henry dropped the snare drum stand he was holding, a stand he'd scored from Corydon High School that morning: wobbly but fixable. He was building Melissa's drum kit one piece at a time, a bent that now seemed ludicrous. "What, they turned up?"

Morain shook his head no. "I'm still trying to tie the story together, but apparently, they stole Rayne Winterfield's Ford pickup idling in the Hy-Vee parking lot, near brand-new I'm told, and were last seen heading east out of town past the sale barn toward the interstate. Apparently, Rayne had stopped at the grocery to quick grab an item or two. All I know so far."

Henry fought to remain standing, speechless. *Stolen truck!* Legs wobbling, he sat. He'd served, '66 and 67, in sunny Southeast Asia, some days beaten down more than others. He shivered, feeling the years-ago, without-warning, dreaded military rush of the "bad": *Oh, shit!*

Morain recognized the shock. "Just go home, Henry. I hear more, I'll call."

Esther took one look and said, "You heard?"

Henry nodded. "From Bill out at the halfway. Temps are turning arctic. I'll be out in the shop boxing up the glues to bring them inside." What he didn't need right now was a spousal row. The two add-ons at the halfway house had become a sore spot between the two of them, a sore spot mixed in with all the others, all festering as soon as the conversation heated.

Pulling up on the always-sticking shop door (was he ever going to goddamn fix it?) and entering, he shook from the chill. With the space heater running on low, his workplace felt like a walk-in cooler. Boxing up his glues and lubricants, his heart racing, Henry tried to take stock: *Where to even begin?*

They had been making progress. Baby steps at the start, growing into a loose-limbed strut. Despite the crappy equipment, they'd forged ahead further than he'd dreamed. At first, they were all song-oriented, but lately they'd begun jamming, taking a riff and running off somewhere with it. Henry, strumming rhythm on his guitar, was beginning to lock in with Melissa and sense where Gretchen was going with the lead, anticipating her changes—which was pretty cool considering that all-over-the-frets Gretchen had pretty much no clue where she was headed. The three of them were holding a conversation—with instruments! There were times they would fly off and even find their way back, a melodic boomerang that produced surprised shy smiles, even laughter. He was learning a foreign language, and no one was laying down rules. They were discovering a weird togetherness all on their own – and he was thrilled with the discoveries. He'd stumbled into a world he didn't know existed. The dayroom trio had become a euphoric drug, and he was hooked.

He also wasn't blind and realized that more often than not he was a rock 'n' roll party of one.

"Get a life, Hollins."

"I'm just saying, Gret, that maybe we might get together more often."

"I believe I hear your wife Esther saying the exact same thing."

Melissa piled on. "Don't turn delusional, Henry."

He wasn't listening. "You guys are a mountain of talent. I sense I'm getting better—"

"We're in semi-lockup, and if we get out and are picked up again, they are going to toss away the key. End of story. End of rock 'n' roll dreams. You're not growing delusional, Hollins, you're already there."

"I'm not, Gretchen. I'm just day-to-day, practice-to-practice. Stretching. We're stretching out … a good thing."

"Bullshit, piano man. This is all just a fucking speed bump in my life."

The gloves were off, and not the first time.

"Well, that's another good thing, Tarbat, because you need to slow the fuck down."

Henry recalled the verbal combat with a bitter laugh. Standing solitary in the shop, an icy cold snaking its way through the drywall seams and thin flooring, he shook again from the chill. His space heater was fighting a losing battle. He slumped against his workbench, elbows and hands holding up his head, catching and confronting his shadowy reflection in a paned window. "They were right. What a fool you've been. What a stupid, delusional fool."

chapter five

Cecil Sidel hankered for a glass of cold beer. Didn't make much sense, but frigid nights often brought on a lager craving. Flipping the light switch, navigating down the basement steps, he opened up his '50s Frigidaire: empty. With a grunt, "damn kids," he retraced, pulling hard on the banister, hauling himself back up to the warmth of his old farmhouse. Cecil shook out the basement damp. "We're out."

"No, you're out of beer." Mary, knitting by the fire, put the emphasis on the *you're*, then added a faint, "praise be."

"Last I looked, there was plenty. Have you been filching, Mary Lee Blair?"

Mary didn't lose a stitch. "How long have we been married, Mr. Sidel?"

"I'd say four decades are long enough for you to turn your afternoon tea parties into … what's the lingo used nowadays? Beer bashes."

"I'll sit right here and wait until you finish."

"Beer bashing while I toil in the fields."

Mary suppressed a grin. "Aside from my tea parties, I'd suggest interrogating your two grandsons. They stopped by …"

"While I toiled in the fields. Thieves, both of them."

"... to watch a Hawk game in the den."

"I've worked up a bull's thirst getting down and back up the stairs. I've a yen for a glass. I'm off to the store."

Mary stopped mid-stitch. "It's bone-chill cold, snow's surely drifting in the wind, and near dark, Cecil. Your yen can hold off until tomorrow."

"If I'd waited on a yen forty-six years ago, I'd have been too late corralling you, Mary Lee Blair." Cecil showed off his new dentures.

Mary eyed him, flabbergasted. "And I would not be sitting here trying to talk common sense to a fool's errand. Bravin' a blizzard for a six-pack? And, I declare, Cecil, not in my car. No sir, and the old pickup can't be trusted in the bitter cold. You know that. Come sit by the fire. Mercy."

"I'll take the tractor. She's winterized and fit." Pulling on an overcoat over his overalls, Cecil added a leer in Mary's direction. "A good warm-up be a plus for the old gal; the oil hot, the joints lubed."

"Ma always said, 'You can marry him, dear, but I fear there be no end to him.'" She gave her husband a stern look. "Rational thinking no longer resides in this house. Tarnation, Cecil, if this isn't the craziest. Have the two-way on. Flashlight and road flares ... don't forget."

"Half-hour at the most, Mrs. Sidel. Cab will be warm."

"Check in with me at the store."

"I'll radio, Captain."

Seated in the Massey Ferguson 135, Cecil eyed his oil and fuel gauges, shifted his levers into neutral, depressed the clutch pedal, advanced the throttle, pushed the shutoff, and turned the key. *Clatter—boom!* Forty years farming, he never tired of that guttural diesel roar—the rolling in the thunder. Heater on, letting the engine warm, he added hat and gloves. Finding a gear, he cautiously made his way out the barn, navigating the curved driveway, adding speed on down the mile of county gravel to the state highway heading west. Wind-driven snowflakes filled his headlights, swirling on past a windshield that thankfully remained clear. Two miles in, headlights signaled another vehicle headed his way. Though still a distance apart, he edged right to allow safe passage. The oncoming lights suddenly swerved left then overcorrected back right, spun sideways, backwards, then disappeared completely.

Someone had lost control, or the winter storm was playing light tricks. Cecil prayed for the latter. Regardless, only darkness ruled his line of sight. Decades of farming mishaps took control. Slowing right to the shoulder and stopping at a best-guess spot, he grabbed the flashlight, exited the cab, and walked the tarmac. The wind and cold had him top-buttoning his coat. Peering down from the southside road edge, he felt his neck hairs stiffen. Centering his light, four tires stared back. A pickup, with its headlights still on, had flipped at least once down the embankment. What looked like a Ford F-100 had come to a rest on the passenger side, up against a tree.

Cecil slid on down. There was no fire. At least not yet. He called out. No one answered. The silence and stillness of the winter night felt ominous. Shining his light against the shattered windshield revealed two bodies squashed together on the passenger side, neither moving. The snowfall grew heavy. His eyes watered. He battered his heavy flashlight against the remaining glass and hollered again. Nothing. No response. "Sumbitch."

Breathing deep, fighting the elements, his age and his nerve, Cecil noted the pickup was lodged against what appeared to be a massive burr oak, the ground rising to the tree. The rise had him thinking. He made two decisions.

First, he'd call for help. Returning to the tractor was no easy task. The embankment proved steep and slick. Crawling provided the best traction. Back in the cab, massaging his beating heart, breathing hard, he unhooked the radio mike. "Mary, pick up."

"Cecil?" Her tone held an edge.

"There's been an accident on 69."

"Oh no."

"Not me. A pickup in the ditch. Two passengers hurt. Neither responding. Just a mile east of the interstate on 69. Call police dispatch. Get them out here quickly."

"Will do. Are you okay?"

"A mite winded. Tell Rex, if you talk to him, he'll need an ambulance. Mary, this is serious."

"I'm on it. Stay safe."

"I'll have a flare lit on the side of the road. I may be down in the ditch doing what I can."

"You stay where you are."

"Make the calls, Mary. Out."

Locating and opening the metal box stashed behind the seat that housed the hook and tow-chain triggered a sigh of relief. Cecil recalled Matt and Jody recently borrowing the chain for some such. "By gum, they returned it proper. Good lads."

Decision two: He'd right the pickup. He'd noted room to maneuver the Massey at the tree and that the roadside embankment flattened out back eastward, allowing access. "Okay, we'll keep the grandkids, now let's get turned around, old-timer."

Though operating on farmland inclines was second nature, Cecil took care backing down into the ditch, continuing on a backtrack to the crash site guided by the flipped Ford's still-burning headlights. "Stay lit, sweethearts." Hooking the chain from the tractor hitch to the Ford was solved by smashing the driver's side window and wrapping the chain around the truck frame back out through the gaping hole in the windshield. Back in the cab, Cecil said a quick prayer and inched the Massey forward. No good. He was pulling the truck, sliding it, losing his ground angle, making the situation worse.

Back outside, with the flashlight and an urge to haste, the cold forgotten, he searched for logs, rocks, anything he might jam against the pickup's right-side wheels, to keep them bedded. With a "might work," he located what appeared to be old split telephone pole remnants. Burying and wedging both rock and the pine logs up against and under the tires, he climbed back up into the cab, and with near frozen fingers crossed, inched the tractor forward. The pickup slid, then caught. Cecil added power, and in what felt like slow motion, the Ford wrenched and fell back onto its rubber side with a thud. He was out the cab, near back on the ground, when roadside voices and lights zeroed in on his location.

Cecil watched as two young women were quickly snatched from the wreckage and carried by stretcher to the waiting ambulance, then sped to the county hospital. He was told they were both alive, at least for now.

Seated in a warm patrol car, Police Chief Rex Hardin could not resist. "I get you witnessed the spin, the pickup coming your way. I gotta ask, Cecil, what in the world are you doing out in the dark, minus two last I checked, road slicker than snot, with your farm tractor, for God's sake?"

Seventy-seven-year-old Cecil Sidel spoke matter-of-fact. "I was makin' a beer run."

Rex Hardin shook his head. "I say to myself, some twenty-five years in, that I've seen it all. But you're proof, Sid, I ain't even close." His laugh was more a relieved snort. "Mary know about this?"

"Mite contrary, she was."

"Do me a favor, Sid."

"Sure."

"You look beat. I'll have one of the boys get the Massey back in the barn. You ride with me."

"Only for one in return, Rex."

"Name it."

"Let me know how those two youngsters make out up at County."

"Bank it. You realize, sir, you might have saved two lives tonight. If you hadn't seen them fly off, ditch that deep, no one passing by would have taken note. I'd surely had me two frozen corpses tomorrow."

Cecil held a worn-out look. "The savin' might be cause for a glass of beer."

Rex gripped and squeezed Sidel's shoulder. "Yes, sir, and I'm buying."

chapter six

"Dinner's warming on the stove," Esther said. "I went ahead with mine. I'm off to visit Molly next door. She needs help with a pattern." Standing in the kitchen, she hesitated. "I've heard bits and pieces. I know you're upset, Henry. I'm sorry with what's happened."

Without thinking, Henry turned defensive. "Sounds more like 'I told you so.' Go ahead and say it, Esther."

"I just feel—"

"Let's not do this, okay?"

"Don't make me the bad guy here, Henry."

"I'm not. I just can't handle you throwing this in my face right now."

Esther stood chilled. Not all of her shakes were coming from the winter weather. *I'm either losing him or I've lost him already. Damn this, I have every right to be angry.*

Weeks back, she'd been informed, sucker punched really, that Henry's two "add-ons" at the crime house, recovery house, whatever it's called, were in fact a couple of young female runaways. Liberty was a small town. Stories traveled quicker than sundowns. But more than a questioning look from a neighbor, it was Henry's masking the true nature of the get-togethers that annoyed to no end. He was spending more and more time with his add-ons. *What in the world?* She felt betrayed, even a smidge jealous, which she hated.

"I don't get the trickery; actually, the lying, Henry."

"The smokescreen, yeah. Guilty as charged. I didn't know what to say at first. I mean, the two at the halfway house, who they were, that's not going to go over well … with you, with anyone. I did play you the tape that first day. What's surprising—"

"And, oh boy, did I get surprised, too. Let me see … age bracket, close to a generation's difference …"

"Eight years. They're around twenty, I'm still stiff-arming twenty-nine."

"… gender, that they are convicted criminals. Melissa *Minch*. Gretchen *Tarbat*. Add-ons, Henry, really?"

"The names. Sprung from a Dickens novel, right, and all I meant with the term was, like, finally 'adding on' to my chickenshit solo playing."

"Bullcrap, and I'm dead serious here, mister."

"I'm playing guitar and piano with them. We sit in the dayroom once or twice a week and learn songs, even make up a few. First time for me, Esther. The loner tuner is in a band! Holy Buddy Holly. I'm using the 'band' term loosely, but be they criminals, orangutans, male, female, runaways, giraffes, Confederate gray, Union blue … makes no difference. I've stumbled onto a couple of Crickets, I'm having fun."

"There *is* a difference, Henry, a huge difference. This ongoing infatuation of yours … hurts. Hurts *me*. That should matter, Henry. *We* should matter. Rural Iowa. People are talking. It's demeaning. You care more about—"

"Don't say that, Esther. Not true."

The Rise of The Mad March

Weeks passed. Their arguments escalated.

"I'm determined to keep on at the halfway while I can. At some point, Melissa and Gretchen will no doubt be released and gone."

"When?"

"I don't know. I'll regret the end. I *will* be a better musician. You won't even try to understand my side, Esther."

"Nor you mine."

Now, an escalation to an explosion: "Molly called earlier. She heard there's been a bad accident out on 69. If it's the add-ons –"

"Just go help Molly, Esther. We'll argue this out later."

Henry spent the next two hours both fretting about Melissa and Gretchen and wallowing in self-pity. The more bourbon he drank, the "wallower" he got. At the vanity mirror, he began shouting at someone he barely recognized. "You actually believed they cared! They took off, loser man, laughing all the way. You didn't see that coming, no sir, because you weren't fucking looking, ace. They've been laughing at you for weeks, the weirdo piano loser. Did you get a goodbye? Hell, man, you never had a hello. Well, they didn't get far. Bad accident. Maybe they're dead. Happy now?"

A bourbon refill found him at his piano. His self-castigation turned to longing as he pounded away at what he later called "Say It Isn't So," a dirge with the shouted refrain: *Don't go*. At least it rhymed. Two chords, repeat for two minutes. With a final run-through, he offered his critique to the Baldwin upright: "more rock 'n' roll garbage from a nobody who refuses to grow up."

Returning from Molly's, Esther heard the pounding, peered into the piano study, saw the depleted fifth of Wild Turkey, turned away and headed up to bed. The piano went quiet. She paused mid-step. With quick glances, searching, their eyes met. Esther's dismay locked into Henry's humiliation. Not a word was spoken. As if defeated, Esther raced up the staircase. Henry sat, heard the bedroom door shut, began counting up his losses, stopped, staggered to the phone and woke up Bill Morain at home.

"There was a wreck, Henry. They're alive. Minch is listed as serious. Tarbat stable. No details. The stolen truck was Rayne Winterfield's. He'd parked at Hy-Vee facing the road and left the engine running to keep the cab warm. All they had to do was release the brake, shift into drive and go. Rayne's on record hoping they survive so he can strangle them both with his bare hands. This is bad in a lotta ways, Henry. I know from our files here, Tarbat's sitting with priors. Mostly misdemeanors, but auto theft and the destruction thereof might lead to hard knocks."

"Mother fuck."

"Stop right there. I can tell you've been drinking, Henry—eighty-six-proof fumes are coming through the lines. Long day. Hit the hay. I'll call tomorrow."

Eleven p.m. Another piss and a last stand at the mirror. "You are at a crossroads, Mr. Delusion. A left or a right? What's it going to be, cowboy? The devil's waiting. This is as black and white as it gets. Go right. Right as in right. Forget about them. Don't even think about them anymore. Erase the halfway trio from your memory; a folly that had no freaking rational to begin with. They made their choice." Henry finger-jabbed the glass. "Law and order will deem their fate." He gave himself a nod of satisfaction and approval. "All I've lost is a little time, and according to Esther, a little self-respect."

Henry stood rooted. His mirror image faded and shifted to a dusty, empty street. Two gunslingers faced down one another. High noon in Dodge City. Stetsons blocked the sun. Gun belts with holsters were strapped low on the hip. Hands hovered over Colt .45s.

"Or … go left, Wyatt Earp. Come push, shove, whatever, fight for them. Turn left. They have no one."

Henry's mirror self-image returned. "What direction, cowboy?"

Draw!

Grabbing his guitar, his winter coat, his keys, Henry stepped carefully about the icy outside, crammed into the driver's seat, started the van, the battery with a last gasp winning against the cold, found reverse, backed out, shifted to first and turned his head. The upstairs bedroom was dark. Snow was falling. His headlights reflected a white blanket, street centerlines nothing more than a guess. Clutch, gas, rolling now, his back end slid right, Henry corrected right, then left, and drove on.

jersey moon: tour interview #2

August 1973

Jersey: Can we go back and talk about the stolen pickup?

Gretchen: No. I thought this diary thing was all about the music, Moon.

Jersey: Journal thing. And I'm sorta poking around at the whole "band" story—the big-picture thing.

Gretchen: Wha … you going to drag up my entire trashed life? Is this a school project? What are you in, eighth grade?

Jersey (bristling): Ninth.

Gretchen: All this garbage about the pickup for what, a grade, a useless junior high school B+? You're out of bounds, cow.

Jersey: Whoa. Not digging for garbage here. I'm only asking what happened. Geez.

Gretchen: Yeah? Well, what's happening is … get fucked, Jersey.

Jersey (beet red): I'm not even fourteen, but I hope to eventually, and with someone nice. Not like you, Gretchen.

Gretchen: This is so over.

chapter seven
February 1972

Henry skidded sideways to a stop. Fourteen slick miles to the Lyon hospital—white-knuckle all the way. Grabbing his guitar, slipping and falling twice, navigating the snow-blown unplowed parking lot, barging past the glass door entry, shouting at the admission desk, "visiting Tarbat and Minch," he furtively made his way down a dimly lit hallway. The old brick county hospital was not a big place. The new private nursing home out on Route 2 probably held twice the space. Peering into patients' rooms left and right felt creepy. He reached a nurses' station. The staff phone was ringing. A white uniform hollered, "Stop right where you are." Henry swept past, picked up his pace, locating them at last, room 118, bedded side by side. Nightlights glowed. Nearest to the door, Gretchen lay awake. On the window side, Melissa slept dead to the world, tubes running every which way. Henry bowed in despair. Only the perceptible rise and fall of her chest allowed an exhale of relief.

Her whole body one giant bruise, Gretchen struggled to sit up. She'd been praying, begging for forgiveness: for the booze, for stealing, for losing control of the truck. Whoever was listening, she'd bargained away her own life twice over so that Melissa might pull through.

Earlier, the sheriff had stopped by. After inquiring as to the theft and a heartfelt how-was-she-holding-up, he let on that criminal charges would probably be filed. He more than hinted at the dire circumstance Gretchen was facing. "Bad decisions hold consequences, young lady."

———

Along with her prayer for Mel, Gretchen added a worldwide SOS.

And who stumbles in at midnight? She was wide-eyed dumbfounded: the piano guy – three sheets to the wind.

Henry squinted at the wall clock, showing two hands a few ticks past vertical. "Note the time, Tarbat. You and Minch missed band practice. No gold stars for you." He held up the guitar with a goofy grin. "Good thing I've arrived for the makeup."

"Are you like totally insane?"

"No, I'm like a songwriter, and I wrote one tonight." He shouted, "Mel, wake up! I'm gonna play us a new song." Dragging a fold-up metal visitor's chair between the beds, screeching all the way, he sat, digging into his jeans for a pick. At the ready, he took a moment to grab and shake Gretchen's toes. Reaching across, he gently patted Melissa's knee and looked up. *Both warm. Blood flowing. Thank you, amen.*

On his ride over, he'd passed Johnson's Auto. Bathed in parking-lot pole lighting, Winterfield's totaled pickup was still hitched to the garage's massive tow truck, facing up into the storm like a reared stallion. Henry stopped and sobered as he viewed the wreckage. *How did they survive this?* Some kind of impact had squeezed the cab like an accordion. Standing on a crate, peering inside through the shattered windows, his heart skipped a beat. Gretchen had escaped the halfway ward, but she'd brought her guitar—wedged behind the seat but still seemingly in one piece. "Hold on, no-name. I'll be back."

"I changed the name of this song on my way over. It's now called, 'Hey Baby, At Least Stay Long Enough for My Funeral.'"

Henry's opening chord coincided with the arrival of hospital security and two nurses.

"You! Out!"

Henry made a groggy turn. "First, kind sir, a lament, then I leave in peace."

"Bullshit. Night patrol's been called. County cops are on the way."

"Just one song, Mr. Security, then I'm ..." Henry focused. "Rowdy? Damn. Better not have a baseball bat in your hands."

"Is that you, Hollins? Christ, what are you, drunk?" Rowdy Jarrett, on the job three months, was facing his first security crisis. *Hollins! The skinny fucker who had doubled home a winning run last summer and busted up our undefeated season.* Rowdy tapped his nightstick into his open palm and made a move. *Payback time.* Gretchen halted him mid-stride.

"Let him play the freaking song, then hogtie him out of here."

Rowdy caught the patient's tone and held up. Henry launched into a minute of "Funeral," with its hard strumming and a new, never-ending wailing refrain, *"keep the beat, beat the casket."*

Rowdy was shaking his head, bewildered. The nurses covered their ears. Gretchen suppressed a grin. Melissa, eyes closed, never moved. Two "counties" stormed in at Henry's whiplash finish. He stood, hands up. "Done. I surrender." At the door, being hauled off, he beseeched the nurses, "They're going to be okay, right? Mel's just sleeping?"

Henry never got an answer. He hung onto his guitar right into the holding pen in the courthouse basement. He had a cellmate, unhappy with the wee-hour intrusion. Henry introduced himself and offered to serenade Victor with a song.

"Fuck off, punk." Victor's snarl became a snore. Henry waited, his mind drifting back to a jungle highland mountaintop, a lone chopper, M-60 rounds pouring through the treetops, a dive for cover, a personal vow made. Chilled, still holding the guitar, he softly strummed Dylan's ode to the lost, his plaintive voice echoing about a dark cell: *"How does it feel, to be on you own, with no direction home ..."*

Not until days later, after Gretchen had rehashed the crazy midnight-rambler story, did a slowly recovering Melissa Minch let on that she'd somehow heard Henry's racket. "'Funeral' needs another chord."

chapter eight

Henry reached the phone on the fourth ring, right before the answering service kicked in. "Piano shop."

"Henry, Clara Pickford."

"Golly, Mrs. Pickford, are those tuning pins in the bass still not holding?"

"Henry, please. Clara. And the grand is fine. I've a proposition, sir. Have you a moment?"

"Absolutely."

"I'll get right to it. We've talked these past few years. I know you love this old house."

What was not to love? Built a mile west of rural River Grove, Iowa, population two hundred, up a long tree-lined rock driveway, high in the hilly glacier-region countryside, hidden and shaded by tall oaks and maples, the old Victorian stood majestic—two-storied, topped with a widow's walk. Henry looked forward to his yearly service calls, being inside tuning the mighty Mason Hamlin AA six-foot grand, the musty fragrance of the place, spacious rooms, high ceilings, white lace curtains, the scrolled oak interior woodwork. The house defined benign neglect but seemed to still flourish, adding luster, as another century marched on. Casual dress seemed inappropriate. On more than one tune-up,

Henry had admonished himself for his Lee jeans and sweater attire. You half expected to see Vivien Leigh, one hand atop the ornate banister, stepping down the wide staircase.

"Our children are rooted in California," Clara began. "Sherman and I are relics, Henry, and relics can't maintain this museum. The Pickford place has housed this family for generations. I've no wish for that to end, but Sherman requires proper care, and I'm not far behind."

"Nonsense, Clara. If I need a partner for beach volleyball, I'm signing you up."

"Hah! Thank you, Henry. I'd consider your offer, but right now Sherm and I have a residency awaiting our arrival at Windsor Manor up north in Indianola. Helpful needed assistance, Henry. Life is what it is. Now then, I desire a live-in caretaker here at the house. Temporary, until some sort of permanent decision is made at my end. When last we spoke, you mentioned you were at loose ends. I'm wondering if Pickford might be at least a fill-in for you?"

Henry nearly dropped the phone. "For how long, Clara?"

"I've no idea, sir. This will be a handshake, Henry, one step at a time."

"Can I tinker?"

"You can renovate to your heart's content."

"Are you and Mr. Pickford returning at some point?"

"Like I said, Henry, life is what it is."

"Can I fix the coop? Raise a few chickens?"

"I'd love that. The house needs life, Henry, not two old coots spending half a day reminding themselves to take their medications."

"Am I leasing? Renting?"

"You're moving in. Money doesn't enter into this proposition. I should be paying you. As a matter of fact, I'll handle the utilities. Least I can do."

"I can't give you a firm yes or no right this minute, but I

promise a quick decision and I'm thrilled, Clara. I'm also taking advantage."

"Alright, sir, we'll agree to a lease at one dollar per month. How does that suit you?"

"I've my piano service van, Clara, a good mover. Do you need help getting your things to Indianola? Are you packing up the family ghosts roaming the widow's walk?"

"We've enough help. The house means the world to me. Think my offer over. Let me know. Bless you, Henry. The ghosts remain at Pickford. I'll make them aware, no shenanigans."

"Be firm."

"I promise. We're due at the manor in ten days. Stop by beforehand, when your schedule allows, for a Pickford tour. Fair warning, Henry: Plumbing, heating, electric, what-have-you … everything here is a bit worn and idiosyncratic."

Henry broke the connection in wonder. He'd risen from a jail cell to Tara in a week.

chapter nine

"Do you love me? Don't answer that. Have you ever loved me?"

"Yes."

"Past tense so noted." Esther appeared to wilt. "From our very beginning, Henry Hollins, I've always had this sense of sharing you. You were never quite all mine."

Henry's attention drifted from Esther to centering on a barely visible meandering plaster crack in the kitchen ceiling. Esther waited.

"I loved Eddie Cochran. I loved Chuck Berry; I loved Dylan and Grace Slick. I loved the Creedence rhythm section. I love T-Rex."

Esther threw up her hands to stop the traffic. "Enough. That I know little of who or what you love speaks volumes. But this Tarbat and Minch?" She let go a bitter laugh. "You went to jail for Tarbat and Minch, two street urchins from 'David Copperfield.'"

Henry cracked a half smile at the book reference. "Urchins. You might be right ... but don't be cruel."

"I'm not cruel. I'm lost. Half drunk, you go racing out in a winter storm in the middle of the night like some knight-errant. Chasing after two young women who apparently, from what I've learned, were in fact running away from this town, running from you, Henry."

Henry followed the jagged ceiling crack feathering out at the corner. "I read somewhere that for every hotshot who picks up a six-string, there are only one or two players on Mother Earth who have the chops to join up, shout, *she loves you, yeah, yeah, yeah,* and ignite a magical musical spark. Think about that. Would there be an Elvis without Scotty Moore? Without Ray Manzarek, Morrison is still entering poetry contests. Don't you see, Esther? It's all about the pairings, the magic. Ancient Norse mythology states that axe players only get one transcendental connection. I mean, does Led Zep exist unless Page meets Plant?"

"Really lost, Henry, and you're so full of shit."

"Right from the start, Esther, with the two of them, I heard this musical link. Felt it. I played you that tape. No doubt, we're pretty terrible and our equipment is worse. But together … strumming and drumming … something is happening."

"Well, Mr. Hollins, apparently you were the only one picking up the 'something,' because your playmates were headed off, destinations unknown."

"True. My mystical connection became a humiliation, one bitter-cold roller-coaster February day."

"Fueled with whiskey."

"Guilty, your honor."

"And in the sobering here and now?"

Henry braced. "They have nothing and no one."

Esther was a mess, her heart hardening while a tear escaped down her cheek. She was shouting. "Wrong, Henry, they have you!" She grabbed a tissue, dabbing her eyes, despising her distress. "Humiliation fills my day too, Mr. Hollins. The wandering husband on everyone's lips. We're no longer a team. Oh wow, were we ever?"

"I'm not deserting Melissa and Gretchen. Not now."

"You're deserting me."

The Rise of The Mad March

Henry detested turning defensive, but there it was. "It was *never* my intention to walk away from anyone."

Esther sighed, dead tired. "You've wrapped me in chains, Henry. If you keep on with the two of them, I lose. If you're forced to end this, this adolescent fantasy, I lose again. I'm starting to hate you."

"And I'm tired of being the bad guy."

"Let me ask you something. Where do you think you're heading? I've heard you tinkering away at the piano for years, more than one 2 a.m. recital I might add, and I'm not hearing a professional recording artist. Sorry."

"I'd never met my match."

Esther drew back. The way he said, "my match." Not kidding around. No sly put-on grin. Dead serious. He meant his *musical* match. She knew that. But he didn't say that. And the past tense 'I'd,' not 'I've'—as if now, with the add-ons, he had. "Oh my. I'm losing you." Esther ran fingers through her hair. "We need a timeout, sir. I need a timeout. Maybe I'll go visit my sister a spell."

"Don't let her say, 'I told you so.'"

Esther flared, "Why not?"

"Because your family has never been my fan club. Their ongoing snarky insinuations: 'Fully recovered from your military service, are you? How much do piano tuners make these days? Maybe the two of you ought to allow more time.' Oh, and my favorite: 'Mark called.' "

"I apologized to you profusely... for all of that."

"Nothing like dragging out the old fiancé, still beloved by all."

"Enough, Henry, you've made your point."

"Their smugness still rankles. How long the Ruth visit?"

"Depends, sir. Why do you care? Go save your, your something."

"Ruth's not working anymore. Have her come here instead."

Esther gave him a quizzical look.

"You can't just walk away from your job, Esther. We're in a timeout, fine, but your employer, Banta-Smith College, is not in a timeout, nor is my piano service business. Ruth, being here, can keep tabs on my customer phone messages."

She hooted. How could she not? "Oh my. You've no end, Henry Hollins."

"Just have her list the clients' names and callback numbers and drop them on my workbench in the shop. I'll pick them up. Everyone needs to get off the high horse and understand this timeout, whatever it is, cannot bring on financial ruin. We've both worked too hard to stay afloat."

"Where will you go? Where will you stay?"

"I've a possibility."

"Aren't you the lucky one."

"Don't be –"

"I need to be *something* too, Henry. Why can't I be *your* something?"

"We've weathered bigger storms."

She nodded. "We have, but they were internal. You, me, my rude family. This feels like an outside betrayal."

"No one is being betrayed, Esther."

"Not yet."

"Not fair."

"May I ask you one thing, Mr. Hollins?"

"Of course."

"Did you ever let on to Melissa and Gretchen, the two of us?"

"No. They found out from a third party."

"And?"

"You want their side of this? This is a first."

"Don't be condescending, Henry."

"Tarbat was teed off. I believe she called it 'the final fucking red flag.' Minch allowed me some rope. In the end, though, they both didn't much care that I was married. And the reason for that was because, at the halfway house, they didn't much care about anything."

Esther was flustered, bewildered, you name it. "So, if *before* their escaping and stealing the truck, you had told the two of them that the dayroom get-togethers were over, done with, that I was upset, that you weren't returning—"

"They would have, no doubt, not given a pig's rump."

"So why, Henry?"

"The music, Esther."

"Good Lord, I don't get this."

Henry nodded. "Nobody does."

chapter ten

An earlier agreed-upon time had been postponed, but Henry's top priority remained meeting one-on-one with Sheriff Marion Buckpool. Days had passed, lessening the ignominy of his overnight lockup. February was giving way to March.

While he was waiting on the sheriff, life rolled on. Esther had driven straight-away to Lincoln. She and Ruth were due back by the weekend. Amid the home-front chaos and catching up on his service calls, Henry had stopped at the Pickford house up in River Grove, met with Clara, and made arrangements to move in. The decision to relocate seemed surreal. *Was this really happening?* He and Clara discussed utilities, the basement sump pump; they toured the drafty barn. Henry eyed the long built-in tool bench; a makeshift piano repair shop was certainly doable. Henry said: "I might get a dog. What do you think?"

"Good for you. Keep you company out here. You appear stressed, Henry. Is everything alright?"

"Life is a circus, Clara."

She patted him on his hand. "Take it from an old ticket holder, Henry, try to enjoy the show."

"I'm the piano tuner up at Simpson College, right where

you'll be situated in Indianola. I'll stop by and keep you up to date on Pickford."

"Perfect. I'd love the visit."

"After all, it won't be long before I have the pot farm in full swing. You'll want to stay abreast."

"Hah. I knew I'd made the right choice. Take care of my home, Henry. I know you will."

He reached for her. They hugged. A first hug that proved a long one. "Thanks for choosing me, Clara."

But Esther's travels, Henry's service business and moving to Pickford were all white noise. First priority—Sheriff Buckpool. Another callback secured a morning hour at the courthouse. Henry did have a tie-in, much different than his recent overnight in the county holding cell. Marion was a longtime customer.

"Grab a seat, Henry. I'd say things around Decatur County are falling apart when the local piano tuner turns desperado. You'll be named on the sheriff's blotter report in both county newspapers. They publish Thursday. Can't say that'll be good for business. Speaking of which, my B flat above middle C has gone sluggish. Driving me crazy."

"Might be a tight key bushing or a damper spring."

"Whatever. Put me on your list. Beth's home most weekdays."

Henry made a note. "I'll call this afternoon. I mean, I'm already here in town. It'll be a quick fix."

"Good. And how was Decatur's accommodation the other night?"

"Far cry from the Cobblestone Inn."

"Meant to be, Henry, meant to be. Now, down to brass tacks, the hospital has dropped the forced entry charge." Buckpool sat back in his swivel, hands behind his head. He smiled. "You're facing a clean slate, apparently on the insistence of a healing patient. I've got her very words right here in front of me." He reached and grabbed a sheet of paper. "Quoting a Miss Tarbat: 'Nobody that mentally unstable should be locked up.' "

With a grin inverting to a grimace, Henry sat shaking his head. "Probably true." His demeanor changed. "Can you tell me what's coming down on her and Minch?"

"I reckon they are looking at auto theft, destruction to private property, not forgetting their unauthorized departure from the Liberty Halfway House. That's the cake. Blood tests at the hospital confirm that neither would have passed the drunkometer. I suspect driving intoxicated will be the icing."

"Are we talking about conviction and jail time?"

"Let's stay with the booze testing. You weren't, Henry. You're welcome. But I'm giving warning right this very minute, Mr. Hollins. Alcohol. Driving. You want to maintain a service business, knock that shit off."

"Yes, sir. The lockup spoke loud and clear."

"Okay, that's settled. Back to the kids."

"State prison? Really?"

"Most likely the reformatory at Anamosa. These are serious charges, Henry."

"I'm serious, too. Two girls, barely twenty. Locked away? Goddamn, Sheriff."

"I hear you. Nobody's smiling at this, but laws are enforced."

Sitting was impossible. Henry was on his feet. "There is a Grand Canyon divide between a calculated criminal act and a spur-of-the-moment mistake."

"I'll buy into that." Buckpool waited.

Henry sat back down. "What is Rayne Winterfield's take?"

"He may have liability issues with his insurance. Keys were in the truck; the vehicle was left running. Rayne was keeping the cab warm. Smart lawyer might get Tarbat and Minch off on a joyriding charge. Regardless, they totaled it. The rumor mill has Rayne installing a guillotine in his backyard as we speak."

"Oh, man." Henry fought to regain some composure. "I stopped and saw the truck that night. Wow, what happened?"

"First up, you being in the middle of all this somehow escapes me."

"Simple. Band meeting ... our trio. Melissa, Gretchen and I were scheduled to be together the very day they ran off. I wasn't about to let them get away with that. We needed the practice."

Marion looked on in wonder and finally said, "Don't we all."

"I sound beyond stupid."

"So, Mr. Hollins, close to midnight, you drove twelve miles in a blizzard to—"

"Show I cared."

"Enough said. As to the night in question, coming at them from the east, Mr. Cecil Sidel saw them fly off the highway. He called in the cavalry. Bottom line, if the old coot isn't out there bravin' the storm on his tractor, I've got two young women found frozen to death the next morning. The embankment they cartwheeled down was steep and out of sight."

"Jesus Christ."

"Well, somebody was looking after them. Amen, brother."

"Saved, Sheriff Buckpool, but saved for what?"

"Follow up, Henry. You want to be involved? Talk to the principals. Start with old Ironsides Patch, who thinks wearing a black robe makes him nobler than me." Marion stood. "Sorry partner, time's up." He gave Henry a reassuring tug on his shoulder. "Mind your hospital visiting hours, Hollins, and don't forget my B flat."

chapter eleven
March 1972

Seated in a cozy, book-lined study, Henry spent close to an hour with Judge Wendall Patch the following afternoon. Patch didn't play the piano, but his wife, Evelyn, accompanied the choir and congregation at the Lyon United Presbyterian. So, there existed another link, loose as it was.

Patch was nodding. "First off, Evelyn wanted me to thank you for fixing that damn pedal squeak on the Yamaha. Second, small town, Henry, I've heard bits and pieces as to the events you spoke of on the phone. What can I offer?"

"Say, sir, they plead guilty or say they are tried and found guilty. What happens?"

"You are here today as?"

"A friend. A worried friend."

"You are jumping to sentencing, Henry. You are overlooking the possibility of a pretrial settlement. And guilty of what? What will the prosecution charge?"

"Auto theft for sure."

"Okay, that being so, 'intent' will be the focus as to a misdemeanor or a felony. Let the facts play out, Henry."

"I can't do that. I can't sit helpless. Back to sentencing, Judge Patch, worst-case scenario?"

"The two so-charged stand trial. The prosecution presents a

case that the accused meant to permanently deprive Mr. Winterfield of his vehicle. Grand theft. A guilty verdict. Incarceration, a very real probability."

"How long?"

"Priors?"

"Not sure. They *were* at a halfway facility. Let's say yes, but minor."

"A record of repeated offenses and a failure to reform will be noted, Henry, lessening the weight of any contributing factors. They might serve years."

Henry blanched. "So, you're saying community service and the like would not be considered?"

"That is correct."

"Road trash pick-up? Come on, sir."

Patch shook his head no.

"That's horrible."

"That's the law, sir. Being sorry is not a defense. Simply begging for yet another chance will fall on deaf ears."

"And I can't fathom the law sitting on its high pedestal, staring down at two girls, scared shitless, not old enough to vote, dismissing any and all forces that brought them to trial, and proceeding to toss them in the garbage."

"Apply to law school, Henry. I'll pay the tuition."

"No offense, Judge. This can't happen."

"What are you asking, Henry?"

"What can I do?"

"Get the charges dropped before the court hearing."

Henry sat up.

Patch saw the hopeful look. "You're giving the truck owner a thought or two, aren't you?"

"Of course."

"Have you a pen, perhaps a notepad?"

"Sure." Henry dug into his shoulder bag. "Ready, sir."

"Write this down, Henry: Victims do not drop charges, the law does."

Henry nodded.

Patch noted his dejection. He offered what he hoped was encouragement. "Winterfield, Sheriff Buckpool, the county prosecutor. Get them on your side, Henry."

"That's a minefield, Judge Patch."

"Tread lightly, son."

Two early March days passed. Esther and Ruth had returned to Liberty while Henry found himself some thirty miles north, roaming about his new digs at the Pickford house. First night, dog-tired and stressed to the max, he slept fourteen hours. Later, at the hospital, he was denied visitation, but in badgering the medical staff, he was told Gretchen was held over with a concussion and fever while Melissa, after a fraught first twelve hours, was listed now as stable.

"Stable from what, Nurse Winslow?"

"Blood loss, partial lung collapse, severe shoulder trauma."

"Trauma?"

"Fracture. Dislocation."

"When can I see them?"

"You're on the visitor-banned list, Mr. Hollins. We'll let you know."

"Has anyone been to check on them?"

"The Sidels. Are you aware the story?"

"I am."

"Cecil and Mary arrived to visit the day before yesterday. Room 118 finally wore a smile."

Another night at Pickford allowed for contemplation. Cecil Sidel had averted a tragedy. Henry needed a beer run of his own.

chapter twelve

With a deep breath followed by a very deep breath, Henry shook off the night's cold, planted his feet firmly on the top step, and rang the Winterfield doorbell. A young girl answered, asked him who and why, revealed that she was daughter Paige and showed him into a large, high-ceiling living and dining area. Oak furnishings and a huge area rug gave the room a cozy feel. He met Case, Paige's six-year-old brother, and mom Paula. Towhead Case was the only one smiling. From somewhere, Paige, and he was guessing her age at thirteen or fourteen, looked familiar.

After introductions, Paula asked, "And what brings you out on a cold night, Mr. Hollins?"

Henry had debated long and hard about what his approach might be, the possible songs and dances. But now, in the opening act, he dropped all pretense and came straight to the point. "I'm here to ask your husband to seek to drop the charges against Melissa Minch and Gretchen Tarbat."

A voice boomed from the kitchen entry. "Why not ask for world peace while you're at it?" A strapping six-foot-plus Rayne Winterfield followed his question to the dining table.

If Henry might possibly be *more* intimidated, facing the

scowling Marlboro Man made him so. The month was March with a twenty-degree wind chill. He was sweating.

"Grab a seat, Hollins."

"I'm okay standing. I won't be long." *Chin up. Shoulders back. Don't wuss out.* "Only you can maybe save them, sir, provide them another chance."

"If they got the electric chair, Hollins, I'd plug it in."

"Daddy!"

"Yes Rayne, please. You're still upset. We all are. But the histrionics—enough." Paula held a beseeching look.

Rayne waved a pained compliance.

Paula turned to Henry. "But why let them off, Mr. Hollins?"

Henry noted the touch of empathy. "Bottom line, Mrs. Winterfield, a conviction now might sentence them to a penitentiary, lock them up for years."

"What's a pentenery?"

Paula looked to her children. "Paige, take Case up to his room."

"Mother, we're staying put."

Rayne headed off a spat. "The kids are fine, Paula. Mr. Hollins is leaving."

Henry grew desperate. There would be no step B and C without step A. "Minch and Tarbat are slipping through the cracks. Prior to the halfway, they were homeless. Homeless ... just a few years past Paige here. Two lives in a shitstorm, Mr. Winterfield. They got nobody."

"Let's all knock off the Mr. and Mrs. crap. No one is getting married here." He pointed his finger. "Nobody? Are you a nobody, Hollins?"

"I met them by chance."

"You're the piano guy in town, right?"

Henry needed a moment. This was going nowhere. What to add? His roving eye centered on Paige. "Where have I seen you?"

"I help out some in the kitchen at the halfway house. My Aunt Rosalie supervises cooking most days."

Henry saw a ray of light. Small-town life. "Do you know Melissa and Gretchen?"

Paige was thrilled to be joining the conversation. "No. I'm in the back kitchen. I've no connection with any of the residents."

Henry still marveled. "But I've seen you."

"Dayroom cleanup, maybe."

Rayne wanted the intrusion over and done. "And why are *you* at the halfway, Hollins?"

Henry quickly related to Winterfield the donated piano, the repairs, getting with Tarbat and Minch to play some songs together.

"A nice tale that leads to the trashing of my Ford F-100. Your thieves made a bad choice. No one at this house is shedding tears on their behalf. $3,500 total loss. You got $3,500 in your jean pocket, Hollins?"

Don't back down. Repeating ... don't be a wuss. "What I've learned, sir, is that dropping the charges at your end changes nothing. You actually have to persuade the sheriff and the county attorney to agree to the same."

"Are you even listening to me, Hollins?"

"Right this evening, I pledge to you, sir, that I will make good the loss of your pickup. I'll see you the sticker price. I'll assume liability. Pay you every dime you need to replace. I'm aware the Ford was fresh off the lot. I know it was beautiful, but so are Gretchen Tarbat and Melissa Minch."

Rayne made a parental gaffe. He paused.

"I've watched from the kitchen and heard them play. They're pretty cool."

"Tarbat and Minch are anything but cool, Paige."

"They were running away from something. We don't know anything about what the something was. Maybe that matters. Maybe they were afraid."

"And maybe they were just pissed off. Well, so am I, Paige."

"Rayne! Please." Paula felt the escalation had gone on long enough, then watched with uncertainty as her growing-like-a-weed, headstrong daughter, hands on hips, drew close to her father.

"So, change everything, Pops. Make them smile."

"And why should I do that?"

Paige about-faced, grabbed Case by the arm, and headed for the stairs. One step up, she turned. "Because you're my cool dad."

The kids headed to their rooms. Henry and Paula exchanged confused glances. What just happened? The father-daughter exchange leaped by so fast. Rayne appeared rattled, still staring at the empty staircase, and now a bit starstruck, like the very air in the room had changed color from shadowy gray to Caribbean blue.

Paula broke the awkward silence. "Get you anything, Henry?"

"No, ma'am. I've had my say. Coming here tonight—this hasn't been easy."

Rayne was struggling to collect himself. "At the hospital, how are they?"

Henry related what he knew. At the door with Paula, they both heard Rayne's callout: distant, resigned. "I'll think about your offer, Hollins." Paula followed with a quick hand squeeze.

In the Winterfield driveway, letting the motor warm, Henry caught his reflection in the rearview. "Well, good buddy, first off, thank God for thirteen-year-olds and second, as a reminder, the payback offer was not in the game plan tonight. Not ever. What were you thinking? Not about $3,500, that's for goddamn sure. You don't have it, good buddy."

Long drive back to Pickford, late evening, emotions running high, Henry drank two bourbons on the rocks, found his nerve and placed a call.

"Buckpool. What now?"

"Hollins again, sir. I've talked with Winterfield. I could use your help."

"Henry. Thanks for my B flat. What's on the stove?"

Henry quickly detailed his past few days, took a sharp breath, and ran on to the sheriff the who, the why and where he might turn to next. Finished, he gripped the phone like a life raft, crossed his fingers and waited. *Just get me to first base, Sheriff Buckpool ... a bloop single, a walk, a hit by pitch. I'll take anything.*

"Okay, pardner, no promises. I'll make a few calls and get back."

chapter thirteen

Starting the day with a hangover hardly helped. At least he'd slept. The Winterfield visit resulted in aspirin, hydration, and one giant exhale. Granted, Rayne's last-minute "thinking it over" was all he had, but Henry stayed positive. Buckpool, Patch, and Winterfield hadn't thrown up any stop signs. The quest to help Minch and Tarbat remained improbable, not impossible; it was a far-fetched, evolving mission, to be sure. So be it. Bring it on. Henry forged ahead as if success was a given.

Many rural Iowa towns, regardless their size, support and maintain a community center. River Grove proved no exception. At noon, Henry pulled up to a center-of-town, low-slung, white brick rectangle building and struck gold. The meeting hall was holding court to a potluck luncheon; locals and long-time farming friends, up in years, mostly retired, filled the seats—just the folks he was hoping to find.

Henry pushed in past the screen and storm door. With the entry of the outsider, the ongoing conversations took note and died down. Someone recognized him. "You here to tune the pie-ana?"

Henry acknowledged the query with a frozen smile. Why wasn't he an anonymous something: a truck driver maybe, an accountant, a forensic pathologist? "Not today. Forgive me for barging in. I'm looking for some help. Perhaps one of you might guide me in the right direction."

"Battery dead?"

Tables arranged end to end had them all together. With twelve attending, Henry hadn't spotted who'd fired the question, but he had everyone's attention. "Nothing of the sort, sir. Truth being, I'm looking to hire a housekeeper."

"Where at?"

A dozen pairs of eyes on him. Henry felt his nerves chip away his resolve. *Maybe this was a bad idea. Maybe my whole life is a bad idea right now.* "A household of sorts out at the Pickford place."

"So, you're the fella Clara warned us about."

A roomful of good-natured chuckling followed.

"Henry, Helen Slade here, what's this I read in the Journal-Reporter this past week?"

Henry stood rooted in place.

"The police report, Henry?"

I've way too many piano customers. Decatur County towns are way too small. "Hello, Mrs. Slade." He felt himself redden. "Actually, there's an explanation for that."

"A hospital break-in. A Mr. Henry Hollins charged and retained." Helen loomed, questioning, a bit amused.

Folks waited. Henry tried acting with nonchalance. "A visiting hour dispute, Mrs. Slade. Nothing more." Henry hoped his sheepish smile might afford him a pass. In a rush, he moved on. "Look folks, I'm glad Clara has made you aware. I've got me a big house. I guess right now I need a part-timer: some cooking, sweeping up, someone who knows his or her way around a toolbox, maybe a chicken coop. Right now, little is settled. Just someone handy who might be willing to sign on and help out."

"Live-in?"

"No. Well, I don't know, sir. That'll be ironed out. I'm just underway at Pickford. Hopefully, I'll know more in a few days. So, patience is required and," Henry sighed like a man with a plan unraveling, "a sense of humor and a rock 'n' roll fan would be a plus."

"You offerin' proper recompense?"

"That'll be a talking point, sir."

A long silence followed. Faces cast toward the far end of the table, and the end chair caught the attention. "And why is everyone looking my way?"

No one else spoke. Henry felt out of place and finally said, "Sorry to interrupt your luncheon. I'll leave a few business cards with my Pickford and piano shop number." He extended a one-hand wave and headed for the door.

The "my way" voice rang out, "Carsten's passed some two months. Lost my boy to the war in '66. I'm alone now. Not sure I'm what or who you're looking for, Mr. Hollins. I suppose I do have the time, not sure the inclination."

Henry peered at a slender woman in a print dress, dark blue with flowers. A light-green cardigan draped her shoulders.

"I can hammer a nail if needed. In my day, from the saddle, I helped drive cattle to greener pasture. Not much for knitting. I am a reader. Name's Dorothy Gunzenhauser. I'm not much to humor these days, but I was once an Elvis fan."

Making his way closer, Henry jokingly asked, "When can you start?"

"I'm only willing, sir, to take a gander."

A friendly voice was heard. "Make sure that's a long gooseneck gander, Dorothy."

More light table laughter followed, and Henry witnessed Dorothy's slight smile. She had face lines that drew from past summers in the sun. Overalls and chaps would be as natural a fit as the dress she wore. Moving cattle, indeed. Abundant hair, parted and combed back on past her shoulders, flowed as fine white thread.

"I doubt I'm your Pickford housekeeper, Mr. Hollins."

"Well, perhaps you'll consider an offer, Mrs. Gunzenhauser. If you're open to suggestions, so am I."

They exchanged phone numbers and addresses. They shook hands. Hers felt cold. Dorothy offered that she lived in town, one block west of Main.

Henry took note that despite the slight smile, it was forced and perhaps rare. A sadness enveloped the woman. Crow's feet marked the gray in her eyes, a color that matched her disposition. She sat round shouldered, defeated in a way. There had been good times, perhaps the farming years, but her demeanor showcased that her recent personal losses had piled up. They'd been severe. In the ashes, a graceful woman was not aging gracefully.

Henry let on he'd be in touch.

"Just so you know. I'm not taking on until I know what I'm taking on, sir." She raised an eyebrow. "You did say household, did you not?"

"I did, but at the moment I can't quantify that word. Sorry. Right now, I'm performing in a vaudeville variety show, Dorothy. I'm juggling baseballs, maybe bowling pins. They are all up in the air."

"Well, Mr. Hollins, whenever they fall and whatever you catch, I'll still be here. I'm sixty-four, sir, Paul McCartney's worst fear."

Henry cracked a knowing, beaming smile. "I'll send you a valentine, Dorothy. I promise."

Out the community center door, sitting in his van, Henry exhaled, glad he'd made the effort. He liked Dorothy. Life had dragged her down, but she had a stout heart. Resilient. Anyone could see that. The Beatles reference proved it.

Starting the Ford, a sudden, cold realization set in: not to get his hopes up. Mrs. Gunzenhauser was more than likely all for naught. Baseballs and bowling pins? Bullshit. He was juggling grenades. And no way was he going to catch them all.

chapter fourteen

"Let the minutes show that Sheriff Marion Buckpool, the injured party Mr. Rayne Winterfield, Mr. William Morain from the halfway facility, Mr. Henry Hollins, recorder Mrs. Jan Sackett, and myself, county attorney Martin Riser, were all in attendance on such and such. Whatever transpires here will be transcribed for the county record. Good morning, lady Jan and gentlemen. And allow me to begin. Whatever you've cooked up here, Marion, I'm against it."

"Dammit, Marty, hear these fellas out. Don't be goin' all DA. A proposition has been raised. Let's see if we can all find some common ground."

Marty raised an eyebrow. "Patch know about this morning's stunt?"

"He suggested we meet, Marty." Marion sighed. "There's no reason to get all henhouse here."

Marty defiantly straightened his tie. He eyed the table's far end. "Thanks for attending, Bill. Bring us up to date on the perps at your end."

"Okay. Minch and Tarbat are state guests, having pled guilty to misdemeanor charges of petty theft. They've three weeks remaining prior to release, a time span likely to augment with regards their recent escape. At my shop, running off before time served has legal consequences."

"Theft?"

"From a Dahl's supermarket in Des Moines."

Riser nodded. "First Dahl's, now a pickup." He turned to Winterfield, waving a paper file. "Somebody coerce you into this, Rayne? You bein' blackmailed?"

Across the table, Marion felt his hackles rise. "Sumbitch, Marty. You Columbo now? This ain't no goddamn TV show. Pardon the language, Jan."

"That's quite alright, Sheriff."

Marty wasn't listening to Buckpool. "Last I heard, Rayne, you were beating the death-penalty drum. Am I reading this right?" Riser cracked open the file and found his spot: "Wishes to drop all charges?"

Winterfield looked uncomfortable. "Restitution still stands."

"Damn right it stands."

"Tarnation, Marty, we maybe got something to resolve this morning. Let's resolve it."

Marty was back at Buckpool. "Resolve what? This was no joyride. They were not returning the truck back to Winterfield with an empty six-pack scattered on the floorboards. They drove straight to the interstate, no doubt planning to head south. Only the tore-up blocked entrance ramp kept them from Missouri to Texas. The county is filing a stolen vehicle with an intent to flee. Grand theft. I've the case reports right here. The People vs. Tarbat and Minch is open and shut."

"They might have changed their minds. Maybe they were looking to turn around when they fishtailed off 69. Dark, narrow, hilly road. Icy. Happen to anyone."

"Yeah, right, Hollins, swing it around, pick up Rayne and his sack of groceries walking out of Hy-Vee." Marty scrutinized Henry. "And I'm aware you're wrapped up in this, I'm just not sure I want to know how. But while I got you, get your tools on out to the Westview Care Center and tune that damn piano. Every week, I'm there visiting Grandmama Riser, listening to some kid play "Für Elise" that sounds like Chinese water torture."

"I'll call and—"

"Just get it done, Henry, and send me the bill. Jesus. Now, where were we?"

"Restitution."

"Thank you, Jan." Marty refocused. "You are the victim, Rayne. But we are looking at two thieves without a penny to their name. Iowa drops all charges relating to theft. They walk. You wind up with nothing."

Rayne pointed. "Hollins here swears he'll make good."

Marty sat back, arms folded across his chest. "Really. How many service calls to fork over the sticker price of a new F-100, Henry?"

"I made Mr. Winterfield a promise. I plan to keep it."

Marty flipped his own pen onto the table. "Damn, Marion. What am I missing?"

"Marty, we've an accord here. Rayne wants the charges scuttled. I'm not opposed. Moreover, regards the pickup, I'm aware liability is a stickler, but Rayne carried comprehensive on his policy, so there is that."

"I don't give a hog's snout about State Farm this or that, Marion. The State of Iowa doesn't let perps walk because someone is waving insurance. What else you got?"

"We're all concerned with your law, Marty. Tarbat's got priors. Nothing real serious, and you know that. You get your verdict, comes the sentencing, Patch says judicial hands may well point at hard time. Decatur County's got two delinquents that messed up big-time, to be sure. But two gals—what, maybe twenty if a day?—facing years at Anamosa? That rankles, Marty. Take that young niece of yours —"

"You know better, Sheriff Buckpool."

"I do. I'm just saying. The drunk driving stands, as does

restitution. Bottom line, why not payback and probation? Now hold on Marty, let me finish. Set a duration. Hollins here has proposed he be appointed as some kind of guardian. He's got a place just outside River Grove. He's got a full-time housekeeper. He's willing to take responsibility. For certain, more appropriate living quarters can be worked out on down the line, but right now, let's keep these kids away from lockup. We're far from squared away, I admit. Regardless. This is our chance."

Marty redirected. "Wow. I'm looking at a real Galahad, here, eh, Hollins?"

Henry ignored the sarcasm. His recent flare-ups with Esther had left him immune. "It's the Pickford place. Twelve miles from the courthouse here. Fell into my lap. Clara Pickford will confirm the arrangement."

Marty tossed a wave of dismissal. The room quieted. With a ponder, thumbs twirling, the county attorney began anew. "How's about another scenario, gentlemen? Three months go by, they split again. Steal another vehicle. This time, they run haywire and cause a pileup. Someone dies. How do you think our little 'backroom' today is going to look? How much guilt are we prepared to shoulder?"

"My housekeeper and I will run a tight ship."

"So does Morain, Hollins."

Buckpool's fist slammed the table. Even the coffee cups jumped. "Five years. That's what Patch is seeing. Five years, and we wind up with two head cases released, ready to set fire to the whole damned state."

Marty stewed. Everyone waited, and if waiting was hoping for a change of heart, they waited in vain. "What gives, Winterfield? Why aren't you backing me?"

"There has been enough damage. No need to add to it."

"Sounds like a Gandhi quote."

"Try thirteen-year-old Paige Winterfield."

"Ah ... not sure being a dad is material to —"

"I went to see them."

Marty sat up. "Jesus Christ."

"A promise to my daughter. At the hospital, I had my say. Gave the two of them both barrels. Minch tried to own up. I saw their faces, the lost look in their eyes. There are emotions that can't be hidden. I saw enough. I left."

"The visit was hardly authorized."

"Find a wife, Martin. Have a kid." With fire in his eyes, Rayne Winterfield zeroed in on Henry Hollins. "When we're done here twisting the prosecution's arm, when you get Minch and Tarbat tucked away up at Pickford, you get nose-to-nose, Hollins. You lay it on thick to those two hijackers that their fucking screw-up and the fallout is no longer just about *them*. You catching my drift?"

"Like a blizzard, Mr. Winterfield."

"Lay it on those two hellions in spades, Hollins."

"Yes, sir."

"Excuse the F bomb, Jan."

"I'm adding, all parties … emotions running high." Below the table, Jan crossed two fingers. She sensed a compromise at the gate.

Everyone waited again. Marty sat, removed his glasses and rubbed his eyes. Anything to add, Bill?"

"The state-run halfway is a transitional stop, Marty, there to provide individual support and structure. I'm thinking two choices: we, at some point, transition Gretchen and Melissa back into the street life or we push now toward the Hollins setup. Again, support and structure. Your decision, Marty. You've got a lot on your plate, but you asked, and at my end I'll recommend to Iowa time-served, waive the AWOL and point toward a fresh start at Pickford."

Marty sat with hands in his lap. The thumb twirling restarted, a nervous gesture that radiated about the conference room. To Henry, the ongoing silence sounded like the ocean's roar.

"Alright. Probation. Two years. They check in here at the courthouse each and every month. They break this gift, so help me God I'll have Marion's hounds on the loose. Restitution and drunk driving fines: their problem, your problem, Hollins. Your name will be on the dotted line. Time served at the halfway awaits disposition. Payments on time, Hollins. I hear one complaint from Winterfield, Iowa cracks the whip. Are we clear?"

"Yes, sir."

"And Decatur County Hospital does not operate pro bono."

"Sir?"

"The perps were never officially arrested, ergo the county is hardly responsible for their medical welfare. You catching another drift, Hollins?"

"There will be an ER bill in my mailbox." Henry appeared to wilt as if a rhino was added to the elephant on his shoulders.

Marty rolled on. "You in the Army ... Navy, Hollins?"

"Yes, sir."

"Social Services will visit, Hollins. I will read their reports. This Pickford place had better be STRAC, otherwise —"

"Anamosa prison. I understand."

"Ho boy. I'm not sure I do. Okay, Mrs. Sackett, make note that the Decatur County attorney has lost his mind while concluding his recommendation to said county judge to remove the Tarbat-Minch court hearing from the docket; that the State of Iowa has an acknowledgment of guilt from the perps, paperwork to follow, that we have a pretrial probationary agreement."

Jan smiled. "Shall I put 'lost his mind' in italics?"

"Capitalize every letter, Jan." Marty stood, "Fun's over, gentlemen." Rayne Winterfield continued to sit, looking skeptical.

Sheriff Buckpool stood and offered his hand. "Well done, Marty."

Henry was the first to leave. He turned back at the door, staring at the five of them. "I'm not sure how this is all going to turn out. But I do know there are decent folk in this room. Big hearts." Nodding at Jan Sackett, the sheriff, Riser, and with a thankful glance at Morain and a raised, clenched fist of gratitude at Winterfield, he left.

chapter fifteen
March 1972

The county prosecutor's reprieve let loose a rockslide of change. An ever-expanding to-do list dominated Henry's every waking hour. There were release forms and sundry complications exiting Tarbat and Minch from the halfway house. Piano parts and tools were transported whenever possible from his shop to the new makeshift setup inside Pickford's barn; a personal life doing a figure eight while the professional side marched with straight-line precision.

Continuing quarrels with Esther shook his fragile self-confidence. Were they separating, divorcing? Was she staying in Liberty? Was he ever coming back? What about the house? Was this truly what they both wanted?

"You are losing me, Henry. I never imagined."

"I've begun something that's reached a pace that's hard to slow."

"And that, Mr. Hollins, is total horseshit."

"I got them another chance, Esther."

"This is a poker game, and you're upping the ante till I bow out. And you know what really galls me?" Esther was at wits' end. "Someday, when the dust settles, I'll be the shrew, and you'll stand as the wild romantic."

"I'll stay in touch, Esther."

"Spare me, Henry."

There was Ruth.

"You're breaking vows made to my sister … at the altar!"

"Actually, I'm not. Look, thanks for helping out, keeping tabs with the service calls and all."

"I'm not happy about it, mister."

"No one is, Ruth."

———

Then there was Dorothy Gunzenhauser.

"Let me get this straight, Henry."

"Okay."

"You told the county attorney I'd already taken the job?"

"I may have fudged some, yeah."

"And the reasoning behind this fib?"

"Desperation."

"And I'm to give up my peace and quiet for these two hooligans that comprise this so-called household?"

"Gretchen will arrive first from the halfway facility. Alone. Melissa is still in the hospital. We need to get the upstairs rooms ready."

"We?"

"Give us a start, Dorothy, a few days. I know I'm off on the wrong foot here."

"Is Clara aware the arrangements?"

"Some. I detailed all about the band, a place to practice, et cetera."

"Did you mention the stolen pickup, the probation-bound convicted felons?"

"I hedged a few details."

"More fudging? No siree. Make her aware, Mr. Hollins. I'll not abide dishonesty in any detail. And do so right away, face-to-face. Fully informed, if Clara is still in, I'm in. I'll give you a week at Pickford, helping out, then we'll see."

"Yes, ma'am."

"And now I've a dog."

"I see that. I was greeted at your door, and I use the term 'greeted' rather loosely."

"Basically friendly. At least he hasn't eaten anyone I know of yet. As you can tell, mostly Lab and something else. He kept showing up at church some weeks back, rail thin. No matter my path, he'd follow. I got to thinking that my recently buried husband was making an effort of some kind. The mutt's had hard times. Ever since Carsten passed, I've felt the same. Carsten always said his company sergeant, John Parker, protected and kept them all alive through the winter 'German Bulge' in '45. John failed to survive the war, but the man was never forgotten in this house. I've decided to allow this dog here to take on John's surname. Hope I'm not bein' presumptuous."

Parker was a lumbering short-hair, his silky, cinnamon-brown coat turning light tan around his huge snout and floppy ears. Henry took note the uncertain look in his gray-green eyes. "At the door, I didn't see a tail wagging."

"Still to come, I reckon. Takes time to build trust, Henry."

"Yes, ma'am, and he's more than welcome at Pickford. I talked to Clara about a dog myself. You think he'd protect a henhouse?"

"You aimin' to find out?"

Henry stood to leave with a weary sigh. "It's on my list. Right this minute, providing Clara okays the setup, I'm penciling in Dorothy and Parker for at least one week." Henry stepped forward with a purpose.

"Gracious, sir, a kiss to the cheek was hardly necessary."

Henry offered a shy smile. "Yes, it was."

jersey moon: tour interview #3

August 1973

Gretchen: Why don't you interrogate somebody else?

Jersey: I will. So, Gretchen, looking back. The Pickford house ... an answered prayer?

Gretchen: I'm in a van with the piano guy. I'm leaving the jerkface louts at the halfway. I'm not going to trial. I'm not headed to Alcatraz. On the outside, I'm suspicious. On the inside, I'm caught in disbelief.

Jersey: Suspicious. You mean bitchy.

Gretchen: Why am I even talking about this?

Jersey: What's with the attitude?

Gretchen: God, Moon, talk about attitude. Are you writing a journal here or just plain pissing me off?

Jersey: Sorry.

Gretchen: Look, I loved my room upstairs at Pickford. Okay? Bigger than all the boxes I'd lived in combined. The musty smell, big windows that cranked open, the pale pink flowered wallpaper, the creaky floorboards. And damn, a double bed. Mel's room down the hall was basically the same. All light green, wildflowers on the wall, and between us, our own bath, with a shower stall like, you can just walk in. And hugging Parker. Love at first sight, man. A fairy-tale dog.

Jersey: So ...

Gretchen: I was like ... in the back of my mind ... what's the catch? All this just to start a band? Are you kidding me? What about Henry's own house, his piano service business, his workshop? He was married. What the hell? A guy chucking it all for two losers? Like, no fucking way, Moon ... and don't tell your mom I said that.

Jersey: I won't

Gretchen: My room at Pickford, as cool as it was, still had four walls. Every place has rules. Prisons come in all disguises, Jersey. Were Henry and now this Dorothy person any different? I don't follow anyone anywhere. The world was still a shithole.

Jersey: Life is a trip, and you meet good people along the way. You know that Gretchen, right?

Gretchen: Moon, the shining light. Give me a break.

Jersey: But when and where did the shithole stuff take hold?

Gretchen: I'm so not going there, Moon.

Jersey (standing): You must have told others. Tell *me*, bitch.

Gretchen: You want to know something? This tour is not good for you. You're barely a snot-nosed teenager, for crying out loud. And wipe that goofy smile off your face.

chapter sixteen

March 1972

Henry arrived at noon to pick up Melissa at the hospital. There were balloons and well-wishers from the staff to see her off. Pneumonia and infection had kept the doctors and nurses on edge. She'd become more than just another patient. Minch had battled through. Medical staff smiles and "take cares" filled the entryway.

Aided into the van, comfortable in the front seat, she peered at Henry and said, "Gret couldn't make my grand departure?"

"I didn't let on my taxi service, but she knows you're on the way."

"We're like sidestepping her? What gives?"

"I wanted just the two of us."

"And you again, Mr. Piano. I was expecting Mr. Morain with one of those rickety medieval horse-drawn jail wagons."

Henry laughed and let on their destination's whereabouts. "Be about twenty minutes north, up near the small town of River Grove." He provided nothing more, wanting to surprise. "The Pickford house calls for a long story, Melissa. I'd prefer another time. First things first, I salvaged your drumsticks from the wreck."

"I don't want to talk about the wreck."

"Roger that. Here's what I'd like to talk about, if you're willing. You, and how you and Gretchen met up."

"Ah, so this secret one-on-one, you want my back pages?"

"Yes, ma'am."

"Wow. This isn't easy for me, Henry."

"Take your time."

Melissa appeared to dwell on the request. Hollins had *been* there at the hospital, and it wasn't just to play the goofy song. He cared. The why didn't matter. She decided. "I'd been living with my grandmom for two years. I was close to sixteen when she passed. I'd no other family, so I was back with the state people."

"Where were you?"

"Stockton, California."

"So, high school?"

"Yep. Go Rams. Tenth grade at the time, and this was going to be my second go-round with the foster placement service."

"What year are we in?"

" '69."

"Can I ask about your folks?"

"You can. First, my actual dad was always a question mark. Mom had been a beatnik. You know what a beatnik is?"

"The 1950s. I read *On the Road.*"

"There you go. Back then, my mom traveled a lot. She had stories. I think she knew Kerouac. Regardless, she possessed a wanderlust and had lovers, none of whom stopped writing poetry long enough to claim a daughter. And I guess the natural order of things led Mom to eventually swing on over to the '60s hippies in San Fran, child in tow. A commune was our home. People were transient, some stayed a spell, others went truckin'. I recall the police and the whole farm being busted one time. You can guess our main crop. Everyone scattered." Melissa gripped her hands and squeezed her eyes shut. She sat very still. "This is hard."

"You don't have to continue, Mel, I'm sorry."

Melissa barely paused. There was a catharsis at work; her life, and no one had asked for a long time. "I believe Mom tried her best. All it took for her, in that Summer of Love, were too many spiked acid trips, the last with a no-return flight, a monumental final mistake. The state snatched me, and I was hooked up with Granny. All pretty confusing. I was a thirteen-year-old skinny runt. Still am, I guess."

"All I see is a really good person, Miss Minch."

"Thank you, Mr. Hollins. And Gretchen and I see you as quite insane."

"No argument here. So, with your grandmother from '67 to '69?"

"Yes. Gran died gracefully in her sleep. Bless her. My anchor. I loved her so much."

"What about friends in school and their families? No one with an extra bedroom to see you through?"

"I was a weird kid."

"Gee, I wonder why?"

"Regardless. No immediate takers, and I'm in limbo waiting on placement. First week in December 1969, a warm day and I'm out walking, simply to help clear my head. I stopped at a lamppost to read a concert poster and a voice behind me says, 'It's today, Stick, you wanna go?' And that's the story. Now, here I am in 1972, just out of the hospital and riding off with the Tin Man to Oz, I guess."

Henry's rock 'n' roll mind was flashing through history. "Wanna go … did you?"

"We did. Altamont Speedway, 12-6-69."

Henry was off the gas, slowing and incredulous. "You and Gret were at Altamont, the Stones?"

"Along with what looked like half the state of California. Infamous Altamont. But according to Gretchen, the fest was perfect, it was free."

"This is amazing."

"No, Henry, it's not. We were way back with the concessions and the outdoor field kitchen. We got roped in as designated soup slaves. They made us line-servers, slopping cooked beans onto paper pie plates ... which was okay because we were there for the food, not the Rolling Stones. We stuffed ourselves."

"Were you aware of the Hells Angels, the bloody violence at the stage, then all the stolen cars and shit?" Henry backed off the gas again. "Tell me you didn't steal a pickup truck at Altamont?"

"We didn't."

"Just teasing."

Melissa threw him a look. "I doubt that."

"So, winter of '69. That was over two years ago."

"Two years on the road, Tin Man. Tarbat was a free spirit when I met her. Still is. I became the rank and file. She knew the ropes: the missions, metro-shelters, Salvation Army centers, encampments. Nothing hassle-free, but places safe enough: cold months in New Mexico, summers in upstate New York ... overhead accommodations and free kitchens."

"You're vagabonds, a couple of gypsies."

"We held jobs at some places, but yeah, that's what we are, I guess."

"How'd you get around?"

"Rides. A sister knows another sister with wheels, in need of gas money. We have some. Other road trips with the thumb."

"Jesus."

"Gret can spot road danger like a lizard a fly. We backed off plenty of ride offers. We hopped onto a train once, rode the rails."

"Really?"

"Actually, really scary."

"No doubt. Thank you, Miss Minch, for the history lesson. Now, listen carefully to the present. You are on probation, Mel. Definition: 'On the Road' is over. Monthly mandatory check-ins. Drug tests. Social service inquisitions. In a very real sense, I'm on probation, too. We need to follow the rules. I cannot emphasize this enough."

"Gotcha."

"And what about the authorities in Stockton?"

"You think foster care is still looking for me, Henry?"

"I'm in a new world, Mel. I don't know. You're probably on some list somewhere. You're also past eighteen. So ... New Mexico and New York, how did I find you in Liberty, Iowa?"

"Pretty simple. You always mess up when you least expect to, right?"

Henry acknowledged with a grunt and a knowing nod. "Some folks are saying that about the county's piano tuner these days."

"Hah. And I'd be one of them." Melissa paused. "You really want to hear all this stuff, boss?"

"I do."

"Okay. Our travels had landed us in Des Moines. Gret and I were hungry. We were broke. We are outside a large Dahl's supermarket. I still remember the store name. We're set to enter and fill our pockets when we see an elderly lady roll out a cart with grocery bags crammed full. She stops and says, 'Shoot,' then leaves the cart and rushes back inside."

"She forgot an item, maybe a whole bag."

"Our conclusion exactly."

"Maybe left her checkbook at the checkout. I've done that."

"Who hasn't? I look at Gret. She looks at me. We stroll nonchalant, grab the cart and make way towards our imaginary station wagon that will carry us to our imaginary homes and our imaginary kids and husbands."

"Instant decision."

"For sure, and we weren't going to take all the goods. We are not monsters. What are we going to do with frozen raw shrimp, coffee beans, a hunk of Parmesan and canned veggies?"

"You probably don't have an electric can opener."

Melissa laughed. "We don't. So, we reach outer parking, commence rummaging the cart, not even aware the unmarked patrol car circling. In haste, we broke a street rule: in all endeavors, one's a doer, one's a keep-watcher. We weren't on guard, Henry. We felt scot-free until this burly guy pulls up in a sedan and gets out saying, 'Did you remember to pick up some aspirin? Because you're gonna need it.'"

"Let me guess, the forgetful cart owner is the wife of a cop who's waiting for her and sees the whole snatch."

"Worse. She was his mother. Bottom line, our excuses went nowhere. Our Bambi eyes found no sympathy. We were printed and booked. Gret had some priors, nothing serious, so we got carted off to the Liberty Halfway House, two small fish in a big pond."

"Stockton?"

"I let on nothing about Stockton. Tarbat made stuff up, and I went along for the ride. Gret wasn't concerned about the misdemeanor. We were either gonna do the time or check out early. Impulse would decide. Thus, a possible end to the story, but then, holy moly, we had this run-in with a deranged piano tuner." Melissa took a long look at Henry and said, "A guy we know nothing about."

He nodded. "There's not much to me. I've no famous rock concerts and gypsy travels to relate."

"I'm listening, boss. Your turn."

"Okay. After high school, not showing much direction or ambition, eighteen, I enlisted. That was in '62, and then, making my worst decision ever, I re-upped in '65. I didn't even know where Vietnam was."

"You okay from that?"

"I'm in one piece." Henry was caught off guard. Years had passed since anyone had asked about the war. "You're an American soldier, Mel, the good guy. You're in a foreign country to help, right? I survived. In '68, I got out. The country was on fire, I escaped into music. Guys like Pete Townshend were singing directly to me."

"So, *you're* the pinball wizard. I can't wait to tell Gret."

"I was more a purple haze."

Mel's stare held keen interest. "Eighteen in '62. That makes you today a ripe-old twenty-eight."

"And pretty soon … not to be trusted. Better watch out."

"Can I ask you something else?"

"Sure."

"The band thing."

"I'm caught up in a promise I made to myself years back. Not to be a drama queen but, at the time, I was in a tight spot."

"What promise?"

"If a chance came my way to try with the band thing, I'd make an all-out effort. You and Gret are my chance."

"We're nobodies."

"Well, I'm seeing a lot more of what you say isn't there. Let's just play this out and see. Look, Mel, if what's up ahead falls apart, I'll be fine, I'll accept my fate. Bottom line, I gave my long-ago promise my best shot. Case closed. You and Gret are on your merry way. But –"

"Uh oh."

"There's another thing, even more important. Something has gone very wrong with rock 'n' roll, and we need to fix it."

"You, me and Gret. Yikes."

"It's all rock gods now with full orchestration, touring giant arenas with the entourage and the runway-model girlfriend in tow. Nobody's rocking and pissing off the masses. Where are the 'hide away the kids' bands? Rock once howled from a scary back alley, now it's shopping music. Gentrified. Over-cooked. Rock's gotten fat, Mel."

"Okay."

"We dig for a different groove. I want us to be a 'what the hell was that' band. I want us playing and seeing bodies running for the exits."

"Can you hum a few bars, boss?"

"Not yet. First, we get good, then we change the world. A new heading, a new howl, Minch, and I'll know it when I hear it."

Looking about, Melissa felt a slight unease thinking, *but where are we heading right now*? Having exited off the main highway, they'd been riding on a rural county road awhile. "Wait, Henry, what's this? We're taking a dirt road?"

"Long driveway to the house, Mel. Up this hill a hundred yards and around a bend. Hold on." Slowing, Henry pointed through the trees to the high ground. "There it is: Pickford Manor." Continuing on, rounding left, house in full view, Henry stopped and shifted into neutral, motor running. "Before we pull in, Mel, a few final questions?"

Melissa focused on the house. "Fire away."

"Meeting up for the first time at a historic rock concert, that's cosmic."

"Yeah, Altamont, historic for all the wrong reasons."

"True, lots of bad that day, but there is a duality in nature, Minch. Maybe something really great happened there, too."

Melissa's gaze fell back to Henry. "You talking about me and Gret?"

"What else?"

"Such a romantic. You are beyond help, Hollins."

"I've been told that. So, the walking day … out for a breather … the concert … you never went back to Stockton foster care?"

"Tarbat was what I needed. She was my placement."

"At times, the last couple years must have been lonely, even frightening."

"Scary, yeah, never lonely."

"Gretchen's past—did she ever relate a this or that?"

"I asked early on, us being Butch and Sundance. She let me know I was off-limits. I let it go. I'm not sure Tarbat is even her real name. She told me once: 'an ugly name for an ugly girl.' "

With a hand on the gearshift, set to drop into first and go, Henry held up. "I want to say one more thing. Listening to you, comprehending all you've been through, and now sitting here in this van … I've an urge to give you an 'it's all going to be okay' hug, even though I don't know if it's going to be okay." He laughed at his mixed-up words.

"Well, you can't. My shoulder." She grinned.

He did the same. "Right. Okay Sundance, let's go find Butch."

Henry parked at the front porch, honking the horn; Melissa slid out, feet on the ground, and took in the two-story Victorian, the barn, the bounding dog headed her direction, an elderly gal stepping lively to greet, and a frantically waving Gretchen following right behind. She quick-turned back at Henry, her expression wide-eyed, attempting to convey a "what have you done?"

Gretchen and Parker met Melissa with kisses.

Henry shouldered next to Dorothy and said, "Here we go."

chapter seventeen
July 1972

At the afternoon's final service call, a broken bass string repair had Henry running late. As he reached Pickford, the sun was somewhere low in the west; the usual magical colored sky hidden by the dull gray of a stormy day. Pulling the emergency, hopping out, he felt a tightening in the pit of his stomach. Something was wrong. Dorothy's Ranch Wagon was gone, but it was Thursday, and she had her quilt group at the community center. That made sense, but the hens were cooped up. That was odd. Reaching the porch, Parker was at the window barking nonstop. Barging inside, moving past the foyer, looking about, Henry's heart sank. Parker had ransacked the place. "Holy shit." His heart pounded the obvious: Gretchen and Melissa were gone. A race upstairs confirmed the worst. Back down by the piano, Henry picked up what was left of his chewed and torn jean jacket. Parker lay slumped in the corner, laboring, nose to the wall. Henry knelt down and tried to reassure and console the big guy. "It's okay, buddy, you couldn't stop them. You tried. I know how you feel. Let's you and me check the barn."

All the band equipment lying about felt like the lowest blow of all. Gretchen had split; her Mosrite guitar stood propped against a support beam, left behind. Mel's drum setup appeared complete. Not even a stick was missing. Henry closed his eyes. Sorrow, anger and resignation allied into his now worn-out face. The progress they'd made in the last one hundred days; sounds of riffing guitars, beating drums and spunky vocals danced behind Henry's eyes. Standing with Parker now, he could almost visualize that built-up energy within their makeshift practice den seeping out past the barn door.

———

At Pickford in early April, they'd first set up in the downstairs parlor beside the grand piano. But Dorothy began spending more and more time at the house, and the daily racket was driving her upstairs. That wasn't fair. Relocating, they'd all worked like demons clearing out and cleaning up barn space. With summer coming on, the new Cecil Sidel Beer-Run Studio proved ideal. The barn was already wired. Electric was called, and outlets were checked and added. The pine and oak exuded a fragrance of eras past: leather saddles, the hot oil of a Model T, the birth of a calf. Most important, they had their own vibe swirling about in their own space. The attached hen coop clucked up a storm but, then again, newcomers Keith, Mick, Brian, Bill and Charlie clucked at everything. Secluded and cozied up as they were, Henry, Melissa and Gretchen had to be the best-kept rock 'n' roll band in the universe.

To celebrate Beer-Run Studio's grand opening, Henry surprised big-time, driving them up to Stoner's Music in Des Moines. Gretchen chose an electric Mosrite Venture, pale yellow with a black pick guard along with a Fender Mustang eighty-five-watt amp and speaker. Mel got a sorely needed new round-style drum throne, adjustable and padded just so – her choice after sitting on and critiquing Stoner's entire inventory. Henry paid via BankAmericard. He'd fret over the charges and interest on down the road. A peck on the cheek from Melissa was down payment enough for now. Riding back, Gretchen simply glowed; that part of her, so safely hidden away, hidden no more.

"What was that there, Miss Tarbat, a smile?"

"Don't start, Hollins."

Forced to collar Parker racing about the driveway, intent on picking up the trail, Henry's reverie was shattered. "Stop, Park. We need to think this through. More rain is on the way. Let's head back inside."

A thorough search only confirmed the fact. Coats were missing. The band slush fund was filched from the kitchen cookie jar. Henry's eye caught the wall calendar displaying a circled black-marker X. Melissa and Gretchen were due for a probation call in three days. "Oh, man."

Henry reheated a cup of morning coffee and sat. Parker, eyes forlorn, rested his head on Henry's leg. "They hiked out. Probably hitched a ride on the county road to the interstate. God knows where to after that." Sitting thinking brought on a surge of dread—the ramifications. He thought about switching to beer, tossing in a few shots, getting to the point of chewing up the furniture, just like the dog. Instead, he phoned Dorothy at the community center. "They're gone."

"What? Who, Henry?"

"Been here close to an hour, trying to get a grip on a slew of questions with no answers. They packed up, took the little money we had, and split."

"Gracious. How long, Henry?"

"When did *you* leave?"

Dorothy's mind was racing. "Midafternoon. Close to three. I had chores to run before meeting the group at the bee."

"It's close to eight now. So ... five hours at the most. They locked up the hens and left Parker inside the house. He went crazy and tore up the place. Your kitchen aprons are among the casualties."

"Where would they go?" Dorothy had no use right now for aprons.

"Summertime. They'd head north."

"You okay, Henry? You holding yourself together?"

"No and no."

"Listen to me, Henry, north is too general. All your conversing these past few months … anything that was said?"

Driving Melissa to Pickford from the hospital, her back pages – Henry grabbed a snippet. "Upstate New York."

"How would they travel?"

"Hitch to Des Moines … the bus depot. They'd have enough cash for two tickets. Buffalo … maybe Rochester."

"Go find them, Henry."

"I'm grasping at straws, here, Dorothy. I'm throwing darts at a map of the entire United States."

Their line went silent for a spell. Dorothy waited, feeling more and more heartsick for the three of them. To keep the conversation afloat, she said: "Don't despair. A step forward, a step back, you know that, Henry."

"This is a thousand steps back."

"Wait, they've got a probation date just around the corner."

"Yes, ma'am. Three days."

"What happens?"

"There will be a massive 'told you so' screamed my direction from all directions. But that is minor, hardly on the radar. Iowa will issue a warrant for their arrest. Attorney Riser will lead the posse himself."

"Are you absolutely certain they're gone, Henry? Maybe new friends in town … they're visiting."

"Wishful thinking, Dorothy. Mel left a hasty note on her pillow. One word: *sorry.*"

"Let the sheriff know, Henry. We need help."

"Okay. I'll call Buckpool."

"No, wait. I'll babysit the phone at Pickford, just in case they call. I'll notify the sheriff. You skedaddle. Go and find them."

"Why should I search for them just to murder them?"

"Go!"

More line silence. Dorothy, waiting, mouthed a silent prayer.

"I'll take Parker."

Sick at heart, Dorothy replaced the receiver. She knew she'd gotten too close – to all three of them. She'd even admonished herself time and again for doing just that, all the while slipping into roles she wasn't seeking. Mothering? Oh please, no. Nevertheless, she had faced the mirror more than once asking why she was trying—no, yearning—to win their trust? And she knew the answer. Right from the start, back in March, the small victories began to pile up.

Parker, Gretchen and Melissa were one. Within a week, she began leaving the big mutt at Pickford. She had to. In town, Parker's constant moping drove her batty.

There were those beginning early mornings that had Dorothy and Henry buffaloed. No matter what time in the a.m. she and Henry started their day, Melissa and Gretchen were already up and about: walking Parker, tending the chickens, making breakfast. There were mornings that Henry arose before dawn to write. As if he didn't have enough on his plate, he'd started a short story that had kept growing into a full-bore Civil War novel; up at 6 a.m. to research and type for two hours before heading out to his piano customers. He'd kept at the book because he loved working on it. Why do we do most things? What proved baffling was that, regardless of the time Henry fell out of bed, Melissa and Gretchen had preceded him. Since when do two twenty-year-old girls leave their warm beds to catch the sunrise every morning?

jersey moon: tour interview # 4

August 1973

Jersey: Backing up to the early days at Pickford. Did the shoulder heal up okay?

Melissa: Pretty much, Jersey. For weeks I took it real slow with the drumming. Easy tempo. I'm sure that helped. When Gret went electric, I kicked up the beat a few notches. At that point, I honestly felt the drumming would hurry the heal.

Jersey: You know, if you were in like, a police lineup … to pick the suspect drummer, I'm not choosing you.

Melissa: Thanks a lot.

Jersey: Come on. The hundred-pound blond elf? Rock drummers are gorillas, right?

Melissa: Keith Moon is not a gorilla. By the way, any relation?

Jersey: Doubtful, I'm sure. But tell me, where did the I'm-gonna-play-drums come from?

Melissa: I was the eleven-year-old bongo player in my mom's commune band. Not that they were ever a band. Later, when I lived with my grandmom, there was a guy on our street who practiced a lot in a basement apartment. I'd stand outside on the sidewalk and listen. One day I caught him sitting on his stoop. I asked if he'd teach me. Can't believe I had the nerve.

Jersey: Definitely nervy.

Melissa: Not so much. Simon drummed in a jazz quintet. He was a professional. I got to see him perform in a street fest benefit one time. Check this out. The day was hot. Easy to get sweaty. Playing the gig, Simon loses a stick. Lunging to grasp it, his arm nearly topples a cymbal, then another. Trying to recover, he's missing heads, hitting rims. Simon's flailing away at his kit like he's chasing butterflies. Finally, he replaces the runaway, recaptures the beat and settles into his groove. The tempo's back, no problem. I mean, it was like the whole gaffe was planned. Simon's a cool cat. Not many watching and listening even caught the stick chase. The piece over, his band is all pointing and grinning. He looks over at me and says with a twinkle in his eye, "I need to practice more." Golly, that was so funny. But he made me feel that day as if I was part of something special. I was hooked. I wanted to *be* him. I mean, he was never my longtime personal instructor or anything, but he got me started on the basics: gripping sticks, staying relaxed, practicing the high hat, counting, a few fills. There was a kit at school. My band teacher encouraged. I pretty much lived in the practice room.

Jersey: But why an obsession with drumming? Any idea?

Melissa: I never fully grasped my growing up. We are whatever surrounds us, right? I just knew lots of stuff in my life wasn't cool. Maybe I was frustrated. Maybe drumming helped. But listen up, don't go and paint me all Oliver Twist. My growing up was screwed up, but I met saints and angels along the way. You got me?

Jersey: I do get you, Melissa. Let's get back to Pickford early on. Gunny told me once that you guys had this morning thing, like up at dawn.

Melissa: Oh yeah. Easy answer. Wandering about the USA with no direction home, the big decision each and every day was to locate a safe place to bed down. Nothing was more important. Before we hooked up, Gretchen, being alone, was attacked once in her bedroll by a psycho with a kitchen knife. It was like 7 a.m., maybe earlier. Totally terrifying. From a deep sleep to scrambling for your life, half awake, fending off a madman. You never know the mental problems or what drugs they're on. Luckily, another from the shelter was up, intervened and chased him away. Gretchen was cut on her hands, arms and neck. Shaking in fear, she threw up right then and there. A vow was made: She'd be first out of the sack wherever she slept. No zombie would ever surprise her again. Our whole time together, we did just that. We had run-ins. With crazies and street drugs, confrontations were bound to happen. But we were up with our own knives at the ready. And we simply carried on the same at Pickford. Yes, Henry was cool, but that was when we met and practiced at the halfway house. Gunny was new and unknown. We weren't totally sure, got me?

Jersey: Absolutely.

Melissa: Parker was with us and Pickford was so obvious a gift, a haven. I flat-out told Gret: "We're as safe as can be. I'm sleeping in my own bed and waking up when I damn well please." She held onto our first-up rule for a few more days, then joined me. Gretchen and I went from always being first to rise to dead last; the unbelievable joy of feeling secure and sleeping in, so long in coming, so wonderful when it arrived. Gunny couldn't wake us up with cherry bombs.

Jersey: Oh golly, I love that.

Melissa: Me too.

chapter eighteen
July 1972

Sitting beside the phone in an all-too-quiet house, Dorothy continued soul-searching the early spring victories along with the trials.

Melissa's delight in cooking for the first time; Gretchen feigning little interest.

The four of them restoring the coop, the "Rolling Stones" hens arriving and Gretchen, despite manifesting an indifference, instructing Parker his fowl-protection responsibilities. They lost Mick to a predator early on. A few days later, 5 a.m., all hell broke loose. Squawking and barking filled the predawn air. Dorothy and Henry had raced outside with flashlights waving to find Gretchen standing by the coop holding a croquet mallet in one hand and a dazed raccoon by the tail with her other, a big grin on her face. Gretchen cared.

Neither Melissa nor Gretchen had graduated from high school. Their probation conditioned that both pass the GED exams. Melissa dived in. Gretchen proved stubborn. Dorothy began tutoring the state programs and practice tests in reading, writing, math, social studies and science. Prepping the GED proved a bumpy ride for all three of them. The two students weren't quite ready to take their finals yet, but they were making progress.

The Rise of The Mad March

If any one event truly highlighted the first 100 days at Pickford, the Gretchen Tarbat and Harry Caray link reigned supreme. The ongoing band practice generated little interest to Dorothy, but she recognized the importance of Harry Caray in the excitement of their voices. She sought to comprehend.

"So, you've had some sort of musical breakthrough, Henry?"

"We may have something, Dorothy."

What happened was that on a warm evening in June, Henry was watching a Monday Night Baseball game from Comiskey Park in Chicago. Gretchen plopped down on the sofa during the seventh-inning stretch.

"What's this, Hollins?"

"Harry Caray is serenading the White Sox faithful with 'Take Me Out to the Ball Game.' The NBC guys talked him into it. This is great."

Gretchen watched. "I love this guy."

"All the Southsiders do."

That was the extent, their whole exchange. Gretchen up and left. At Comiskey, Harry Caray shared another joke with the MNB crew, made his way back to his local radio broadcast and the game resumed.

Ten minutes later, an electric storm blew out from the barn. Gretchen had her Fender amp at ten. The riffing was furious fast, the sound of a razor shaving a tough beard, and if you kept your ears glued and clued, you could make out the "Take Me Out to the Ball Game" melody line weaving its way through the growling tempest.

Henry switched off the game, stood and listened. Gretchen ended her metal serenade. Before she started in anew, Henry turned to Dorothy and said, "She found it."

Of course, the first few months fostered days of downside. Gretchen could be maddeningly defiant with Melissa backing her at every turn. And speaking of moments, there were those mornings, with the two of them sleeping in, when Dorothy found them cuddled up together; her raised eyebrows resulted from a long life of traditional expectations. Convention did veer on occasion. She never told Carsten she'd voted for Kennedy. Lesbian relationships were hardly unknown, but Dorothy would be honest and admit she'd never encountered them directly. At Pickford, with the three of them often together, Dorothy could not resist commenting.

"I couldn't tell this morning if that lump under the covers was one body or two."

"And, Mrs. Gunzenhauser?"

"And Miss Tarbat and Miss Minch, I've a few questions pertaining."

"Are you shaming us?"

"Hardly, Melissa. I'm intrigued."

Yes. There were moments to savor. Moments now set to be tossed aside and forgotten. *Oh my, what was being lost?*

She sat conflicted. *I didn't ask for this. There's been enough hurt in my life.* But she was heartsick for them. She could not help feeling otherwise. Two young lives. An opportunity here at Pickford – being missed. She called the sheriff.

"Buckpool."

"Dorothy Gunzenhauser, Sheriff."

"Tell me some good news, Dorothy."

"Can't. They've run off."

"Goddamn it! When do they violate probation?"

"Three days. Henry's out searching, thinking they're headed for the bus depot in Des Moines."

"Destination?"

"Buffalo, New York. A pure guess, Sheriff."

"I'll have the DMPD spot-check the station. Next, how long ago, Dorothy?"

"Best guess, five hours. And they left on foot. Carsten's old pickup is still here. I'm by the phone. If I hear anything, I'll call back. I'd appreciate you doing the same."

"I will, Dorothy. Central Iowa's had thundershowers all day. Someone's going to take pity on two hikers getting soaked."

"This is all so sad, Sheriff."

"We all took a chance. I'll leave you with this—I'd do it again."

———

Cursing his low fuel, Henry, sharing the front seat with Parker, was running west on rural county pavement toward the interstate. The rain had slackened and had brought in a sharp temperature dip. July is not always July in Iowa. Chilled, he cranked the heat fan. Lightning lit the western sky, storm clouds extinguishing whatever daylight remained from the sun dropping below the horizon. Henry downshifted as they approached the County Road J55/Route 69 two-way stop intersection. Parker began growling. Given dusk, the drizzle, worn wipers, low beams and an underpowered defrost, Henry failed to make out the bundled-up figure standing alone at the southeast corner. Parker, now whining, was turning circles. Henry's foot stomped the van to a stop. "What's got you riled, big guy?" Parker's nose pointed the way. Rotating the window down, Henry peered out. *It couldn't be.*

It was. Henry leaped to the tarmac and had Melissa in a smothering hug. She was soaked and shivering. "Look at you, Minch, let's get you warm." Parker, demanding a hug of his own, was at last pushed and prodded to the back. Everyone sat. For what felt like an eternal half-minute, no one could bark or think of a word to say. The van seemed to shrink down to jewelry-box size.

"I'm not as wet as I look. My jacket held up pretty good."

"Where is she?"

Melissa didn't dare look at him. She closed her eyes and started in. "We'd gotten a ride as far as the Winterset 35 exit. We had a terrible row. I wasn't going any further. I wanted to go back. Gret was freaking out. She hurled her world at me. All that she had done, where would I be without her. She was like, 'Why just this far? Why now, traitor?' I'm yelling, 'I want to sleep in my bed; what about Parker and the Stone hens?' We were on an entrance ramp. It began raining again. A car stopped. I was crying. We were in a screaming match. I'm pleading, 'Don't do this.' She shook her fist at me, ran, peered in, hesitated and grabbed the ride. I walked across the bridge to the southbound side. A family station wagon took mercy and dropped me back at the River Grove/Grand Garden exit. Then, nothing, no traffic, more rain. I've been walking miles. I'm cold and really tired, Henry. We've split. We're over. I can't believe it."

"Where is she headed? Parker! Settle down."

"We were going to decide when we saw the bus schedules."

"Shit! Can you stab at a first choice?"

"Denver, then down to Santa Fe and back east to Las Vegas, New Mexico. We have connections there."

"Hah. I wasn't even close."

"What?"

"I had you both heading to Buffalo."

"Maybe. Finger Lake region is another possible. We've stayed in Geneva. She's got these hangouts, Henry. Safe havens, or what were once safe havens. She had paying jobs at these places, too … knows people."

"Definitely bus?"

"No. She'll keep an eye out for anyone looking for her. She's got a sixth sense, always able to blend with the shadows. Did you call the police?"

"You've a mandatory with the probationary officer in three fucking days, Mel."

The Rise of The Mad March

"I know."

Henry hardly heard Melissa's whispered answer, just the sniffles.

"Not to mention band practice. Hah. Where have I heard that before?"

"I know."

"And sitting here crying is going to get us nowhere, Minch." Henry stewed. Deep inside, he half wanted to hug Melissa once more, so grateful to have found her, a prayer answered. His other half was so angry, so let down. He eyed the rearview. "We need a plan, Park, and back off, beast. Nuzzling Mel's neck is not a plan."

They drove north ten miles to a truck stop in Osceola. Henry gassed up and called Dorothy, then he called the bus depot. Denver had left thirty minutes ago. Chicago to points east was just now loading. And ... "Just came on duty. No, sir, I can't say if there has been a solo dark-haired backpacking girl ticketed."

Henry chose Denver. They'd skip the first Nebraska stop at Omaha and intercept her at Lincoln. They cleaned the windshield and drove 180 miles, reaching the Jefferson Bus Lines terminal in Lincoln around midnight. There had been a bus repair delay in Omaha. The additional hour wait was maddening. Melissa walked Parker. Henry barely answered a clue in the Des Moines Register crossword found left in the waiting area. His lost patience turned on the puzzle. *Goddamned N.Y. Times crossword. Always so goddamned impossible on Fridays.*

When the bus arrived, hissing and whispering to a stop, they both hid out of sight. Many on board disembarked to stretch and find a snack. No Gretchen. They boarded, swept past the vacant driver's seat, and searched on down the center aisle, eyeing the asleep and half awake. No Gretchen. Henry had guessed wrong. Heartbreaking. Pull-the-hair-out frustrating.

Melissa was famished. They found a twenty-four-hour

Denny's and treated themselves to breakfast. Leaving the restaurant, Melissa leaned close and quick-kissed Henry on the cheek. "I'm so sorry." She stayed dispirited and catnapped all the way back to Pickford. Parker finally laid down and quieted. Hardly a word was exchanged during the long return. Henry pulled in beyond tired at 5:30 a.m. Dorothy met them at the door. Melissa fell into her waiting arms. Henry's eyes told her all she needed to know about Gretchen. "The sheriff hasn't called, Henry. No news. He did promise earlier to send someone out this morning to take down our statement or some such."

All Henry longed for was a huge bourbon, a hot shower and bed.

Dawn broke, the sun was rising in a clear sky as Henry related the night's search to Dorothy. He sipped his bourbon to the last. Melissa was asleep on the couch. Dorothy elected not to disturb her and fetched another blanket. Parker barked. The doorbell rang.

Dorothy called out, "That'll be the deputy from Lyon."

Parker was pawing the floor. The cop was now knocking. Obviously, the night and now new day were never going to end. He swung the door wide: Gretchen Tarbat. She was shaking, her arms wrapped around her waist. Her wet windbreaker held little warmth. From the storm elements long endured, damp hair plastered against her head and neck, framing a face best described as moldy gray.

Henry stood numb. Why not end this odyssey on the least expected? Spanning ten seconds, he flashed from gasping surprise to explosive anger to exhausted resignation. She'd won. Tarbat was everything everyone had warned him that she would be. His eyes met hers. "You should have worn a hat."

She said, "I forgot my …" and staggered. Parker, at her side, kept her from falling. Henry provided a shoulder to lean on and hollered for help.

The Rise of The Mad March

Melissa had Gretchen in a hot tub. Henry poured another bourbon and heated cans of Campbell's chicken noodle. Eventually, four half-dead souls convened at the kitchen table. Dorothy threw Henry a searching, go-easy look. Melissa and Gretchen, downcast, appeared set to fall headfirst into their soup bowls. Henry was buzzed. Two bourbons had him feisty and combative. The phone rang. Dorothy got up and picked up.

"They're both back. Yes. This morning." Dorothy held the phone away until the shouting died. "Okay, I'll put her on." She pointed. Gretchen dragged herself over and took the receiver. "Tarbat here." She stood listening for a ranting minute, answered, "Yes, sir," and hung up. Back at the table, Melissa sat, questioning.

"That was Mr. Buckpool, the sheriff, screaming that the police spent $22,000 in man-hours searching for us. He's going to take it out of our hides."

Henry slurred a chuckle. "The good sheriff is tallying up. Aren't we all?"

Gretchen peered up. "Don't go smug."

"You're grounded for the rest of your life, Tarbat," Henry was shouting, "and if you do hightail it again, and say, find someone, fall in love, get married, and have a kid … the kid is grounded, too. That's a Woody Allen joke."

"And I fail to find the humor, Hollins. Mel and I are not your fucking slaves—but don't you wish."

"And I fail to find the humor in my last twelve fucking hours, Tarbat, searching all night for two imbeciles, ready to strangle—"

"Enough, Henry," Dorothy interrupted. "For heaven's sake. Language! Mercy. The both of you. We've all been through enough for one night. Go. Get some sleep. All of you."

Henry scowled at all three, stood up, wandered over to the

couch and fell face forward. He was lightly snoring before he hit the pillow.

Dorothy, Melissa and Gretchen sat stoic. Dorothy said, "You're wearing him out, you two."

"Works both ways, Gunny."

"He thinks the world of both of you."

"He's a dreamer."

"Last I heard," Dorothy raised her eyebrows, "there be no crime in that, Melissa. Let's all get some shut eye."

The two were halfway up the stairs when Dorothy called out from below: "I overheard you at the door. What did you forget, Gretchen?"

She and Melissa both stopped. Gretchen slowly turned. "I never got on a bus, Gunny. I never bought a ticket. I just strayed outside and sat on the bench there and started thinking back to when we were in the hospital … so scared that Mel might die. I prayed 'please help.' I made a promise not to mess up and to be there for her, always. I don't even know who I was praying to. Somebody. Anybody. So, I'm back, because I had forgotten my promise."

Catching everyone by surprise, Henry sat up. Parker barked once like a biblical herald. Trance-like, staring at no one, Henry shouted, "You're both in the penalty box, but I know a way out."

Dorothy, Melissa and Gretchen waited.

"We play a live gig." Henry fell back, dead to the world.

jersey moon: tour interview #5
August 1973

Jersey: The Pickford split, July of '72.

Gretchen: Oh crap.

Jersey: I mean, what were you thinking?

Gretchen: You mean the great escape? We were gone one day, Moon. Nothing more.

Jersey: Except for all the near heart attacks suffered. Gunny, Henry, Parker … the sheriff.

Gretchen: Hah. Typical writer. Take a little rain, turn it into a hurricane. Look, Moon, how about this? I came up with this wacko riffing for "Take Me Out to the Ball Game." At first, Henry loved it. He's like, "You found our *groove*, Tarbat," blah blah blah, and we started working it up. Mel matched my tempo. She and I were a train roaring through a tunnel. Henry wove the melody line on top. Day in. Day out. And guess what, Moon?

Jersey: What?

Gretchen: Henry was never happy with what we had. He's all over me. "It's still not fun, Tarbat. It's all white noise. Your changes aren't clear. Nobody's gonna get it."

I'm like, "Me? I'm the problem? Are you serious? You can't play jack shit. You're tied to a chord chart, Hollins." He's all, "I'm working on that, but 'Ball Game' is all sharp edges, you need to 'round' the sound. Everybody's got to know what the hell it is we're playing. You're holding a guitar, not a dentist drill."

I could not take him slamming my playing, Moon. No ma'am. I fucking left.

Jersey: Gretchen, look at me.

Gretchen: What?

Jersey: I'm thirteen, not three. That's what.

Gretchen: You're a pain. That's what you are. Alright, for the sake of posterity … why we left. And I explained this to Gunny way back when. I dragged Mel along and took off because that's what I'd always done. For years. Keep moving on, babe. Don't let the dust settle. Just because I run into Santa, that doesn't mean I have to stay at the North Pole.

Jersey: Okay. Let's say I'm buying the "dust" thing. But why? What are you *not* telling me?

Gretchen: There you go again. Up yours, Moon.

Jersey: My mom is so not going to be happy with that.

Gretchen: Funny, runt.

chapter nineteen
August 1972

For the rollout gig, Henry considered Hitches. The bar was close-by, twenty minutes, located just off Interstate 35 at Van Wert, a town of maybe a hundred. The schoolhouse was long-ago closed, a sad, hollow shell; a small grocery was hanging on. Main Street was abandoned brick buildings in various states of disrepair. Hitches, the post office and scattered churches fought to stay open.

Dex Knotts owned and ran the bar. Heading home from work and passing through Van Wert, Henry had stopped in on more than one occasion for a five o'clock beer. And chatting up Dex, tall and rangy, a back-home Haight-Ashbury survivor, was hardly a problem. Hitches, a long, gloomy rectangle housing a permanently soiled wood floor, a black tin-tile ceiling and glowing with corporate-beer neon, was usually as empty as the town. Henry made the call.

"Hitches ... he just left."

"Dex, Henry Hollins, the piano tuner."

"Hollins! Where have you been hiding?"

"You wouldn't believe. Hey, calling for a favor. A request, actually."

"Bring it."

"I'm in this band. Just getting started. We need a live gig

under our belts. I thought maybe we might do a short show at your place."

"No shit, hombre. Hitches is honored. You realize this dump hasn't had any live music probably since VE Day in '45. Jukebox only works when it wants to."

"Look Dex, there's just three of us. We're pretty rough, so no cover charge, no payouts or any of that stuff. Ears listen for free. We just blow through a few songs, have a brew. That's it."

"I've got a raised corner up-front. No idea why. Might stand in for a stage of sorts. There are a few outlets, and Henry, before we go any further, one other thing. I hardly have any customers, and for the few old codgers I do put up with, rock 'n' roll ended when Presley began wearing army green."

"That's what I'm hoping for, Dex. We don't need much. We've a couple amps and speakers. We'll hook up a vocal microphone somehow. Chance to test the nerves with a few locals. Hitches will be perfect."

"When are you gonna show up?"

"How about the eighth, a week from Tuesday? Say at nine?"

"Sure. Every day is next Tuesday at Hitches. This ain't Liverpool, Hollins."

"We ain't the Beatles, Dex."

———

Despite Gretchen's loud protestation ("an oncoming fucking train wreck"), the three practiced like crazy to put together four songs. Along with the jitters, the Hitches gig had them focused: hit the nail or surrender the hammer. They would open with "Ball Game," follow with two originals—Henry's "Stay for My Funeral" and Gretchen's "Shut the F**k Up"—and finish with a Neil Young cover: "Everybody Knows This Is Nowhere." Considering Hitches, an apt closer.

Gretchen had a new song, "Cecil's Beer Run," that they all

liked; not quite ready, but if they actually had a call for "one more," dream on, they might wing an encore.

At breakneck speed, none of the songs lasted more than two minutes. Melissa said it best. "We'll be a shot, a beer, a goodbye."

Henry laughed. "The few there won't know what hit them until we're packed up and gone."

Despite focusing on the gig, the day-to-day at Pickford struggled to return to normal. Built-up trust on all sides had been erased on Depot Day, the tag given July 22, the day that Gretchen and Melissa flew the coop. Gunny sat them both down to comprehend the why or whys they left. Little was resolved. Gretchen did swear on the Gunzenhauser Bible to stay put through the probationary period.

Henry put anger and disappointment aside, eager for the band to jell and help ease the friction that still existed. To that end, he drove up to Stoner's Music and shelled out for a magnetic pickup for his prized Martin. With Gretchen blasting away on her Mosrite electric, Henry was looking to balance the drums, vocals and guitars. The new Martin pickup would aid and abet. He eyed Bill Stoner hopefully. "The acoustic amp's a loaner, right?"

"The amp's a one-gig rental with an option to buy. Special to you only, Henry."

"You're killing me, Stony. There's no end. Melissa's begging for a new kick pedal. Hell, she needs a complete upgrade. She's playing a patched kit of middle school rejects."

"Melissa deserves the best. I've got a Ludwig set. $750. Perfect. Burgundy beautiful."

"I haven't got seven-fifty."

"Rock 'n' roll has no fear of Master Charge, Henry. Why

save for your casket? I'm starting to love you guys. You're playing a gig. What about guitar stands, you need stands?"

"What? We need a microphone … with a stand. Can I plug a vocal mike into Gretchen's amp?"

"With an adapter cable, but not a good idea. You *need* a PA, Henry."

Henry sighed. "And a ride to the poorhouse. We're gigging at a nothing place. Small tavern. No one will be there, Stony. The big-ticket items will have to wait."

"Squeaking by is going to produce nothing but a squeak, Henry."

"Maybe that's all we're capable of, Stony."

Henry had troubles. But needed band equipment was not keeping him awake at 3 a.m. Since the early weeks at the halfway house, Melissa and Gretchen had surprised him. The blond with her spoons and boxes could really drum, and the trash-mouth had a righteous ear. Prepping now for the Hitches gig cemented what Henry had known all along: how musically talented they both were. From the very beginning, keeping up with *their* progress became paramount.

August had arrived. Henry had contracts at three separate colleges. With the new school year near, late summer/early fall was the busy time for his piano service business. Yet, the situation was ideal. He gave up his novel writing for a daily early a.m. start. Tuning, cleaning and repairing instruments all morning, he then stole away into a practice room with his Martin for a few hours each afternoon, there to riff chord changes, build speed, to work on Gretchen's songs, and to arrange his own stuff. That is, to tackle the mystifying act of transcribing what was in his head down to his fingers and strings.

The practice paid off. Moreover, he discovered writing and

arranging new songs was up his alley far more than memorizing covers.

Together in the barn, they'd all agreed. Covers were secondary. Neil Young's "Nowhere" seemed to work. Great. But they'd concentrate on their self-penned songs. "And keep it simple" became a war cry. No one knew how to play decent guitar leads—thus, no leads. If Clapton came calling, axe in hand, he'd be shooed away.

All summer, both Henry and Gretchen took to composing songs. Riffs, mostly. Chord progressions to sing around. Lyrics were added. "Ball Game" gave them a reference, and they duplicated Gretchen's hard-and-fast tempo with everything they tried.

The mood in the barn was upbeat. There were times they laughed at how bad their efforts sounded. There were times they stared in wonder when something seemed to work. By chance, Gretchen and Henry traded off vocals on "Beer Run," one male nasal tenor up against one female contralto. Minch sat at her kit, amazed. "Hey, you guys need to do more of that." And they did—because Melissa seemed to have an uncanny talent for suggesting changes that gave plain straw songs a golden tint.

They were hit and miss. And if Henry lacked the musical flair of his bandmates, he fell back on what he considered his strength: that he recognized what *did* work.

What frustrated at times were jam sessions in the barn seemingly full of possibilities that didn't pan out. Changes failed. They lacked the chops to find the ingredient to whatever was missing. What was swimming about in Henry's head was not coming through the speakers. He felt strongly that the difference between a cool song and bland noise was often as slim as a guitar pick. Gretchen was often on frustration's receiving end. "You've the ear, Tarbat, use it. We're playing like a jackhammer crew."

She was not amused.

And now, post-Depot Day, those frustrations had become magnified. In the growing tension of the upcoming gig at Hitches, seeded hurts rocketed to the surface.

"Maybe this song is not working out because you don't give a shit one way or another, Tarbat."

"And your loser-playing is making everything worse, Hollins."

"Maybe you'd rather go running off to Buffalo."

"Will a blow job make you go away forever, Hollins? Because I'll go down on my knees. Whatever it takes."

"Jesus, what planet did you come from?"

"I wish I fucking knew."

"Cool it. Both of you. How about we try it this way." Melissa sings.

Parker accompanies with a howl.

They give the new change a run-through. Ears got scratched; affirmative nods and forced smiles returned—until the next lash-out.

But no one called off the Hitches gig. There grew a combative "I'm-gonna-show-you" vibe that drove them on. If antagonism produced art, the Pickford barn band was more than suspect.

chapter twenty

Eight riders from the Ravens M/C had spent the weekend at a state-line motorcycle rally in Eagleville, Missouri. Mechanical headaches kept them held over. With a late start, heading back toward home base outside Iowa City, they hammered north up Interstate 35, stopping to camp near rural Grand Garden. Harboring a rider's thirst, they asked about until a local offered, "Sure, Hitches be open, ten minutes away up in River Grove." They took the gear wagon and five bikes. It was a Tuesday, the eighth, 9 p.m.

At Pickford, darkness arrived, as did the jangled nerves. No one had tossed their cookies all day. A good sign. Jitters were expected, as well as the occasional "I hate you for this" tossed Henry's way. Henry wasn't worried. He knew the songs. He knew the changes. Singing was a slight concern. He fell back on those rare occasions when he'd spoken in public: a town council meeting, a wedding toast. Yes, he'd suffered stage fright, but he always relaxed as soon as he began. Hitches would be no different.

They arrived late, somewhat surprised at the number of cars and pickups in the lot. Hauling in the gear, owner Dex Knotts hollered over Henry's testy look. "Hey, I mentioned it to a few people. Shoot me."

So, they'd play to a dozen or more. Not what they wanted, but doable.

Henry was soon cursing they hadn't set up earlier: have everything ready, then simply hit the stage, plug in and start playing. Why hadn't he thought to do that? They used tuning forks to keep the guitars on pitch together, always a problem in a noisy bar. *Shit.* Everyone was staring at the confusion in the corner. Hitches was grim and dim. They needed more light. They didn't have a damn flashlight. Locating the outlets and setting up the drums in near darkness took freaking forever. Guitar cases were tripped over, amps were knocked over, Mel's hi-hat cymbal fell over. What camaraderie existed upon arrival was lost in a tortured, whispered jibe, "We're the three fucking stooges," while making jackasses of themselves.

Set at last, Henry stepped to the mike. "Hi, we're new. Obviously." His nervous laugh was awkward and too loud. "We've a few songs to try out. Thanks for showing—"

Henry's "up" was drowned out by a motorcycle roar outside. Everyone in Hitches turned a questioning look at someone else. In moments, eight burly black leather jackets, who'd been passing around a bottle of Jack both before and on the way over, stormed in past the rickety front door. Patrons gave room. Barstools were commandeered. Tables and chairs were shoved together. Beers were ordered. Dex got busy. The band was noted. There was a shout, "Let's get the party started."

Spooked by the swelling rowdy crowd now before him, Henry needed two hands grasping the microphone to stand steady. *How can this be happening?* Gretchen grabbed, pulled and dragged him back to Melissa. In the low light, welcome now, she whispered, "We're busting out. Now. Nobody says a word. We'll take the guitars, make for the van and return for the drums later."

Henry was a third in shock, a third in fear and a third in

dismay, but Gretchen's proposed dodge really sucked. "You just named the band, Tarbat. The Chickenshits. Nice choice."

"Who cares, Hollins?"

"I suppose I do. Your decision, Mel."

She did a drum kick and a quick snare roll. "We're fucking here. Let's fucking play."

Both Gretchen and Henry took a step back. Neither had ever heard Melissa Minch use the f-word. They played.

"Ball Game" was an unequivocal disaster. They had a false start. They didn't come in together. Their labored-over-forever instrumental intro, practiced 500 times, was botched. Riffing at breakneck speed, timing was everything. They knew that. Starting again, underway, the balance was shit. Gretchen was way too loud, even too fast. Even worse, if that was possible, mike distortion turned the vocals to garbage. They even messed up the all-together one-two-three (strikes you're out at ...). How was that freaking possible? How can you not even count right? Henry butchered a chord change. Embarrassing, but maybe not, given no one heard him. He couldn't hear himself. At the song's merciful end, Henry ripped the microphone cable from Gretchen's amp. With an angry, "who gives a shit," they'd sing into a dead mike.

The cacophony had been such, for what seemed a never-ending five seconds, Hitches sat and stood in stunned silence. Laughter began and grew. "What the heck" proved a popular response. There was a shout, "I need way more beer for this," and Dex grew busy behind the bar once again. One biker, stocky, piled black hair tangled and curled, a week's worth of beard stubble, staggered close to the band's corner, eyed Melissa and Gretchen, and said, "What have we got here?" Henry drew back, wary, and turned to Melissa, who counted off, "Three ... two ... go," and they launched into "Shut the F**k Up."

It felt like they were playing for their lives. But more at ease with their own stuff, there was a semblance of tempo and timing. The give-and-take vocals were shouted. Given all the screwups, Gretchen was furious, and she played that way, but at least her Mosrite growl was now free of feedback. With an abrupt ending that almost worked, Melissa kept up a light drum fill, determined to keep the playlist moving. Two more songs and out the door was all that mattered. She was at "Three … two …" when someone hollered, "Dudes, spare us." That was when the already stage-front curly-haired biker badass stumbled closer and shouted, "Dudes? I think we got ourselves a couple dykes." Melissa quit her countdown and held her sticks. Hitches quieted. The biker stood swaying a foot away from Gretchen. "Damn. What are you, sugar or salt?" He held up his empty beer bottle, muttered, "shit," and staggered back to his table and chair.

The continued lull was unnerving. Dex Knotts had witnessed rural bar-ugly a few times. If possible, stop it early. He discreetly speed-dialed County dispatch, "Hitches. Send a patrol car," and hung up. On stage, Henry feared a Tarbat lightning bolt laying waste to the place. Instead, she wilted from the drunken putdown. In total defeat, her guitar dangling on her shoulder, she closed ranks and whispered, "I'm done, Henry."

Startled by the resignation in Gretchen's voice, Henry knew straightaway that "I'm done" meant far more than the Hitches gig. Despite all Gretchen's bluster, her vulnerability, ever-present but hidden, was now on full display. *I'm done* was not a night's end, it was *the* end. The rollout show had become a requiem, a Mass for lost dreams: two botched numbers, one inebriated slur, one band kaput.

Henry shouted at the ceiling, "No, no way." He looked for a place to secure his Martin, frustration and anger boiling over. "Why don't we have any goddamn guitar stands?" Quickly leaning his still-plugged-in guitar up against its amp, the Martin promptly twisted left and fell onto the cement floor. *CLANG!* Screeching feedback filled the bar: the final straw, the

The Rise of The Mad March

final screwup piling onto all the previous screwups on this screwed-up gig. He exploded. Henry, now Henry the Avenger, a role he had never played in his entire life, turned with fists clenched and made for the bikers.

The badass was sitting facing out. He was wide-eyed but unprepared as Henry shouted, "Apologize. Apologize to her, to both of them." Then without waiting, he grabbed the metal seat with both hands and flipped the biker over backward. Adrenaline flowing through Henry's veins, the leather-clad Neanderthal and his fresh beer bottle were sent sprawling – but not before he grasped the avenger's shirt and catapulted the two of them to the floor. The Ravens stood and gave room. Henry wound up on top for one more spit-fueled, "apologize," before being unceremoniously flipped over. The badass was strong. Henry was straddled and looking up at bloodshot eyes, a raised fist and a grin. "Mess with me ..."

That fist was halfway to Henry's eye, cheek, or jaw when Gretchen flew past the circled Ravens, and giving her all with a baseball bat swing, shattered the back of an acoustic guitar against the biker's skull, catching him at the hairline above his right eye. The sultan swat cut the biker open. Head wounds are bloody. This was no exception.

Back on his back, the stunned biker groaned. Henry scrambled to his feet. Before another Raven made a move, a Civil War-era musket fired a black-powder-only round at the tin ceiling. *Crack!* Everyone flinched. The deafening shot had all eyes zeroed in behind the bar. Dex raised his Springfield like Billy Yank at Antietam. "Battle's over, boys, stand down."

With cosmic timing, two county deputies entered just as Dex fired. Side belt pistols were drawn. Everyone settled. Fingers were pointed. Names were taken. Dex produced a clean bar rag to stem the blood flow from the biker's head.

The Ravens had a ringleader. "We need to get Granite here stitched up, chief. Where to?"

"County hospital ER. Fifteen minutes south on Highway 69."

"Our wagon's outside, Chief. No need for an ambulance. We'll take him."

"You do that. And take a shotgun rider to keep him stable. I'll lead with the siren. The rest stay put until we iron this thing out."

Being led toward the door, pressing a bloody towel against his head, Granite eyed the local cop and said, "Nothing to iron out, Chief. I count myself a music critic. The guitarist took offense. A misunderstanding, officer. Don't turn this into something it's not."

"Looking at you, what did you give them, ace, a one-star review?"

The seriously cut Raven grunted and turned defiant. "No charges pressed against the band. Write that down. Just let them go." Near the door, he was close enough to catch a stare from his assailant, a young woman still holding onto a shattered guitar. "Don't forget to mop up the blood, Cinderella."

"Only if your brains are included." Gretchen was shaking.

"I'd have only tapped him."

"Bullshit."

One officer stayed to take statements. The other led the Raven van to the hospital. Everyone else gathered at the bar to check out Knotts' Springfield musket. Dex had a ramrod and gave a demo on how to load. The Ravens bought the house a round, then another.

Henry grew fixated on Gretchen's head-basher. She took note the sadness in his eyes and held up her battered club, now in two pieces held together with steel strings dangling in all directions. "I brought along the halfway house no-name, just in case we closed with an acoustic 'Cecil's Beer Run.' What a dreamer, huh?" Henry turned and eyed the guitar still laying by his amp, no doubt dinged but alive and well. He exhaled a sigh of relief. He'd survived—so had the Martin.

Without another word, the band packed up. Equipment loaded, names and address provided to the cop, Henry was last to leave Hitches. Knotts caught him at the door.

"Was that really supposed to be 'Take Me Out to the Ball Game'?"

"Don't go there."

"Everyone okay?"

"Physically, yeah. We got some self-esteem that needs a prop. Regardless, this was probably the end for us."

"Listen up, tuner man, Van Wert hasn't had this much excitement since the boys returned from Shiloh. Admittedly, you guys are raw oysters, but there was something coming from that stage. Pretty well hidden, but something. Band got a name?"

"We ain't the Chickenshits."

chapter twenty-one

Henry delicately placed a huge platter of hash browns and scrambled eggs onto the table, added a serving spoon and said, "We have girls in the band."

Gretchen and Melissa eyed breakfast with ravenous looks, Henry with blank expressions.

"I'm stating our reality. Isolated rural bars, beer, whiskey, weed, roughneck male horseshit, rock 'n' roll, and cute girls on stage. Yowza! Now there's a combo ready to combust into a wildfire. Case in point: last night."

"Get to the point, Hollins."

"Common sense, babe." Henry aped Gretchen's stare. "Security is a factor for us, a must."

"She's not a babe, Henry."

"She is, Dorothy."

Gretchen grunted, pointing to herself. "Is it a Jane, a Joe … somebody take a guess. Those bozos last night didn't know what I was."

"But I do, Tarbat. And I don't care so much about your fears or lack thereof, I care about mine."

"And that calls for the Marines?"

"Yes, ma'am. A size extra-large roadie who is also keeping an eye out for trouble. In case you didn't take note at Hitches,

I'm not Tarzan. Pass me the platter and tell them I'm right, Dorothy."

"Henry's right. Gracious, the more I hear about last night, the more appalled I get."

"I'm done, remember."

"You're an admitted pain, Tarbat, but you are not a quitter. Mel, I need the ketchup."

She clutched the Heinz bottle close to her chest. "Did you say cute?"

"I'm dead serious here, Minch. If anything happened at a show or after a show to the two of you, I'd never forgive myself. There have been plenty of Grace Slicks up-front in rock, but you two are slinging a guitar and beating on a drum. It's 1972. You are not the first but you're rare, quite rare, and, if we keep the band going, you're going to endure a load of caveman crap because …" Henry was pointing fingers, "girls don't play guitar. Girls don't play drums. Don't you know that?"

"I don't give a shit about the loser cavemen. Sorry, Gunny."

"That Raven you bashed last night comes with the territory, Tarbat, and one scary fist-flying faceoff was one too many. We need a defender-dude. I'm not backing down on this." Henry held out a hand. "Gimme the ketchup, Minch."

Gretchen slammed her fork. "You're still talking like there's going to be a tomorrow. Totally delusional, Hollins. Who'd want me anyway?" Mockingly, Gretchen slung her shoulders back, chin up, and posed.

"Don't you put yourself down, young lady. I won't stand for it."

Henry seconded Dorothy: "I'd pass up a six-pack just to steal a kiss."

Gretchen made a face at the two of them.

Henry stayed laid-back but determined. "The Neanderthal did us one favor last night. Dorothy, the salt and pepper, if you please."

"What, pegging me and Minch for dykes?"

"Why don't you two just admit you both stood up for each other at Hitches? Big-time." Melissa was jabbing a butter knife at both her bandmates. "And *that* was cool. Two round-table knights battling the dragon. I'm proud. You should be, too. What we really learned last night was never, never plug a microphone into an axe amplifier."

They all laughed.

"The Raven's favor was in not pressing any assault charges, no matter how bogus. We don't need any earthquakes making waves in the county probation pool. Buckpool would be pissed to the max. And I'll tell you something else we learned at Hitches." Henry waited.

"What?"

He pointed next to Melissa. "I'll take that last piece of toast. We need a bass player."

Gretchen slumped, head bowed, eyes closed. Fragments of conversation danced behind her eyes: *Never forgive myself, not a quitter, steal a kiss.* "Tell me there is an end to this madness, Minch."

"Can't, Tarbat."

jersey moon: interview #6

October 1973

Jersey: Thanks for inviting me and agreeing to do this, Mrs. Gunzenhauser. Pickford is such a neato house. You know what shakes? All this modern stuff stashed inside a hundred-year-old kitchen.

Dorothy: And if we were able to conjure up the original homeowners, what would they marvel at the most?

Jersey: The dishwasher.

Dorothy: Hah. Spoken like a true teen. What are we up to, Miss Moon?

Jersey: Well, back in July, Mr. Hollins tapped me to keep a journal about the tour.

Dorothy: I wasn't on the bus, as they say.

Jersey: I know, but I ended up writing a bunch of before-the-tour stuff. Ace reporter. My new Lois Lane fixation. Anyway, the story of how the band began became an itch I kept scratching. I've got gaps, and you're the voice in my journal not yet heard.

Dorothy: Who are you writing for?

Jersey (grinning): That's just it. Henry wanted an outside-the-fishbowl "tour-look" thing. So ... him and nobody, I guess. Maybe an English class essay mainstay: How I Spent My Summer Vacation.

Dorothy: You enjoy writing.

Jersey: I do. Weird.

Dorothy: Suits me fine, Lois. Fire away.

Jersey: This is awesome. First question. Rumor has you financing the tour. Care to comment?

Dorothy: Can I retract my "fire away"?

Jersey: No quitting, Mrs. Gunzenhauser.

Dorothy: Okay. The rumors are nonsense. I provided a small emergency fund and some tires. Not that the girls at the quilt bee will ever let me forget: "Why don't you just find a bookie, Dorothy, and throw your retirement money at him?" Gracious.

Jersey: You sign on and partner up with Mr. Hollins at Pickford. Any second thoughts, early on? Misgivings?

Dorothy: Well, Pickford was certainly more than I bargained for. Henry was running a service business. He was out and about each day with customers. And us girls were left shadowboxing one another. Eventually, a small trust was earned. Both ways, mind you. But those two young women needed more than rock 'n' roll music.

Jersey: Meaning?

Dorothy: Oh goodness. Where to start? Neither could scramble an egg. Lord knows what kind of diet they'd somehow survived on. They needed jobs. Their combined apparel would fit into a carry-on. Neither had a license to drive and barely knew how. No wonder they had that awful wreck. My late husband's old farm pickup was soon parked at Pickford. Henry and I taught them. Melissa struggled at first but proved game. Gretchen loved driving both the beater and my car. So, there was passing the state DOT skills test and all of that.

Eventually, Melissa helped run the town library. Gretchen assisted the custodian at school. And they both worked hours with the crew restoring the old hotel in town. I'll admit to pulling some strings getting them on a payroll. I could go on.

Jersey: The GED …

Dorothy: A bumpy road. Lassoing Gretchen to her study chair crossed my mind on occasion. The GED was the first inkling I had that both of them were whip-smart. They caught me off guard.

Jersey: They can do that.

Dorothy: And Einstein I'm not. Going way back, I was a "middling" high school student. Thus, my tutoring included a fair share of personal boning up. But caught off guard again, I relished every minute. When they passed, I'm not sure who was most proud.

Jersey: I hate to bring this up, but the two taking off like they did must have been a shock.

Dorothy: I'd label it a disappointment. But let's not forget, Jersey. At the time, we were unaware why they'd left. And I was more worried than shocked. I'd come to care. Women are prone, I guess. I'd lost the men in my life too soon. My son and husband were gone. When Henry came calling, I was wallowing—as good a word for my state as any. Then, without any preconceived notions, there came a time at Pickford that I found myself embracing two beating hearts. I swear there were occasions I took stock and mentally apologized to Carsten and Daniel for letting them both slip from my thoughts.

But Pickford proved a mighty chore. I'm not much for patience, and there were many times what little I had was sorely tried. As such, I needed a reminder, every now and then, that the good in the world can be overlooked and misplaced as easily as a stray calf. Can I relate an odd turn? Promise not to laugh?

Jersey: Yes, yes.

Dorothy: There was one morning, at wits' end with both girls, and not even a snicker from you about this, Jersey Moon, our hens, strutting about, suddenly gathered together and stared me down in the coop with looks and clucking that said,

"Calm down, don't miss out." I was so taken aback. There I stood, egg pail in hand, being admonished by my peers. Beady-eyed they were, all four of them. My heart skipped a beat. But the end result was, I did calm. I didn't miss out.

Jersey (laughing): Best interview ever. I'm not laughing, Dorothy, really.

Dorothy: Melissa and Gretchen were guarded, suspicious, argumentative and angry. There was deep-seated hurt. I accepted that. I didn't probe. But they were never petty. They were straightforward, never devious. They were never cruel or malicious. In an odd fashion, they were opposites. Melissa was like a sponge. Get her started, say cooking, and she'd have at it. She embraced. Gretchen would be wary of a piece of chocolate cake.

Jersey: And yet onstage, playing, they are like one person.

Dorothy: I'm not surprised. They lean on one another. They adore one another. Yin and yang. Hard to fathom … so I didn't. I just accepted what was and what they became: a gift.

Jersey: I have to ask. Running away that one time, why didn't they take the pickup?

Dorothy: You know, I never asked. Maybe the old rattletrap wouldn't have taken them far before breathing its last. Maybe they felt they'd be spotted and pulled over right away. But I believe that taking the truck would have been, for them, too much a slap in the face to both Henry and myself.

Jersey: Melissa told me a "keeper." In the middle of the falling-out that she and Gretchen had at the Winterset interstate entrance ramp, right before they split up, she'd shouted, "I want to go back. We have candlelight every night at dinner."

Dorothy: Sometimes, Jersey, little things matter, can matter the most in fact. Something else along those lines. The county authorities had serious reservations about the whole Pickford setup. Henry's unraveling marital status raised questions, and broadly hinting, they wanted my eyes to be their eyes. They asked for written reports. One evening at supper I related to the three of them the situation I was in. They were upset, being spied on and all. But I got the sense that my token honesty went a long way. Little things, Jersey.

Jersey: One last. The "Gunny" tag. Bothersome?

Dorothy: I'll never forget Melissa dropping in on our quilt bee at the community center and nonchalantly saying, "I'll just hang around here, Gunny, and ride back with you." Around the table, there was a sudden awareness of the close bond that existed between the two of us, and everybody's eyebrows shot to the ceiling. That was a moment to cherish.

chapter twenty-two

September 1972

Henry, being the piano technician at Banta-Smith College in Liberty, had no problem reserving the music department's instrument-rehearsal room on a Sunday afternoon for two hours—a spacious studio, ideal for the bass audition or simply having fun playing the huge Yamaha G5 grand— if no one showed.

For Gretchen Tarbat—adding another band member to what was already a joke was deranged. "You play bass, Hollins."

"I'd be forever getting up to speed. I'm not sure bass players are made, Gret. I think they're born."

Breakfast-inspired or not, Henry's audition plea won out. Melissa's backing—"I'm game, my kick drum needs a playmate"—was a big assist. Flyers were posted around campus. Henry put the word out to his music friends. An ad was placed in the local advertiser. He snagged a bass amp loaner from the BSC jazz band.

"How many do you think we'll get?" Henry said.

"Zero."

"Maybe if our band had a name, Tarbat."

"Maybe if the band was actually a band, Hollins."

They got four.

The Rise of The Mad March

First up was tall and burly, plugging in and leaping about like a puppet on a string with a slap bass technique, adding fills and lines no one followed—a gyrating jammer who, despite all the practice space, barrel-rolled into Henry without looking and sent him sprawling.

Gretchen screamed for a halt. "Asshole, what are you on?"

"Flying, baby."

"Coked up? Really?"

"You offering me a line?"

"Thanks for coming, dude."

Henry was rooting hard for the next two serious science lab-type guys. One after the other, both proved far better musicians than the no-name band holding court. Their caustic comments left Gret, Mel and Henry little to grow on.

"I cannot possibly relate to whatever you're playing."

"I'm into improv jazz. You're into what, exactly?"

"Is that really your drum kit?"

"Are there changes? Am I supposed to stand in the far corner and pluck one string all night long?"

Henry, though he never uttered a word, kept his fingers crossed that a *guy* would prove a good fit. But first Charles, then Gregory, were gone in a wasted-time huff and really didn't appreciate Gretchen's "fuck you, too," at the door.

Enter Christine Bertram Baird.

Shoulder-length light reddish-brown hair, side parted, high-bridge straight Roman nose, eyes wide-set, tall, slender, shapely, hesitant and nervous. "Am I too late?"

"Yeah, you are." Gretchen began packing up, keeping a watchful eye.

Henry countered. "No, no. Come on in. No problem. It's not like we have anyplace to be."

"Hey, Hollins, we could go drink a million beers."

There were quick intros, Christine offering up her three names, Henry hinting at Gretchen to back off the snide remarks. Baird was a BSC student, a senior from Michigan.

Pleasantries, as they were, passed. She was given the chord changes. An informal jam would kick them off.

Plugging in, she said, "I borrowed this, so … not too familiar. I'm sort of starting out here."

Melissa was giving Henry a sly comic look easily transcribed: *You're drooling, Hollins, and I get it, she's in without playing a note.* He smirked back. Henry should have been eyeing Gretchen, already mentally sticking pins into a redheaded voodoo doll.

The early jamming was comic. They tried a cover that went nowhere. Christine was totally lost. She said, "Play that first thing we tried one more time and I'll just listen." With yet another run-through, she tentatively joined in. Stop-restart. Stop-restart again. Twenty minutes passed. With another "from the top," she began to latch on. Her eyes closed as a bass line flowed and grounded the music. Everyone was taken aback at the finish. Miss Baird was obviously green—but talented enough to walk a melody. Regardless, Henry just knew. She was perfect. Melissa and Gretchen were noncommittal. Henry took her name and number. They'd be in touch. Christine was gracious for the tryout. Henry gave her a thumbs-up at the door, and the war began.

Shots were fired in the rehearsal room, the fighting escalated on the trip back to Pickford and exploded full-scale at the barn.

"It's obvious that the girl can play, but also obvious at the start that she never had. Does that make any sense?"

"Not much, Mel. And who turns up at an audition with a borrowed guitar? She was making it up as she went along, like a newborn taking a first step and then, voilà, at the end, she's hotfooting about pretty good." Henry held a positive look.

"Miss Bertram's a lost country club debutante who strayed into a blue-collar pool hall."

Henry laughed. "I thought maybe she wandered into the

The Rise of The Mad March

wrong audition, that the theater department was filling roles for "My Fair Lady" somewhere on down the hallway."

"She was an Amazon … and I saw the looks, Mr. Hollins."

"Gimme a break, Minch. I say, let's invite her out to the barn and see what happens."

"What was that little-girl-lost charade?" Gretchen aped a Marilyn Monroe purr: "'Is this the band tryout?' Holy bombshell, what a phony. And keep it in your pants, Hollins—she's out. I mean, the moment she tiptoed in acting all mousy and shit, my ears were pinned back."

"You hardly gave her a chance, Gret. We might have played more. Just a half-hour and you're like, 'That's it, babe, adios, the door's behind you.' Jesus Christ."

"I'd take the savior himself before that pretender bitch."

"We connected that last run-through, Tarbat. Admit it. Cut the crap. We'll call her back."

"She's never played bass." Gretchen moved closer to Henry, her voice rising. "We're nothing but a prop. She's writing an essay for her debs-only English Lit class. She's never experienced anything in her tight-ass life, so she chose us to at least come up with an opening paragraph."

"She was nervous, that's all."

"It was a fucking act, Hollins. How can you be such a gullible moron?"

"There was something there, Gret."

"There is always a 'something there' for you, Hollins."

Henry was red-faced, straight-armed and pointing. "Yeah, you!"

Silence ruled the remainder of the ride back to Pickford. In the barn, Henry tried again. "I say maybe we hit paydirt. We ask Christine up to the house, get to know her, rehearse and go from there."

"Oh, you do that, Hollins. Break out the fine china and English tea for Miss Bertram Baird." Gretchen feigned a gag. "But I won't be there for the meet-and-greet because if she's in,

I'm out. I fucking quit this fucking fantasy of yours—which still isn't working because that first blow job is only in your dreams."

"Fine! Go on and quit. And don't bother running off this time. I'll drive you to the bus station. Destination your choice. I'll buy you a ticket ... as long as it's *one fucking way!*"

Henry was out of breath. They both were. He turned. "Mel?"

"I'm not stepping into the middle of the ring to get kicked by two jackasses."

Feeling worn out from another dead end, finding a needed best-friend in his usual place, Henry bent down to provide Parker a reassuring scratch behind the ears. "Come on, partner, let's go chase a rabbit."

chapter twenty-three

September—November 1972

Henry labeled what followed "the phony war," appropriating a phrase coined early on in WWII. One hundred autumn days of steely-eyed coexistence, everyone going their individual way: giving space, making space, contact and conversation at a bare minimum. Dorothy and Parker grew fit to be tied, but all their pleas for peace fell on deaf ears. Jobs and GED studying abetted maintaining a wartime separation. The barn was used on occasion, but never together.

The phony war proved a time to reflect. Henry had to laugh: *reflect needed an adverb—like bitterly*. He was struck that in reading Rolling Stone the past three years, some sixty issues cover to cover, never once could he recall the magazine detailing a rock band trial the likes of which he was experiencing. The stories were all headlining-show recaps, ego interviews and party photo ops. "It's all bullshit," he wailed. Where was the truth? The endless practices that crushed what was once an active life, the brooding contempt that festered and grew, the endless togetherness that turned solidarity into a "screw you, too" show?

For sure as hell, the phony war had never been in his dreams. He was learning the hard way. Every classic rock album had a history of drudgery and angst within its grooves. That was the God-given truth. He'd bet the farm.

A second reflection brought a chill. From the start, when looking back from the road he was on, there was always a lamplight burning, always the choice to try to reconnect with Esther and admit, "The band thing was all a bad mistake." Now, into the phony war with Gretchen, he grew aware that a point of no return had been passed. No home lights glowed in the rear. There was nothing but a dark gray haze obscuring what once was. The only direction was forward—a one-way ticket, indeed.

But Henry surprised himself. He batted down his sulking and alarm. He concentrated on the same o' same o': answering or returning business calls, scheduling appointments, servicing piano customers. Being away each day from Pickford felt tactical. His Martin acoustic accompanied each and every working day. He practiced his licks solo, wherever and whenever.

Gretchen did not ship off for ports unknown. Promises were promises, and "probation" stood at the exit door: *Stop. Do not pass go.*

At night, with everyone a stay-at-home, Pickford played the big house—easy to find a spot and hide away.

For Henry, with fall-term semesters underway, college tunings took precedence to include the Baldwins and Yamahas at Banta-Smith in Liberty. One late afternoon, working among the music-faculty studio grands, he spotted Christine. They both waved a recognition and drew close. He began with, "Hey, sorry about –"

"I never in a million expected a callback, Mr. Hollins."

"No, no, it wasn't like that at all. What's happened is hard to explain. Say, could we knock off the formalities? I'm sure it was never Mr. Jagger and Mr. Richards. Christine, right?"

"Sure, and Chris is fine."

Henry leaped. "So, you still have the bass?" She was still perfect. "You want to get together?"

"To like, jam? Are you serious?"

"I am."

"No bass. I've got a six-string stashed back in the dorm."

"A senior, still living on campus?" He smiled.

"Mother Baird. Lord knows all the sinful pleasures out in the real world that would keep me from studying. Dean's list or death, that's me." She half grinned, half sighed.

Ever mindful of the dark hostilities back at Pickford, Henry saw sunlight peeking out from the clouds. "I don't know you at all, Chris. I do know you passed the audition."

"Really? Were you just now truly serious? Can I go get the guitar? You have time?"

He always had the Martin. He'd make time. "Yeah, be great. I need to finish up. Let's meet back here. Gimme an hour."

They made use of one of the few piano-less practice rooms. Christine opened her case. Henry's eyebrows shot up as she slung on a hollow-body, burgundy-finish, six-string Harmony electric.

"Dad and me. Our little secret. When I started pre-med classes in my junior year, he asked if there was anything I truly wanted. And boy, did I surprise him. He kept his word. I kinda fell in love with the look, ya know. She's a model H-72, light weight, and we bought the gold foil pickups." She smiled with a vertical index finger pressed against her lips. "Don't tell my mom."

Henry marveled. Christine wore the Harmony as if the two had shared a crib together. Validating the metaphor, the playing that followed had Henry's jaw on the floor. *Good God, we nearly missed all this.*

"So, the audition?"

"A borrowed bass for sure, Mr., Henry. I never held one in my life until getting with you guys."

Henry grew fascinated. "Why us, Chris?"

"I've been a closet guitar geek forever with whatever six-string I could get my hands on. Here at BSC, nothing's changed. My roommate is set to toss me out the dorm window. For years, I've been embarrassed over playing, over my desire to play. Little-girl dreams of being a jet pilot. Same kind of thing. Weird, huh? And, of course, never letting on with my mom with her classic fallback line, 'Anatomy doesn't allow for distractions, darling.' " Christine hooted over the quote. "Anyhow, I saw your post for the audition in the student union center. Maybe my hiding out just boiled over. I'm at the mirror talking to myself, 'At least try, scaredy-cat.' "

Henry was sold. He'd never been so sold on anyone or anything in his entire life. He felt a kindred spirit. She was perfect—or had he already said that? "OK. I'm offering a closet-breakout. If at all possible, we'll meet here every single day. Standing invite. Let's you and me pick till fingers bleed."

"For sure? Are you willing?"

"I'm self-employed, Chris. I set my own schedule, which now reads each day Banta-Smith College, Music Room 108. Say 6 p.m. until whenever. Can your study time handle this?"

"How about your schedule? I'm so in, Mr. Hollins."

"Hey, no misters."

"Sometimes a 'mister' is a must, sir."

For ninety days, it proved rare when Room 108 lacked the two of them. Henry felt like he burst through a next-level playing curtain on multiple occasions. Christine Bertram Baird was dragging him to heights only dreamed. They covered covers. Riffing turned into improvised songs. They tackled "Ball Game," Henry attempting to duplicate Gretchen's power

The Rise of The Mad March

chording, Christine catching on, matching Gretchen and adding on. Henry was all shits and grins. Baird was a righteous talent. Every session, Henry sought a counterpoint to Chris' Harmony lead, but still staying rhythmic, keeping it simple. They were locking in. If anyone asked, he was sitting next to and playing with "the something that had always been missing."

If Christine did fail to show, she'd say only, "Sorry, boyfriend." Henry took note the boyfriend was never named, never talked about, never smiled about. And if little was made of the boyfriend, the same was said of Melissa and Gretchen at his end. Christine had been early on matter-of-fact. "Gretchen terrified me." Enough said.

There were sessions they didn't play, Henry striving to explain what the band was after – a pure sound: short, rhythmic, fast. No grandstanding. No operas, no arias, no orchestration, no chorus backing, no decoding the universe, no solutions to world peace. No organ fills, no wall of sound, no drum solos, no extended-anything solos. That lyrically, they shouldered Gretchen's broadsides. She'd have her say. Whatever the band was, they weren't cute. "But I promise, Christine, we won't be all gloom. Our sound, if we ever figure it out, is going to lend itself to a few smiles." He fisted an imaginary mike and sang faux basso profundo: *no dice, son, you gotta worka late.*

"Okay, I'm getting this."

"We need our own 'Summertime Blues,' Christine, at a pace that will get us pulled over." Henry smiled. "And it all might work if the players and the playing somehow stay both loose and tight. Oh boy, I'm not making any sense."

"Okay, I'm getting this ... I think."

They both laughed.

And to get loose/tight, they all needed to be together, a togetherness that existed only in tangled dreams. Banta-Smith College was approaching Thanksgiving break. Christine would be flying home. Henry mapped a plan. "When you get back, you and I are busting out of Room 108, Miss Baird."

"Where are we going?"

"We're at an impasse. A barricade stands in front of us, and I'm going to charge hell-bent to the breach. I figure I've got one shot: turkey day. Time to blow the bugles, Chris. Balls to the walls."

"Uh oh. Do I need a steel helmet?"

"Get one."

Henry focused on his Thanksgiving Band-Aid band plan with pure tunnel vision, like he was wearing blinders. So focused, he never saw the ambulance coming, the ER room, the doctors' shouting, "stand clear."

jersey moon: tour interview #7

August 1973

Gretchen: Why me?

Jersey: Better perspective. You were the observer, not the instigator. Plus, Hollins and Minch wouldn't cough up any good stuff. They stonewalled me.

Gretchen: Maybe so, but dredging all this up is not about the tour, the music, or even our screwball beginning. You are out of bounds again, Moon. Hollins needs to shut you down.

Jersey: He did. He got red-faced mad. But sorry. Too late. And, *of course*, it's apropos. Apropos. I like that word, don't you?

Gretchen: Just leave me out of this, Tolstoy.

Jersey: Leave out sex, rock 'n' roll, and a freaking heart attack. What do you think my readers are expecting, a nursery rhyme?

Gretchen: Thirteen, Moon! And this journal is nothing more than adding bells and whistles to a Hollins photo album, a wordy fill-in between all the stupid pictures being taken. Readers? There are no readers, Moonbeam, nor will there be.

Jersey: Almost fourteen. And okay, maybe I'm acting out some. But a story needs every chapter. Pretty please? I'll do your hair before every show.

Gretchen: You already do that. And where did you even hear about this?

Jersey: I'm a journalist. Call me Lois.

Gretchen: Apropos my bare behind, and your mom's going to kill me. Minch, too. Damn. OK, a broad outline, that's all. You owe me, Moonbeam, and there will be payback. What happened occurred during what Henry calls "the phony war," when we were all apart but still thrown together at Pickford. What I call The Big Bad Bass Revolt, last October-November and a strange time. Everyone pretty much doing their own thing. No practicing. The guitars and drums in the barn were gathering dust. Our sea appeared calm, but there was a volcano rumbling underneath.

Jersey: You should be a writer. And the volcano was Melissa.

Gretchen: Who else?

Jersey: Did you sense an eruption?

Gretchen: No. I should have. Mel and me were sleeping separate most nights. We'd had a rift over quitting the band.

Jersey: You were the one who quit.

Gretchen: Regardless, Moon. Everyone at Pickford was hibernating in their own little world. Actually, the only thing that Hollins and I agreed upon back then was that Mel was turning more beautiful every day and she had to stop.

Jersey: But she didn't.

Gretchen: Still hasn't. Who knew the toothpick I hooked up with at Altamont would do the late swan thing?

Jersey: You're both amazing. And?

Gretchen: November, I think. A Sunday morning. We had cleaned the chicken coop. Gunny was at church. She was always after us to join her. She hadn't won that battle yet. Anyway, we're at the table in the kitchen. Mel's across from Henry and says out of the blue sky, "I've been like cuddled up with Tarbat for years but technically I suppose I'm still a

virgin, and I'm wondering how I can overcome that because …
I'm past ready."

She's leaning over, all through this, right in Hollins' face.
She's wearing nothing but a flannel shirt and jeans. She looked
edible. I'm like, *what in the hell?*

Jersey: Melissa Minch: Cosmo cover girl.

Gretchen: Here's a thing. Mel and me have always been
aware of Henry's … call it a crush on us, admitted or not. He
was always the gent, but invisible Mr. Lust was always
hovering about.

Jersey: And you no doubt teased.

Gretchen: No one has ever seen me wearing a halo, Moon.
Anyway, Minch is in heat and Henry's brain needs a few
seconds to gather and grasp the incoming data. I'll give Henry
credit. He didn't lunge over the table, scattering and smashing
dishes about.

Jersey: What did he do?

Gretchen: He dove under. Minch is sitting, and all at once
she's got an alligator from the depths thrashing her direction.
She shrieks while sliding her chair back but she's way too late.
He rises, snatches her up and slings her over his shoulder.
Total caveman. Nine-alarm fire.

Jersey: That's way out of control.

Gretchen: Exactly. Henry, with his wench, is halfway up
the staircase. He pauses. He turns. He races back down, grabs
my hand in a vise grip and charges back up, both of us in tow.
I just recall shouting at my dangling upside-down girlfriend,
"This is all your freaking fault."

Jersey: Oh God, I'm loving this.

Gretchen: We're in Mel's room and she hollers: "The coop.
I'm not submitting, smelling like a chicken. Let me down.
Quick shower. I need a shower." Henry's eyes light up like a
July Fourth celebration. He's shouting, "The walk-in. Every-
one." The water's turned on. In what feels like ten seconds,

Henry and Minch are without a stitch, and then yes, Minch, face alight, is stripping me naked.

Jersey: I'm going to direct the movie. I can't wait.

Gretchen: Three of us. Two bars of soap. Hollins is gawking, "You're both so beautiful." So, you know he's delusional. Minch is grinning, "If this thing is going inside me, it's gonna sparkle. She starts in and to be honest here, Moon, being up close and personal with a shower hard-on was a new morning for us girls.

Jersey: I've never seen one, either.

Gretchen: Thirteen, Moon!

Jersey: Just saying. So, soaping up. That's a way to write this, right?

Gretchen: And that, Hemingway, is when Henry went short of breath. Gasping.

Jersey: Scary.

Gretchen: Confusing. At first, we're like, is this a tease? Then no, it wasn't. He dropped to his knees. We managed to get him out onto the floor. Mel's pleading, "Go call for help."

Jersey: Oh wow. This is awful.

Gretchen: I tore downstairs to the phone and made the best decision of my life. I called Gunny, praying she was home. She'd just walked in. I was probably hysterical. She's like, "Hold on, ten minutes."

Jersey: Good for you, Gretchen.

Gretchen: So now the slapstick starts. The ambulance is on the way. We got a naked guy …

Jersey: With a hard-on.

Gretchen: Thirteen! With a hard-on, sucking like a beached fish, turning blue. There is nothing worse, Moon, than watching the living fighting for air. Jesus. Recalling this gives me the shakes. Getting pants and a shirt on Henry was a chore. We managed, and then slipped into our own duds just as the cavalry arrived. Calls to the hospital were made; an adult male in cardiac arrest was on the way.

Jersey: Holy moly.

Gretchen: Not forgetting the gun-barrel look Gunny was sending our way. Putting the puzzle pieces together was oh so easy. The floor was water everywhere. Everyone's clothes were damp. Our hair was tangled and wet. Gunny wasn't pointing fingers, but she was royally pissed. In her car, following behind the ambulance racing poor Henry to the hospital, she was all, "How could you!" We didn't say a word. Mel held my hand real tight.

We waited quite a spell. The doc finally came out and said Henry was going to be okay, please follow me. In her office, she said, "Tell me what happened?" You could hear a pin drop. Gunny said, "For Henry's sake, you two, spill it." Mel took a deep breath. "A communal shower, the three of us. Lots of soap."

The doc nodded. She said, "I don't believe this morning was solely responsible for putting him in the hospital. Henry and I talked. He admitted being under heavy self-imposed stress for months, coming from all directions: financial, marital, his service business, this band of yours. I'm saying whatever occurred this morning was the tipping point. His blood pressure was probably on the moon before the, the shower. This is not a lecture. Well, maybe it is. I'm asserting in the strongest words possible that we have to get his BP down and keep it down. He's experienced a severe anxiety attack. A three-way anything is not beneficial to the overall condition of his heart nor his recovery. Am I being clear?"

We were nodding like a couple of bobbleheads.

"I'm holding him over for observation. I have him back to you tomorrow. Mark our talk here."

Jersey: So, Henry's back. Days pass. Any change in the phony war?

Gretchen: The war dragged on, and Henry was the problem. He grew testy about everything, muttering about bad timing or some such. Jesus. I mean, he had no patience with anything or anyone. He probably kicked every piano he tuned. He even snapped at Parker. If we *were* practicing in the barn, he'd have been impossible.

Jersey: Pretty simple if you ask me. The shower. He felt like maybe humiliated or some such. A guy thing – I think.

Gretchen: A complete jerk thing, and his being pissed off all the time was not good for the ticker. We had a kit from the doctor. Gunny was checking his blood pressure every day. The way Hollins was acting all bent out of shape, he was giving me a panic attack.

Jersey: So, in the end?

Gretchen (raises an eyebrow): It all happened on a Sunday. I repeat: Sunday. Take a wild guess, Moonshot.

Jersey: You … oh man … I'm thinking I got it. This is so cosmic. I could write the final chapter in my sleep. He hit normal on the BP. He stayed normal. You suddenly got religion with Gunny on Sunday mornings and left Melissa with back-in-the-saddle Henry.

Gretchen: Just for a couple of sermons and that was the end; just so everybody gets whatever it is off their Cosmo/Playboy calendar. And "back-in-the-saddle," Moon? Really?

Jersey: You guys are so cool.

chapter twenty-four

November 1972

Tuesday of Thanksgiving week, Henry cornered Dorothy. "I'm looking for a time alone with Melissa. I need you to run interference."

"I don't meddle in such things, but *really*, Henry."

"No, no. Nothing like what you're thinking, I assure you. Just talk." He grinned. "Honestly, Mrs. Gunzenhauser, Pickford is hardly a bordello."

"Don't make fun, Mr. Hollins. I'm not the one with a stressed heart." Dorothy suddenly felt the measure of loss. Losing Daniel and Carsten hit her at odd times, triggered by the unexpected, perhaps a song lyric or the turn of a poetic phrase. Teary-eyed, staring now at Henry, a recent close call at death's door if ever there was one, she made her way and hugged him with compassion. He surprised her with a gentle kiss on her cheek, saying, "I'll be fine, Dorothy. Just stress. I've no clogged arteries. The doctors aren't overly concerned, and neither am I."

She felt out of breath, dabbing her eyes and fighting for composure. "Gracious, I'm a mess. This is all your fault, young man – you and your household. And now … just talk?"

"Yes. I don't understand my band, Dorothy. Melissa is the key."

"Alright, sir. I've got a special quilting bee this evening. I'll ask Gretchen to tag along."

Henry grew amused. *Tarbat and the quilting group at the community center. What's wrong with this picture?* "That's a long shot, Dorothy."

Dorothy caught his drift and frowned. "She might surprise, and if she does, there be a lesson to gather, Mr. Hollins."

Gretchen went quilting. Henry smartly avoided comment. Lesson learned. With Melissa shelving dishes in the kitchen, he had his chance. "Come sit. We need a heart-to-heart, Miss Minch."

"I hate that. I know where babies come from, Mr. Hollins."

Henry made a face.

"From storks, right?"

He waved away her grin. "I need you to level with me, Mel, like never before."

She sat with him in the dining room. "Sock it to me."

"Gretchen Tarbat and Christine Bertram Baird. What gives?"

"So obvious, mister."

"Not to me." Elbows on the table, palms upraised, radiating a frustrating-questioning air, Henry resembled a Rodin sculpture.

"Okay, listen up. Miss Baird has been and *is* everything that Miss Tarbat never was or will be. Think playing cards in the cradle, Mr. Hollins."

"Still in the dark here."

"Twenty odd years ago, Gretchen and Christine are both newly born, asleep in cribs. Baird is dealt the ace of diamonds. Tarbat draws the deuce of clubs."

"Ah, I'm beginning to catch on."

"I sure hope so. A bet-the-pot wager has our Christine raised with loving parents in a lovely home. Wealth provides perks. Surely there is an indoor/outdoor pool, and Mother Nature blesses the diamond ace with 'runway' good looks and a hot bod, not forgetting to add plenty of dental and dean's list smarts while growing up with friends galore. What have I missed?"

"She's pre-med."

"Of course, she's pre-med, Henry, and she sells more Girl Scout cookies than anyone."

"And?"

"And," Melissa grew animated, "her entire life, Gretchen is standing outside the fancy restaurant, her nose to the glass." Mel held her arms outstretched. "And that's okay. Life isn't fair. There is Marie Antoinette and there are the cake eaters. But Marie never butted her way into the maidservant's cellar kitchen and lorded over the recipes. Am I getting through to you, Mr. Hollins?"

Henry let Melissa's words sink in. "Like a laser. But Gretchen knows she's really cute, right?"

Melissa let loose an anguished sigh. "Spoken like a guy-guy. I speak from her eyes, Henry, not yours or even mine."

"Another lesson learned, Dr. Minch. Now, the dishes can wait. I need to bend the conversation?"

"At last."

"You and me. Just wondering."

"The de-virginizing?"

He laughed a little. "I'd choose a warmer noun."

"No regrets, sir. Never. But," Melissa was up and pacing now, acting as if she'd rehearsed this very moment, "given all the loony tunes, playing from the Liberty Halfway House to Pickford, I believe that mixing in a 'you and me' right now would crush any possibilities we all might have on down the road."

"You see possibilities?"

"Don't you?"

"Are we talking you and me or the band?"

"I'm saying even good intentions go haywire. We leave our

two Sunday morning sleep-ins behind. Over and done. Mission accomplished, lieutenant."

"And madly kissing you at this juncture would not be a good thing?"

"No, it would not."

"There is a restless aftermath at my end, Miss Minch."

"More warm blood flowing to the heart. That's good for you, Mr. Hollins, and I'm still pacing here, I'm not done."

"All ears."

"I think about that pickup skidding out of control, flipping over down into the roadside ditch; Gretchen and I two frozen corpses when we're finally found; being saved by pure chance; being given another lease on life. Regardless of what that all means, Henry, I don't want to waste that second chance, that finger of fate. I see an out-of-control pickup. Now, I see an out-of-control you and me. Nope. Sorry. No way. Can't have another crash landing. I'm not messing with the 'finger.' And there is no 'just me and you.' There is only everyone, the possibility of all of us. Am I making sense, Mr. Hollins?"

"Yes ma'am, the big picture."

"I'm not being completely honest about my feelings, but I don't want to be completely honest."

"Fine. I may bat an eye at your direction when the moon is full. How about that?"

"Fine."

"And, putting the kitchen cleanup on hold yet again, I'd like to discuss something else, Miss Minch."

"Me too. Anything."

"Here goes. I have a big secret to tell."

"Goody."

Henry took what he hoped was a reassuring breath. "Why have I been returning late every night these past months? That's the secret."

"Me and Gret figured you were back with your wife, and she was going to show up at Pickford after dark with vampire fangs, rip into our scrawny necks, blood everywhere, and drain us dry."

Henry slouched, world-weary with his arms on the table, hands cupped hiding his face, thinking, *There are lives being led in this world that are crazy insane, then there is mine.*

"Are we right?" Melissa held a smug smile.

"Not even close, Minch"

"Well then, what's the secret?"

"Sorry, it'll have to wait." He dropped his brooding, finally catching onto Melissa's tease. "You think you're such hot stuff."

"Oh yeah." Her smile was now ear to ear.

He laughed. How could he not? "I'm disclosing all at Thanksgiving dinner. Fortify yourself, Minch. Speaking of which, are you assisting Dorothy with the upcoming feast?"

"Big-time."

"Gretchen chipping in? If she's willing to quilt, she can …"

"Debatable."

"Meaning?"

"Meaning, mister, that the whole holiday is a 'whatever for' to her. Probably because she's never had a Thanksgiving that mattered or had one at all. So, here we go again, the diamond ace versus the club deuce."

Henry nodded a comprehension and found a few words. "There are things we take for granted, Melissa. Things we never should."

chapter twenty-five

Turkey day eve, Henry was back up at Stoner's in Des Moines.

"Renting, Henry?"

"Buying, Bill. I'm going for broke. We need a bass."

"Tag along, my friend. How's my Gretchen? She and that Mosrite in love?"

"Inseparable."

"Hang onto that girl's tailfeather, Henry. She'll take you places."

"She's already done that, Bill. What are you showing me here?"

"Rickenbacker 4001 four-string. "Who's playing—big and burly or a lightweight? You?"

"Not me. On the lightweight side."

"The Rick's all aces, and it's in your band for $550. Easy action, solid tuning, short scale, narrow neck—a work of art."

Eyeing the jet-black finish, thin white body trim, white control plate, Henry's first thought was, *out-of-this-world beautiful*. Decision time, but he'd already decided. "I'll need an amp and cable."

"I've got an Ampeg, great shape, great price. All yours. Watts of power. Bad joke. You need a strap and a case. Who's next? Melissa? We've had this conversation. She needs a kit, Henry."

"I need a bank account. You still have the Ludwigs?"

"Right this way and listen up." Bill laid a beefy hand on Henry's shoulder: "No bullshitting here, your band needs a practice PA, Henry. You can't put it all together without a PA. I've got a loaner I'll sell you. Grab it before it flies out the door and never comes back."

"Do I look like a five-hundred-dollar bill to you?"

"Tune my acoustic pianos here at the store. We'll strike a deal. Work some of it off, McKinley."

"Who?"

"President William McKinley is on the five-hundred-dollar bill."

"No shit. How do you know that? Wait, Bill, wasn't he assassinated?"

"And the same is going to go down on you if you don't grab the PA. I have this vision, Henry: Gretchen, standing offstage, another horrible sounding show, pistol in her pocket."

"Jesus. I surrender. Pile the PA on. Just promise me, Stony, that the collection guys at my front door will be sweethearts. I'm a musician. No finger breakers."

Bill Stoner was of average height, round-faced, balding, wide of girth. His belly laugh was his best feature. "No one ever claimed rock 'n' roll was a honeymoon, Henry."

"I'm only on a first date. Show me some straps for the Rickenbacker."

"Band got a name yet? I'm thinking Stoner's Delight has a nice ring."

"Has it ever occurred to you, Bill, why so many spaced-out cadets come wandering into this place? Hey, can you somehow gift-wrap the Rickenbacker?"

"Where are we, Macy's?" Bill Stoner took the credit card and smiled. "Henry, you're the gift."

chapter twenty-six

Dorothy invited the Pickfords for Thanksgiving. Clara drove herself down from their apartment in Indianola. Her husband, Sherman, wasn't well enough to make the trip. She arrived just as the bird left the oven.

Clara complicated Henry's intended "bombshell," but a change of plan at his end was out of the question. Dinner had been great. There'd been a Pickford truce. Everyone was snark-free, thanks mostly to Clara being a welcome guest. And he was truly sorry now to ruin the holiday spirit, but his go-for-broke plan had been afoot for a week. Money had been spent as if a printer in the basement was working overtime. Thanksgiving was D-day, desperation day. He took a deep breath, tapped his wine glass and rose from the table.

"I'd like everyone to remain seated. Tarbat, you might want to strap yourself in. I'm only going to say what needs to be said. I'm only doing what needs to be done."

"I know you forewarned me, Henry, but is this really necessary right now?"

"Yes, Dorothy, I've been days and sleepless nights setting this up."

Dorothy sighed and turned to Clara. "Our household is

experiencing contentions, Clara. I'm afraid you've found yourself on the front lines."

"Do I need a steel helmet?"

Henry nearly laughed recalling Christine asking the same. Somehow the two "steel pots" felt like a good omen.

"I've five points to make. Kindly withhold your applause or the grenade-tossing until I'm finished." He looked directly at Gretchen. "All five. Please allow me the courtesy."

"Will do, point man."

"Thank you. *One.* I've been getting together with Christine Baird, the two of us practicing at the college nearly every day for these past three months." He sensed Gretchen stiffen. He locked eyes and repeated, "Courtesy, Miss Tarbat?" Along with a scowl, almost imperceptibly, she offered a one-handed wave to carry on.

"*Two.* Christine is an amazing talent and will henceforth be the lead guitarist in our no-name band. *Three.* Christine in, Miss Tarbat is henceforth our bass player." Henry again loomed across the table to a now blank-faced, uncomprehending Gretchen, obviously in the throes of too much being thrown her way too quickly. He said, "Don't move."

Henry left for the adjoining piano study and returned, placing a slightly battered guitar case in Gretchen's lap. "For you. The amplifier and speaker are in the barn. Wear it well."

"*Four.*" Henry dug a Ludwig Drum Company promo from his pocket. He handed it to Melissa. "Some assembly required. The hens are guarding the bags and cases. I figured you'd prefer being hands-on for the initial setup." Melissa stared disbelieving, darting from the Ludwig photos to Henry and back again. "For real? For keeps?"

"No one is more deserving, Miss Minch."

Henry had been anticipating this moment for weeks. His mind was racing: *This is cool, this is a good thing.* Getting bolder, he made for the finish line. "Our no-name loser band is now complete. Christine returns from break on Monday. She will be here, in the barn, on Tuesday for the restart and kick-start. **Five**. Go, go … go … Johnny B. Goode."

Secret out, bomb dropped, Henry sat and waited for the explosion. Eyes darted back and forth across the table. No one was asking for more apple pie. Even Clara Pickford realized in the silence that a gauntlet of some sort had been thrown down. Tension ruled. No one moved except Parker, now pacing, and Gretchen, unsnapping and opening the case.

The worn guitar case was a prank, a mask. Henry loved that. When he spied it at Stoner's standing with the newbies, he was all, "Bill, let me take that one." Now, with the lid up, he nearly missed Gretchen's startled expression as she lifted the Rickenbacker for all to see: black body, white pickguard, with a black-cloth wide strap embroidered with white tiger lilies.

If the chosen electric bass looked sharp among all the others at Stoner's, the gloss-polished 4001 proved a stunner at Pickford. Henry quietly said, "I don't know what's more beautiful … maybe you and the Rickenbacker together."

Gretchen had scant time to comprehend. She'd been staggered. She figured, given the drawn-out "phony war," he'd be up to something. But a Thanksgiving sneak attack, a "holy cranberry" Pearl Harbor? She studied Henry's face, searching for any hint of smug self-satisfaction, finding only a guy needing to cease holding his breath and exhale.

Allowing for an impulse to take root, Gretchen carefully replaced the guitar back in the case, snapped it closed, twisted right and threw her arms around Dorothy who, though caught by surprise, did the same. Breaking free, Gretchen stood. Guitar case handle in her left hand, she up and grabbed Melissa with her right. Arm and arm, they made for Clara at the head of the table. Gretchen bent to Clara's ear and said, "The ghosts upstairs whisper your name at night."

Clara slapped her hands together and gave a delighted hoot.

At the door, Gretchen turned back to Henry, chin out, stoic. "Mel and I need to practice."

They were off.

At the table, Henry took one breath, then another. *This is very good.* He fought back a tear. He looked to Dorothy, still in the throes from the long hug, and said, "I heard there was champagne."

———

The day required an addendum. That night after ten, Henry wandered upstairs, finding them together in conversation on Melissa's bed. He drew a tease from the drummer.

"Man on the floor."

He slid a wooden high-back chair up close, turned it backward and straddled it.

"If you're looking for eternal gratitude …"

"Cease, Tarbat. Don't go there. I took stock. I decided. Now, it's your time to decide. But that's not why I'm sitting in this den of conspiracy. I've another point to make. This is for you both, but mostly for you, Gretchen. **Six.** *If* we are all in the barn on Tuesday, I'd like you to start keeping a subtle, keen eye on Christine, each and every practice."

Henry unstraddled and made for the door.

"What are we looking for? You gonna give Mel and me a hint?"

Fortified by the bubbly and a wee late whiskey, Henry made for the bed, slid the chair aside and dropped to his knees. Their three heads were now but inches apart. He strived to act sober and serious. He said, "Christine Baird is not the ace of diamonds. She is not perfect." In the moment, Henry leaned and gently kissed Melissa on the forehead. Her skin was warm; a small kiss that stirred not-so-long-ago big memories. He pulled back wistfully, turned to Gretchen, and said the same, "Christine is not perfect." Then surprising her all to hell

Robert Espenscheid, Jr.

for a second time on this Thanksgiving Day, he kissed Gretchen's cheek as well, holding his lips in place as long as dared. Without a word, he stood and made for the staircase.

Full-tilt boogie. A long, tense day with fingers crossed can dance just like that.

chapter twenty-seven

December 1972

Gretchen pushed to delay Christine a few days. She wanted extra practice time with just Melissa. The bass and drum had been holding conversations in the barn all Thanksgiving weekend. Gretchen wanted more. There was a freedom in locking onto the kick drum and playing just what she felt. "With you and Baird slinging away, I'd have to follow and walk some kind of line, Henry. I'm not up to speed to follow anything or anyone right now. Just Mel. New razor, Hollins, gimme a break."

"Absolutely." She'd taken to the bass. A prayer answered. Whatever she desired. He'd hang the moon for her.

No one brought up Henry's Thanksgiving late-night kisses. He was convinced he knew exactly their intent: an armistice, an end to the "phony war," a celebratory sigh of relief. He'd bet the future on the Rickenbacker and the Ludwigs. He'd won. Well, maybe with the no-name band, there was no winning per se, but there had been a reprieve. And along with the kisses there was one other recent event that required a peace treaty.

Christine was reset for Saturday. On Friday, with just Gretchen and Henry at the kitchen sink, cleaning up after dinner, she shyly and slyly sidestepped his direction. Standing shoulder to shoulder, eyeing his profile, her hands, with one still holding a dish towel, wrapped around his neck. Pulling him close, her lips grazed his neck. Before letting go she said, "Many thanks for the Rick, boss man."

Henry nodded.

The sly look remained. "Who is the coolest cat in the band – in any band, Hollins?"

He grinned. He was loving this. "That's easy. The bass player."

"And you can play the Mosrite, Hollins. Electric rhythm. All yours. You know that, right?"

They'd never conversed like this, not even close, and he was blushing like a first date. Then she surprised him further.

"And something else."

Henry waited.

"You're holding markers on the stolen pickup and the hospital, plus the band gear. Minch and I are not walking away from all that. Just so you know."

"Okay."

"Okay? That's all you got to say?"

"Well, I'm obliged the stance taken at your end, Gret. For now, let's label any payments due as money well spent. And there is something at my end."

Gretchen was lost in thought. She paid her debts and had wanted Hollins to know that. She was not without honor. "What?"

"I never meant to cross a line, Gretchen."

"You've lost me."

"We've never talked through my dragging you up into the shower with Mel."

"Not necessary, Hollins."

He wasn't hearing her. "Mel and I were a massive train wreck in the making. I realized that truth halfway up the stairs. Running back down to include you was, I guess, some kind of desperate ploy to save the band."

The Rise of The Mad March

"Still lost."

"Minch and me, we were breaking away from the pack. We were deserting you, deserting the band, leaving you stranded. Isolated. That can't happen. That should never happen."

Gretchen stepped back, puzzled. "So ... upstairs. Now there's the three of us."

"Roger that. My body shut down and stopped the train. End of story."

"I get that, but what if the train hadn't stopped?"

"There'd have been wreckage spewed everywhere, to include, no doubt, an appendage of mine I'd rather hold onto." Henry smiled. "But at least it would have been an entire band thing."

"You're unbelievable, Hollins. Enough."

Henry nodded, relieved at his effort to make some sense of a confusing, traumatic, unforgettable day. "And hey, tomorrow, don't forget about Christine. Check her out."

"What you're after, Hollins, I've no idea, but how could I forget about Miss Bertram Baird, galloping into my life with six white horses?"

"Hah. Dylan. What's that from?"

"Are we going to clean and shelf these dishes, Mr. Train Wreck, or not?"

The world changed the next day. Standing at the barn door, Christine, tentative at best, called out a hoped-for icebreaker. "Hello, is this the audition?" Gretchen, Southern accent, showboated a reply, "Why Miss Bertram Baird, I do declare," a reply that had Henry recalling back in the spring when they had all first met at BSC's rehearsal hall. Christine had introduced herself, giving her full name. She'd just been nervous, but Gretchen took that formal intro to heart. Adding the "Bertram" was a strut, being aloof, the high-and-mighty noble looking down at the peasants, and Gretchen Tarbat was not going to allow Christine Bertram Baird to forget the perceived transgression.

Everyone plugged in and found a spot with varying degrees of separation. Uncomfortable (an understatement) in new roles, they began with one of the bass-drum lines Melissa and Gretchen had cooked up. Christine, chording, slowly wove her way. Henry followed. Jam end. Repeat. End. Repeat. At some point, unintentional and near seamless, Christine took charge. The jam held a melodic line, and she branched out. When was that? Practice day three, day five? Did it matter? New patterns emerged. The rhythm section became just that. Henry, with a new assurance, filled and abetted Christine's lead as he had for months. There grew a connection. There were looks all around. A curtain had parted. They all knew it.

They toyed with the PA, finding a balance. Jams gave way to songs. They worked "Ball Game." Gretchen was hardly thrilled showing Christine *her* timing, *her* changes. Christine nearly recoiled having Gretchen so close. But Henry got goosebumps hearing the two of them play the Mosrite and the Harmony together. With Christine feeling the arrangement, Gretchen went back to the Rickenbacker. Henry took up the Mosrite. They played "Ball Game" over and over. They tried various openings. On one, Henry led off, Christine blasted in, Melissa and Gretchen followed together. They loved the sequence and tried another, starting with just bass with lead coming in last, creative stuff they soon transferred to other songs and riffs.

The vocals were somewhere. They needed another microphone. Singing into a propped-up lawn rake was at least funny—so was the occasional Parker howl.

"Do you guys think Park's doing that as a thumbs-up or down?"

"Not sure, Chris, but the howl always seems perfectly

The Rise of The Mad March

timed." Henry bent and scratched behind both ears. "Scat-dog, Parker."

"Maybe Brian, Keith, Bill and Charlie might help too."

"The Stone Hens. A 'cluck' chorus. They'd be awesome."

Mel hit a cymbal.

On one "Ball Game," they had a complete take, start to finish. Great opening, great timing. Everyone hit their mark. A first. Henry felt a chill—the thrill of that.

A week of practice passed, then another. Christine missed a few, was late on a few others, excuses always the same: exam, boyfriend, makeup class. The good news—no one quit. Christine, out of her guitar closet, out of Practice Room 108, was playing the likes of a running buffalo herd. And Tarbat's bass was driving her. Always rhythmic on lead, Gretchen approached the Rickenbacker with equal technique and intensity. The musical chops were growing, the timing locking in, the tempo picking up. They were working on original stuff – more good news.

Thus, the proverbial stew was on the stove heating up. But to Henry, at least, key ingredients were missing. There was no esprit de corps. Yes, they had moments kidding about with the Stone Hens – but not nearly enough. Smiles. Where the hell were the smiles? How can you be together yet apart? You can't —not at the station they were at. Too often, the passing looks among bass and lead barely rose above condescension and fright. Frustrated at a Friday practice end, Henry did what he always did with yet another ugly ogre blocking their road. He threw a rock at it.

"Before we split, BSC's got a fun talent show at the student union center coming up before the Christmas holiday break. Christine is a student. I'm the music department's piano tuner. Ergo, we qualify. Ergo, I signed us up. We're on the playbill."

"No fucking way."

"Yes way, Tarbat. We do one freaking song. December 20. Mark your calendar. Next, what song do we play?"

"On the 'bill' under what name?"

"I signed us in as *Baird*, Mel. Spur of the moment."

"We suck."

"No band stays in the garage forever, Gret." Henry was needled with Tarbat's crass negativity. "We need a mindset to play shows every chance we get. I don't care a rat's ass about who shows up to listen. We're trying to win ourselves over, not them." He was shouting, "We know what we want to sound like, and goddamn, we'll raise a glass when we get there. But we're not there. We need a push. The talent show's a push."

Melissa and Christine both slowly swung their hands together. The clapping resounded about the barn beams. He was being mocked. Probably deserved. Henry bent and bowed, turning, a complete 360. They all laughed together—a first, at last.

And here was the thing. They didn't suck, and Gretchen knew that. Henry was in awe of her progress with the Rickenbacker. She was experimenting, chording her lines for a fuller sound. He made a passing comment one night at supper. "You were born to play bass."

In awe he was, but hardly surprised—given the two of them. He loved overhearing Tarbat and Minch get it on at the dinner table or anywhere for that matter—the two of them holding court over, say, the GED. They had both passed. They were now high school equivalents. The teasing swung back and forth.

"You must have cheated."

"Yup, but not from you."

Relentless and fun. One would begin a sentence, the other would finish. Henry realized that was exactly how they were playing bass and drum. Theirs was a comfort connection born of a shared life. They had been "one" for years. Now they were exchanging words for notes and beats, one knowing exactly where the other was heading.

"The Equivalents. Hot band-name choice, Henry."

"Maybe, Gret. Let's hang that one on ourselves a while."

The Equivalents faded. Henry was all marble-mouthed trying to pronounce it, and no one was quite sure what the word meant.

Early on, he had urged them to listen over and over to "Green River." To Henry, the Creedence song was the rhythm-section pedestal in catching that mercurial loose/tight sound always rumbling about from his bobbing head to his tapping toe. They listened. "Green River" became the band's catch-phrase for a song well played. Melissa went a step further. "Green River. Not a bad tag for us, Henry."

Gretchen cupped a hand to her mouth. "Ladies and gents. Welcome to the Hollywood Bowl. Let's give it up for Grrrreeeennnn Rivvvver!"

They all agreed, an awesome name, but soon retreated. They would never live up to CCR's status in rock's pantheon, never do the song justice.

With no intention, Henry had become the leader of the band. He was the one roping everyone together, now pushing gigs. He was the one spending the bucks. But the role was an ill fit. For starters, he was the worst musician. Yes, he was living his pipe dream, but he had never been the leader of the pack in the dream. He *believed*. There was that.

Henry knew Christine well enough now to know she was not a take-charge type. Playing guitar—that was her Zen. Melissa always surprised but was satisfied being Tonto. Gretchen was the Alpha. No question. But did she *believe*? Not yet.

Henry led by necessity. Someone had to get pissed over the BSC Talent Show negativity: we suck—blah blah blah. Pissed enough, he was, to push-push and make another call.

"Dex. Henry. Remember me?"

"I recall the clock reaching midnight ... Hitches still standing."

"How about another date?"

"I'll have the Marines on standby."

"We've added a player."

"More chaos. Excellent. Got a date in mind?"

"Not yet. Are you in with this? This is a feasibility call."

"I'm game, Hollins."

"Thanks, Dex. We'll be more, I'm guessing, professional?"

"Switching over to easy-listening shopping music?"

Henry laughed. "Hey, no way, you don't have fresh produce and a canned goods section. Might be a few weeks, Dex, after the new year. I'll get back."

"How about I post a few flyers this time? No more hiding, Henry."

"Sounds good, Dex."

"Hey buddy, I'll need a name."

jersey moon: tour interview #8

August 1973

Jersey: When I say, "talent show," what first comes to mind?

Melissa: This is weird. I always flash to Gretchen grabbing Chris' dad's tie, up near the knot, getting right in his face and shouting, "No quarter!" Wow. Just the explosive ferocity of that, the wild look in her eyes. That moment still sends shivers.

I'd seen Gret become emotional lots of times. Never to that extreme, though. At that talent show, I remember thinking that I was glad I was on her side, and that *being glad* is what led me to latch onto her when we first got together at Altamont—that she would take care of me. And she has. The talent thing at the college, when that awful day was finally done, I was like, oh golly, Tarbat, who is going to take care of you? Sorry, Jersey, rambling here.

Jersey: No, no. This is great stuff.

Melissa: You really want me to walk through the entire show?

Jersey: That'd be awesome.

Melissa: First, there was the stage fright. When our turn to play came, Henry turned porcelain. What a bunch of newbies we all were. We never once gave a thought that the "show" was going to be a whole new world. We had only a dark, grungy bar with a few beer-drinking rowdies to fall back on.

We were at the tail end of the playbill. We show up. The student center is huge. The place is packed. Bleachers on one side. On the other, people were sitting on folded chairs or standing in the back. Students, parents, faculty, townies. Holy SRO, there are hundreds crowding in under the bright ceiling lights. I think we all pretty much stopped breathing.

Jersey: It was not a great show for you guys.

Melissa: That is the understatement of the rock 'n' roll century. I mean, everything went bonkers. We were the Marx Brothers setting up and hooking up to the college PA. My drums took forever. You could just sense the restlessness of the crowd. Henry's microphone and speaker were positioned all to hell and, before we struck a note, the feedback was horrible. Imagine, an entire crowd covering their ears, their pained looks. Someone shouted out, "next," and that was so bad. Gretchen goes, "Let's get this over with." We kicked off. Total scrambled eggs, Jersey. The start was botched. Chris was way too loud. I couldn't hear Gretchen's bass. Henry apparently missed a change, maybe two. I was never even aware. I couldn't hear him, either. Acoustics in gym-type places are awful. We sounded worse. What a combination. We were not a band. We were a garbage disposal. We ended somehow. The silence from the stage and the union center was deafening. We ran off.

Jersey: What did you play?

Melissa (laughing): That's just it. We had argued over what might work best: a cover, an original? All the rushing around, being so nervous, we were still confused and probably played two different songs at once. Talk about screw-ups, can you believe that? Has any band in history ever been that terrible? We were morons.

Jersey: And the storm was just beginning.

Melissa: Exactly. We trooped back to this dressing room used by all the performers. Only the next act getting ready and a few others were there. Anyway, Gretchen is screaming at

Chris and Henry for messing up. I can still hear her. "What's that slung over your shoulder, Hollins? That thing with the strings. Do you even fucking know?" She was yelling at all of us, "A mountain of practice; a pile of shit. That's our name, P ... O ... S ... A Pile of Shit." On and on she went. That's when the door burst open and Chris' parents barged in.

Jersey: And this is a big-time surprise for Christine, right?

Melissa: From the very beginning when Chris joined up, she had never mentioned her parents. Of course, we had never asked. We later learned they'd arrived at BSC to drive her home for Christmas, and they never would have showed up to something like a goofy talent show except that they saw a posted flyer with *Baird* listed to perform. Anyway, you have to understand, Jersey, Mrs. Marion Baird is a formidable lady. She had no idea her pre-med daughter was spending a ton of time in a horrible loser band. She had no idea Chris played guitar or even owned one. What she did know, apparently, was that Chris' grades had been slipping, that she had been sounding sullen over the phone, that something was off-kilter. And now she knew.

Jersey: And that "something" was you?

Melissa: Absolutely. Marion Baird, probably intimidating on a good day, rushed straight at cowering Chris and started in. She was furious. It was like she was picking up where Gret had left off. I really can't recall all she shouted. There was an "I had to look three times to assure myself that the creature on stage was actually my daughter." She eyes us. "And who are these trashy, irresponsible ..." She could not come up with a proper noun, Jersey, just a disgusted face.

Jersey: And that, so I've heard, is when the world tilted on its axis.

Melissa: I love that. Yeah. Gretchen leaped to Christine's defense. Golly, if only someone had a movie camera rolling. Mrs. Baird is a full-figured, shoulders back, force of nature. General Patton ... battle-ready. I mean, everything but the uniform. She's pointing an accusing finger at Chris, "I'm both bewildered and appalled." Then, like out of the blue, she's blindsided with a Tarbat finger in *her* face.

"But I'm not. Don't you ever talk to my lead guitar player like that again."

Mrs. Baird is rocked back on her heels … but this is Patton. She fires away, "I'm her mother."

Gret doesn't even take a breath. "I don't give a flying fuck who you are."

Holy hellcats, Jersey, the brawl was on. The fireplug dressed in formal gray with black pointed pumps versus the raggedy thin reed and her falling-apart sneakers; both the same height, head-to-head, letting loose. Really something.

"You have one second whoever you are to step clear, away from myself and my daughter."

"Not another word from you, tight ass."

Crack! Marion Baird cuffed Gretchen across the face. A firecracker exploding. I flinched. Everyone did.

Gret recoiled with fists clenched. That's when Henry and Mr. Baird grasped and pulled them apart. All of us looked on in disbelief.

Mrs. Baird was irate. "Where are the authorities? I demand this monster be taken away. How dare you? My daughter!"

"Chris? Your daughter? Bullshit. You know nothing." Gretchen was mocking, practically laughing. Henry couldn't keep hold of her. Gret broke free and flew at Chris.

"Strip your top, Baird."

If possible, poor Chris grew more alarmed.

"Take off that shirt. Now!"

Chris reacted like a petrified animal. Gretchen reached and literally tore away the light plaid flannel she was wearing, buttons popping in all directions. Chris was hysterical and begging for her to stop. Ripping away the shirt, Gret pulled and broke the bra clasp. Naked from the waist, Chris bent and cowered, attempting to cover herself. With her hands on Chris' shoulders, Gret was turning her and yelling, "Show yourself, Christine. Stand straight and show your mom."

Christine didn't need to do that. Everyone saw enough.

Jersey: Oh my God.

Melissa: There were a few of those. Both Bairds rushed to Chris. Henry muttered, "Oh shit, worst fear." I was so stunned. Chris' body... she'd been beaten; red, black and blue bruises were visible on her upper chest, breasts and backside. There was some swelling, some scarring. This was beyond awful. I began crying.

Her dad covered her, gently wrapping his suit jacket about her shoulders. He said, "Who, Christine?"

"Bryce."

"Where is he?" His voice was half caring, half crazed tiger.

"Sitting on the risers. Left side. Red shirt, red hat."

As Mr. Baird let go, Mrs. Baird rushed close and cradled her daughter. Chris was all tears, "I'm sorry, Mom."

Marion was crying, too.

Jersey: How did Gretchen know?

Melissa: Henry had us eyeing her at practice. He knew something was wrong, her body language at times. I believe Gretchen caught on right away. At the time, Jersey, I was too scared to know how she caught on. You catch my drift?

Jersey: I do. That brings us to Gretchen's "no quarter."

Melissa: Henry, Gret and Mr. Baird witnessed little of the mother-daughter comforting. They were out the door. I followed. Chris's dad apparently had met this Bryce once or twice before and spotted him right away. He pointed. Gretchen sprung like a pent-up, let-loose black panther, charging through the talent show crowd, locking onto a red shirt in the bleacher risers. Bryce Marrow was four or five rows up, chatting with friends. He might have sensed Gretchen oncoming a second or two before she waded up past the lower rows, screamed, and uncorked a wild left that caught Marrow square in the face. He was sent rearing backward but, comprehending the attack, recovered enough to ward off Gret's second blow. She screamed again as he grabbed and bent her wrist, allowing Henry to shove and slam Marrow into the solid metal and wood seating.

Marrow was a big guy, six feet, maybe an inch higher, square-faced with an athlete's build. Bleeding about the head, he shook off the impact, scrambled back upright, shouted, "what the fuck," and grabbed Henry in a headlock. Hollins fought with rabbit punches that went nowhere. He felt the hold lighten when Gretchen somehow swung her boot into Marrow's crotch. She caught just enough to garner a groan, but not enough to prevent Henry from being thrown three rows down. Students scattered from the melee as best they could. Shouting, "you bitch," Bryce pushed Gretchen backward. She fell and struck her head as she tumbled to the cement floor. With all the shoving, Marrow lost his balance. Teetering, grasping the hardwood bleacher seating with both hands, he prevented a fall, but in so doing he was positioned defenseless and never wised up to the dress shirt and tie now before him unleashing a hard right fist that shattered his jaw. Mr. Baird followed with a "father's-daughter" uppercut that drove teeth through tongue and cracked bone loud enough to emit gasps from those close by.

Marrow collapsed on the risers, his eyes somewhere in the back of his head. Security arrived. Walkie-talkies had an ambulance on the way.

Jersey: I'm sitting here wishing I could kick the fucker, too.

Melissa: Jersey! We shouldn't even be talking about this. We're such a bad influence on you.

Jersey: No, you're not. So, did someone, like, drive a stake into Marrow or something? How do these sick psychos even exist, Melissa?

Melissa: Gret's skull required six stitches. I'm like, "Hey, just like that biker dude." She failed to find the humor. Henry checked out okay, just bruised and a sore neck. The student body had broken his fall. Mr. Baird fractured bones in his hand. Later on, we all signed his cast.

Chris finally confided the hell she'd been living. Days after the talent show, as if it were her fault, she tried to leave school. Hah. As if Gret was going to put up with that. "You got classes, Bertram, a backbone to grow, and a shit-ass loser band to rock." Nobody lays it out better than Tarbat.

Jersey: God, I love Gretchen.

Melissa: Weird, but eventually, so did Chris' mom. Listen up, Jersey. If Chris had run away, she'd be in the college rumor pipeline forever. By staying put, by returning the stares with one of her own, eventually she was off page one, and everyone moved on. There is always another social-headline story in another dorm. Got me?

Jersey: Gotcha. Was Christine alright?

Melissa: Tough question. With prescribed salve and time, the physical scars faded. We subjected her healing to a weekly inspection, a fun thing: lots of kisses. Lord knows, Baird's gorgeous boobs are worth safe keeping. They're the only ones the band has. But I don't mean to make light, Jersey. To lose innocence and trust, to lose your way, to have to come back from being so far down. Maybe you never do.

Jersey: What happened to the cretin?

Melissa: Hopefully, he was permanently disfigured and ate with a straw like, forever. We heard the Marrows were big-time donors to the college. Maybe the wheels of justice got greased with movers and shakers needing the ugliness to vanish. Is the "shit" somewhere far off waiting to strike again? I don't know. I wish life was all black and white. Truth is, Jersey, I don't have an end to give you.

Jersey: You do, Melissa. We're here on tour with Christine. We see the end every day.

chapter twenty-eight

December 1972

Marion Baird faced an awakening. She had failed. Her pivotal role: guiding her daughter's well-being—and she had failed. The horror of Christine being abused and remaining silent bred in Marion both depression and confusion. Christine's guarded admissions, revealed in bits and pieces, brought only anguish.

—"At first, I was his everything. Then, everything I did was wrong."

—"I got so lost just trying *not* to make him angry. What was I doing? I felt like the fault was all mine."

—"God, how Bryce hated my guitar practicing with Henry."

—"The punching and biting. I was driving him crazy. I was *making* him hurt me."

—"If I threatened to break up, he said he'd kill himself."

—"I got too scared to do anything, to change anything."

—"I'm ashamed, Mom, and I refuse to talk about this anymore."

Marion asked herself where to turn. How do I undo? How do I help? Wes had warned more than once she was over-controlling, to give the reins some slack. She hadn't listened.

Had her masterminding led directly or even inadvertently

to this horror? Had she squashed her own daughter's self-confidence? Had she pushed Christine to a complacency that allowed a sick creep to render her powerless? She shuddered at the answers.

Marion knew one thing: The guilt felt massive. She had dismissed Christine's meek retorts: "What's wrong with a B? All this pre-med, Mom, really?" Her daughter had hinted at other interests. Marion had turned a deaf ear. She'd taken a hard line. *She* knew what was best. Christine would thank her later. *My God!*

What mattered now was both comprehending what the past had wrought and yes, the future. Indeed, she could change. She vowed to change. She would not lose touch with her only child.

One fact sat rooted like a tall redwood. Marion would wager her jewelry box that, going forward, this Gretchen Tarbat monster would be in the mix. Marion held a mental picture of Gretchen returning to the rehearsal room, bloody and unbowed—what that picture meant. The foul-mouthed Tarbat held sway with Christine. There was a connection between the two. Marion drew a deep breath. Without being aware of the how or why, she had to be accepting and never forgetting her vow: She could change. The monster had stood up. The monster had bellowed, "No quarter!"

Her daughter was going to survive the horror of Bryce Marrow, and if it took a street urchin and a rubbish rock band to enable, so be it.

"Feeling okay?"

"Can we not talk about it? I'm going to be fine, Dad. How about you?"

"I ache and I itch." He raised his cast. "But check out all the signings." He grinned. "I was just wondering, given that

Christmas has come and gone, if there was anything in your heart's desire, that your mom and I missed?"

"You both could stop feeling responsible."

"You didn't answer my question, Christine."

"Okay. First up, Mom unwrapping that Woodstock T-shirt you gave her, the look on her face, priceless."

"Think she'll ever wear it?"

Christine laughed. "I only know you're the best." She cradled his ink-signed cast with both hands and kissed it. "Back to me. To be honest, Santa forgot one thing."

"The sleigh is still out front, Christine. Name it."

"I'd like Melissa and Gretchen to visit here for New Year's."

"Consider it done."

chapter twenty-nine

January 1973

Kicker reached the goddamn, pain-in-the-ass phone on the sixth or seventh ring. "Clubhouse."

"Don't you fuckers ever pick up?"

"Who the hell is this?"

"Gretchen."

"Doesn't ring any bells, sweet mouth."

"Gretchen from the Van Wert bar. Hitches. The bitch who caved in some asshole biker's cranium with my guitar. Any bells ringing, Raven?"

"I believe there's a price on your ass. Every time you hear a Harley, Gretchen, run."

"I'll wear my sneakers every day. Tell Granitehead that the band's …"

"Wait a second. I'm recording this. We can do that now."

"Do I sound like I fucking give a shit? Jesus. We're playing back at Hitches in early March. This is a Raven invite."

"You're inviting the whole club? You got a set of balls, sister."

"Pay attention. There are girls in the band. Leave the tit-size jokes in the parking lot … and I'd appreciate a cheering section from any of you leather zeros that show up."

"Females. No tit jokes. Early March. Bring the cheerleaders.

Robert Espenscheid, Jr.

Got it. Let me tell ya, crusher, that's a few weeks out. Still, our social calendar might be filled."

"Who's the smart shit I'm talking to? "

"Kicker."

"Granite doing okay?"

"He's alive. I'll relay your concern, young lady."

"Fuck you, Kicker." Gretchen slammed the phone down.

Kicker gently laid his in the cradle. "Now that's what I call a hotline."

chapter thirty

The hardest part was getting them on the plane. Neither Melissa nor Gretchen had ever flown.

"If I think back long and hard, I can still remember when I made my own decisions. Fuckin' A, Hollins."

"It's New Year's Eve, Tarbat. There's not enough time to drive, plus the weather. The reservations are set."

"Four days with Baird's battle-ax mom? Are you kidding me? And what if the jumbo jet t-squares into the Great Lakes?"

"Planes fly and land every day. But hey, if the bird crashes, I'll take the credit." Henry smiled.

"I'm not scared."

"You are, too. Mel's the same. Hold hands. You'll be fine, Amelia."

"I'm not waving goodbye to you at the airport. Just so you know."

"Just give Dorothy a hug and play nice with the stewardesses."

Wearing a smart-aleck smile that Gretchen matched, Melissa piped in, "You'll miss us."

"I need a favor, Mrs. B."

"Sure, Melissa."

"If you actually manage to get Gretchen into a dress, let's call a halt right then and there."

"But I wanted to buy dresses for the both of you." Marion frowned.

"Let me take a raincheck."

"Heavens, sweetie, why?"

"I want my girlfriend to have this special day all to herself."

Marion eyed Melissa with admiration, an affection somewhat lost as Gretchen emerged from the dressing room with yet another perturbed, questioning look on her face. As calm and encouraging as possible, Marion said, "Not quite. Let's try another." Gretchen stuck her tongue out and disappeared behind the paneling. Melissa and Christine laughed. Marion sighed. She and the "monster" had battled right from the beginning.

"I've never worn a dress in my life, Baird."

"Always a first, Tarbat. We're all going. You'll try a few on. Humor me. My treat, take advantage."

"I don't want a dress, Baird."

"I don't care, Tarbat."

Gretchen appealed to her cast-handed soldier in arms. "Save me, Chris' dad. Do something."

"I'll drive."

"You can't? I'm appalled. Melissa?"

"California raised, ma'am. I swim."

"You'll learn, Tarbat. At college, I swam competitively. Being able to swim is vital to your well-being. I'll teach you."

"It's winter, Baird."

The Rise of The Mad March

"The pool's enclosed and heated, Tarbat."

"Mom, is it possible for you two to at least address one another by your first names? Good grief, people. Dad! Go find them a peace pipe."

Gretchen was barely listening. "I don't have a suit."

"We'll find something or, with just us two, you can skinny-dip. Divine. Trust me."

Gretchen held back and wore a knowing smile. "I sense an ulterior motive here, Baird. Like, like an accidental but not accidental drowning."

At first, Marion responded with a why-do-I-keep-trying sigh. The child was exasperating. But her demeanor abruptly switched gears because *she could change*. She whispered so only the two might hear. "I'd pull you to safety, Gretchen, just as you pulled Christine."

Five try-ons on, becoming more vexed with each one, Gretchen sashayed out number six in sleeveless silk and cotton: peach-colored with white dots, V-neck front and back, wide calf in length, bodice gathered at the waist with a tied belt. A gorgeous dress on a gorgeous girl that had everyone nearly faint in awe. Jaws dropped. Hands clapped. Faces radiated delight.

Reading into the late afternoon, Henry failed to turn a page and said: "Minch was right. I can't fathom how much I miss them."

Dorothy slowed her stitching. "Pickford feels like a silent movie. And poor Parker."

"The new year, Dorothy, and I'm a far cry from festive."

"There's beer in the fridge. No bubbly."

"They'll be back in two days, right?"

"Not the end of the world, Henry."

The phone rang. Henry made the grab. There was no hi or hello – just a contralto, near singing and ending on an upbeat.

"I'm in Bloomingdale's."

Gretchen Tarbat in Bloomingdale's. What was oh so incongruously right about that picture? Was there another soul more deserving? He belly-laughed. He couldn't help it. Talk about a gambit. "Buy something."

"Okay, and if I can survive one more fitting and one more lap, we'll see ya Wednesday, boss man."

She was gone. Just like that. Henry hated replacing the phone, signing off. *Fitting? She had bought something. Lap? What was that?* He could wait.

"What did she say, Henry?"

"It wasn't what she said, Dorothy, but how she said it."

Driving back, the three were squeezed up-front in Dad Baird's 1970 Bronco, a surprise gifted loaner for the spring semester; a gift met with cheers and hugs. Looking about the back, Melissa said, "Where's the dress?"

"At the bottom of the pool. Don't worry, it's heated."

Behind the wheel, Christine laughed. Melissa didn't. "Don't you dare tease, Tarbat. Where is it?"

"Way in the back in a box. Mom Baird packed it like it was the Mona Lisa."

"It is. It's so beautiful. You're so beautiful. When are you going to wear it?"

Gretchen stared at the open road ahead. "I have no idea."

Scrunched as she was in the middle, Melissa grew serious, shifting even closer to Gretchen, wedged against the passenger door. She spoke quietly. "I know you sense change, all that's been happening, all these new people in our lives, like we've crossed a bridge or something. I see the changes and worry some, too. Like, what's ahead? I know one thing. None of this will separate us. We will stay together. I promise." With no reaction, Melissa added, "What I'm feeling is that we need to trust."

Gretchen rested her head on Melissa's shoulder. She whispered back, "That's hard for me."

chapter thirty-one

February—March 1973

The band exploded. As January passed the baton to February, the musical awakening in the Pickford barn felt like a crescendo. They were "one." They practiced as "one." They teased and joked as "one." The talent show debacle was figuratively stashed away to a top-floor closet – shelved high up above the coatrack. They moved on anew. Rant songs pumped from Gretchen. Christine began writing. The pace grew faster, bass and drum tighter. They seemed to reach a high-water mark, then another. Henry labeled the output: *Evolved mayhem*. Grandstanding leads were non-existent. Rhythm ruled. Going biblical, they brought down two commandments from their own mountaintop.

Songs will be short. Two minutes tops. Sing it. End it.

The music was both exhilarating and punishing. Playing, they wore themselves out pretty quickly, and listening ears would be no different. Gig sets would run twenty minutes, no more, then a break or an escape back home.

Would their playlist connect to an audience? They didn't care. They had evolved into what they were. A freak show? They didn't care. The band was a buzz. They felt it.

In early March, Dex from Hitches called Henry. The gig was confirmed on the ninth at 10 p.m.

"I'm willing to put up flyers. I still need a name, bro."

"I'm on it, Dex, I swear."

"Something else, Henry, something black-jacketed and surly."

"What?"

"Brace yourself. The biker's here, searching for you guys."

"Oh shit. The one Gretchen hit? The Raven?"

"From the neck up, he does look a little lopsided."

"He's the last thing we need. Hold on." Smothering the phone, Henry called out, "It's Dex. Granite's at Hitches, tracking us down."

Standing in the kitchen, Gretchen grasped the countertop to steady. She always knew there would be hell to pay. Images from the first gig melee flashed behind her eyes. Shaken she was, but also sick of waiting for the inevitable. "Circle the wagons, boss. We'll meet him head-on."

"For sure?"

"He can only kill us once, Hollins."

"Dex?"

"Yeah."

"Buy him a beer. We're on our way."

"Okay. Your tab, killer."

Late mild morning, pulling into Hitches, the sun reflected off one, and only one, black and gold Harley-Davidson parked out front leaning a hard left on its kickstand. Barging in, door slamming behind her, Gretchen marched straight at the watering hole's sole customer, standing at the bar, beer in hand. Caught off guard at the rapid oncoming confrontation, Henry and Dex drew a collective breath. Near snuggling in, close up, Gretchen eyed the biker's forehead hairline scar. "When did the threads come out?"

"Pretty quick. Late last summer, 'round Labor Day."

Gretchen stepped back. "What do you want, Raven? Another shot at Henry here? Me? One fist in the mouth for every stitch?"

"A how-the-hell-are-you would be nice." An obvious shaving with now incoming hair above her left ear caught the Raven's eye. Leaning close, aping her chutzpah, he laid a hand on her jaw and gently turned her head. "Another nasty scar. What happened to you?"

"Another gig."

"Damn, what is it with you guys?"

"Since you didn't ask, Raven, I'll survive."

"What's your band's name, hotshot, The Headhunters?"

Henry relaxed some. The biker appeared a far cry from that infamous August summer night. He was sober, looking through probable prescriptions, inquisitive and alert. Actually, Henry had to admit, given the stocky build, the black mass of curls, the chin stubble, the square jaw, the prizefighter nose, the Raven was a decent-looking guy, more Ivy League professor than Hells Angel, and he was zeroed in on Gretchen. "Dex tells me you're on bass."

Gretchen stepped back once more and stared.

"How do you generally plug in? Solo amp? Through a PA?"

Gretchen stared.

"Everyone in the band needs to hear a clear bass feed from their monitors, don't ya think?"

Gretchen stared.

"What is this, a contest? You called the club, Tarbat. Kicker? The invite? Remember? This isn't a search and destroy. I'm here to help. I'll be the FOH."

If Gretchen had gone mute, Henry was now intrigued. "FOH?"

"The front of the house guy. The one at the sound check who's listening to the levels from the stage to the back shitter.

The one who can maybe turn your wall of distorted garbage into something else."

Henry shook his head, totally confused. "Help, Granite? Like how?"

"I work for Hawkeye Sound out of Iowa City. Part of the stage setup crew."

"You're a band tech? A professional? I don't believe this."

Still eyeing Gretchen, Granite said, "I am what I am, and it would pain me to hear your garage band repeat its colossal fuckup."

Gretchen stuck out her chin. "You were the fuckup."

"Agreed. Fuckups all around. Do you even know what a stage monitor is?"

Gretchen stared.

They were close, but Granite was shouting. "I was a drunken ass. I admit it. I'm sorry I said whatever I said to make the two of you go batshit crazy. This is an apology, Tarbat. Is 'sorry' enough? How about stemmed roses? Do I need to paint your toenails? Would that work? I'm offering to lend a hand to set up the show. You look lost on stage. I know the rock shops in Des Moines. They know me. Maybe, for the one gig here at Hitches, I can beg and borrow the gear that might work for you. No guarantees. I can try."

"Why?"

"Why, Tarbat? Jesus. How about to see and hear if the band's worth five cents?"

Henry was all over this. "He made the trip, Gret. On his bike. In March! We need help. Our sound is crap. You know that."

Once again, Gretchen slowly weaved her way close to Granite, eyeing the scar. On her tiptoes, they were inches apart. "You have headaches and shit?"

"No. I'm fine. You get any closer, girl, I'm not liable."

"Take me with you."

"What?"

"Stoner's, wherever else. I want to learn tech stuff. We'll take the van. Okay, Henry?"

Henry's thoughts were scattered. This was moving way too fast. "Our reality is, equipment-wise, we don't know enough to know what we need."

Granite was struck at the two of them. *Gretchen: ballbreaker or nursemaid, take your pick. Humble Henry: a rock 'n' roll first.* "Where's your practice setup?"

"Ten minutes from here, southeast."

"Can you run through a number or two for me?"

"Then what?"

"I'll offer suggestions, Henry, then maybe Tarbat and I head up to Stony's and the like and see what shakes out."

"The gig's but a few days away."

"Time enough." Granite spied Dex. "Show day, can we do an early sound check, say at six or seven?"

"Anytime, bro."

Henry felt the pace reaching breakneck speed. "Whoa. You are rolling past me, Granite. We've never had monitors and such, not even proper mikes, and I need to know what you are going to cost me. I already owe Stony a trust fund I don't have. You're not hooking up with Steppenwolf here."

Granite sat on his barstool with his hands outstretched, "I'm not a barge-in, takeover type guy. I'll suggest, okay? You need this, you upgrade with that. Maybe I can grab some gratis for just one show. Rock shops have worked with me before. They're aware I send bands and sales their way. As for me hooking up, I'm repairing fences to the both of you. I'm on vacay from my job for a week. Lemme do what I can."

Damn, the biker's a gift. Henry, deciding on the spot, suddenly knew exactly what Julius Caesar was thinking as he eyed the English Channel for the first time. *When was that? Around 50 BC?* Henry found himself nearly laughing. "Let's do this. Dex, you'll get a name. Granite, come listen to a run-through and see what you can add. The van's yours. Gretchen too!"

She was wide-eyed. "I'm your forever girl and then you pawn me off to the first barbarian that comes along?"

"You volunteered."

She appealed behind the bar. "Dex, what should I do?"

"Go learn stuff."

In what seemed a swiftly passing thunderstorm, they convened at the Pickford barn, played two songs, and waved as Granite and Gretchen headed north to Des Moines with the van. Henry was having second thoughts. The Roman invasion never went well.

chapter thirty-two

"Can I ask you something?"

Heading north on I-35, Granite was driving. "Sure."

"No bullshitting me, Raven."

"Got it."

"Why are you here? Why are you doing this? And please, no song and flowers about making our loser band better."

Granite shot her a glance and then had his eyes back on the road. "I'm here because you're here."

That was unexpected. Gretchen folded her arms across her chest. "You're here because your biker buddies have razzed you to no end about being coldcocked by a ditzy dyke who needs to grow a pair, and you had to do something."

"Do you actually stand in front of a mirror every day and practice tearing yourself down? Is that like a morning ritual with you?"

"You showed up to be with me? What a crock."

"In the middle of the night, I'm dreaming about adjusting the timing on my piss-poor-running Harley and I can't set the specs because your face keeps butting in. So, you're right. I had to do something."

She half laughed and studied his profile. "Your nose is crooked."

"Been reset a time or two."

This guy was a first. "Look, Granite, here's a snapshot. I'm on probation for theft. I've got priors. I'm wanted for worse."

"And I wanted to see you again."

"Chrissakes, man. And by the way, have you got, like, a real name?"

"Tony Destino."

Gretchen perked. "Italian?"

"Nothing but spaghetti."

"So that's Tony as in Tomás?"

"Antonio."

"Antonio Destino." Gretchen rolled the name on her tongue, repeating it out loud to herself, adding without thinking, a quietly spoken "beautiful." She collected herself, sitting up straighter, embarrassed. "So … big familia?"

"Ah, 'The Godfather.' The word's famiglia."

"I like that better. Big famiglia?"

"Three sisters. Two older, one younger. Way too many cousins. How about you?"

Gretchen pulled back. She was wading in, the water rising too deep. "Let's just focus on the mission, Destino."

"Yes, ma'am. So, sound-wise, what bothers the most?"

She exhaled, relieved to be back on solid ground. "Keeping the guitars tuned and tuned together."

"Problem with every band I know."

"We're using Henry's tuning forks. They're a pain."

Granite nodded with a sympathetic look. "Onstage, bands tune to portable keyboards—those that carry them."

Gretchen took an immediate interest. "At Gunny's church, I'm killing time one Sunday snooping around in the basement. They've got this tiny electric organ stashed in a corner gathering dust."

"A Farfisa?"

"Don't know. Worth a look?"

Granite held a wolf's smile. "I'm getting that old-time religion, Miss Tarbat. Next up, vocals."

"Henry and I trade off so two standup mikes would be a plus. Basically, the vocals are secondary to Chris' riffing, but if they're too submerged, we're a nothing band."

"I'm thinking, for Hitches, we'll keep the setup simple. Maybe mike everything through the PA. Worth a shot. Melissa has to hear you. They all do. Look, Gretchen, a righteous setup is hardly cut and dry. Like at Hitches, the band's all jammed into a corner. We'll set one monitor out front and see what shakes out. Every venue is different and, listen up, this is important. It'll pay for you to be hip and stay hip on the production end. Recordings, live shows—new gadgets are being introduced in this crazy business every day. I know money is tight for you guys, but Baird, for one, needs to at least be aware that different amps, and pickups can more than tweak her sound. If you hear a band that sounds awesome, it's probably because they've trolled the tech side and found what was inside their heads. There are payoffs for comprehending where all the stage cables are running off to. Capisce?"

"Cool."

"And I'll explain the PA mixer as we go along, okay?"

"Double cool."

"We'll balance the mikes at the sound check. Any lights onstage?"

"None. Pretty dark up there. Not a whole lot of outlets, either."

"Okay, a junction box and at least one light stand is on the wish list, or better yet, maybe a couple footlights—if only to spotlight the vocals."

"Henry is not a real singer. He's got this nasal whine with a lisp." She hooted. "If we were a church choir, it'd be like, 'Where do we hide this guy?' But there is a difference between irritating and interesting. Hollins is the latter, and he and I sing back and forth. Our trade-offs hide the simplicity of our stuff.

Melissa says our voices mesh. I actually go lower than him. That works, too."

"The sultry sexy thing." Granite grinned.

"Wrong, spaghetti." She felt herself blush. "I'm guessing you're a momma's boy, right?"

His grin stayed. "Absolutely."

Gretchen totaled up what she now knew. For reasons best left unsaid, a sadness crept in. "You're a hundred floors above me, Antonio."

Only his mother used his formal name. He fought to stay matter of fact. "Use the elevator."

"I surrender. You're here to be with me. Let's leave it at that. I get it, I guess."

Granite playfully nudged her shoulder. "No, you probably don't, and that's okay because neither do I."

Reaching Des Moines, they exited City Expressway 235, crossed University to Beaver Avenue north, braved the tight traffic and pulled into Stoner's Music.

"Scoring what we need here would be a big win for us. Can you bat a sultry rock 'n' roll eye at Stony?"

"You got the wrong girl, bro."

"Do it for the Rickenbacker."

"Okay."

chapter thirty-three

Rigg Moon was tightening lug nuts on a tire rotation when he spotted Henry standing in his service bay. "Hollins, Liberty's man of the moment."

"Hey, Rigg, got a minute? I could use a hand."

"You're at the top of the rumor-mill mountain, my friend."

"What's the town saying?"

"I like 'Henry's harem' the best."

"You're kidding."

"Small town, partner. An assist?"

"I'm looking to hire paid help."

"Now you're talking."

"I've got this band, Rigg."

"So, I've heard."

"We've a gig at Hitches up in Van Wert on Friday."

"You providing body armor?"

"Hah. Were you actually there at the fiasco, back in August?"

"Nope. Just heard the stories. Did Dex actually fire his musket through the roof?"

"Black powder only. The blast caught everyone's attention. I'll say that much. So, the band could use a roadie. Equipment transport, loading, unloading, lugging amps."

"What am I going to cost you?"

"But that's not what I really want you for. Besides a camel's back, I need an eagle."

"Not sure I follow, Henry."

"Melissa, Christine and Gretchen. I want someone watching whoever is watching them: guys drinking heavy, bad asses, space cadets high on whatever. It's rock 'n' roll. It's a bar. They can party hearty but anyone unwanted who stalks too close to MCG takes a step back."

"This a real threat, you figure?"

"No. But if anything happened to the gals—wow, I don't want to even think about it."

"But you are."

"True. We have a gear guy running sound. Dex is busy behind the bar. I'm playing guitar. We can't be the eyes we might need. Look, the band's got rules. We arrive together, we leave together. Nobody wanders off alone. You're the insurance guy expecting the unexpected."

"And if I'm out brawling ten gorillas, defending Melissa's honor, I've got major medical, right?"

"How about twenty bucks to cover Friday?"

"Question, Henry. Are MCG aware my hire?"

"Not yet. You agree, I'll let them know."

"And?"

"I suspect their reaction will be Gretchen speaking for all three: 'I can fucking take care of myself.'"

"Cecil Sidel's runaway girl. What's not to love. Why me?"

"I want Wyatt Earp. You fill the mirror, Rigg."

"Me wearing a tin star. I can't wait to tell Ty. I'll do it. Twenty plus gas expense."

"Welcome to the circus."

chapter thirty-four

Having Rigg Moon on board was a major win. Henry's bandmates would kick up a fuss, but he'd put his foot down and keep it there. Moon was a soft-spoken, easygoing guy, but a big enough bull to corral a herd if needed.

Henry recalled being at Moon Auto months ago waiting on an oil change. Rigg's wife, Tyler, dropped by. He was close enough to overhear and sense their exchange. They loved one another. Nothing was more obvious. The grease-stained mechanic and the trim, impeccably dressed school administrator exchanged this and that with teasing smiles, the two a perfect match. Henry paid his service charge and drove away from the repair shop that day envious as hell.

Rigg was the right call. Welcome to the circus, indeed. One key appropriation on Henry's "must" list was checked off, one more to go.

"I understand we have two graduates at the table tonight."

"Don't make fun, Hollins."

"Never, Tarbat. History was a GED subject, was it not?"

"Need more research help with your Civil War novel, boss?"

Henry sighed. His story had taken a back seat of late. "I'm dropping back further, Minch. 1776. Christmas. The middle of a bitter-cold winter's night. Washington's army crosses the Delaware River, surprising the hungover Hessians at Trenton. Victory. Yes, sir! In the aftermath, Big George has only one problem, and what *was* that, Miss Minch?"

"Gee, I dunno. Trouble getting back?"

"I love how this woman thinks. Exactly, and Lord Cornwallis commanding the redcoat regulars twelve miles north at Princeton sees what Minch sees and double-times his army on down, trapping the whole rebel enchilada with their backs up against a raging river.

"Now, it's the night before the coming battle, and George holds a war council. They could surrender. They could fight to the death. Or they could do a little of both. The American Revolution is near its end, folks, and then …" Henry waited.

Gretchen, both caught up and exasperated by being caught up, pounded the table. "What, Hollins?"

Henry nearly grinned. He'd roped her in. "A local farmer is at the war council. Why is he there? Nobody knows. Regardless, the farmer lets on that there is an old hidden goat path that winds around the British position, frozen and passable. Big George is all smiles and leaves the campfires burning while his army slips away in the dead of night."

"And somewhere in that bizarre brain of yours, there is a reason for going on and on with all this, right?"

"Oh yeah. Cornwallis awakens to a miserable morning. And it isn't the coffee, Miss Minch. Not only have the rebels escaped, but they are attacking his left-in-reserve force in Princeton. He turns to an aide and says," Henry's smile is ear to ear, "Mr. Washington is on a mad march."

Listening intently, Dorothy, Gretchen and Melissa all registered incomprehension.

Henry drumrolled the old oak table. "Lord Cornwallis named our band."

Three still-bewildered faces stared back.

"The Mad March."

Parker barked.

Henry laughed. "I read that last night. The quote from the British general just leaped off the page. A mad march. That's what we are. Just like the American rebel army in 1776, that's what we're on."

"The Mad March. And where are we going?"

"We don't know, Gret. That's the point."

Melissa ended any argument. "Wonderland Alice and the March Hare. I'll paint a big white rabbit on my kick drum."

———

"Hitches."

"Dex, we got a name." Henry dropped the designate.

"Puts Pink Floyd to shame, and about time, tuner. I'll get the flyers made up and posted"

At the bar, Butch Boxer was having a beer with two cronies. Late afternoon, they were holding up the place. He'd overheard the telephone exchange. "Damn, Dex, not those punks again."

Mick faced Boxer with a smile. "The house is buying the next round. Thanks for the flyer header, dog."

chapter thirty-five

If anyone had asked Christine Baird how she managed to soldier on at college after her torment and tormentor became public knowledge, she'd have said, "As long as I continue here, I get to go to band camp." True, the behind-the-back daily stares and murmurings of her fellow students were tough to handle. Getting to and from class was not fun. On one occasion, she'd been asked to chair a seminar on abuse awareness. She begged off. Too soon. She wasn't ready. Classes were endured. Band camp at the Pickford barn became an Eden. That's what the Mad March was, a glorious escape. She was the happy-go-lucky camp kid, trading lanyards for guitar strings. Euphoria was storming her guilt-built castle walls. A new Christine Baird was slowly taking shape.

None of Christine's joy escaped the eyes of Gretchen Tarbat. She was torn, still wary of the rich bitch for being a rich bitch, all the while coming to terms that they shared a horror best survived and overcome together. For Baird, the poison in her life had been unveiled and vanquished. She had once walked with her shoulders on the ground. Now she was Olga Korbut.

They had finished an early dinner, five tonight at the table.

Christine was there. Hardly a surprise, she'd been camping out at Pickford more and more, staying over on the weekends.

Gretchen had been out of sorts the whole meal. Hardly a surprise. Nobody probed. Gret was Gret. Sullen moods were not new. Still, the Tarbat cloud tonight felt like a thunderhead. Dorothy and Henry stood to clear plates. Gretchen said, "Wait."

There was no introduction, hardly a chapter one, and no explanation as to why now. Gretchen was a few matter-of-fact lines in before a realization dawned that strapped everyone to their chair.

"He was on top of me. I was suffocating. God, the stench of him. He penetrated me and it hurt. I fought. He hauled off and pounded me in the face. My jaw went numb. I tasted blood in my mouth. That shut me down. I was going to die, and I couldn't wait."

Everyone sat very still. Gretchen's deadpan monotone kept on.

"It was days later at a free clinic in Tennessee that I had myself checked out. I was cut, infected and bruised inside. No traces of semen were found. The nurse listened to my story and reasoned that if my attacker was as drunk as I said—that he was, in all likelihood, unable to get an erection, and that he'd finger fucked me and cut me with a filthy nail. I mean, how did I know the difference? I was fourteen."

"Jesus, Gret." Henry was hardly able to swallow, much less get a few words out.

"Lemme do this, Hollins!" Gretchen had shouted the last. Hands clenched in her lap, she closed her eyes and calmed. "Like I said, the hard punch to the face stunned. And then with a shaking and a shudder, he like flopped still, not moving. There was just this guttural gasping coming from his fat face. I waited. He still didn't move. Thirty seconds? An eternity? I only know I could barely breathe from the weight and pushed with all my might and rolled him over on his back. He just laid there on the bed, passed out I guess, still gurgling like a clogged drain, and I stood naked, and I felt between my legs and saw blood on my hand, and I went berserk."

Christine sat riveted.

Melissa started to cry.

"He wasn't the first. There had been others. But he was the first to attack and hurt me. He was the grossest. He was the worst. I did what I could to prepare for them. I had a baseball bat and a short flat shovel under my bed. That night, I blindly grabbed, and the shovel was in my grip. With two hands, I raised up, screamed, and hit him in the face with everything I had. My room was pretty dark, one nightlight burning. He sat up. I was scared shitless and reared back and hit him again. Back he fell. I swung and smashed him again and again and again. Not sure how many times, but enough. Blood soaked the sheets. His face was a pizza. My hands bled from gripping the handle. Without warning, I gagged. I raced to reach the bath and vomited all over the hallway. On my knees, right then, I stopped whimpering. A kind of eerie weirdness came over me. Like I was now dead and just a ghost. Moving with a purpose, snatching paper and a marker from my desk, I wrote 'rapists die' and pinned it onto his slimy chest. I tossed on jeans, a sweater and packed a suitcase. I pocketed what jar money I had and went downstairs. All was still. She looked lifeless lying half on, half off the sofa, her head dangling at an odd angle, an arm extended to the floor. She was always a 'her' or a 'she,' never a 'mom.' I'd told her over and over: 'I don't care what you do or how wasted you get. Just never, *never* leave me alone with them.' "

Gretchen was tearing up. Dorothy offered her napkin, which was waved off. "Port Huron's a small town. Where did she find these dirtbags? Why did she bring them to the house?"

Dorothy leaned to comfort.

Gretchen backed away. "Let me finish. There was a notepad and pen by the phone. I scribbled, 'If you try to find me, I will kill you,' and stuffed it in her bra, because that was pretty much all she was wearing. Her skin felt ice cold. I was losing my weirdness. I was freaking out. I took the dollar bills she had in her purse, my coat, and left. I never looked back. Walking the roadside, the first headlights that stopped I knew from school. Midnight, and Jeffrey Hodges was taking his dad's pickup out on a joyride. I told him he could feel me up under my tee if he took me to a bus station. We rode to Jamestown. I told a boozer guy there I'd give him money for a thirty-two ouncer if he bought me a ticket. He did. I had enough on me for Memphis."

Dorothy was pale. "Merciful heavens. At home, how long had this been going on?"

"Wasn't a home, Gunny. It was bad for over a year."

"Wasn't there anyone you could turn—"

"School. My guidance counselor. I let on only that I was scared, never the bad stuff. They would call her in, and holy Emily Post if she didn't turn on the charm. But even sober, she was a lying shit: 'Oh, gracious. Everything is fine. You know the age. Their imaginations just run wild.' I guess the principal never had enough cause to tie her to a stake and light a match. I mean, straight, there were times she could be remorseful and stuff, get me to believe she was truly sorry. The straight life never lasted."

Gretchen shut her eyes and stayed silent a spell before beginning again. "I cuddle some nights with Mel because I love her. I also sleep with her because she is my security blanket. And if I've shared my sack lately with Chris, the reason is the same. Fear doesn't leave, Gunny. Even if everything changes in my life, it hovers. Bad dreams: heavy thuds coming up the stairs, chair against the door, trapped again. It's no fucking wonder I wandered about the country living without walls for so long.

"And the cops are hunting for the pizza-face killer. If they catch me, I'll be sent back. But I'll never allow that to happen." Gretchen stood up. "I don't hate myself. I'm not looking for a new me. I don't want to be sweeter, Gunny." She bowed her head. "But I want what Christine has. I want the fear to go away."

From around the table, outstretched arms reached out. Gretchen declined. No one said a word. What could anyone possibly say? She wanted only Parker and the great outdoors for a spell.

Henry, Melissa, Dorothy and Christine had all longed to know the anger, the source. Now they knew.

———

Much later that evening, Henry caught Gretchen on her way up to her bedroom. "Hey, about the shower thing."

"How's your ticker holding up these days, Mr. Hollins?"

"I don't feel like a panic attack victim, that's for sure. But I recall Melissa on my shoulder, your hand in mine, racing up the staircase."

"Look, boss man, you've been through this, don't ever be sorry about the three of us in the shower. The shower was cool." She drew coy. "At least until you stopped breathing."

"Well, the two of you were sort of breathtaking. Wait, I don't want to joke about this."

Gretchen said, "Mel was so excited and full of fun that morning—the way it should be."

"Roger that, but given what I know now, what I'd really like is one big bear hug. From me to you?"

"Okay."

chapter thirty-six
March 1973

Dex Knotts had owned Hitches long enough to develop an innkeeper's sixth sense at avoiding serious pitfalls. Case in point, he'd had his re-enactment musket primed and ready to fire the first time the Mad March played—just in case. Bottom line, without the black powder prep, Hitches might have been totaled that night; chairs, tables and broken glass all piled in a heap—cops or no cops.

Tonight, the band was back, and damn if his premonitions weren't working overtime. A wild aura hovered over his ramshackle place—strange howls, growls and a clattering. The Bronx Zoo was on the roof. He went with that.

Dex's anxiety might have been lessened had he been better informed. He remained clueless that Gretchen had called, and both invited and challenged the bikers. Worse, he knew nothing of the band's growing and now near-legendary status in the wake of the BSC talent show and its violent aftermath, that the BSC Student Center cork board was filled with tacked notices: "need a ride to Van Wert on the 9th."

All Dex recognized was that unknown forces had him on edge enough to invoke the bar owner's manual, Rule Number One: Don't run out of beer.

"Maggie, I've called Bob's Place and the Blue Moon Saloon

in Lyon. They've got inventory. Take the pickup. Tell Bob and Charlene I need every can they can spare. Make sure you total up the cases and get a signed receipt. We'll store everything down in the basement if needed."

"I'm on it, boss."

"My toes are wiggling. I'm thinking a crowd tonight, Maggie."

"We've never had a crowd."

"I hear you."

Dex designed a bold heading: **The Punks are Coming**, added a self-styled graphic, listed the specifics and ran off a bunch of flyers, posting them in downtown Lyon, Liberty, on the square up north in Osceola, and a few in between.

Maybe Henry's band was a start. Why not remake Hitches into a live venue joint? Put in a proper stage. *Something* was needed to stir up the moribund place. With twenty printed promos scattered about two counties, he was hoping for a doubled headcount at the door—maybe even fifty.

chapter thirty-seven

Parked at the curb, the street name and house number matched what he'd entered years past in his worn leather "blue" book. All the homes appeared the same. Sal surveyed the surrounding well-kept lawns and driveway basketball hoops: a mid-America, middle-class, ranch-style suburban development and an odd locale for a professional music studio. The previous visit date was posted right there under venues. Two years had slipped by, but Sal didn't forget a face and, standing now on the front stoop, the guy at the door proved he was at the right place. "Richard, right?"

"You look familiar."

"Sal Tuchinardi. Viking Records, Minneapolis. Been awhile."

Richard Herrera, stocky, short stature, dark-complexioned, square-jawed, healthy-looking black hair trimmed short, a good-looking guy, registered delight. "Sure, sure. Good to see you. Welcome, señor." Richard offered a gratefully accepted cup of coffee and led Sal downstairs to his basement recording studio. "I've added upgrades since your last visit, Mr. Tuchinardi."

"Hey, amigo, nobody but Sal here."

"Yes, of course." With a look of pride, Richard was pointing toward the obvious, "Our Steinway model S. A difficult delivery down the stairwell, but as you can see, a perfect fit."

Richard went on detailing his technical improvements as Sal viewed the large west wall filled with group promos of Herrera's recorded sessions. "So, what's happening in Iowa, Rich? Have the next Beatles shown up, the new voice of a generation?"

Richard grinned. "Still waiting. The usual, Sal. Country cover bands and duos. Solo voice with piano. A school choir last week."

Sal took note the mixing board control room, the open mikes, the soundproofing. Small, compact, every studio square foot being put to good use. Richard loved his business. It showed. Sal had cottoned to the guy when they first met. Yeah, Herrera sported more hair (who didn't?) but they were both short, a couple of NBA basketball refs always looking up, but together they matched eye-to-eye. "Dylan grew up in Hibbing, Minnesota. Talent can spike anywhere. Don't forget that, Rich."

"If Elvis wanders in to make a record for his mom, I have you on speed dial, Sal. We are past noon, how 'bout I take you for dinner?"

They went to The Depot just off the square. Over the "cafe special," Richard asked, "Are you still the corridor king?"

"I cover every live music venue, Minneapolis to San Antonio. Pick any bar, I've kissed the maid, or at least tried. I hit snarled traffic on Interstate 35, the coppers recognize the Caddy and wave me on around." He smiled. "How you doin'?"

"Growing some, with groups from Omaha, Des Moines, Kansas City looking for fair-priced studio time. They lay down tracks. Go back home and say, 'We had a good session at Herrera's.' Word is passed. Another band calls. I am very glad for this visit, you keeping my studio in the loop. You are a good man, Salvadore Tuchinardi."

"We're in a crazy business, pardner."

Sal insisted on paying. They walked the town square, passing Gambles Variety, Flowers N More, True Value Hardware and Templeton Insurance, making their way to the corner. Sal took note of a handbill taped to the light pole: **The Punks are Coming.**

"What's this, Richard?"

"Has to be recent."

"Hitches close?"

"Ten minutes south on 35. The Van Wert exit."

"Know the place?"

"A dive. Right there east from the turnoff. A live band? This has got to be a Hitches first."

Sal gave the flashy promo a second look. An eyebrow jumped. "The show's tonight. Let's go. It's what expense accounts are for."

chapter thirty-eight

An early spring warmth in the air, the band van pulled into Hitches at 7 p.m. for setup and a sound check. Their first! One battered Ford pickup sat in the lot. Inside the tavern, two codgers drinking Hamm's cans held the fort.

Dex Knotts behind the bar looked on wide-eyed as first guitars and drums, then amplifiers/speakers, a PA, one monitor, two microphone stands, and stage lights were hauled in and plugged together. "Lights? Are you shitting me, Henry? What am I here, the Fillmore Midwest?" The biker, Granite, was directing traffic. Surprise, surprise. So, he and Gretchen hadn't murdered one another. World peace at last.

Granite stood out front from the makeshift stage checking balance and volume. The footlights and both vocal mikes were toyed with as the band ran stop-and-go through two numbers. Dex was taken. "*Holy shit.*" Along with the new Amazon on lead, these were hardly the green nervous nellies from months past. "Not sure this joint has enough juice in the walls for you guys, Granite."

The Raven held a Cheshire grin. "We're gonna light up Hitches one way or another, Knotts."

At the bar, Butch and Cass had another Hamm's and couldn't take their eyes off the tall burgundy bombshell slinging the burgundy guitar. Dex felt a high tide rolling in. Thank God Maggie was off stockpiling the beer inventory.

With Knotts promising to keep an eye, the Mad March marched off for the diner in nearby Decatur City. Over a meal, they worked on their butterflies and finalized the playlist. They leaned on Tony Destino like rookies would a grizzled veteran coach. Gretchen had the final word. "At last, somebody actually knows what the fuck they're doing."

Given the weeks, the days, the umpteen hours spent practicing, they professed a determination to get at least one gig right. They opted to open with "Ball Game," then five originals, and end once again with Neil Young's "Everybody Knows This is Nowhere." Maybe, if they held the crowd, if there was a crowd, everyone would sing the chorus and laugh at Dex at the same time. "Nowhere" had been the supposed closer the first time. Smashed guitars and musket fire led to an early retreat. Now, they were back. Melissa Minch, Rigg Moon, Gretchen Tarbat, Henry Hollins, Tony Destino and Christine Baird put hands together and agreed the number that showed up, be it four or an unimagined forty, was of little import. They'd get to "Nowhere" and they'd "Green River" it. They would put on a solid show for themselves.

That last-minute diner resolution evaporated to startled incomprehension as they returned to Hitches to find the street packed with an overflow of cars, pickups, even a few motorcycles, all snaking north around the corner to the Assembly of God Church parking lot.

"There's got to be a couple hundred here." Henry scanned about, incredulous. Christine shouted, "Are you kidding me? Look there!" By the church, a number of horse and buggies, five to be exact, nestled under an old elm.

Tony did his levelheaded best to settle a herd of would-be

The Rise of The Mad March

rock stars set to bolt. "You built this beast; now's the time to cut it loose. Why have you been writing, arranging and practicing? Why have you been going over the same song a million times?" He was waving at the massed vehicles, horses too, trying to make light. "Even the nags are here. Hands together again, troop." They grasped one another and Tony said, "I don't want to see any robots onstage tonight. Play below the belt." Gretchen shot back, "Screw you too, Antonio." Everybody laughed. Right then, Tony knew. They were going to tear it up.

Gretchen stepped to the mike. What looked like an ocean of students, bikers, cowboys, cowgirls and local farmers stood and crowded stage-front. At the side, a tight knit of Amish stood out with their uniformed white shirts, suspenders, black coats, and black hats. She deadpanned, "We're all on a mad march. Batter up." Melissa shouted her countdown, "Three, two, go!" And they were off.

Were the stars aligned? Was there a full moon? Did they really pull off "Take Me Out to the Ball Game" without a glitch? Halfway through, the crowd recognized the rip-roaring take and called out the "one, two, three strikes." With the final note, someone hollered, "Play ball!" The originals that followed weren't perfect, but then again, perfection was never really the point. Twenty to thirty minutes were spent rocketing through sound barriers. There were moments. Christine, wired up, rocking "Shut the F**k Up," screamed, "repeat, repeat, don't stop." On they went, their two-minute commandment ignored. The improvised tight groove ignited the now shoulder-to-shoulder fist-pumping crowd. "Cecil's Beer Run" stunned. Christine found a spot before the third verse. She shouted, "I'm off," and launched into not so much a lead, but a low-end chord shedding, a twenty-second grinding buzzsaw. She stood stage-front, her head rocking side to side, her long red locks flying off in all directions. Henry, transfixed, nearly stopped playing before trading off on Gretchen's pleading vocal.

> Cecil, make a beer run
> Catch us in your lights
> Cecil, make a beer run.
> Trapped and dying in the night

Henry's ode to a wanderlust girlfriend, "Stay for My Funeral," switched gears and brought some laughs.

Melissa stole the show. She said afterward that it was all adrenaline, all instant decision. They had one original left to play when she left her drums and stood alone at Henry's center-stage microphone.

"I just want to say that if anyone here tonight is caught up in a bad relationship, an abusive relationship, end it. If someone is building walls around you, climb over the top. Free yourself. Find a way. Look to family, friends, teachers, cops and firemen. Get help. Don't be afraid. End the abuse. No one —I mean fucking no one—should live their life in fear."

She went back behind her drums, screamed "three, two, go," and Gretchen's ferocious, menacing, powerful "Shovelhead" nearly blew the walls down. They ended with a tribute to Hitches and yes, two hundred-plus voices sang to Dex: "... *everybody knows, this is nowhere. Sha la la ... la la ... la la.*"

Henry hollered to a liquid crowd, "Get home safe," the few ceiling lights that worked brightened, and the gig was history.

By all rights, champagne corks should have popped, but the reality was, everyone was spent. The whole mob scene unfamiliar, the March commenced doing what all bands do when the houselights come up: tear down and pack the gear. There were, among themselves, "good-show" hugs and kisses, a ritual that became a band tradition. Well-wishers, tentative at first, mingled on the made-do stage.

Tony Destino decided then and there he'd take an extended leave from Hawkeye Sound. *I may lose my job, but I'm not going to lose this band. I may miss my job, but I'm not going to miss Gretchen Tarbat.* Dressed simply in a black long-sleeve crewneck Henley, jeans and sneaks, she nevertheless stood out, be it hovering close to the drums, up-front at the vocal mike, or on occasion, rocking face-to-face with the crowd. Tony swore he'd never witnessed stage charisma like tonight. Never forced, not knowing, she just possessed the proverbial *it*.

A shy Amish man approached Christine, whispered, then quickly left. She was casing her guitar with a huge grin. Everyone took note.

"Well, what did he say?"

"Spill it, Baird."

"He said," her grin staying put, "next time we'll bring the sisters."

Later, the raised corner left bare, the van near packed, a black leather jacket cornered Gretchen. "Near two dozen lubricated bikers. No tit jokes. How 'bout that shit?"

She could not help but smile. "Kicker. Did I see fists raised? Was that a Raven tribute, a Raven cheer? I swear, you outlaws will never live that down." She offered a "thanks" high five. He took it. He stepped back, staring. She grew leery. "What, Kicker?" He leaned back close with a conspiratorial gaze. "Take good care of our brother." With a wink, he melted back into the milling crowd.

Henry was at the bar trying to get Maggie's attention. He *really* wanted a beer."

"Was that it?"

Henry looked down at a balding round-faced guy dressed for the 1950s. "What?"

"The show over?"

"Hey pal, we played all we know. And look around. Everyone's had enough."

"Twenty minutes? A half-hour? You're not going to win a Grammy for time served, partner."

Who is this? "Maggie! One beer, anything. Make it two." The guy wasn't going away. Henry defended the show. "Swing for the fences, leg out what we can. That's our gig. You want a meandering three-hour endless jam, go buy a Grateful Dead ticket. Look at this crowd. You think anybody right now is begging for another set?"

"What *was* that?"

"What? Our music?"

"Music? No shit. You fooled me. All these chainsaws on stage. I'm wondering, where's the tree?"

Henry did not need this. "Who *are* you?"

"Sal. Friends call me Sallie."

"Okay, Sal, you're asking what's the Mad March? Listen up. We're a rock 'n' roll band."

"Not like I've heard, partner."

"A few chords and put the pedal down. Pure and simple. You can join the ride, Sal, or not. We don't care."

"Where are you going?"

"We haven't a clue. Rock 'n' roll rebels, Sal. If you're not incensed, hiding the kids or writing your congressman, we're not doing our job."

"Rebellions, my friend, often fail to catch on. You see any success with this march?"

Henry, still buzzing from the show, pointed toward the stage. "I've got Baird, Tarbat and Minch. I've got a shot."

"I wanna meet the band."

Henry kept pointing. "Right over there. Keep your negatives to a minimum. The bass player's thin-skinned."

The Rise of The Mad March

Sal handed Henry his card and said, "Viking Records. Minneapolis. I scout talent, I book shows. Where can I find the Mad March tomorrow?"

Maggie handed Henry two beers. "Well earned, showboat."

Henry was reading Salvadore Tuchinardi's card. He thumbed to his right. "Give one of those to this guy."

———

"Hey Christine. Kip Lee. I'm in your Contemporary Art class."

"Oh, hi."

"Awesome show."

Kip was tall, Asian slender with a quick smile. He did look familiar.

"Wow. Thanks. To be honest, we've never been that good, not even in practice. Kind of shocking, really."

"So, I'm facing this art-design project. I was wondering if I might sketch out a Mad March tee, and if you guys thought it cool, contact a screen printer and—"

"You mean sell band T-shirts at shows?"

"Only if the design works for everyone. We'd have sold a few tonight."

Christine registered surprise. "Yikes, really? I mean, yeah, sure. Just grab me in class with a mockup. I'll let the guys know."

"Great. This is like an instant decision. No ideas right now." He held up his beer bottle. "Maybe when I'm sober."

She laughed. "Take a shot. Anything would be cool, Kip, and hey, Melissa needs a badass rabbit on her kick drum. Any chance?"

"Yes, yes. Awesome. I'll get with her. And about the T-shirts, it might be helpful to know the how and why of the band name."

Christine's laugh continued. How could she do anything

Robert Espenscheid, Jr.

else after tonight, a dream fulfilled? "General Washington goes to Princeton."

jersey moon: tour interview #9 (part one)

August 1973

Jersey: Can we talk about writing songs?

Henry: Gretchen is our principal go-to. She needs to be here.

Jersey: So not happening. Quoting the bass woman: I'm not only a witch, I'm stirring the pot.

Henry: I'm guessing she's a rough interview.

Jersey: Stormy doesn't begin.

Henry (laughing): Look, whatever I say is not going to mean a thing. From what I've read or heard, every band does it differently.

Jersey: The Mad March, Mr. Hollins. All that matters here.

Henry: Basically, I plunk around on the piano. Usually, a lyric line is first up, then I fish around on a keyboard for a melody that fits. But my song catalog contains exactly three songs, so any band relying strictly on me is going to starve pretty quick. I believe Christine is just getting started. Her latest, "Bloomingdale's," is really good. Plus, she offers stuff like in final draft form—just add accompaniment. By the time my songs go through our rhythm-section wringer, I barely recognize them. That leaves Gretchen. Her stuff is tough and personal.

Jersey: She's the brick, you're the feather.

Henry: Yeah, that works. Her songs matter, but like I've told the whole band, nobody goes to a show to get totally pummeled with negativity. "Shovelhead" works if the crowd is taken by surprise. I mean, thanks to Mel's spoken intro—always improvised, by the way—and the fact that the song sits near the end in the playlist, "Shovelhead" kills at shows. The song empowers, and that works best when given the chance to stand out.

Jersey: So, was "Shovelhead" like, total Gretchen, or a band effort?

Henry: For us, a finished song at the get-go is rare. It happens. but usually it's more like hey, I got this idea I've been playing around with, and we get started: working the melody line, adding lyrics, what-have-you. Changes happen playing and practicing. I've always liked those stories where someone's got something going nowhere and someone else is in the same stew and then the band puts the two together and bingo! Which brings me to the Mad March ace.

Jersey: Meaning?

Henry: Melissa. She's inventive. She takes a piece, "What if we drop this? What if we add *this* bridge?" She sings the changes. Her uncanny talent is that so much of what she offers works. Tiny change. Big difference.

Jersey: She's a confluence! I like that word.

Henry: Here's a blueprint. Gretchen creates. Christine complements. She takes Gret's canvas and adds color. I'm the critic and Mel's the fixer. Lots of times, that's how the songwriting works.

What's vital, what defines the Mad March, is that what's coming from the stage is real with a capital R. The lyrics and sound are born from personal past history. Angst, anger, occasionally a big shit-ass grin ... we are all about what we are or were. Nothing is made up just to please an audience. That's not happening. That's not our makeup.

Jersey: Do the workups get feisty?

The Rise of The Mad March

Henry: Nobody's got a pumpkin head. We're not a my-way-or-no-way band. Testy at times? Hell, yeah. I'm at Gret, "lighten up." She's, "no more bubblegum bullshit, Hollins," but no one is throwing punches. At least not yet.

Jersey: The Beatles started out all chummy.

Henry: Good point.

Jersey: "Starting to Hate" is not chewing gum.

Henry: "Hate" is from my ex, Esther, saying, "I'm starting to hate you." A stressful time for us. The song's honest and personal, a first and last for me. And according to Tarbat, a breakup song worth at least a teardrop. She insists on singing the vocal. Feels weird, but I'm fine with that. "Hate" is a tough fit. We don't play the song much.

Jersey: Bubblegum? "Bone Pile" is hardly that.

Henry: Tony and I are '60s army vets simply catatonic that the Nam war grinds on. Gretchen contributed lyrics and structure. How did she do that? She was like, age twelve during our oversea tours. Gret has no creative limits. Given a chance, I'm convinced two hundred million Americans would sing along. The band was never meant to be overtly political, but I'm glad we own that one.

Jersey: So, the future—is the Mad March's second album going to be better than the first?

Henry: Hot damn, Moon. Absolutely.

jersey moon: tour interview #9 (part two)

August 1973

Melissa: Can I read what Henry said in your songwriting notes?

Jersey: Sure. You're the rose.

Melissa (reading): Yeah, right.

Jersey: Are you okay? I'm hearing stuff.

Melissa: Why is everyone my doting grandmother? I'm fine. Geez. Okay, Henry left out something so vital. He does that; on stage or off, he never draws attention to himself. First up, with songwriting, we have something lots of bands don't have, Jersey. At the start, we didn't realize how lucky we were. Can you guess?

Jersey: Parker?

Melissa: Hah. Him, too. No. We had the barn, Jersey, that wonderful old Pickford barn: our makeshift cozy studio. Our sound, our songs, are all part of that old oak and pine. On countless nights, we'd stop playing and just sit. Maybe everyone sips a beer.

Jersey: Maybe smokes a little weed.

Melissa: Don't put words in my mouth, Miss Moon.

Jersey: Sorry.

Melissa: Henry might uncork his sipping bourbon. We

talked music: what we were listening to, what we loved, what other bands were doing, what we wanted to be, what we wanted to sound like, even to look like onstage. I mean, we didn't want to be different. We just needed to be us. In Henry's world, the Mad March would play out our own story in two-minute snapshots.

The fragrance of the place, Jersey. Parker resting in his favorite spot by the sliding door, a few hens roosting about, the moon maybe peeking in, the quiet all about us.

Jersey: Wow, Melissa, the poets have nothing on you.

Melissa: From the start, Henry was always moaning what a no-talent he was. Bull. He shined those nights at the barn. Gret and Chris are the songbirds, for sure, but Henry has the vision. He wanted Christine to sound like the Vikings coming ashore in Britannia, the Confederate onslaught at Shiloh. He'd tell the stories at length. Spook us as if we were kids sitting around a campfire. Toss us back to a time and place, and we'd try to put that sound to our own stories. Henry saying, "It's all there in our strings and drum skins."

Jersey: Sounds like …

Melissa: Okay, okay, maybe a bong gets passed around. You are so bad, Jersey Moon.

Jersey (smiling): I don't live in a nunnery, but I'm a good girl.

Melissa: You better be. Anyway, someone says to me after a show, "You sound like an oncoming freight train." I'm like, *we did it.*

Jersey: So, Christine is onstage playing, hair flying in all directions, eyes closed, and the song is maybe about trying on a dress in a department store, but it sounds like a cattle stampede.

Melissa: Exactly.

Jersey: Hoo-ha. This stuff is very cool.

Melissa: I know this seems strange and eerie, but that old drafty stable, with its own history swirling about, conjured up a band, Jersey. You ask where the Mad March was born? We were conceived in the Pickford barn at midnight.

Jersey: That is so fucking rock 'n' roll, Melissa.

Melissa: Your mom and dad are going to murder us.

chapter thirty-nine

They all met at Hitches the next day. Inviting the unknown Sal Tuchinardi to Pickford didn't sit right with anyone. They settled on a neutral site. Dex opened at noon. Gathered about a makeshift table, they had the tavern to themselves. Introductions were short but hardly sweet.

"No fucking way some big-city music hotshot is gonna take time for a loser band. This is a scam, Tuch. You're a scam and we got no money, so the joke's on you."

"All this hostility at an intro?" Sal peered around the table. "Who is this? Godzilla? I'm a booking agent, toots."

Henry called out: "Cool your jets, Gret. Give the guy a chance. We called and checked with Viking. They confirmed Sal's the real deal. You know that."

Gretchen didn't budge. "A scam with phony business cards with phony phone numbers. Who did we talk to? Who'd you pawn us off to, Tuch, some in-cahoots girlfriend?"

"If I said yes to that, toots, what are my chances of asking you to the prom?" He grinned.

Gretchen appealed to Melissa and Christine. "Can you believe this, this –"

Melissa broke in, "What were you even doing at last night's gig, Mr. Tuchinardi?"

The Rise of The Mad March

Sal took the question, but his eyes never left Gretchen. "Mister? What is that, toots, manners?" Gretchen failed to bite. Sal went on explaining to everyone his job at Viking, Herrera's Osceola studio, lunch at The Depot and seeing the posted flyer. "First question. Have you any recorded demos?"

Henry shook his head no. "Last night was our third gig. We've been together three months."

Sal nodded. "I want to be straight with you. Breaking bands is never dull, but never easy. I wear a lot of hats in this business. As a talent scout, I tell Viking I've hit on something. They give a listen, maybe a recently recorded "Shovelhead." You gotta understand, kids, they'll laugh me right out of their ivory tower. Why, you ask? Well, they're recording industry big shots with top-floor office space, thousand-dollar desks, plush carpeting, and gold records hanging on oak-paneled walls from the likes of Nat King Cole, LaVern Baker, Perry Como and Bobby Darin. These guys, say, they audition the Beatle mop-tops back in '64; they're up in arms: 'Whataya bringing us, Sallie? What is this crap?'"

"Start your own label, Tuch."

"Don't confuse my already confused life, toots. So, I'm saying, I'm with Viking yes, but in a sense I'm on my own here today. Look, I'm an old hand. I've been beating the bushes off Interstate 35 since Jerry Lee and Little Eva. When I hear something that registers, my ears twitch. Last night, I got two jumping jacks."

Gretchen sidled up close, focusing. "They're kind of hairy."

"So's everything else, all except the top of my head. Wait. What was that, toots, a smile? She smiles, Henry?"

"What are you actually saying here, Sal?"

"I go to bat for you, Henry. The noise you make is raw. I know the clubs that might fit. Three gals. No offense, Henry, the heart of the band. Like three female astronauts. Ba-boom, fly me to the moon. That's over-the-top brand-new." Sal pivoted. "What planet did you come from, Miss Baird?"

"Grosse Pointe."

Everyone laughed.

"Let me guess, scout man, your booking commission is only 90 percent of the take."

"Only for you, toots." Sal grew animated. "Look, I see everyone here taking wild chances. Why not the same at my end? So, I'm saying, Henry, a possible late summer tour. It'll take time to put together."

"A tour?" Henry was floored, thinking, *Gretchen is right. This guy is from "The Twilight Zone."* "How long? Where to?"

"That's my job, Mr. Hollins. Meanwhile, third gig, Jesus, you do yours. You play local every chance you get. I don't wanna hear three gigs. I wanna hear fifty gigs, and then some. I'll work the street, you hone the stage chops."

"Midwest, right?"

"Wider net, Henry. Like this new stuff, Velcro, right? We toss the Mad March out and about, see where the band sticks."

"Gretchen doesn't lie, Sal. Money. You're not looking at the Four Seasons or the Four Tops."

"Speed bumps, Henry. Up and over."

Sal turned to Granite, sitting apart on a barstool alongside Dex. Granite had spent the night at Rigg's. Rigg had insisted he forgo the long drive back to Iowa City. Henry had called early morning and asked both of them to sit in with the Viking rep. Granite had said, "Sure. We'll meet you there. I'm honored," thinking, *first the gig, now the talent scout – what next?*

"Tony Destino, right?"

"Yes, sir."

"Are you still in their corner, Mr. Destino? Because, if I ever put together a tour, the band's going to take some serious hits, blood on the highway, and they are going to need a patch-man."

There are moments in life when there's little time to make a big decision. Tony didn't hesitate. "If they're okay with me, I'm in."

The Rise of The Mad March

Melissa, Christine and Gretchen reacted like a last-place team that just signed Henry Aaron. Melissa was the first to find a voice. "And you're driving the tour bus, right, Mr. Tuchinardi?"

"I'm not driving the bus. I'm not your manager nor your nursemaid. I'm not holding your hand, Miss Minch. I contract a club date. You show up."

Henry tried to play the straight man. "I know jack shit, but come on, Sal, this isn't the way the game is played."

"Okay, tell me my job."

"A band signs with a label, they get some money. They make a record. They go on tour to promote the album. If there's a buzz, there's something to sell. We got zilch, maybe a few future T-shirts, maybe not. What you're offering is ass backwards."

"You're absolutely right, Mr. Hollins. If I can put a club tour together, the Mad March is driving to hell and back with the cart before the horse. But don't forget, pal, I've got years in this business, twitched ears and coast-to-coast connections. Like last night's show … are there more Mad Marchheads out there? There's only one way to find out. You kids take the tour, gimme a buzz to work with, then I crawl on my hands and knees to Minneapolis and go, "They're making a splash. Cannonballs, Viking, do something!"

Henry wasn't sold. "Could that happen?"

"Let me add something." Sal hadn't intended a hard sell, but the vibe at the bar table felt worth an effort. "And Gretchen here is gonna roast me for this." She smirked. He waved her off. "Before you heat the oven, kid, let me finish. Last night doesn't exist in a vacuum. The Mad March is not a lonely and only warrior. Around the country, scouts and agents with ears exist. There's a linkage. For the past year, a bunch of us with our sixth sense supposedly close to the ground have heard a train coming, a storm brewing. Whatever cliché fits. The usual hot spots are reporting in: New York, LA,

England again. No one's quite got a handle on this roar. No one's connecting dots. Yet. There is just an awareness, an awareness that even a so-called loser band in the rural Midwest is maybe part and parcel of the makeup to whatever kind of wave this thing is. And if that's a possibility, and if the Mad March is out touring countrywide and finding fans, who knows? Look at me, kids. With or without LPs in the bin, brush fires spread."

"Big guessing game, eh, Tuch? You really see something in us?"

"The sun at dawn, toots."

Gretchen stood and commenced slowly circling the table, eyeing Tony intently as she swept past the bar. Everyone remained very quiet. Completing her roundabout contemplation, she slammed back into her seat. "Regardless where this shitstorm blows, make me a promise, Sallie."

"I'm listening."

"When the ship founders, all hands going down, that you'll be there for us."

"I'll be manning the lifeboats, Gretchen, I promise."

Dex Knotts broke an awkward silence. "You guys need to gig. I'm looking for a summer house band."

Amid the laughter, Henry took a silent vote around the table. Melissa showed a half-hidden thumbs-up. Gretchen an OK shoulder shrug, Chris a nod. "Do we need to sign anything?"

"We'll deal up fair and square with our names on the bottom line. I've never had an act sing the blues over my being their rep. But business is business. I wish it was all 'Sugar Mountain,' kids, but it ain't."

"And maybe we're leaving too soon, Tuch."

"A million years ago, toots, I was a Marine."

"Don't they have like a height line?" Gretchen regretted the stupid tease as quickly as the words escaped her mouth.

"Everyone looked down at Napoleon. Big mistake."

The Rise of The Mad March

"Beyond dumb. I'm sorry, Mr. Sal, I didn't mean –"

"Don't sweat the small stuff, toots."

Amid light laughter, Gretchen flipped. She really liked this guy.

"And if you're a Marine once, you're a Marine forever. End of day, end of mission, no soldier is left behind. Semper Fi. You following me, toots?"

"I'm right with you."

Sal turned serious. "I need you to promise *me* something, Gretchen. All of you, in fact. I've witnessed ugly last chapters. Bands once whole left torn apart. Guitars and drums scattered and shattered. Best of friends now sworn enemies. Ambition, sex, money, drugs – name the killer, name the poison. Just one is a big enough disease to swallow the whole." Sal eyed them all, practically begging. "Promise me you will care for one another. Promise me you won't lose track of who you are. Promise me that waking up freezing in a broken-down van in the middle of the mountains of Montana is not going to lead to a bloodbath."

Melissa raised her hand. Everyone chuckled. She said, "Actually, we're a 180 band, Mr. Tuchinardi. We blew apart at the start. Hostility ruled." She glanced over at both Gret and Tony. "A few stitches were needed. Our beginning, I guess, was like another band's ending. Now, well," she discreetly slid over and sat thigh to thigh with Christine, "we've a bunch of scars healing over."

Sal found himself taken. Probably not a good sign. "So, you're saying, Melissa, civil war raged. Was there a truce?"

"I'm saying, Mr. Tuchinardi, the Montana mountains are diddly-squat. This is my family."

jersey moon: tour interview #10

August 1973

Jersey: New York, Mr. Hollins. You lied to her.

Henry: You sure know how to kick off an interview.

Jersey: Obviously, you planned the whole thing, right?

Henry: The band was a Pan Am 707, circling, waiting for clearance to land. March gave way to spring and summer. Sal's tour was taking shape to begin in late July, maybe early August. So, we had like four or five months to play, play, play, iron out any and all foul-ups, and get ready. All in all, a really good growing period. I mean, after the Hitches gig, we thought we were hot shit. But Sal proved right. We got a lot tighter. In late May, I told everyone I had a Piano Technicians Guild convention to attend in Philly. I was going. Four days. We were a band, yeah, but money-wise nobody was quitting their day job. Especially me. I owed Stony my shirt plus the whole damn closet.

Jersey: All bogus.

Henry: Only Dorothy knew the truth, that I was heading to Port Huron. If I'd told Gret, she'd have carved me up.

Jersey: You were taking a mighty big chance, sleeping dogs and all.

Henry: For sure. I spent a lot of nights sweating the whole idea. Dorothy and I weighed everything. Huge decision. We knew that. At Pickford, when Gret revealed her past, the horror, she'd let slip her home state and hometown. I'm positive she hadn't meant to do that. I took the slip as a sign. Plus, the timing was good. We all needed a break. I flew to Buffalo and rented a car.

Jersey: Where'd you start?

Henry: At the Port Huron public school. Five or six years had passed. The school counselor, Janet Allard, had retired. Luckily, she still lived in town. We met at her home. I say, "Gretchen Tarbat," and she says, "Gretchen who?" and I say, "the Gretchen from the late '60s who ran away from her classes and her hometown for parts unknown." And she says, "Gretchen Tarbeaux altered her name," and I say, "Spell it." A physical description and timeline followed that substantiated that both of us are referring to a young girl, one and the same.

Jersey: Holy wow, she's actually French. Tarbeaux, and you're saying "tarbow" as in bow and arrow? Yikes, it's like knowing someone and starting over.

Henry: Exactly. From a "bat" to an accented "beaux." But there was no restart. I was direct and honest, that I knew Gretchen and had been told what I prayed was the worst from her past. My directness turned Janet pale.

"You need to speak to the sheriff, sir."

"That doesn't sound like a good idea to me, Janet."

"Is Gretchen alright?"

"She's fine."

Janet's hand covered her heart. "It's vital you meet with Stephen, our sheriff. He was on duty back then and still holds office. Promise me you'll think about it."

Our talk had been hesitant and formal. At the door, set to part, emotion overwhelmed her.

"Try to understand, Mr. Hollins, I was an academic counselor. Personal matters with the students were rarely discussed. A fault, perhaps. I've never forgiven myself for failing Gretchen. Not for a day. Back then, she'd been absent from class for two days. My calls to the Tarbeaux home went unanswered. Being aware of Gretchen's contentions, I contacted the authorities. Eventually, patrolmen checked the house. When I heard … oh Lord."

Jersey: And there was no stopping with Janet, right?

Henry: The poor woman nearly collapsed. I struggled to hold her as we made back to a sofa. Yeah. I turned Sherlock and chanced contacting the cops. I was nervous as hell, seeing myself destroying any and all of Gretchen's chances in life.

Jersey: But you knew the truth. She was beaten and assaulted! And maybe not the first time.

Henry: I could not let it rest with Janet Allard.

Jersey: You saw the sheriff.

Henry: I did:

"What can I do you for, Mr. Hollins?"

"Gretchen Tarbeaux."

Raised eyebrows. "You know where she is?"

Deep breath. "I do."

"She okay?"

"She is."

"It's close to noon, Hollins, you up for some chow?"

Surprise. "Sure."

"Give me a minute. I've got to make a call."

Finally exhaling. "I'll wait outside."

Ten minutes later, Sheriff Lozniack and I took a patrol car to a countryside café. We grabbed a table, and I'm introduced to Paul Wills, retired county medical examiner.

Jersey: Are you holding up?

Henry: I've jumped off a cliff, Jersey. Her name change has me dazed. I'm free falling. At the café, Lozniack didn't waste a second.

"Carol, principal over at the school, called and let me know your inquiry this morning. Appreciate you following up with me, Hollins. Did Tarbeaux detail her side?"

"Just recently."

"Care to repeat it?"

I did. I replayed that terrible night. Probably embellished some. At least, I hope so. And ended with, "caught a ride to Jamestown and jumped on a bus."

Lozniack leaned back in his chair. Our waitress arrived. "You got a spot of whiskey back behind the counter, Flo?"

"Things that bad, huh? Now, you know we ain't licensed, Sheriff."

"Well, you ought to be. We'll have three noon specials."

"Brown or white gravy?"

Flo noted her order pad and winked. "That, and I'll see what I can drum up."

Suspense building all day, I was probably turning blue. I blurted out, "You looking for Gretchen?"

"Tell him, Paul."

Wills removed documents from a file and said, "I examined the bodies of the deceased, estimated time of death."

"Bodies? Gretchen's mother was dead?"

"Cased as an alcohol and drug overdose. You want the postmortem specifics, Mr. Hollins?"

"No, sir."

"Upstairs, one male, a bloody mess, blunt trauma, a short-handled shovel, the obvious weapon lying on the floor. Cause of death ... asphyxiation, a clogged airway due to acute alcohol intake. Seriously inebriated and anesthetized, the deceased vomited. Not recommended. Accidental, I suppose. Not a word I'd choose. I also suppose that the county sheriff here might have charged Gretchen with disfiguring a corpse, but I'm not aware, given the circumstance, that the State of New York has any such statute on the books. This here's a copy of the official report, Henry. See that she gets it."

Lozniack homed in. "If Port Huron is searching for

Gretchen Tarbeaux, it's to apologize for not protecting her. There's more than one guilty conscience living in these parts. I can't change the past, Hollins. I wish I could."

Plates of chicken fried steak, corn and mashed potatoes arrived plus three small juice glasses each with an ounce of Kentucky's finest. Sheriff Lozniack offered up a toast. "A Port Huron day we've been waiting for, Hollins. Bottoms up and tell us something good."

The bourbon burned. An elephant lifted from my shoulders. "She's in a rock band. She's dynamite."

"A rock band, no kidding? Good for her."

Lozniack took his time for Flo's lunch special and to collect his thoughts. At the last bite he felt ready. "I'm sworn to protect, Hollins, but you learn early on you can't protect them all. But the Tarbeaux signs were all there and overlooked. Your subconscious won't admit vicious depravity exists in Port Huron. That's for faraway shithole places. But there are still times that a fourteen-year-old girl hovers over me at 3 a.m. I don't welcome her presence." He sipped his coffee. "What's she like?"

"She's bottled up inside, Sheriff. Defensive. Anger's a factor. Her cursing can make a sailor blush. But there she is at 4 a.m., fighting off a raccoon trying to nab her chickens. She's got a big heart, Sheriff, a kind heart. The best of her lies ahead."

Paul Wills said, "Tell her that the Port Huron pavilion awaits her band."

"We play this song she wrote: 'Shovelhead.' "

Lozniack nodded. "I'd love to fucking hear it."

chapter forty
June 1973

"What's this?"

"What does it look like? It's a ring."

"I know that, Destino. But what? For me? A gift?"

"Yeah. I had my ironhead Sportster motor rebuilt months back. Bunch of worn-out parts were leftover laying on the workbench. I saved that." Tony smiled. "You never know."

"So confused here, Destino."

"You're being wooed. I had it polished and sized – a good guess, I hope. Engraved, too."

Gretchen, disbelieving, inspected the outside band inscription. "G2 H 8-8-72."

Tony slowly deciphered. "Gretchen ... Granite ... Hitches gig, the night we met."

"You called me a dyke. I smashed your head. Six stitches."

"Eight stitches. Love at first sight." Tony held his smile.

She wasn't going near that and held the ring up, inspecting. "What was this?"

"Good question. I'm not a serious motorhead. Sly Fox at the machine shop figured maybe an added pushrod shim. Beat-up Harley Sportsters, always being tinkered with, you never know."

"You're a piece of work, soundman, you know that?"

"So are you."

"When Mel sees this, she'll be bug-eyed."

"She already knows."

Gretchen shook her head. "A piece of work, Destino. What did the minx say?"

"And I quote, 'Do I get hugged and kissed, too?'"

"She would."

Tony grinned, then scolded. "Damn, Gret, I'd never push you away from Minch, you know that."

She stared at him and said, "I do," her heart pounding. "Total turmoil here, Raven."

"I wanted us to have a keepsake. What am I supposed to say? If I've stepped over the line with this, I'll take it –"

Gretchen flew from confused to alarmed. "No freaking way am I letting go of this, but you are complicating my life."

"Like you haven't complicated mine."

"I'm not the one changing jobs and engraving rings, Destino."

Tony's words just flew. "I've never been in love. I've never even caught a glimpse –"

"Bullshit. You love your Sportster."

"Maybe, but I never gave the bike a ring."

Exasperation was written all over Gretchen's face. She was waving his gift. "That's because she already had one."

A moment passed, a realization, and they both began laughing.

Gretchen returned to the confusion she held in her hand. "Can we just let this whole summer blow around like a kite in the wind? God knows where it's headed, or where we're headed. And like I was saying, you've become Antonio Complicated, and I can't handle 'complicated' right now."

"We can. But rock 'n' roll, Gretchen. Picture an upcoming gig night. The band's setting up. We cross paths by chance behind the amplifiers, a darkened stage, a moment. I steal a kiss."

If there is such a thing as a confounding smile, she wore such and gave a little ground to boot. "I'm going to wear this, Antonio, 'round my neck on an old piece of string. Safe and tucked away."

"Lucky shim."

"First the dress, now a G2 ring. I mean, can I just play the fucking bass?"

"What dress?"

chapter forty-one

Weeks flew by. Summer played its games. Sal stayed in touch. He wanted demos. There was debate over buying time at Herrera's in Osceola. Henry had tuned the recording-studio Steinway a number of times. He was friendly with Richard and maybe might work a deal. In the end, they weren't quite ready, plus they didn't have a dime to spare. Granite, marking time both in Iowa City and Liberty, brought in and hooked up his own Teac reel to reel. They recorded themselves right there in the barn. Tapes were sent. Sal's get-back was always the same: *Keep working*. Forging an ever-growing commitment, they did just that.

There remained two rocky hills to climb. One, the prosecutor.

"This is a bigger reach, Hollins. The two of them crossing state lines to visit the family of a friend in Michigan over the holidays was marginal but allowable. But this," county attorney Marty Riser held up Henry's submitted typed 'tour' request, "is way out of bounds."

"This is how I see a solution, Mr. Riser –"

"Knock off the 'Mister' shit, Henry."

"A solution, sir: Melissa and Gretchen check in with their probation officer a week early in late July, then get right back on schedule in September. They've been solid for sixteen months, Marty."

"Two hijackers on a state-sponsored countrywide joyride? The DA would have my ass."

"I'm simply trying to kick-start a rock 'n' roll band, Marty." Henry was already on edge. It hadn't taken long.

"What are you implying, like that's work?"

Riser's accompanying snort pissed Henry to the max. "You ever tried it? You want to slave away hundreds of hours, fork over thousands of greenbacks, take on a mountain of anxiety? I need a probationary allowance, Marty. Gretchen and Melissa have a valid work-related reason to extend their jurisdiction. Five weeks. Nothing more." Henry glanced around Riser's office, tucked away inside the county courthouse building. The certificate-covered walls were closing in. "Just let us go. Christ, I sound like Moses."

"Wait six months." Marty shrugged his shoulders. "Probation served, both of them are on their own."

Henry lost all pretense and bore into the prosecutor with all he had. "A contracted five-week rock 'n' roll opportunity that cannot and will not wait, Marty."

Marty sighed and closed his eyes. "I'll need more than just *your* supervision and say-so."

Henry drew an ace from his sleeve. "How about Clara Pickford?"

"What's my Aunt Clara got to do with –?"

"Both Clara and Dorothy Gunzenhauser have an active interest in the welfare of two young women under your thumb. Clara and Dorothy are a formidable duo, sir. Cross them at your own peril. You need a second for the probationary allowance? Call Clara."

Marty grew testy. "Under my ... a reminder, Hollins. It was my recommendation that led to probation rather than incarceration."

"Yes, but don't turn the better of the two into a Caribbean cruise. I've accompanied the monthly mandatories and can vouch they can be a humbling and humiliating chore. Until you're forced to pee into a cup with someone hovering to make sure the urine's yours, don't wrap a bow around the show."

"Probation is tough for good reason."

"They've been abiding, Marty. All we're asking is that the chain be loosened for a few weeks."

Marty sat back, inscrutable.

Henry was dying a thousand deaths over the stalemate.

"You know, Hollins, I had you pegged as the quiet, unassuming type."

Henry waited, thinking, *What next?*

Hands in his lap, Riser took up a Buddha-like pose and began, "The murder mystery is near an end. The inspector paces the room moving from suspect to suspect until finally reaching the piano tuner and I'm watching this on the TV and saying to myself ... *it can't be that guy.*" Marty leaned forward. "How could I have been so wrong? You're the murderer. You turned Winterfield. You somehow pocketed the sheriff, even Judge Patch. My Auntie Clara now? Jesus H. Christ! We're all puppets dancing on your strings."

"It's just a rock 'n' roll band, Marty."

Riser was on his feet, raising his voice. "And my aunt is hardly going on a summer rock 'n' roll tour, Hollins. Give me something or somebody else. Give me some back-pocket insurance I can pull out for the judge and say, 'The State of Iowa is fine with this.'"

Henry grabbed a sheet of paper and wrote down a name. "Here's your insurance."

Marty took the paper and said, "Bullshit. How did you drag Mrs. –"

"I haven't. Not yet. But if she's on the bus, will you talk to her?"

"Is everyone losing their mind around here? Damn straight I will."

The second hill proved nearly as steep.

"You're a Batman badass, Hollins: The Meddler. And you too, Gunny? How could you?"

"I agreed to what we thought was best. You're hurting, child. You've been hurting for a very long time."

"But this is *my* life, Gunny." Gretchen pounded her chest with her fist. "*My* life, Hollins."

Henry remained stoic. He'd returned from New York and, on the QT., made all at Pickford aware what he'd found out—all but one, until now. "Besides the examiner's report, I typed up both my interviews with your guidance counselor and the sheriff, what they said to me, word for word. They are included in the file. You have everything."

"Oh, so now I feel so much better. How about you, Baird? Are you in on this? Did you rob your trust fund and buy Henry's plane ticket to New York, first class, all expenses paid?"

"No, *Tarbeaux*, but I would have."

Melissa had heard enough. "Gretchen! Shut up. Take Parker and go for a hike. Find a shady spot, sit your butt and read everything Henry brought back. Go."

"Another Judas."

"Go!"

With a final withering, "meddler," at Henry, Gretchen and Parker were out the door. Pickford exhaled.

Supper began without her. Gretchen and Parker's walk was taking hours. Granite arrived and was briefed. Henry had

The Rise of The Mad March

called him for support. Forks were set aside when the front door slammed. Everyone stayed seated. The only happy face was Parker. Gretchen made straight for the table. She lunged into a huge hug with Dorothy. Granite drew a surprised glance. She took her place, all the while staring at Henry with an impossible-to-fathom face. One elbow on the table, hand cupped under her chin, she said, "You roll the dice with your own life at stake, Hollins. Not mine. Care to comment?"

"No."

"You wrecked your marriage."

"Now, hold on."

"You shut up, Hollins. I've the floor here. I'll rephrase. You dumped Esther, you lost your house and home, you've been jailed and hospitalized, you're in hock, dead broke, there have been smashed pickups and now a mutilated dead body. How do we possibly summarize this meddling, walking disaster, Miss Minch?"

"Words fail, Miss Tar ... what was that name again?"

Melissa's snide question annoyed Gretchen to the max, but one backstabber at a time. She struck again at Henry. "Thanks to your kamikaze mission, Buckpool could be knocking at the door this very moment with a warrant for my arrest and with transport to railroad me back to New York in chains. Care to comment, dice man?"

"We'd hire a lawyer. We'd hire the entire United States Supreme Court. We'd have Sallie call the Marines Corps. Come hell or high water, we'd get you back."

She was shouting. "Fucking A—why, Hollins?"

Henry turned. "You answer her, Christine."

"We need a bass player."

Gretchen sat—a loss for words.

Henry silently declared victory.

With one hill topped, the other halfway up, freewheeling practices and gigs bent old songs for the better and gave life to new additions. Small southern Iowa towns played host to the band. Nary a summer sweet-corn festival snuck by without the Mad March. At afternoon "all ages" shows, they were loud, they were fast. To the farming bib overalls crowd, they were a "what in tarnation?" To the elementary kids, they were a Saturday morning cartoon. To a pack of teens, they were a new "cool"—the band was theirs.

Confidence onstage soared.

chapter forty-two
June—July 1973

W*e are the Beatles in Hamburg* became Henry's rallying cry. Like the Fab Four early on in Germany, the Mad March was forging an identity. Henry the mastermind, Henry the coach; his team jelling and winning.

In truth, the Hamburg guise was all a false front. Night after night, the wee hours had Henry on his back staring up at the ceiling, seeing cracks in his masterpiece slithering every which way. Over and over, he listed the negatives.

He was falling behind. Practicing until his fingers bled wasn't keeping up with the band's raw talent. Memorizing song structure, there were times he felt straitjacketed as improvisation all around him roamed free.

He was becoming superfluous. Gretchen was singing more, and why not? How does a duck lisp compete with a sexy contralto? And Tarbeaux had evolved a rhythmic chord-like bass playing that deepened their sound which, when combined with Baird's riffs, begged the question: Did they even need a rhythm guitarist?

He was a guy in a gal band, close to a generation older, facing gender potshots tossed his way. Rigg's joke—*Henry's Harem*—still rankled.

All of the above rattled his self-confidence, never his strong suit to begin with. There was a reason he was a behind-the-scenes piano tuner. There was a reason he chose to play music with two thieves from a halfway house rather than join his open-jamming contemporary friends.

Then there was Esther, another head-on collision, a self-made mess. Former lost love Mark had returned, saw a second chance and proposed. She'd called. "I'm not waiting forever, Henry." Time passed, as time always does. A letter followed to inform that she'd accepted Mark's ring.

Why *hadn't* she waited? Was it even fair to ask such a question? The final chapter of his life with Esther brought on an unnerving panic.

He recalled again the promise he'd made to himself on a Vietnam hilltop with machine gun rounds ricocheting all around, that if he survived, he would live a dream. But that promise, that drove him still, never laid bare the pitfalls he was encountering.

And perceived negatives or not, there grew a massive desire on Henry's part to counter his building stress. Another SOS call to the EMTs for a gasping coronary would surely be the last.

At supper at Pickford, Christine staying over, Henry said, "I've been having the same dream over and over."

"Are you sleeping with two of us or all three?" Gretchen parlayed her usual smart-ass grin.

Christine, laughing, added to the tease. "Do we have a big enough bed?"

Even Melissa could not resist. "Golly, Henry, think of your heart."

Henry waved for a ceasefire. Truth being, he was thinking exactly that. "I'm serious here, wenches. The dream has the three of you sitting at a sidewalk café, filled wine glasses gracing a small round table, an afternoon in Paris."

"Wow. Can we see the Eiffel Tower?"

"Why not, Chris? You're on a European tour. The conversation drifts from the upcoming show to the band's beginning. And Chris, you say, 'Who was that guy in Iowa back when we first started?' Dust-covered first names get tossed around. Was he a Harry, a Hank? Was his last Huggens, maybe Higgins? Then Mel says, 'I know, the piano guy – his name is on the tip of my tongue.'" Henry waited. No one said a word. "That's the dream, except for the ending that finds me alone in a small apartment, watching the Lions play on a small portable black-and-white with rabbit ears, and the reception is terrible. It's Thanksgiving, I've a fold-up TV tray and a Swanson dinner in the freezer, and that's when I wake up."

"Rabbit ears? And this is a recurring dream, Mr. Hollins?"

"Yes, Miss Minch, nearly every night."

"Esther has kissed you goodbye. You told us. The dream is a pity party, Hollins."

"Esther is not in the dream, Gret, you are."

Christine sighed with a grin. "At least we have Paris."

Henry wasn't laughing. "I don't want to be left behind and forgotten."

The statement sounded like a tolling bell. Henry hadn't intended to let loose a cry of desperation. But there it was. The conversation was now officially awkward.

"It's just a dream, Henry."

"Well, Miss Minch, dreams are important. This one is screaming rejection and loneliness. And today, right this minute, I'm attacking this nightmare head-on. Lock and load. I'm not waiting around for the inevitable."

Melissa, Christine, Gretchen and Dorothy all exchanged looks of alarm.

"I've got the name of a Des Moines law firm. I propose to

look into legally adopting Melissa Minch and Gretchen Tarbeaux."

Seconds ran off the clock as the female team was held speechless.

Dorothy finally managed a, "You can't be serious."

"Dead serious, Mrs. Gunzenhauser."

Christine was still grinning, "Pardon me, sir, what was your name again?"

Nervous laughter collected around the table.

Gretchen said, "Call Esther, Hollins, maybe it's not too late and she'll take you back. Dream over."

"She's already called. She heard all about the talent show. She wants me to buy a very large life insurance policy and list her as the chief beneficiary. Look, I'm always harping on Hamburg, right? Comparing the Beatles' beginning to our beginning. But I don't want to be Pete Best, or worse, a completely forgotten Pete Best. We're all about the music and the band. But we're about each other too, right?"

"You're not making any sense, Hollins."

"I am too, Gret."

Melissa shouted, "You want to be our dad?"

"No, I do not. I want us, ten years down the road, together at Thanksgiving. Say the Mad March as such is long past. Kaput. Say you and Gretchen are playing and performing God knows where with God knows who, which is fine—Paris even—but you are adopted. We are legal tender. We are a family. Late November has arrived, and we have get-together plans for the holidays because that's what families do. We are not flamed-out rock 'n' rollers who can't remember who they shared a stage with. We are, and will always be, a caring tribe."

Chris said: "I think this is actually kind of cool. And if all else fails, maybe my folks might file the same."

The improbable had turned absurd.

Melissa playfully punched Gretchen in the shoulder. "Are

you Peter? Am I Tink? When did Pickford fly off to Neverland?"

Gretchen, looking first to Christine, then Henry, took her cue. "Question is, Minch, do we join forces with a heated swimming pool or a small black-and-white TV?"

"Rabbit ears, sister, we need to consider the reception."

They were laughing and high-fiving one another.

Henry sat glum. "This isn't a joke."

"And we needn't tease about Henry's serious intent, no matter how farfetched. Both of you. Stop. I won't have a hurtful manner. That's not who you are."

"Sorry, Gunny," Melissa said, "we're trying to catch a breath here."

"Pete Best, the canned Beatle? Really?" Gretchen answered her own question. "We played a good show at Hitches. Sallie shows up and all of a sudden you have a lot more on your plate than you bargained for. You got two cold feet, dreamer man. The dream is all about stage fright. Nothing more."

"Bullshit." Henry stayed serious. "The only fear I have is losing you, Christine and Melissa forever. And I wish to add a coda." Henry paused, gathering his thoughts. Instinctively, he stood and straightened. The table waited. "I was given an honorable discharge from the United States Army. I am an honorable person, ergo, this is an honorable proposition."

Darting eyes partnered with raised eyebrows. Gretchen said, "Is that it, Hollins? The defense rests?"

"Yes, ma'am." He sat.

Amid the quiet that followed, Gretchen hardly needed an okay "second" from Melissa. Abandonment was their middle name. "Then goddamn, make the call. Go see the family adoption lawyers. They are going to laugh at you, Hollins."

"Are you?"

"Of course not. Mel and I are honored."

"Is being in this band," Ruth Mott referred to the paperwork, found what she was looking for, slid her reading glasses to the tip of her nose and peered across her desk, "the Mad March, your principal means of employment, Mr. Hollins?"

"No, ma'am. It's all there on the form. I'm self-employed, a piano tuning and repair business."

"I'm finding it difficult to take this application seriously, Mr. Hollins."

"Why does that sound familiar?"

"I am concerned here, as will be a judge."

Attorney Ruth Mott wore a healthy glow, silver hair brushed back, keen eyes that bore a seen-it-all countenance. Henry had noted the wall-framed certificate: Drake University Law, class of '46; he noted, too, the corporate plaque, her apparent full partnership in Kaitz, Mott and Lang. He'd been intimidated at first sight.

"I'm saying, sir, that even with the parties' involved written consent, I don't envision a judge finalizing this adoptive request."

"Make it happen, lawyer Mott."

"Your application notes your being single. Perhaps, if you had a wife, Mr. Hollins."

"Actually, I jumped the gun there. At present, I'm wrapped up in a finalized divorce proceeding."

"Oh my."

"Nothing contested. I just thought 'single' would prove less confusing."

"To be honest, 'single' makes your application indeed less. Do recall, sir, that birth, marriage and divorce certificates are part of the submitted process."

"Please, Ruth Mott. Just Henry here. Melissa's birth certificate might be a problem. A beatnik hippie mother living off the grid, now passed. Father unknown. State foster care. Lord knows if there were any birth files or records kept anywhere."

Ruth sighed. "Anything else you're not telling me, Henry?

As I warned at the start, any intended misrepresentation at your end will be an immediate cause for dismissal."

"I've been honest to a fault here. I've listed Melissa and Gretchen's ongoing state two-year probation sentence with the cause thereof. They have no immediate family, no relations. I long for a legal bond." Henry gazed about the rich tapestry of Mott's office. "This is a free consultation, right?"

"Nearing an end, sir."

"I may rethink the application."

"Given present circumstances, my legal opinion exactly, Mr. Hollins."

"Rethink that my 'single' marital status, as you've said, carries weight."

"You wouldn't dare."

"Are you available, Ruth Mott?"

"Hah!"

Henry held the gleam in his eye. "Is it Mrs. or Miss?"

"I'll not be shanghaied on a mad march, Henry."

"Touché, madame."

———

Another Pickford supper, another shocker.

"So, a dead end?"

"Pretty much. Attorney Ruth Mott didn't pull any punches."

"Hey boss, Gret and I are one. We're awed by the effort."

"I'm not done, Melissa."

"Uh-oh."

"Thinking about the adoption application all the way home, I ended with a *why not*?"

"Meaning, Henry? Hasn't this gone on long enough?"

"Simple, Dorothy. Lawyer Mott left the door ajar: The application has a better shot if I've a better half on my arm."

Gretchen butted in. "You're going down on one knee, begging Esther to reconsider."

"No, I'm not."

"What are you saying, Henry?" Dorothy felt at wits' end.

"We all go to Vegas. Melissa and I marry. We all return. The two of us refile jointly to adopt Gretchen."

Not even Parker moved.

"You've taken leave of your senses, sir. You have taken a preposterous situation to begin with and—"

"As to Melissa and myself, ours will be a marriage of convenience, to assist the application process. Unconventional, yes. Do I give a damn? No. The marriage will end whenever called upon to end."

"I won't stand for this, Henry."

"We need your blessing, Dorothy."

"Don't Dorothy me, Mr. Hollins. I declare."

"You'd be my daughter." Melissa sat, staring at Gretchen in wonder.

"Fucking A."

Melissa stood, one hand on her hip, another outstretched with a finger pointing. "One more F-bomb from you, young lady, and my husband and I are grounding you for a fucking month."

Gretchen and Melissa flew into hysterics. How could they not?

Dorothy's two hands rested on her forehead. "Goodness gracious."

"Parker, let's go check on the Stone hens." Henry slowly got to his feet. "Leave the dishes, ladies, my turn. I've a Mad March proposal on the table. There are two conditions attached. One: we don't go to Vegas without a Gunzenhauser *and* a Gunzenhauser blessing. Two: Miss Melissa Minch has the final say."

"Dorothy, you need to change your thread color there."

"Gracious, Fran, look at me. Sorry, ladies. My mind's drifting."

"Drifting where to, Dorothy?"

"Tomorrow I'm off to Las Vegas, Nevada. American Airlines. A gambling junket."

The community center quilting bee slowed to a halt.

"Fares are dirt cheap. American is practically paying all of us to go. Subsidized by the casinos, I reckon."

Mildred scoffed, "What wins, Dorothy, a flush or a straight?"

"I don't know, nor do I care to. I'm accompanying one of my daughters. She's getting married, and apparently an Elvis is singing the ceremonial benediction."

"What daughter?"

"Melissa."

Across the table, faces eyed faces. A concerned quiet was finally broken. "You don't have any daughters, Dorothy."

Dorothy Gunzenhauser snapped, "Of course I do, Mildred. Caring hardly rests with personal childbirth." She felt herself warm. She eyed across the quilt table. "You had three, Grace Minnick. As a mother, you monitored their happiness, and we're all here witness to the fine job you did. I've two of my own now, and I'm following your lead, madame."

Another unspoken break followed. The quilting restarted.

"I sincerely hope you're keeping tabs, because you might decide to write a book about all this someday, Dorothy."

"Pickford's lively, Edna. I'll say that much."

Edna stamped her foot in frustration. "We're just concerned, Dorothy. We know you've grown fond of that wild bunch out at Pickford, and don't you say a word. We've all heard the rumors, the stories, the what-have-you. Land sakes, the only poor soul more ripe-for-plucking than an old woman in this world is an older old woman. There. You carry on. I've said my piece."

Dorothy allowed for the concern, then said, "I appreciate your keeping an eye out for me, Edna. I'd do the same."

"I know you would."

"What's Elvis going to sing, Dorothy?"

She turned and smiled. "We're taking requests, Sybil."

Sybil, quilting away, stayed matter of fact. "I'd go with 'Can't Help Falling in Love' from 'Blue Hawaii.'"

Willa Vandermark pointed a finger directly at Dorothy and, dropping her voice as low as she could go, began singing. *"Wise men say, only fools rush in ..."*

Laughter filled the community center. Dorothy led the way.

jersey moon: tour interview #11

August 1973

Jersey: Can we talk Vegas?

Melissa: Oh, goody.

Jersey: Unconventional even for an unconventional girl.

Melissa: Precisely.

Jersey: Is there one word that can possibly sum up that, that whirlwind?

Melissa: Fun. How much fun it was. Golly, Jersey, at the chapel we were the fifth couple in line, waiting.

Jersey: Like an assembly line? One wedding after another? Really?

Melissa: You got it, kiddo. There was this big front room. We were five couples in all. One of the grooms popped a bottle of champagne. Why wait, right? Everyone was in such high spirits, and we all had this weird desire to explain ourselves.

"I told him, if the ball lands on black, we walk the aisle. Bingo!"

"He thinks he's the industrialist and I'm the trophy… but it's really the other way around."

"Her third. My second. This is a gamble so why not roll the dice at the mecca?"

"All our kids are outside in the car, freaking out."

What a hoot they were. We exchanged addresses and planned a five-year reunion.

Jersey: I'm thinking the other couples had you representing the traditionalist?

Melissa: Hah! No way. Henry told them I was a mail-order bride from Bulgaria. They loved that. Trying to explain our convoluted wedlock was way too confusing. I let on, "We're in a rock band," and somehow to them, that made perfect sense. Everyone wanted a Mad March album. Vegas was such a loony tune. I loved them all. I really did."

Jersey: What did you wear?

Melissa: Just a frock thing. Gretchen was delegated Best Man and she let Henry borrow Tony's ring that he'd given her. Actually, she was peeved that it fit my finger. Hah. Gunny was tabbed the Maid of Honor.

Jersey: Did Elvis make it?

Melissa: He did. He was a tad overweight. We asked him to sing "All Shook Up."

Jersey: *That* sure fit. Christine wrote *Gambling Girl* for you, right?

Melissa: She made up the song right there in Vegas.

Jersey (singing):

> Staked her life with a roll on red
> Was she misled?
> Now she's wed.
> Maybe better off dead.
> Hey, Marie… off with her head.

Melissa: I always feel that Gret sings those lines with way too much relish.

Jersey: So, the vows await and—

Melissa: The Hollins-Minch party was last on the docket. We had the waiting room to ourselves. I catch Henry staring at me. Our eyes lock and I knew the whole thing was over. Off by ourselves, he told me he was taking his Mad March proposal off the table, that his so-called honorable proposition was anything but, that he'd been thinking only of himself when, in fact, he hadn't been thinking at all. There was a muttered, "so selfish." I offered the obvious, that everyone who rejected him, forgot him and abandoned him to that lonely Thanksgiving in his dream had all travelled over a thousand miles and agreed to his Vegas plan because—we didn't want to lose him. Fighting back tears, he nodded a confirm and said, "How about a rain check?" He dug out a business card, and on the back, wrote:

Rain Check—redeemable—one marriage—anytime anyplace.

Henry placed the card in my hands, covered them with his, and whispered, "For safekeeping." He leaned in and kissed me, really kissed me. I sat a little stunned as he made his way to Chris, Dorothy and Gret, got them all caught up, gave each of them a monster hug, and then, Moon, we all went back home.

Jersey: So rock 'n' roll.

Melissa: Back at Pickford, we tagged the Vegas venture the *Sanity Soundcheck*. Henry took some serious ribbing. Everyone was emotionally spent. Maybe there was a lesson-learned for each of us. Chris whined she'd already written an Off With her Head wedding song. Gret's stab: "First I'm adopted and now I'm back in the shelter?" was probably meant to be funny —but it wasn't. Henry, more himself, countered. "We'll play it anyway, Baird." As for Gret... well, Jersey, even an emotional wasteland can bloom.

Jersey: Meaning?

Melissa: Meaning that Henry, ever so casually, let on, "The adoption rolls forward. The latest from Lawyer Mott is that our filing has a better shot now that my name on the application has been replaced with Dorothy Gunzenhauser."

Jersey: Oh, wow.

Mellssa: A bombshell. Not sure what Gret and I will offer Gunny in the future, but we started off with whopping embraces.

Jersey: So, maybe sisters. Hmmm, I still think that it would have been cool if you wound up Gretchen's mom.

Melissa: I've already had plenty of practice. Oh God, don't tell her I said that.

Jersey: I love these juicy nuggets. Sorry, kidding.

Melissa: The adoption thing is processing, I guess. To be honest, with Sallie's tour, the filing has been off the front page for a while.

Jersey: Just so you know, I'm sending all my notes on Henry's Grand Proposition to the TV soaps.

Melissa: Not funny, Moon.

Jersey: Quick take. You're OK for sure, right?

Melissa: Meaning?

Jersey: I was at the last show. Sometimes Dad sneaks me in, offstage. You were the usual drum-tornado, but the usual joy was missing.

Melissa: Nothing but a stiff shoulder.

Jersey: Hope so. Here's my final. You're a minute from the altar. Any what-ifs?

Melissa: You are so bad. Well... maybe a little something.

Jersey: You still got that rain check, right?

Melissa: Oh, yeah.

chapter forty-three

July 1973

Time was short. The State probation-allowance was now on the front burner, red-hot—a problem that should have been reconciled weeks ago. Without Iowa's permission, Sallie's tour stood padlocked in the starting gate. Prosecuting attorney Marty Riser wouldn't budge on his recommendation without more of a guarantee that Melissa and Gretchen were coming back. Recklessly, without corroboration, Henry had provided a name that proved good enough for Marty's so-called back-pocket insurance, but that's all Henry had—a name; a name without confirmation and a long shot, at best.

Riser was waiting.

Standing now at the Moons' front door, what Henry *did* have was faith. All that he'd been through, all that he'd put others through, he still had faith. If anyone asked him, "Do you still believe?" the answer was yes, he did.

"Henry Hollins. What a surprise. Come on in."

"Hi, Mrs. Moon. Hope I'm not barging in. Rigg home?"

"Tyler. Please. I'm Ty to everyone. He is, and so is dinner. Join us."

"You don't have to—"

Henry was roped toward the kitchen, Tyler shouting, "Jersey, set another plate."

"This is way beyond the call."

"Stop, Henry." She wore a big smile. "We haven't had a rock star to supper for ages."

Henry conceded. Tyler Moon, Donna Reed attractive, projected that good-hearted ambience that won world wars. He was captivated and quickly caught up with the give-and-take at the table. Rigg had a pain-in-the-ass Pinto he couldn't get to run right. Jersey was contending with a still-being-mean former friend. He waited for an opening and said, "I'm here tonight with a proposition."

Rigg scrutinized his dinner guest. "Better watch out for this guy."

"The band's been gigging around locally."

Tyler clapped her hands. "I happened to be at Hy-Vee the afternoon you played in the parking lot. The music kicked in and shocked shoppers lost control of their grocery carts both coming and going. That was funny."

"That was a tough crowd." Henry smiled.

"Mom, you should have had a camera. The Mad March is in the background, rocking up a storm, as a little old lady, pushing her piled-high wobbly cart, desperately tries to escape the killer zombies with the guitars. Perfect album cover."

"That's awesome." Henry laughed. "You have a graphic designer daughter, Rigg."

"I'm not quite sure what we have, Henry."

Father and daughter were making smug faces at one another as Rigg asked, "What's up?"

"One week from now the band is leaving on a tour set up by this booking agent we met at Hitches. Sounds crazy, but we believe he's legit. My old piano-service van being packed and going cross-country; talk about a mad march. Anyway, we're determined to give this a shot. The tour is all new to us. The band is both pumped and petrified, if that makes sense."

"Expect the worst, hope for the best."

"Exactly, Rigg."

"Wow. You guys are going to be famous rock 'n' roll stars."

"I suspect, Jersey, we'll be more like lost sheep."

"And you want me to go along." Rigg dropped the obvious.

Henry hoped he didn't look needy. "I want you 'on the bus,' Rigg. Tony's on board, a huge plus, but you are just as vital. Everyone can roadie, but gig security ... so important to me. We've talked this through before."

"Leaving in a week, Henry? Not a lot of lead time here, and I'm staring at a dubious spouse. What did the Viking Record ace come up with? Where to? How long?"

"Sal—that's the booking agent, Mrs. Moon—is still working on dates. Apparently, he's got club connections on both coasts. That's where it's happening, he says. That's where we need to be. We'll be on the road some five weeks. We head east to New York City at the start in late July and finish in LA early September."

Rigg let loose a whistle and sat shaking his head. "So many red lights, Henry. Time away from the house, commitments at the repair shop. All around southern Iowa, I've been glad to help you guys out. Tony's become a friend. But cross-country, whew, and I'm a big guy in an already crowded van."

"Crammed with great-looking gals, I might add, Mr. Moon. And I suppose, Mr. Hollins, having a professional automotive mechanic in an old cranky van traveling thousands of miles has a wee bearing on your requisition tonight?"

"Mom, hello ... we're having a friendly dinner here."

"I'm not sure your being part and parcel in this discussion is appropriate, Jersey."

"A bulldozer couldn't budge me, Mother."

Henry saw his ploy fading. "Wait. Everyone. Mrs. Moon, guilty as charged. Rigg the mechanic is a monster factor. But I'm after more than security and a torque wrench tonight."

Tyler, Jersey and Rigg waited.

"I want all three of you."

Jersey said, "Huh?"

Not comprehending, Tyler cocked her head. Rigg was a mask.

Henry tried to make sense. "The tour will be like the Mayflower sailing to the edge of the earth. Not so much where we drop off, but when."

Rigg cut in. "Everyone stuffed in that van is a lit dynamite stick, Henry. Pick a state. Where do they blow sky-high?"

"Roger that. So, how to navigate and save us?" Henry was staring at three blank faces. "We take on a captain. A road manager. A general-in-charge. And that would be you, Mrs. Moon."

"What?"

"Mrs. Tyler Moon. She runs an entire school. Surely, she can run a rock 'n' roll band." Henry tried a crooked grin.

If Tyler had been asked to pilot Apollo 11, she would have not looked more surprised. "Road manager?"

"Yes, ma'am. You'll wear lots of hats, making sure everyone is aware the day-to-day where and when."

"You can do that on your own."

"The coming and going. Where are we staying? Counting heads on the bus."

"You're surely joking. You don't have a bus."

"I'm not. Sorry, figure of speech."

Tyler felt Mr. Hollins had gone on far enough. "You want a playground mom."

"A manager. A manager to act as the liaison with the club and bar owners. Stage times, sound checks, contracts and money due." Henry paused to shore up courage. "We're playing. Rigg's security. Tony runs sound. But it's your show, Mrs. Moon. Someone has to stand up and shout, *'Everyone shut the hell up and listen to me.'* "

"I'm an assistant school principal, Henry. I know nothing of what you speak."

"Neither do I, Tyler, and according to our own Miss

The Rise of The Mad March

Gretchen, 'Not having some know-it-all on board is best. Sink or swim. It's our expletive-deleted ship.' "

"Mom! You'll also need to hang with journalists and radio rock jocks. They'll be after interviews and stuff. You're the go-between."

Henry laughed. "You are a dreamer, Jersey. Nobody is going to care about us."

"I will."

Henry never forgot Jersey's surprising two words – and Rigg's daughter was quick to follow up.

"You said the three of us, Mr. Hollins."

"I jumped the gun. I shouldn't have said that, Jersey. First things first. A proposition—and your mother and father have to decide."

"Oh please, Mr. Hollins, let's have your whole scheme."

Henry was close to accepting defeat. Tyler's mocking tone augured an end-all. Proposition was at least a fifty-to-one long shot on the racing card. Thus, with nothing to lose, he bet the trifecta.

"Jersey will be along too, as the tour recorder. I've a deep-seated sense that whatever happens, this summer will be like no other. I want someone writing down the day-to-day, keeping track. And nothing cut and dry from you, Jersey. Be smart. Be sharp. Note your observations and interactions; what you are seeing and hearing with your own eyes and ears: the good, the bad, the complete disasters. The tour, from stage right. I'm commissioning a written journal, Jersey." Henry smiled. "You can also help sell T-shirts."

Jersey sat back astonished, a Moon on the moon. "Dad, I can also lug a microphone and a speaker. And Mom, I can scream at the sleazebag bar-owner guys: *Where's our money, you expletive-deleted, expletive-deleted?* Oh wow, are you actually serious, Mr. Hollins?"

"I am."

"Enough, sir. You have overwhelmed us." Tyler recognized

right away her allowing Henry to detail Jersey's role was a huge parental blunder. If Rigg sided, they'd gang up on her. Wouldn't be the first time. But forget their jobs, forget that school began right after Labor Day. Forget every responsibility that ever existed? Tyler Ann Moon: rock 'n' roll band tour manager? That was utterly preposterous.

"We'll discuss this as a family and make a decision. Fair enough, Mr. Hollins?" Tyler offered a pleasant smile that was anything but.

"We leave in a week. There's scant time. I'm sorry about that, but given Rigg's been a band member all summer, I'm not sorry about being here tonight and—"

Rigg's universal one-hand stop-sign signal held Henry at midsentence. "That makes eight in the van, Henry. With the gear, that's laughable."

"We were thinking maybe an equipment trailer."

"That van can barely power up a hill as is. And what about overnights, Henry?"

"Rigg, I'm not sure this is necessary given we haven't yet talked."

"Details, Ty, let's hear him out."

"I can't promise a Holiday Inn every night, that's for sure. I suspect accommodations are going to vary."

"And I don't want Ty and Jer cuddled up together for a long night in a cold van parked in a rest area with a loser band out in the middle of Wyoming. Loser band. Your description, Henry, not mine."

"Dad! What do you suppose scout camp was like this summer?"

"Just trying to get a handle here, kiddo."

Henry stood to go. He'd tried. "Touring is all new. I don't have a crystal ball. I can't promise any rainbows on the trip." He threw on his coat. "I do know that Melissa said it best: 'With the Moons, we couldn't hope for better.' "

The Rise of The Mad March

Four days passed. Three days left. No word. Not waiting for an answer any longer, Gretchen, Melissa and Christine drove down to Rigg's shop. They didn't find themselves "just us three" that often and relished the ride. On the way, they bought and passed around a celebration cold Falstaff quart. Arriving, they were informed that Rigg was out on a stalled vehicle call. Minutes later, they parked and entered Liberty High School. With only a summer admin staff on hand, they wandered deserted hallways on into a department-head meeting. At the conference table, Tyler Moon peered up startled, seeing trouble.

"May we help you?"

"We need a decision at your end, Mrs. Moon."

"You're Christine, right?"

"Yes, ma'am."

"I'll call tonight." Tyler glanced around the table and offered an embarrassed, fumbled apology for the interruption.

"We can't wait any longer."

So, this is the infamous Gretchen. Tyler iced her tone. "Yes, you can. Our family has been shouting at one another for days. This band of yours has upended my household."

With Tyler sitting on the far side, Gretchen circled her way around, squeezing past occupied chairs, finally zeroing in nose-to-nose. "You don't look like you have the balls to run the show, Moon."

"You've been drinking, Miss Tarbeaux."

She hiccupped. "And Rigg would be so ticked at me."

"So am I. All of you, leave this instant!"

Gretchen rallied. "Are you in or out, sister?"

The teachers and administrators attending sat serene, but there was no doubt what would dominate tonight's at-home dinner conversations.

Tyler was on her feet. Two sleepless nights and now this

half-looped headache in her face. She shouted, "We're in. Take *that*, sister!"

Christine grabbed Gretchen from behind and hauled her toward the door. Melissa slipped past the confusion, made for Tyler and kissed her on the cheek. Tyler drew back in surprise. *What have I done?*

The drummer collected her bandmates, and together they backed out, waving. Two department heads meekly waved back.

Rigg picked up on the first ring. "Moon Auto."

"I committed us, Rigg. They were here, Melissa, Christine and Gretchen, all three of them. At the school. They barged into my faculty committee meeting. I lost my cool, then I lost my mind."

"I love you, Tyler Ann Benson Moon."

"They just really pissed me off, Rigg."

"I've been thinking."

"About what? How to save us, save me?"

"We'll take the pickup. It'll sit three and with a covered bed, haul a lot of gear."

The silence on the phone line was deafening.

"Our young daughter caught up with this, this Gretchen creature."

Rigg waited.

"I never really had a choice, did I, Mr. Moon?"

"You did. I was on my knee with a ring. You had a yes or a no."

"Aha. You just proved my point."

chapter forty-four

Salvadore Tuchinardi showed up at Pickford as promised a day before departure. Tony and the Moons had driven up earlier. Chairs were added. Counting Dorothy and Parker, ten wary souls filled the dining room, and the more Sal detailed the upcoming tour, the more stressed the room grew. Playing at Hitches before twenty fans was one thing. Playing in front of millions of New York City cosmopolitan strangers was in another galaxy. The Beatles refrain, *get back to where you once belonged,* was resounding in everyone's ears. Sal wasn't picking up on the spiraling-downward vibe. He should have.

"In a nutshell, kids, that's the itinerary so far. What's the playlist look like?"

"We've a couple new numbers, it's running thirty minutes tops."

"For bar gigs, Henry, play away. But for the club-theater dates with a two or three band lineup, cut it to twenty. We're a last-minute fill-in or add-on. We don't want to step on anyone's manicured toes or ruffle anyone's gilded feathers. We slip into the program. We slip on stage and wham, you punch 'em in the mouth. Twenty minutes. You're gone. No encores. Everyone attending, standing or sitting, is looking at everyone else: 'What the hell was that?' By the time their headlining dog-ass guitar heroes take the stage and begin their set, all anyone in the seats is thinking about is the badass Mad March."

"In your dreams, Tuch."

"No. In yours, toots. Listen up. And I'm looking straight at Tyler and Tony here. We're nobodies, and we're gonna get treated like nobodies. Big stage venues have seen-it-all managers and heard-it-all sound engineers. Don't be a schmuck. Work with the showcase people. Get your band what they need. Pinheads in this business are like raindrops. Most of the time it pours. They're all God's gift. But, bottom line: Be nice. Respect is the last thing they expect. You surprise them, they might surprise you."

"Care for more shrimp salad or tea, Mr. Tuchinardi?"

"Are you kidding me, Dorothy? Of course. Explain to me, how does a woman with obvious taste get mixed up with these hooligans?"

"We all get lucky every once in a while, don't we, Salvadore?"

The phone rang. Sal stood, checking his watch. "That's for me, Dorothy, an expected Chicago callback." Receiver by his ear, he winked and whispered to everyone crowded about the table, "Maurice Roseborough, Crown Theater, big wheel." Then, "Hey beautiful, tell me he's in."

"For you, sweetie, always. Where are ya?"

"Somewhere in Middle-earth."

There came a Chicago holler, "Mauri ... Sallie on one, pick up," the female nasal accent a thing of beauty, coming through a line connection as clear as if Pickford was on speakerphone.

"Sallie." The new voice was guttural and raspy. Scary. "I figured you died. I'm sitting here. After all I've done for Tuchinardi, why wasn't I invited to the funeral?"

"You're confused, Maurice, I'm *your* pallbearer."

"We're both overdue, Sallie. What have you got?"

The Rise of The Mad March

"I need a Crown date. Middle of August. I'm open to suggestions, Maurice. Find us a spot."

"What, you got the Stones now? Just elbow on in whenever."

"We'll open, we'll warm the seats up while the headliners smoke another joint they don't need."

Pickford sat transfixed, striving to listen, as Maurice began tossing lines in two directions.

"Celeste, where's the damn lineup? Sal, who am I turning into superstars this time?"

"You have never heard of them. You have never heard anything quite like them. You have never seen a band quite like them. The Mad March. Three Janes and a Tarzan."

At one end of the line, Celeste, with exasperation, placed her Crown events calendar on Maurice's desk.

On the other, Gretchen slid her chair closer, primed to catch every word.

"Only you, Sallie. I'm looking ... wait. Where are my goddamn glasses? Cel?"

"They're sitting on your head, Mauri. For crying out loud. Have you taken your pills this morning?"

"Maurice, when are you retiring the fair Celeste to that Florida condo she so richly deserves?"

"You tell him, Sallie."

"You're killing me here, the two of you. Enough. I've Three Dog Night, God help me, headlining the sixteenth, Blood Sweat and Tears the nineteenth."

"We'll open the sixteenth. Give us twenty minutes, Maurice."

"The show's sold out. Three broads? Are they ready? I got standards. No fuckups, Sallie."

Gretchen lunged and grabbed the phone. "Are *you* ready, Mr. Fuckup? Standards? Yeah, we got standards. Like, do we even want to play in your fucking dump?"

"Who the fuck is this?"

265

"Gretchen. The bass player. One of the broads."

Sal, pale as a ghost, wrenched the phone back, shouting "You're a train wreck, toots." Raising a threatening fist at her, he ran his hand through what little hair he still possessed, fighting to calm. "I swear ... Maurice?"

"What, I give you twenty minutes and you give me Attila the Hun?"

Still eyeballing Tarbeaux in disbelief, Sal spun an apology: "She's got spirit. They all do."

"You're killing me, Sallie. Put her back on."

Gretchen recoiled, shored up a last smidgeon of courage, grabbed the receiver and said, "I'm not scared of you, Mr. Roseborough."

Chicago was in turmoil.

Celeste was shouting, "Blood pressure, Mauri, don't do this!"

Maurice was louder. "You there, kid?"

"Yeah. Maybe you should listen to Cel."

"You want a lace carpet for your arrival, hotshot? You want me to redecorate the dressing room? Send me a fucking color chart!"

If Maurice had reached a heart-attack level, so had Gretchen. "Just something without a fucking urinal!" Gretchen tossed the phone back and threw up her hands, registering complete innocence.

Sal dangled the phone, head bowed.

Henry closed his eyes. *Maybe this will all disappear.*

Christine and Melissa were one. "Oh wow."

Tony and Rigg fought gallantly to suppress their smiles.

Dorothy was finger-pointing at her wayward charge. "Enough from you, young lady. Gracious."

Tyler was caught completely off guard, her worst fears realized. *My God, the language.*

Jersey was in awe. *Gretchen is beyond cool.*

Sal prayed for peace. "Maurice. Still holding?"

"Cel is shoving pills at me. Tell Gretchen she's now headlining the Roseborough shitlist."

Desperate to salvage the wreckage, Sal changed course. "Maurice, do you and Harry still tip a few on the Southside?"

"Still arguing over the tab, too."

"I've got this idea."

"Oy, more trouble."

"What's this for, Gunny?"

"Special occasion money."

Melissa gave her a look. "You bought the van four new tires. More is too much more, Gunny."

"When the ladies at the bee find out I've helped outfit a rock band for the road, their dismay will have no limits." Dorothy grinned. "I see the excitement in all the faces here at Pickford. Just stick the envelope in your bag to have 'just in case.' "

Melissa gave her a hug.

"And promise me you'll look after Henry. He's a worrywart and he can be fragile. You know that."

"Our boss man will reap what he has sown, but we will be there for him. I promise." Melissa unwrapped from Dorothy and dropped to her knees, both hands scratching behind floppy ears. "Take care of Gunny, watch over the Stones and don't you dare show me those big dog eyes." Parker got a hug. "I'll be back, double promise."

part two
Road Songs

chapter forty-five
July 31, Philadelphia: Bijou Café

"Do I even look like a soprano to you, Hollins?"

"I screwed up, Gret. Nerves."

"We just played a mountain of local shows to drive that shit out of our system. Fucking A, Henry."

"The Bijou felt different. Like the major leagues, and a long way up from double-A Soybean City."

"No excuse. Our national debut. Our freaking very first song and you got your capo on the wrong freaking fret. You're pitched sky-high and we gotta stop and start over. The whole place was laughing at us."

"They were laughing because yelling that you were 'going to murder me after the show' into a live mike was pretty dumb."

"Playing in the wrong key? I should have murdered you right then and there."

Christine was laughing. "Oh stop, you two. It was funny."

They were gathered around a table, their show over, everyone trying to calm. Behind the bar, Manny Polshaw, wiping down spilled drinks, failed to find any humor.

"Twenty minutes? That it?"

No one said a word.

"So, what do I owe ya, twenty bucks?"

Eyes drifted to Tyler, who cleared her throat and said, "We drove a long way, sir."

Manny draped a bar towel across his shoulder. "Whatever the hell you were playing, you were too loud."

Tony stood, defensive. "The PA levels were checked and rechecked. I'm in the back. You could hold a conversation."

"You guys cleared the room, buddy."

"More blew in during the show, towel man. We ended with a bigger house."

Manny, horse-faced, beefy and tall, sporting a gray wavy pompadour, eyed the dark-haired smart-ass munchkin. "You wanna get personal now, sweetheart?" He pointed. "You see those gentlemen seated in the back? They're the 'show' tonight. Crystal the comedian, funny guy, and the Chick Corea Trio. Anyone coming through the door during your jackhammer set is laying claim to the best seats for tonight's show – you, they waited out. This is a professional establishment. Corea and Crystal are professional entertainers." Manny held up a twenty. "I got a Jackson here. My advice: Take it, buy some gas and go back to the garage."

Tyler stood. Her first show. Conflict. More worst fears realized. Patrons sitting and standing about the bar, pausing in mid-conversation, were beginning to take note. Steeling herself, she said, "We are contracted for another show, Mr. —"

"Polshaw. More trouble. A second gig. I forgot. What was I thinking?"

"On ..." Tyler, all nerves and shaking, dug into her shoulder bag, to find and refer to her pocket logbook, "August 5."

Manny, in obvious displeasure, got back to tending his bar.

A male string bean, his palms clasped to the sides of his head, approached Christine and Melissa. "Awesome show. Far freaking out. You guys stormed, man."

Recognizing a possible gift, Tyler shifted from Polshaw and

quickly locked arms with the bean. "We need to find a quiet spot and talk, just us two."

"Far freaking out."

Jazz lovers were arriving. Crystal and the trio had relocated to the front. Rigg and the band were finishing clearing the stage and loading up. The trio setup was underway. Amid all the activity, Tyler returned, took a deep breath, and confronted Manny Polshaw. "The kids played their hearts out. What am I supposed to do, call the Philly mafia to get our money?"

"Not recommended, sweetheart. You never know whose side they're on. You got musicians. They break fingers for a living."

"Tyler."

"What?"

"My name, sir. Are you a betting man, Mr. Polshaw?"

"Manny."

"Okay, Manny, I've a question on the table."

"I've seen a horse run."

"Here's my offer. I accept your twenty, but if we draw a hundred plus on the fifth, you pay double the contract."

Eavesdropping, Dave Holland, Corea's upright bass player, had a gleam in his eye. "I like this woman."

Manny fired back with a grin. "What are you, sweetheart, a gift? Your troop with 'no cover' barely drew a handful tonight, and most of them looked like they'd been blindsided and—"

"Name's Tyler."

"Bulldozed. And who's to blame? Girls playing guitars? Bunch of social misfits playing too fast. What am I hearing onstage? A band or a pulled fire alarm? If you show up on the fourth, yer on, babes, another Jackson or double down."

"I'm tacking a band promo flyer to your performer's board, another in the front window. Grant me that." She offered her hand saying, "Don't forget, Tyler here."

"Got it."

They shook.

Manny's putdowns were heard. Gretchen sidled up next to Tyler. Crystal and the Corea trio at the bar were growing more amused.

"I don't want more trouble from you, kid."

"Too fast, Manny? Next time, I'll play a fucking twenty-minute lullaby just for you."

"Get your smart mouth back on the bus. Outta my shop."

Gretchen leaned across the bar. "I passed the GED this summer. High school grad here."

Manny raised his arms in mock praise. "You're literate. I'll alert the *Inquirer*."

Gretchen fired at the white of his eyes. "And you're the kind of schmo who's behind this bar in 1776. Franklin's here. Jefferson too, and he's reading his Declaration thing and you're screaming, 'Get off my stage, you fucking misfits. Get lost. I never heard such a pile of shit.' "

Tyler forcefully about-faced Gretchen. They made for the van.

Manny stood speechless.

Billy Crystal was writing it all down, word for word, busting his gut to keep from laughing. "I just might use this tonight."

At the door, much to Tyler's dismay, Gretchen shook free and turned.

"Brace yourself, Manny, she's coming back."

"Jesus, Billy, what do I need, a flyswatter?"

Back up against the bar, Gretchen stood on her tiptoes, as tall as possible. "You got homeless around here, Manny?"

"Not on this block, kid."

"Where?"

"On up north. Stay on Broad. A west-side park, just past the expressway. You'll see a few tents, a few boxes. You searching for somebody, kid?"

Gretchen hesitated, stepped back and said, "There are times, Mr. Polshaw, I take a good look at myself in the mirror."

Crystal couldn't resist. "Damn, *Mr.* Polshaw, I think the headliner just left the building."

"Hey, Billy, am I wrong? Chick, am I?"

"The lead could play, Manny."

Manny grunted. "They were an 'L' wreck."

"But they still runnin'."

"I think you've been played, Pols."

"You guys can't be serious. Holland, Barry, really?"

"They be fast, angry and sayin' their piece."

"They brought something, towel man."

Everyone laughed, even Manny.

In the van on the way to Camden, everyone gathered near Tyler. "I gave away your hard-earned twenty to Adam." Allowing the groans, she said, "That skinny guy who thought you 'stormed'—loved that, didn't you?—has thirty of our flyers. He'll mark the time and place and post them all over Temple University. He's going to spread the word: the punks are coming—scorchin' band—don't miss the show. According to Adam, attending classes himself, thousands of students and boredom reigns at the summer sessions. When we return, we got a shot at a full house, troop." She went looking for high fives and drew a bunch.

Jersey sat in the back staring at her mother in wonder. *Betting, doubling down roughneck bar owners, maybe pulling a fast one. Who is this person?*

chapter forty-six

August 1, Camden, New Jersey: Dio's Supperclub August 3, New York, New York: Max's Kansas City

"No boys allowed. Shoo. Out. Girls room here." Christine shoved the protesting male out into the hallway, slammed the hotel room door, about-faced and said, "Where was I?"

"Hair?"

"Right on, Minch. Our hair is screaming 'makeover.' Gret, Mel, *hello*! The Big Apple gig is on our doorstep."

"Be nice if something went right," Melissa moaned. "You broke a string last night, Baird, right in the middle of the set."

Gretchen held up fingers. "Two strings."

Christine laughed. "They were tired. No biggie. Rigg and Tony to the rescue. I switched to Gret's Mosrite."

"Which wasn't tuned. Another screw-up." Gretchen snorted in disgust.

"We can't have timeouts in our set. All our 'mo' was lost. And it felt like we never got it back."

The bass player slung an arm around her drummer. "Not that it mattered, given so few were there, to include the ones who walked out. Did you catch the beady-eyed glares when we played "Shut the F**k Up"? That song is supposed to be funny. We're basically laughing at ourselves. They didn't fucking get it." Gretchen slapped the side of her head. "Damn. Sorry, Mrs. Moon."

"You're turning my daughter into a sailor, Miss Tarbeaux."

"Better a sailor than an expletive-deleted rock musician."

Everyone laughed.

Gretchen said, "I say we change our name to The House-Clearing Band—go with what we do."

"Here's another: The Walkouts. Hah. The Mad March can empty a room faster than any band in rock 'n' roll." Christine was all smiles. "Actually, that's pretty cool."

Tyler leaped at that. "Back in the mid '60s, Dylan pretty much emptied out the Newport Folk Festival. A few weird-sounding rock songs were all it took. That was badass."

Whop! Christine pounded a bedside table. "And so are we. Big show coming up. We need to get ready."

"Hey, not everyone walked out last night. I sold three T-shirts. We got three Camden, New Jersey fans." Jersey gave them all a thumbs-up.

Unloading her bag, Chris was pulling out scissors, a mirror, a large brush, cans of hair spray, dye and shampoo. She had joined the band late and had always known her place; the strong, silent type lurking in the background, a comfortable place given her reticent nature. But she'd been writing songs, her input growing. And Henry was a nag, always urging her to step up. The makeover push felt right.

"Jersey's three tees in Jersey. Right on! According to Mr. Arlo Guthrie, three's an organization, right?" Christine was a huge grin. "'Alice's Restaurant,' guys, and if we sell fifty shirts in New York City, what's that make us?"

"A movement."

Her mother's hip, quick answer raised Jersey's eyebrows.

Christine clapped her hands in delight. "Another 'right on' for Mrs. Tyler Moon. Let's get started."

"I'm sort of fond of my locks, Chris." Melissa was eyeing the scissors.

"Chicken heart. Remember that night in the barn when Henry went all weird about the band sounding like the Vikings coming ashore in Britannia, a pulsing, ominous, dark, mysterious, relentless …"

"He was a little stoned, Chris."

"A little?"

Laughter filled the room again. Tyler rolled her eyes.

"Thing is, I took Henry to heart. Somebody wants my guitar to sound like a Norse invader, I'm all in. I researched. I plowed through a bunch of books and pictures: what the Vikings wore, what they looked like. Fierce stuff. Their *hair*, troop! I decided. Mel, you and I will braid our locks."

"Oh no, not some mohawk thing." Melissa was waving, "no way."

"Yes, but different."

"No clue how to braid here, Baird."

"Ah, I can help. I've been experimenting on Jersey for years." Tyler eyed her daughter. "Cross under into the middle, right?" She grinned.

Jersey waxed sympathetic. "My mom's Viking braids? Ho boy. What's your pain level, Melissa?"

"Are we serious? Really, Chris?"

"Why the hell not, Minch? But listen up, my true Viking vision lies with Gretchen. She's got the look, the face. We trim the mop top, dye it jet black, clump it, pinch it, twist it and gel it."

"Wha … like my fingers in a light socket?"

"The Vikes had a nasty weapon, a spiked ball on a shaft. They called it a 'morning star.' Spikes, baby. You feeling brave, Miss Star?"

Gretchen was half intrigued, half guarded. "Holy Eric the Red."

"Exactly." Chris let loose a whoop.

They spent the whole afternoon, evening and the next morning styling, failing and restyling. In the end, Mel's locks remained unchanged. Her drumming had long blond strands flying about in all directions. She was an electrifying sight onstage that the band did not want to lose.

Christine in the chair, Tyler's arms and hands grew weary but eventually wove one long side braid, six pencil-like back braids with lots of open strands falling between. Christine checked and rechecked herself, the right-side braid resting on her shoulder. "Damn, Mrs. Moon, I love this."

Jersey was in awe. "No wonder England crumbled."

Gretchen survived two top-down cuttings, four shower shampoo restarts, coloring, not so much styling – more like finger plucking, and way too much hair spray. At the finish line, small spikes of hair jutting from the top, sides and back had Jersey in a swoon. "I'm losing it. You are so exotic."

Young Jersey was right. Christine and Gretchen looked scary sensational.

Guys had been knocking on the door the whole time. "We're seeing the sights, join up. There's this Italian place to eat, what gives?"

Replies behind the locked door were always the same: "Bug-off, gents. We're busy. Hey, bring us back a pizza."

Gig day, Tyler proposed that everyone meet at the sound check. Yes, Gotham! Max's Kansas City club! Park Avenue! Whoa. In truth, the band's stay in NYC was testing Tyler to the max. They had checked in at the Chelsea Hotel because everyone that Tyler dared talk to about the tour said, "you *have* to stay at the Chelsea," and it was exciting to be in the city and why not splurge for one night? Rigg, Henry and Tony were charged with parking the vehicles somewhere somehow and *yes*, they were scheduled for a sound check—another Tyler/tour first.

The guys drove the van for the setup. The gals followed

soon after in the pickup. Gretchen and Christine waltzed into Max's arm in arm and heads turned, eyes grew, and jaws dropped. Stagehands, waiters, bartenders and early birds all wolf whistled, waved white napkins in mock surrender or bowed down at the auburn and black locks. Christine bent and kissed Gretchen on the cheek, whispering, "Rock 'n' roll, punk."

chapter forty-seven

"So how do you do that?"

Gretchen looked up. She, Christine, Rigg and Melissa were taking a break after casing up the equipment. The van loading could wait. A victory beer couldn't. Sitting at a table, bottles were clicked to acknowledge a good show. As the smiles and the "Green River" tag passed among them, no one noticed the near cadaverous looking stranger approach, grab the one empty chair, and fire off his meaningless question. Gretchen resented the intrusion. "Do what, man?"

"Sing and play bass at the same time."

Tarbeaux was now officially pissed. "What the fuck, New York, I've never even thought about it. What are you trying to do, psych me out?"

"Our bass player can't play and sing together. The whole band is ready to dump him into the East River and start over."

Gretchen always prided at pegging the bullshitters right off. This guy was no bullshitter. She played him straight. "I was never the singer to begin with. I just backed Hollins here and there. But the more we played, the more I stood at the mike. Switching to the bass, I never gave the two together a thought."

"Making you a switch hitter. Pisses me off."

Rigg's back straightened. You never knew.

"I'm not your problem, New York."

The cadaver half smiled at Gretchen. "We're not club gigging yet. We're close. But shit, Dee Dee is holding us back."

"Try somebody else. Let Dee Dee just play the freaking bass."

New York nodded. "Joey's a possible singer—our drummer. But Joey up-front is a stretch. He looks like one of those cathedral gargoyles."

"Go with Joey at the front mike. Now, all you need is a drummer."

The intruder was narrow-faced and thin-lipped, a wispy build needing a few more red blood cells. What appeared healthy was the full-bodied, page-cut, Prince Valiant locks, touching his shoulders that swirled slightly as he turned, stared, and said, "Maybe I'll steal away blondie here."

"Fuckin' A, man, you got a name?"

"Yeah—Fury, John Fury. That suit you? Suits me."

Gretchen was now focused. She sensed John's intensity, the attitude, maybe the dedication. He wasn't kidding around. The "real deal" was written all over him. He and his not-quite-together band were going to find a way. She was certain. The fake-named Fury would lead, and you couldn't sculpt a better lock-up-your-children rock messiah if you tried.

She slowly turned to Melissa. Ever since the Iowa halfway house, her co-pilot had been growing leaps and bounds in a hundred different directions: interests expanding, talents and looks exploding. The moment at Max's felt like a crossroads, the deciding fate of a thousand days and nights spent together, now at a precipice. If you truly love someone, you let them go on to great things. "This is maybe how our world ends, Mel. Right here."

Melissa read Gretchen's thoughts. They did that. That was

a given. She felt weightless. She'd been pushed, and she was falling. "Not if you fight for me, sister."

"But do I have the right to fight, Minch?"

"I'd battle gladiators for you, Tarbeaux."

Gretchen took a long, reassured breath. "And I'd do the same."

Christine grew alarmed at Melissa and Gretchen's sharp exchange. What just happened? An eye at Rigg saw only his own confusion. The tour was barely underway and already getting crazy. She said, "You're not going to break up a world-class rhythm section, John."

Two laser-like eyes bored into Baird. "I'm at Max's tonight taking in your set, thinking the Velvet Underground have a 'Jane' on drums, so why not us?" He bent toward Melissa. "How about sitting in on a practice session, see what happens?"

Gretchen threw herself back at the invading alien. "Your band got a name, Fury?"

"When checking into hotels on tour, The Beatles would use an alias: Ramone. Maybe we'll steal that."

"Well, bro, along with the band name and blondie here, why not rip off our redheaded lead, too?"

"No offense, but no interest. I'm the guitarist. I got *my* way, understand?"

Christine asked, "You cool with our show, John?"

"Fuck no. You're the competition. Your sound was cool. Lots of potential, man, and if I can't have blondie here, maybe I'll steal a riff here and borrow a riff there." He smiled without smiling. "All's fair in love, war and rock 'n' roll."

"Where's the camaraderie, pal?" Rigg had heard enough.

"Friends? I've never had anyone holding my hand." John the Ramone had mastered his own unbending look. "Rock 'n' roll is a fistfight. My wish right now: Get your van packed up, hit the road and don't come back."

Gretchen could not believe she was actually taking a liking

to this arrogant stick. "Hey, Ramone, you want the truth, we might be the so-called competition, but we really don't know what we're doing."

"But that's what really pisses me off. You do. Adios, switch."

chapter forty-eight

Tyler stood up and waved for silence. "Gretchen asked me to call this band-in-the-van meeting. We're all here for you, babes."

Gretchen slid past to the front by the driver's seat, everyone thinking, *this is a first*.

"My mother died with a needle in a vein in her neck. That was the last I saw her. Dead eyes. Blue lips. Cold skin."

She waited.

Faces stared back. Startled.

"Everyone here is aware of Henry's security hang-ups. Nobody goes anywhere without blah blah blah. He's a mother hen. Fine. But we need a couple more rules for the road. And this is a grow-up moment for you, Jersey. The kind that makes you aware that adults mess up their lives ten times worse than all your distressed, depressed ninth-grade classmates put together. So, all of you listen up, because this has been bugging me for days. That night after the show at Dio's, back in Camden, some guy bragging he was an ex-big-time roadie or something, hit on me, wanting to know where we were from, where the tour was headed. Then he slips me a vial saying it'll keep me on the road forever. He's like, 'Let the good times roll, baby.' I'm like, 'Cool. Thanks, dude.' When I was able to ditch him, I ditched his shit – and that's why I'm standing here. Dio's could have happened to any one of us in this van.

"We all know how hard Ty is working, the club owner crap she's putting up with, not to forget putting up with us. Ergo, Road Rule Number One. The gigs are God. We play on time. We play straight. Lord knows we've had stage screw-ups, but those had nothing to do with anyone being seriously wasted.

"Road Rule Number Two. Box your ears, Jersey. Anyone fucked-up injecting or snorting God knows what and making a mess of things is off the tour. No warnings. The rest of us will rock on and make do. We'll find a way.

"I know we don't have a problem. I'm just saying that creeps like the one that cornered me after the Camden show come with the territory, and we owe these two road rules to Tyler and to Sallie, and you owe them to me, too." Gretchen felt an unexpected chill. She forced a finish. "One junkie is one too many. Questions? Good. End of meeting."

"Ah, wait. I got a question."

"Is this necessary, Moonbeam?"

Jersey nodded. "Yep."

Gretchen sighed. "Send it."

"What am I supposed to do with the guitar case full of cocaine that you gave me?"

The van had never known such silence, not for 164,228 miles.

Melissa was the first to crack up. Her *hoot* had Jersey in a mile-wide smile. Amid more hoots and hollers, Gretchen pointed at Tyler and Rigg. "You two are responsible for this, this smart-ass wormy apple. Ship her back home, Rigg. Exchange her for anything: a pocketknife, a fishing rod—something useful."

chapter forty-nine

August 5, Philadelphia: The Bijou Café August 7, Pittsburgh: The Spot Light Lounge August 8, Pittsburgh: The Decade August 10, Erie, Pennsylvania: The Gaslight

On an off day, the sxith, Tony and Melissa replaced and tuned the new "kick" skin. Melissa performed without her usual flair in Pittsburgh, hardly herself, still a bit traumatized by the second Philly show. She'd lost a counted-on treasure, and when treasures break down, you'd better ease up because they can "oh no" break down again.

They'd won Tyler's bet. Temple University turned out en masse; maybe 150 summer-session Owls, ready to party, jammed the Bijou. The crowd was all new and unexpected. The scene felt electric. Tony slipped into his hardcore biker "Granite" renown, stepped center stage and shouted a first-time wild intro: "Are all you cracked bells ready (*ringing cheers*)? Hey, listen up, find a partner. You're going to need someone to hold onto." The band ran onstage. Melissa opened "Ball Game" with the kick drum, an adrenaline pounding that proved one-too-many as the mallet tore straight through the drumhead. Thud. Game over. She froze, stunned. The "kick" mallet lay buried into the torn skin. The Mad March "opener" skittered to an aborted, cacophonous end. The built-up buzzed crowd deflated. *Woosh*. Rigg and Tony commenced a mad scramble to first locate a roll of duct tape, then makeshift a repair that barely held up. With Rigg taping together the torn skin, Tony crouched close to Melissa. "There are no other bands. We can't borrow another kick. We don't have another skin. But you're not cooked. I'll adjust the beater away from the tear. Hang tough, kiddo. You can salvage this. You can keep the beat."

Set to go, Tony reintroduced the band and had the crowd laughing.

Melissa gave her best, but throughout the set her "kick" looked and sounded like a torn-up, patched-up stock Chevy running 65 mph laps at Daytona just to goddamn reach the checkered flag.

So, pissed off, Christine, Henry and Gretchen tore through twenty minutes like there was no tomorrow. The crowd was wowed, but at the show's ending, everyone onstage felt snakebit.

Lights back up, behind the bar, Manny Polshaw had tried to cheer them.

"Years back, this Grammy-winning pianist, very highbrow at the Bijou that night, tuxedo crowd, is halfway through a Beethoven something. The piano, big as a barge, I swear to God, rolls off the stage. Screw-ups are legendary in this business. Welcome to the club."

The Café had had a monster night at the register. Manny paid the two hundred dollars, kicked in a hundred-dollar bonus and said, "You guys come back for a week, I might squirrel away enough to retire from this madness."

"I didn't play that promised lullaby, but we need one last Bijou bonus, Polshaw."

"Don't push it, kid."

"A hug for Melissa. She had a tough show."

Cheers erupted from the bar as Manny obliged, then with an open-armed gesture, bear-hugged Tyler, too.

A fitting end to a crazy two-night stand.

Robert Espenscheid, Jr.

Pittsburgh Post-Gazette
A&E Home Section August 8, 1973
Earl Duke: weekend editor

Rock 'n' roll haters have another cause to vent. Last night something called the Mad March somehow escaped their home base in Iowa, wound up at The Spot Light and played a set that left the crowd both in awe and scratching its collective head. The March, a quartet with three Lady Janes (yes, that's not a typo) on bass, lead guitar and drums, played twelve songs (I was counting) in twenty-eight minutes (do the math) that was an onslaught of stripped-down guitar speed and rhythm. Pool balls stopped clicking and small talk died. The good-size crowd stood in a stupor, glued to what might best be called a cartoon onstage. Songs (using the term loosely) came and went before you could take a slug of beer. That's not being derogatory. When the band ended, the silence at the lounge felt like a tomb, and all that remained was this huge grin on my face ... and I was hardly alone. Ready for a rock shock? The Mad March play at The Decade tonight.

August 11 and 12: Cleveland, Ohio: The Pirates Cove
August 13: Toledo, Ohio: The Cave

Christine was too sick to play Toledo: no energy, headaches, a slight fever. Everyone blamed the smoky clubs in Erie and Cleveland. Both nights, the cigarette haze hung thick as stew. Just the thought of playing at a club called The Cave in Toledo had Baird turning avocado green.

The Mad March got creative. Gretchen played lead on her Mosrite. Tony filled in on bass. Destino knew the songs. He could play. The set was scrambled eggs, but they got by. Henry never let on the joy felt at having another whiskered face on stage. No matter how much you love the "certain someones," being an "only" can isolate and wear.

The Rise of The Mad March

Christine was below par but pumped for Chicago. Gretchen was leery. Calling Celeste at the Crown Theater and being provided a phone number, Gretchen managed to reach Sallie. There was no hello.

"Roseborough is gonna have elephants. He's gonna draw and quarter me, right on stage."

"Toots! I just checked in with Manny at the Bijou. He's in love. Should I laugh or cry?"

"Long story."

"You're epic, kiddo."

"I'm pissed, Sallie. Erie. This one club had strobe lights and freaking go-go girls. The crowd just stood around like zombies. The dancers are like, 'What am I supposed to do with your crazy songs?' and I'm screaming at them, 'Put on some clothes, get a life!' What the fuck, Tuch?"

"So, I don't hit a bull's-eye every time. That bad book is on me but sometimes you gotta bend in the wind, toots. How's everyone?"

"Christine's a sickie but getting better. Mel's acting weird. Are you listening to me, Tuch? I don't want to be tortured to death in Chicago."

"Weird how?"

"I'm not sure. She busted her kick drum in Philly, but I'm thinking something else is bugging her."

"Ask."

"I'm getting brushed off."

"Stay on her, kiddo. Have Tyler call me at this number. I've got an outdoor festival lined up in North Dakota."

"You're killing us, Tuch."

"What a way to go. What else?"

"The tits and ass took some foul garbage from some Neanderthals in the crowd at Cleveland: '*Get off the fucking stage, bitches.*' Stuff got thrown at us. Someone had an egg. Two lipsticks. What the hell was that? Rigg and Tony came onstage and hurled beer cans and shit back at 'em. The gig got

291

intense."

"We went over this a hundred times. Dickheads don't bring hearts and flowers to shows. You didn't murder anyone, did you, toots?"

"In my dreams, every single one."

"Get to Chicago. Find Celeste. Maurice is like an attack dog with a wagging tail. It's gonna be a full house. Max effort."

"Butterflies here, Sallie."

"A good sign, Gretchen."

chapter fifty

"Hey guys, I need to say something. Serious-like."

"Last time you said that, Hollins, we wound up in Vegas." Melissa smiled.

"Gimme a couple minutes."

"Spill it, boss."

They were at a rest stop off Interstate 80/90 near South Bend in Indiana. Henry had spied his bandmates at a picnic table, sitting and stretching in the shade. He saw his chance.

"Since the tour started in Philly, I know we've had some rough gigs. But here's a thing. There has always been a small group of young women hanging around the van after the show."

"Groupies." Chris laughed.

"Bullshit. Hanging by the van hoping to catch your eye, make conversation, maybe even to get one or all of you to sign something."

"What are you saying, Hollins?"

"I'm saying, Gret, that they don't really want your autograph. That's just a play to make a connection. The connection is what they're after." Henry was looking at three blank faces. "You are important to them. They saw the show. They are double-checking to make sure you're all real."

"Important? Since when is a loser band important?"

"Even you don't believe that, Gret. Look, what I'm trying to inject here is I think it would be super cool if all of you take the time to talk to them. I've seen you do it. I'm just emphasizing that you keep reaching out to the max."

"And the reason?"

"Because, Chris, they're standing by the van seeing courage and conviction, seeing a sister overcome. Maybe they are in the same boat. Maybe they are battling through whatever it is that's keeping them from reaching their own goals, the proverbial glass ceiling. They see your pride and they want to stand up, stand out and take pride in their own lives. If you can compete, so can they. And I guess that's all I got."

"Ah, Dr. Hollins?"

"Don't make fun of me, Mel. You're a Pied Piper, all three of you are. I'm just saying, be good Pied Pipers."

Christine, Gretchen and Melissa all sat with amused looks. Christine said, "And then one of these pride-seekers whispers to me, 'That rhythm guy is kinda cute, right?'"

Henry bowed in defeat. "Are you clowns ever going to take me seriously?"

"No!"

The collective shout brought smiles.

"I play drums, Henry, I'm not the master of the universe."

"But you are, Mel. That's how they see you, and that's a good thing. Look, the three of you never set out to affect others, but there they are, the end result, waiting by the van in Pittsburgh, in Erie, in Cleveland and on down the line, and that's not happening unless what you're doing means the world to them. That's it. I've said my piece. No more, except like Rigg and Tony keep saying, I'm honored to be tagging along."

chapter fifty-one

"I thought we hitched up pretty good the other night at The Cave."

"We did. I was making a mess at lead. You were a mess on bass."

"Not what I was hearing." Tony noted the string braid around Gretchen's neck. "You're wearing the ring."

Gretchen reached inside her shirt. "I am." Holding it, she said, "A sweet guy gave this to me."

"Like I said previous, I keep Melissa well-aware I'm wooing you."

"Wooing? How old are you again?"

"Always liked that word." He grinned.

Gretchen sighed, exasperated. "And I've said this before, you're a complication, Destino."

"What's so damn complicated about a shoulder to lean on?"

She felt herself warm and defensively peered down at her shoelaces. "What did Mel say this time?"

"You won't believe what she said."

"Try me."

"She's got that smart-ass, here-it-comes look on her face."

"Oh yeah."

"And asks me if Sir Galahad had ever found the Holy Grail. I said I really didn't know, and she goes, 'Well, if he missed out in Arthur's time, he's making up for it in Henry's.'"

Gretchen felt sucker punched. Minch could do that. "How is it possible, Antonio, to find a treasure, standing alone under a streetlight, peering up at a rock concert poster? A treasure, when you're not even looking?"

Tony let loose what he hoped was a Sir Galahad grin. "Tell me about it."

She smiled and kissed him. "Can we chill the hormones between us for right now?"

"I can be good."

She nodded, "I know. And given that, Destino, I need some help."

"With what?"

"Get with Rigg. Tell him you're on board for the ride-arounds. He knows the score."

"Ride-arounds? You and Rigg?"

"And you, too. A three-way."

"Total confusion here, Tarbeaux."

chapter fifty-two

August 15, Chicago: The Crown Theater

"So, we'll run the works through the Crown PA tonight?"

"Right, Tony. Easy setup. Problems?"

"Hell no, Andy. You direct, and Rigg and I will mike us up."

"Get your troop on stage early to run through a number. We'll check the levels. Give them a feel. How many vocal stands do you need?"

"Two. And hey, I see you got ceiling mikes."

"You bet, Tony. I can drop them to any level. We get professional live recordings at the Crown. Top-notch."

"How much bread would it cost me to get you to record the Mad March set tonight, Andy?"

"No can do, amigo. That's precontracted shit. Bands give an OK. Record companies have to sign off. Maurice is directly involved. Tape security is a factor. Everyone has a piece of the pie. Even if you had a notion, you've got to start with the boss upstairs."

"But you know how to set and run the system, right?"

"Part of my job."

Tony tried out a co-conspirator grin. "You could pull a fast one if you wanted. Who'd ever know except the legendary Windy City bootlegger Andrew Vantz?"

"You are an evil guy, Destino."

"I'm just asking for a price to hear a loser band performing in a first-class joint, live onstage on tape for the first time."

Andy tried out his co-conspirator grin. "My price is way too high."

"Bring it, partner."

"I wanna meet the lead—the 'scorching' Christine."

"Done."

"And I wanna meet the 'irresistibles': Melissa and Gretchen."

"Done. Shave, shower, comb your hair. Make all your moves, Vantz, you never know."

"I might require a couple beers backstage to loosen up my best lines."

"Done. And you drive a hard bargain, sir."

They shook. Tony couldn't resist, "Is it rolling, Bob?"

The Crown sound engineer laughed and refocused. "I need your word, Tony, that the recording tonight is just between us two."

"You have it, sir. Our secret, until they turn world famous, and the rock world becomes aware of tonight's tape and bows down to our foresight."

Andy Vantz acknowledged with a huge grin. "And in that case, for my meet-and-greet with the belles of the ball, maybe a photo. Me and the future of rock 'n' roll—close-up. For posterity and shit."

"Done."

"What in the hell was that, Maurice? My guys are pissed. Goddamn nobody band playing all that crap. *We* filled this place. Three Dog sold those tickets, and you put cretins on stage to open? A fucking jackhammer band?"

Maurice had come down from his office to wander backstage. "Who the fuck are you?"

"I'm the publicist for a world-class outfit, Roseborough. A band at the top of the charts. Fucking number-one songs. *One*, get it? You don't throw a snarling wolf pack in front of us."

"So, Mr. Publicist. No joy to the world right now, eh?"

"You think that's funny? That tonight's opener was funny? Bitches with guitars. The crowd all riled up. I thought this was a music hall, not the fucking Roman Colosseum."

"Get the hell out of my building."

"I will not. I've a show to produce."

"I own the joint. Get out, putz." Maurice was on his walkie-talkie. "Celeste!"

"What? Where are you?"

"Stage left. Get Max and Andy down here. Right now. I need a piece of garbage tossed from the premises."

"They're on the way."

"You can't—"

"I'm this fucking close," Maurice held up two fingers an inch apart from his startled antagonist, "from tossing the whole band. You can walk or go out face first."

The publicist had one look at the oncoming Max and hightailed.

"Mauri!" Celeste was back, urgent.

"What?"

"The March is packed up and leaving. Gretchen wants to know if she can call you from the road ... just to talk."

"You'd think the two loggerheads Helen and I raised could do that once in a blue moon. Make sure she gets both numbers, Celeste – the Crown and my apartment."

"Done. What am I hearing on the line here ... a beating heart?"

"Don't start. And call Harry. I'll meet him late at Murph's for a few highballs."

"So be a Santa for once in your life."

Harry Caray, the popular Chicago White Sox radio and television play-by-play announcer, belly laughed. "I got the size. But 'major league,' Rosie, you got a bunch of no-name kids, rookies. They botch it, I hear about it for months. Too risky."

Maurice caught an eye. "Carol, can we get another couple bourbons here? Listen, Harry, the kids played it tonight at the Crown. The 'seats' were standing and cheering."

"Different, huh?"

"Like you never heard. Fast. Loud. They'll wake Doubleday from the grave. Listen, you and I—we're showmen. We don't forget that. And Veeck, if he was still at the helm, would jump at this. Hell, he'd have you singing."

"Not with my gravel pit."

"Bullshit. I've already heard you do it. Showmen, Harry. We put on a show."

Caray chuckled, recalling Veeck. All the crazy promo stunts.

"Harry, listen to me, the fans will love it. Fun at the old ballpark. Your words, not mine. One time only, Harry. Next game, you're back to the usual until the season ends."

"I'll need to run this upstairs."

"Sell it to them."

"Can you set it up?"

"Sure. The groundskeeper, Balicki, he's Sallie's Chicago drinking buddy. Small world, Harry, right?"

"Milwaukee's in town. Big rivalry game. Wood's on the mound. Day game in perfect weather. We'll have a good afternoon crowd, Rosie, a lot more than your kids can handle."

"I tell you what. You swing this for me, I'll get Frankie to do a show at the Crown. Best seats in the joint for both you and Balicki."

"Are the two of us attending arm in arm with Celeste?" Harry's face lit up with delight. Nobody's face did it better.

The Rise of The Mad March

"Listen Harry, I'm thinking, I'll have you onstage. Do a number with Frankie: 'My Kind of Town.' You'll bring the house down."

August 16: Old Comiskey Park

Three a.m., Tyler rousted Rigg and Tony for the wee-hour revelation that a Comiskey gig was a go, that a crowd of some eighteen thousand was expected, that they needed to be at the park at the crack of dawn for placement and a quick sound check. "Better wake them, huh?"

Rigg was adamant. "Absolutely not, Ty. Less time for butterflies, the better. Right, Tony?"

"I agree. Day game starts at 2 p.m., figure the seventh-inning stretch around 3:30. Boom. We're on. But how? Eighty-five-watt amps ain't going to cut the hot dog mustard at Old Comiskey. I'm guessing we stage a band setup behind the pitcher's mound and run a mike cable-snake to the park's public address system. I mean, why not? They have a live organ player, right? Maybe the PA horns won't sound too bad. Cable length. Wow. Might be a problem. This is new territory for me. Guess what, I wasn't with the Beatles at Shea Stadium. Lots of possible headaches here."

Tyler smiled. "That's why we hired you."

"Hired? Are you letting on that you're managing a money-making operation, Moon?"

"Only rock 'n' roll so far. Sorry." Their hands slapped together with knowing smiles. "There's more, Tony. Maurice's call came with a warning. Harry Caray might wake up tomorrow, or I guess today, with a hangover and scuttle the whole shebang, but right now we're set. Crack of dawn, Tony, you connect with a Miro Balicki at the park, head of the grounds crew. He's your contact. After the sound check, we'll do the tourist thing: stores, museums, lunch. Keep them busy."

Robert Espenscheid, Jr.

In the top half of the seventh, the Brewers go down in order. Necks,— 19,488 in all—bend toward the press box, waiting on whatever Harry Caray had in store, then twist back in confusion as the grounds crew carefully rolls out a small band-setup on wheels. Drums, amps, speakers, cables and PA microphones all arrive safe in front of second base. Four musicians, slinging guitars and sticks, run and cram onto their flatbed trailer stage.

Gretchen lightly taps her microphone, sensing a mountain of power. Melissa, sitting behind her kit, counts off, "Three ... two ... go!"

First verse (Henry on vocals— tentative), eighteen seconds from start to end. A twelve-second instrumental break follows (Christine shines). Henry repeats the verse, sixteen seconds (faster, better). "For it's one, two, three strikes you're out at the ..."

Roaring from Comiskey's public address system, "Take Me Out to the Ball Game" slam-bangs to a finish in forty-six seconds flat.

Sox fans sit in stunned silence. Players, standing atop the dugout steps, the same. Not Harry Caray. He's leaning out his play-by-play booth with his live mike, shouting, "Now, let's get some runs!"

As if electrically shocked back to life, the crowd roars approval. Melissa stands on her tiptoes behind her drums and raises her sticks. Christine, Henry and Gretchen raise their guitars. The grinning band's salute to the crowd ramps the cheering. In the stands, a roving TV camera catches looks of wonder and excitement from the box seats to the waving, sun-drenched, beer-soaked bleachers.

As the ground crew races to clear the infield, Henry gathers the four in a huddle, shouting to be heard, "Never forget this moment! Never!"

"Mauri, pick up. Sallie on one."
"Toast of the town, eh, Maurice?"

The Rise of The Mad March

"Your kids had mettle, Sal, I'll give them that."

"Balicki pulled it off."

"By the time the grounds crew finished up, the game delay totaled six seconds. Major League Baseball can live with that."

"What's Caray's take?"

"WSNS is 'what the heck was that?' Harry's all apologetic, 'big mistake, big mistake,' then his grandkid calls all excited and suddenly he's fine. But I'm on the hook for Sinatra. You're killing me with this, Tuchinardi."

"Hell of a Comiskey show."

"We lucked out with the young engineer in the production truck. Some supervisor is screaming, 'Go to break, cut them off!' Kid gives him a look and goes, 'Camera two, zoom in on the redhead guitarist.' That was priceless."

"They spotlighted Melissa at the end."

"That pirouette, Sallie, drumsticks raised high, pointing, saluting the crowd, the 360 turn. What was that? MacArthur returning to the Philippines? Balicki and the crew think they deserve an Emmy."

"You did a good thing, Maurice."

jersey moon: tour interview #12

August 1973

Jersey: Finally corralled you. Nervous here.

Christine: Everyone tells me I should be the nervous one.

Jersey: How does the word "trailblazer" register with you?

Christine: It doesn't.

Jersey: It should.

Christine: Look Moon, I get it, I'm a girl onstage with a guitar, but I'm hardly a rock 'n' roll "first." Henry played us stuff from Fanny. All girl band, way before us, and still touring and recording. So there.

Jersey: Never heard of them.

Christine: Well, if my dad hadn't bought me a six-string, you'd have never heard of me, either.

Jersey: I stand offstage, I watch the crowd. I see a whole bunch of Bettys and Veronicas focus on the tall auburn-haired Viking lead guitarist. I see their faces. You are changing and enriching lives, Christine Baird.

Christine: Bull.

Jersey: Maybe they don't leave the show and pick up a Harmony or a Gibson, maybe they're on a whole different trip, but thanks to you, they'll laugh at anyone who says, *"You can't do that, you're a girl."*

Christine: That's such a spin, Moon, and are you in cahoots with Henry? First his Pied Piper lecture, now this trailblazer stuff. Geez.

Jersey: No, but Henry says you learned to play in a closet.

Christine: Partly true. I mean, it's hard to tell a mom you want to grow up and be Mick Ralphs.

Jersey: Sorry, who?

Christine: Guitarist in Mott the Hoople. My inspiration. The way he played, that sound … the nazz, the buzz.

Jersey: That's cool.

Christine: How do I explain Mick Ralphs to my mother? I didn't.

Jersey: Big chicken.

Christine: I was.

Jersey: You're the quiet type.

Christine: Suits me. Hard to get a word in edgewise with Mel and Gret.

Jersey: The two wild geese.

Christine: Hah. Perfect.

Jersey: So, how do you do what you do? What a doofus I am; that must be the worst question you ever heard.

Christine: I take what's in Henry's head, which is full of rolling-thunder history, add Gretchen's rants, put them in a pot and stir with my guitar.

Jersey: So, you're up onstage playing "Shovelhead," eyes closed, dreaming of what … the Spartans at Thermopylae?

Christine: That's me, old slash and burn. With Mel's pounding and Gretchen's shredding bass, it's not hard.

Jersey: And speaking of history, Joan of Arc never hid in a closet.

Christine: I'm not Joan.

Jersey: But you are. You are fucking awesome.

Christine: And you, young lady, have been spending way too much time with Tarbeaux.

Jersey: I love Gretchen.

Christine: Everybody does.

Jersey: One final question. Day-to-day, with all that's happened to you, are you happy, Christine?

Christine: I'm a rainbow, Jersey.

chapter fifty-three

August 18, Madison, Wisconsin: Bunky's August 19, Madison, Wisconsin: Dewey's August 21, Minneapolis, Minnesota: The Turf Club August 23, Bismarck, North Dakota: Dakota Hinterland Music Fest

The Badger Herald
August 20, 1973
ArtsEtc: music
Kara Harmon: associate editor

Gig review: The Mad March at Dewey's

Go on and heckle if you so desire but I'm letting my gender strut with pride here. Last night at Dewey's, sadly for one show only, girls rocked with drumsticks and guitar picks (it's about freaking time). Yes siree Bob, and no one onstage was playing, *I want to hold your hand*. And it wasn't just Christine, Melissa and Gretchen that held the crowd captive, it was the music: a holler-out from the Underworld. With relentless, furious backing at breakneck speed, lyrics damned the piled-up dead in Vietnam, the depravity of sexual abuse, and yes, shopping at Bloomingdale's. Did the gals miss something? I don't think so. Listen, if rock 'n' roll has been acting of late like a dozing bearded deadweight stuffed in a La-Z-Boy recliner, last night's buzz fest at Dewey's was a serious wake-up call. The Mad March ... and I hope it's a long one.

The Rise of The Mad March

"She's runnin' hot!"

East of Oriska, North Dakota, groans and moans followed Rigg's exclamation from the driver's seat as the van puttered to a halt on Interstate 94.

Standing roadside, hood up, hands in his pocket, Rigg peered down at a tattered fan belt. Tyler checked her watch. The Mad March festival time slot was now in obvious jeopardy. Having elected to stay over outside Minneapolis, they had cut their travel time close. Too close.

A decision was made. They are not splitting up. No one is being left behind to have the band reach Bismarck on schedule.

Taking the pickup west to the town of Valley City, Rigg driving, Tyler finally reached a pay phone. At Hinterland, no one knew festival director-of-operations Johnny Aspinwall's whereabouts. She leaves a message: The Mad March is delayed.

An auto parts store located, the belt eventually replaced, the Mad March troop arrived at the festival grounds at dusk, two hours too late. Aspinwall was adamant: He can't stage them.

"Your band was a last-minute addition, sister. A big favor to Tuchinardi, by the way, and now you want to be an addition to an addition? Your slot is history. I'm dealing with enough hassles."

"Name's Tyler. I'm not your sister. And this is a rock 'n' roll festival, Johnny, not a regulation-saddled military operation. Give me that clipboard you're holding. Now!"

Overhearing, Jersey had a thought: A *school? A rock 'n' roll tour? Get serious. My mom could run the United Nations.*

Trials and screw-ups piling up for two days, Aspinwall reluctantly handed over his one indispensable possession, screaming, "It's not a festival, it's not the army, it's a fucking zoo! The cages are open, and the wild animals are all running loose."

In one ear and out the other, Tyler calmly wrote on Aspinwall's to-do list: *Mad March needs a slot. Twenty minutes.* "Pull yourself together, Johnny, and *please* don't forget us."

Aspinwall grabbed his clipboard back with a crazed look. "But I will. I've got a hundred headaches in front of you. Let's take a look here at what tops my list? Oh, yes. I've been informed that a thunderstorm is on the way, and I need to triple-check that my stoned stage crew isn't set to *electrocute a thousand kids*! Out of my way, sister."

The final day of the festival, the Mad March took to wandering.

Henry found himself backstage observing a keyboard crisis; a broken midrange hammer shank, rendering the stage acoustic P2 Yamaha kaput. A quick run to the van and return had Henry piano-technician-on-the-spot. Using a drop of Titebond and a fast-food restaurant plastic straw (why does he carry such stuff … just for this very reason), he quickly glued and splinted the shank: A above middle C.

"When are you on?"

"Soon, Henry. An hour, maybe less."

"Roll it on out. It'll hold, Ben."

Ben Ganst, keyboard player for Alien Corn, had witnessed the simple repair in amazement and now proclaimed Henry the new messiah. "How can we repay you, brother?"

Henry said, "Well, there is something."

Rumbling thunder, rain threatening, festival closer the Doobie Brothers throw their weight around. Preceding gigs are shortened.

The Rise of The Mad March

The Doobies elbow onstage at 10:30 p.m. and play a rushed set before the oncoming deluge.

Still no lightning, the rain holding off and with time allowed, Aspinwall tosses in the Mad March as a festival coda, an afterthought. Everyone pitches in with the frantic setup. If they'd had Parker, he'd have been hauling guitar stands on stage like a steak bone.

Christine has an inspiration. She corners Tony. "You were in the military, right?" Getting a nod, she asks further. With another nod she whispers, "Hum it to me."

Only the seriously stoned and/or inebriated remain. The now thin crowd stands and stumbles about in the dark like pasture cows. Ominous thunder adds accompaniment to a Mad March blistering short set. With light rain falling, Christine asks the festival stage crew for one more minute. They oblige. Walking back out, alone stage center, near midnight, conjuring up her best Jimi Hendrix, she solos "Taps," one spellbinding note after another.

chapter fifty-four

Christine hits the brakes in wide-eyed confusion.
"Tony! Wake up. Something's strange."
Riding shotgun in the pickup, Tony is jolted to life with a stiff neck.

They're stopped, and surrounding flashing red lights have him disoriented. A military-like uniform is tapping his side window with a large flashlight. With a "what the?" he rolls the window down.

"Sir, I need a spot check on what you're hauling."

Tony turns to Christine. "Where are we?"

Panicking, Christine throws her arms up in despair.

Tony, now fully awake, switches back to the officer. "Were we in an accident?"

"That I don't know, sir. I do know you're at the Canadian border, Manitoba Province, and I need to view your bed cargo before you cross."

"My God, Tony. Route 36 west to 83 south, right? What have I done?"

"I suspect a wrong turn, Miss Baird," he can't help but chuckle, "somewhere way back at a dark, lonely crossroads."

In the side view, Christine spots Gretchen fast approaching her driver's side. "Oh shit, and now my life is over."

The Rise of The Mad March

Pounding on the cab window, Gretchen let her have it, "Fucking A, Baird, 150 miles in the wrong direction. Are you kidding me?"

Tony is back at the border guard. "We need to get turned around. This band is supposed to be heading toward Denver."

Noting two eighteen-wheelers lined up behind the van, honking impatiently, the guard ventures, "I hope your songs are better than your sense of direction. Go on through and U-turn. A welcome and a bye-bye from Manitoba."

Gretchen hears only the horns, not the solution.

Three-thirty a.m., she double-times back past the van and signals the semi driver with her thumb and a shout, "Back it up, Mac."

Window cranked, two squinty eyes, tucked between a full beard and a trucker's hat sporting a Texaco logo, peer out and down. "You're holding up international commerce, runt, get your shit wagon out of my way."

"Reverse it, fucker."

Maintaining an eye on Gretchen in her side view, hearing threats and cussing, Christine quietly says to Tony, "Not to disparage my gender, but our bass player really needs to get laid."

"I'm working on it."

"Try harder, sir." She laughs

Tony fails to find the humor. "I just don't want to mess us up."

Christine leans over and kisses him on the cheek. "You two. I cheer for you guys. And thanks for Hinterland, man, the fastest stage setup in the history of rock 'n' roll."

" 'Taps' at the end. Wow. You were a dream, Christine."

Before the border incident escalates, guards manage to calm a hot-tempered transporter and corral the bass player back into her van. The Mad March go to Canada and return.

Everyone waved.

chapter fifty-five

H*i reader. Jersey here. I know I'm supposed to be the third-person story narrator and such, but I'm going to pause and inject a personal account—one time only, I promise.*

We shared an early breakfast at Roz's twenty-four-hour diner outside Spearfish, South Dakota, a meal that has remained for me a signature event on the summer tour—a special time unplanned, not anticipated, but never forgotten. Roz's birthed a camaraderie among us that I treasured and carry with me to this very day.

To set the stage, our entourage included "Granite the biker," who'd ridden to the annual Sturgis Black Hills Motorcycle Rally many times, ergo, with Tony navigating in the predawn, we rolled stealthily into a campground sporting two bathhouses. Praise the gods. Showers—and so desperately needed. We had soap – towels not so much. And, according to our biker dude, the stalls had coin-operated timers that dispensed the water, thus a frantic search commenced that proved quarters were scarce. (Geez, Mom, how broke *is* this tour?) To compensate, we squeezed together into one stall.

Decorum prevailed. All the grody boys were shooed to their own building.

We were giddy in ours. I was shy, blooming bod and all. Mom was all, "When did we shower together last? Why so long? I've missed this."

I'm totally mortified, but mortification was not permitted with the Mad March girls. Thinking back, takeaways from that communal shower abound: the teasing, the laughter, counting down the seconds allotted under the cascading water. "Time's up! Scat! I'm next." Gentle hands washing backsides. Everyone was just so much fun and so beautiful.

Needless to say, later on, the sun breaking, seated at Roz's with menus in hand, everyone felt born again. Famished, platters were ordered, and the real teasing began. For turning north on Route 83 and delivering us to Manitoba, Christine was tagged *The Mad Maple.* Supporting-role raspberries were awarded to Rigg: driving the van and blindly following the pickup, *and to* Tony and Tyler: both falling asleep while on front seat copilot guard duty.

Melissa saved the best for last. "Given that Baird led the way, we're lucky it wasn't the Mexican border."

I laughed so hard I got the hiccups.

Coffee being served, laughter finally gave way to logistics.

"We've a long drive ahead. Van status, Rigg? We gonna make Boulder?"

"Tyler's bra straps have proved an excellent fan belt replacement. We're in great shape, Henry."

"Pun intended, Rigg?"

"Absolutely."

Melissa goes, "Finally, a reason for touring rock 'n' roll girls."

Mad Maple reaches back and under her sweatshirt, unclips and pulls out her bra, holding it aloft. "Pearls to the rock 'n' roll girls."

Huge applause. Wide-eyed smiles. Now I really got the hiccups.

"That's a song title." Gretchen was aglow. "Tramps ride the pickup, ladies in the van. We'll write our first number one hit together all the way to Colorado."

As if a passing gray cloud, Mom took the occasion to detail our financial woes. "Hang on, kids. First up, we were shorted at one of the bars in Madison. I was rather rudely informed, 'Hey, lady, I pay for three hours of covers, not a half-hour rampaging river.' "

"Wait, he actually said that? Rampaging?"

"His very words, Henry."

Henry smiled. "That's a kudo."

Rolling her eyes, Mom moved on. "We received a likewise pittance in Minneapolis. Same story: 'Take it or leave it, babe.' " Mom shook her head in dismay, then brightened, "And now the good news. Thanks to an amazing band performance at the festival, never forgetting Christine's 'Taps,' Bismarck Johnny threw in a hundred-dollar bonus. For the record, if you're not all aware, thanks to Henry's repair of the stage piano, Alien Corn twisted Aspinwall's arm to put us on the docket. You guys did the rest. I wound up in a Johnny bear hug with the guy shouting, 'Nobody died! A perfect ending. Thank you, sister!' Gracious, why anyone gets involved with running these type festivals is beyond comprehension, and there you have it, our northern Midwest leg wasn't all bad."

Henry asked, "Was Hinterland taping, Tony?"

"They were."

"Video, too?"

"I saw cameras. That's what these 'outdoors' do, thinking they've got the next Woodstock movie."

"I suppose I better find out."

"No, Henry. Let Sallie know. He landed the contract. He'll represent us."

Mom finished up, saying, "Bottom line, troops: We're still

running low. Gas money remains our top priority, food second, overhead cover third."

"Gunny gave me some cash."

Gretchen's eyebrows flexed. "How much, Mel?"

"Three hundred."

"You've been hoarding Gunny's money this whole time? I'm gagging on dinners of soggy fast-food french fries while you hide a fat wallet? Minch, you Scrooge."

"Gunny said it was just-in-case money."

"Minch! We got food orders coming from Roz's kitchen we can hardly pay for. I'd call this a just-in-case moment, wouldn't you?"

"Gunny gave the money to me. You'd have blown it all before New York."

"And, with an empty gas tank, we'd be walking the blazing hot turnpike before you let on that you had it!"

"Miss Waste-It-Away Tarbeaux, the human slot machine!"

"Miser Minch!"

"Big spender."

"Packrat."

As I sat trying so hard not to laugh, I conjured up our hour-ago shower together, Gretchen caressing Melissa's shoulders, asking in earnest, "Are you okay?" A nod is followed by a double-check care, "You sure?" In truth, at Roz's, a warmth swept through me like no other. I singled out my parents. Their across-the-table knowing glances at one another, like a couple of kids playing hooky from school. Everyone's playful give-and-take at that breakfast shined like the aftermath of a show, a good show, that glow of having put on a live performance and coming through the fire, the adrenaline still flowing, the shared joy of feeling fully alive.

At that moment, I realized I loved them all so much. And I believe to this day, that at Roz's Cafe, for me, the true nature of love took root. As I grow older, I still ask myself: "This new person in my life ... do I feel the same now as I did at Roz's? Has that lightheaded warmth returned? Because, on that Dakota morning, there was no other place in the whole world I wanted to be, no other living souls in the whole world I'd wanted to be with, and, with the waiter's check in hand, a decision was made. There was a toast in Gunny's honor. The grande dame of Pickford bought breakfast.

chapter fifty-six

August 25, Boulder, Colorado: Tulagi's August 26, Sigma Phi Epsilon, University of Colorado August 26, Tulagi's August 28, Denver, Colorado: Mammoth Gardens August 29, Golden, Colorado: Buffalo Rose

"Mauri, pick up line two, it's Gretchen."

"Hotshot. Where are you?"

"Colorado. Rocking hard. Crazy stuff. A Greek frat party and a town club. Just like Madison, we pulled in more the second night. Pumped us up. We even got paid. I need a favor, Mr. Roseborough."

"Formal, she's asking. Now, I'm worried."

"Me too. Reach Sallie somehow and have Mr. Booking Agent set up an appointment for Melissa to see a doctor in LA. Her shoulder. She's hurting. Five shows in five days. At the last, she was drumming in tears."

"Call the whole thing off. You're all back home in a few days."

"I'm dealing with Minch here, Mr. Roseborough—the blond mule. She won't admit the pain. So, we yell at one another until we're hoarse and then we compromise. We play LA; she sees a doc."

"Celeste. What's Sallie looking for?"

"Shoulders. Bones. An orthopedist maybe. We'll find out."

"There you go, kid, done. What else?"

"If I hear one more, 'Get off the stage, bitch ... cunt ...' I swear. In my dreams, I'm at the microphone with a machine gun, and I let fly."

"Save the ammo. You're out front leading the pack, kid, but there will be hundreds and hundreds more just like you following right behind. Capisce? All the schleps you're facing now have a common future. They're about to get run over. Roadkill. They are nothing."

"I'm not brave, Mr. Roseborough, I get scared."

"Listen to me. The world's at an end. I get to choose one person to save me, I choose you."

Gretchen laughed.

"Do that more often. How's the rest?"

"Crammed in a van for a million miles; a little separation might help."

"Hey, kid. California. Walk the beach."

"Okay. I'll call in a few days to see if Sallie had any luck. Celeste?"

"Still here, sweetie."

"Sallie said he might make the LA gig. Give him a shove west, will ya?"

"Done, hon."

"And let Mr. Cross-country Booking Agent know that I'm going to strangle him when he shows."

"That's my girl."

"And thanks again for Comiskey, Mr. Chicago."

"Harry's still, 'How in heck do I follow that?' Balicki is already onstage with the ground crew at the Emmys bragging, 'Let me tell ya how we did it.'"

"Good guys, all of them. You guys, too. The best. See ya."

———

The Rise of The Mad March

The Rocky Mountain News
August 29, 1973 Thursday
Entertainment
Pro Zeller: reporter at the local

The Mad March at Mammoth Gardens
On this morning after, there's a gnawing sense that rock 'n' roll was born anew last night. The Mad March, a gender-busting foursome (three Eves and an Adam), let loose a dozen thrilling songs at the speed of sound in one quick half-hour opening set. A one-beer-and-gone band. Whew. Maybe that was enough. I do hold there is nothing wrong with reinven-tion. Rock thrives on burying its dead and seeking out yet another bunch of smart-mouth kids attempting to light a new fire. I'll end with this. They played one demented two-minute electrical blast last night detailing a rollover truck accident. Yup, pickup in the ditch at midnight in the dead of winter. Well ... hell. This is Denver, the Rocky Mountains—we can all relate to that.

chapter fifty-seven
August 31, Bakersfield, California: Mudd Jazz Lounge

For the Mad March/entourage, the Mudd Jazz gig loomed as a prelude to LA, a hoped-for all-positive run-through for the main event to follow—all systems perfected and synced for the big upcoming finale.

Setting up onstage there occurred an unexpected high. Take fashion. How do ideas and innovations take hold and travel? Supposedly lots of ways, to include a possible snapshot taken at Max's in New York City and sent from one cousin to another residing in Bakersfield. Christine nudged Gretchen onstage and said, "Check out those two. Wow." Gretchen followed Christine's gaze, turning wide-eyed, seeing two young women close by sporting wild-looking pixie cut spikes, pink and black, jutting every which way. Hair on fire. Christine smiled. "You're no longer alone, kiddo. Let's go say hi."

Good vibes flowing, halfway through "Beer Run," Christine's Harmony lost power. Tony knew right away an amp tube had blown. That he had a replacement, that he and Rigg tore into the amp onstage and made the switch was all a huge kudo—

but the gig never fully regained its mojo. The small crowd was lost.

Bakersfield, so sunlit at the get-go, now hovered like a dark omen. Philly déjà vu. Tony's admonition: "Happens to every band. If you haven't blown a tube, you've never rocked," failed to spell the gloom.

The Mad March was spooked. Rather than a joyful jaunt to Hollywood, the ride to LA felt like they were headed to the bowels of the La Brea tar pits—right where they belonged.

chapter fifty-eight

"Wes?"

"Hey, Henry. Good to hear from you. Where are you calling from?"

"Truckstop, California. Near the end. I want to give you a heads-up."

"Christine?"

"Yeah. Don't tell her I called you. She'll murder me."

"Problems?"

"Our last tour gig is on the 1st in LA. Find a flight on the 3rd or 4th. Fly her home."

"What's going on?"

"Probably nothing. She's just super tired. You're talking to a worrywart here."

"Would it help if we booked Melissa and Gretchen to accompany?"

"You'd do that?"

"Absolutely."

"Mr. Baird …"

"Lots of concern here, Henry."

"I just want to say, Mr. Baird, that Christine is exactly where she wants to be."

"We're still parents, Henry."
"Roger that. Book the flight."

jersey moon: tour interview #13

August 1973

Tyler: Am I going to regret this?

Jersey: Mom!

Tyler: Alright. Sock it to me.

Jersey: Why are Dad and Gretchen always sneaking off together?

Tyler: Ho boy. My kid ain't shy. If I tell you, Miss Tarbeaux will hand me my head.

Jersey: Join the club. She's been writing my obituary the entire trip.

Tyler: Okay. In keeping with Henry's Law Number One: *Nobody wanders out alone*. Your father is backup support. Whatever the city, if there's time, Gretchen seeks out the homeless. According to Rigg, she spots vulnerable young women two blocks away.

Jersey: She out hunting for Melissa Minch and Gretchen Tarbat?

Tyler: Exactly. Then she and your dad go track down a city commissioner, if such a so-and-so exists. Gretchen busts on in and shouts, "You got a problem, Denver," or whatever city we're in.

Jersey: Wow. But this is Gretchen, so I'm thinking Denver has an f-bomb problem.

Tyler: More than likely. Polite greetings are not Miss Tarbeaux's strong suit. So ... two things happen. Either they get tossed or the commish listens, joins forces, and together they hit the streets, talk to the young women in question to make sure they're made aware city assistance is available, that a safe, secure shelter exists, if in fact one does exist. They provide them location info and bus fare to get there. If the shelters are deemed a risk, they talk about the reasons why. Got time for a story?

Jersey: Sure.

Tyler: In Minneapolis, they got tossed. As they're leaving, a secretarial assistant, overhearing, barges in and says, "that was the Mad March, boss, you better listen to her."

Jersey: No way!

Tyler: Yes way. Turns out the health and human services gal was at the previous night's show. Bless her. Far as I know, the twin city commissioner and Gretchen are still talking, exchanging problems and possible solutions.

Jersey: Unbelievable. Well ... Gretchen, maybe not so much.

Tyler: Please, hon, don't say a word to her. Are we finished here?

Jersey: Not quite. There exists the obvious. How does a conventional, sorta square, reserved wife and mother of one, drop all pretense and go coast-to-coast slugging it out with barbarian rock 'n' roll club owners?

Tyler: One, I resent the implications. Two, I once beat up my two odious brothers in a mud fight. Three, Rigg would never chase after and propose to a weenie roast and four, my drama-queen daughter would have died a thousand deaths if I'd chickened out and stayed home.

Jersey: Weenie roast?

Tyler: Wimp. We're done?

Jersey: If only, Mrs. Moon. One final. Brace yourself. There is a wild rumor spreading that you recently slept with Melissa and Gretchen.

Tyler: You are the world's worst daughter.

Jersey: The French call it a ménage à trois.

Tyler: The worst. Having a child is a choice, Jersey, remember that.

Jersey: I'm not the one turning pink.

Tyler: Can I ask you something?

Jersey: Sure.

Tyler: Am I a good mom?

Jersey: I wouldn't trade you for Ernie Banks in his prime. But sex and rock 'n' roll, Mom—changing the subject won't save you.

Tyler: A spreading rumor? Really?

Jersey: Where was Dad?

Tyler: Right next to me.

Jersey (for a moment – speechless): Oh man, this is getting so good.

Tyler: Golden, Colorado, Jersey. The Rockies. That last-minute off-day bar gig at the Buffalo Rose. The packed house and all that wild pogo dancing up front. Remember? Hours after the show, a chilly night, very late, and the two invaders snuck in, like straight from the Coors Brewery, and crawled into our bed. Two giggling young women, neither lacking in the alluring department, are piling in on Rigg. I'm thinking … what now? Then … holy groupie, talk about a misread.

Jersey: They were after the hot road manager.

Tyler: I had two warm bodies snuggled next to me, one on each side. And, how shall I put this? They proved a comfort. I was well-kept, all night long.

Jersey: All those roving fingertips and lips.

Tyler: Snuggled, Miss Jersey.

Jersey: Okay. And where, pray tell, was your car mechanic through all this?

Tyler: Lightly snoring. Obviously faking it.
Jersey: So, I'm left to my own imagination?
Tyler: Dear God, what have I raised?
Jersey: I'm fourteen, and I adore my parents. What's wrong with me?

chapter fifty-nine

September 1, Los Angeles: Roxy Theater

During the setup onstage, the crowd began pointing, acknowledging the female roadies. Now those roadies sat behind drums and shouldered guitars. The Roxy collectively raised an eyebrow and quieted.

Gretchen lowered the center microphone to address the crowd. This was a first. Henry glanced at Christine with an inquisitive head tilt. She tilted the same.

Melissa sensed an intrigued packed house full of anticipation. Given everyone was blown away by the also-newcomer solo act, Tom Waits, who opened, maybe they *did* need to say something.

"Our first gig in LA and rock on, we have to follow a freaking genius."

There were hoots, a smattering of applause.

"So ... we're a loser band from nowhere. I'm a total pain in the ass, our boss man is on rhythm, a shy blond holy terror is behind the drums, and the braided redhaired Viking on lead really is Mott the Hoople's Mick Ralphs dressed in drag."

Christine broke into a wide smile, laughing. The crowd joined in. Gretchen raised the mike and shouted, "Believe it or not, we recently played this before nineteen thousand fans. Count us down, Minch."

"Three, two, go!"

A perfect set? Not quite, but given Tarbeaux's playful intro, the snafus in Bakersfield were shaken off and laid to rest. Nearly every song got a best-on-tour play. "Beer Run" was a frightening juggernaut. "Funeral" drew laughs. "Bone Pile" left a mark. Forging a recent on-the-road, in-the-van compromise, they played "Bloomingdale's" for the first-time adagio-verse, allegro-chorus. The dialed-down then revved-up tempo changes reinvented the song. Sly, knowing inter-band "Green River" smiles greeted the finish.

Eyeing one another, they felt tight. They were locked in. Christine took chances. Henry, Melissa and Gretchen shadowed and supported her every improv adventure.

Near the finish, Melissa stood center stage, as she had on occasion when the vibe felt right, unmasking abuse: "It's out there, it's real, people. Enough! Scream it. Enough! Look at me. No one should live in fear."

The Roxy was packed. You could hear a pin drop; the opening, growling "Shovelhead" chords followed.

The crowd stayed with them till the end.

"We're gonna finish the show with a new song; probably be a train wreck and fit right in. Stay cool, LA."

"Three, two, go!"

The insanely fast self-salute, "Rock 'n' Roll Pearls," closed their night.

Sal Tuchinardi, standing at the back, taking in the set, was stunned at how far they'd come. His intuition and belief were being played out at the Roxy. Along with others in the crowd, shouting the last song's repeated title refrain along with Christine and Gretchen, he raised his right arm in tribute. He'd been right—right from the start, and despite the usual on-the-road pitfalls, there were times that Lady Luck herself had been riding on the bus. They'd gotten ink at three stops, gig reviews that centered on *rock reinvention, a clarion call, an adrenaline shot.* Then the two shots of pure-gold happenstance, the gifts that are only bestowed when you're out on the highway mixing it up and tempting fate: their own Chicago (seventh inning) Fire at Old Comiskey Park and the Dakota "Taps" Girl. Were they just good fortune? No – they were something more.

As the Roxy set played out and the stage cleared for the next act, Sal had his ear tuned to the milling crowd. One passing exchange caught his attention.

"They looked desperate. They played desperate. I loved that."

"Hah, Ex, just like us, and we'd better get used to it."

Sal smiled. He liked that and thought, *Desperate is good, kids, practically a requirement.*

Priorities for the band took shape: a Viking label signing, studio recording time, financial support. Much to do because … there was a train coming. Oh, maybe some other big city bands might engineer the way, but the Mad March, his Mad March, was right up-front. Sal sensed a band breaking out, a "rise." They'd been rising all along—and there was nothing like the thrill of the rise.

chapter sixty
September 2

"Melissa insisted that all of you be here for her prognosis consultation. Unusual, but I've allowed her request. Small office. Sorry that some of you are left standing. I'm Dr. Thomas March."

"No freaking way."

"I ask not to be interrupted, young lady. Now then, we've looked at the X-rays, and Melissa has detailed to me the rollover truck accident a year and a half ago that left her pinned in the aftermath."

Henry was struck, his mind calculating, *Have only some twenty months gone by? Is that even possible?*

"Hospitalized, her fractured collarbone was repaired and reset, as was the proximal humerus fracture in her upper right arm. She was treated for torn muscle and tendon damage in and around the right shoulder socket. Given prescribed rehab and rest, she was able to eventually resume normal activities.

"Today's X-rays show that Melissa has developed a chronic arthritic condition in the injured shoulder. She is dealing with latent bone spurs, inflammation, and, from my view, a concerned narrowing of her shoulder joint rotation. This has led and, without care, will continue to lead to a reduced range in motion, swelling around the joint and burning pain."

The quiet in the room was numbing. Tony spoke up. "How much layoff time until she's 100 percent?"

"A possible lifetime, sir. As an orthopedic surgeon, I apologize for my profession, but arthritis remains an incurable condition, perhaps worsening with time. Right now, Melissa requires treatment to fight inflammation and infection."

"Tyler Moon here, Doctor. I thought arthritis was mostly an old-age condition."

"Arthritic conditions vary, Tyler, different beasts of burden. Past the age of fifty, an erosion of joint cartilage is common. But Melissa's shoulder trauma to bone and tissue plus her drumming have set off a rheumatic internal crisis that we are addressing this very day. IA— inflammatory arthritis—healthy blood cells under attack ... serious business. Pain ... serious business."

"Is she gonna get better?"

"You are?"

"Gretchen."

"To answer your question, Gretchen, yes ... providing." March turned to his patient. "You're twenty, Melissa. You've a long life in front of you. Opportunities. You might become an airline pilot, the mayor of an American city, the queen of Wall Street, a teacher."

"She might become a clown in the circus."

"You are absolutely right, Gretchen, she might become a clown in the circus, but let's make her a ringmaster."

"I'm already a clown in a circus."

Hearing Melissa's first words, the crowded office, worry and stress building, exploded in laughter.

Dr. March waited, then said, "I'm concerned, too, with nerve damage. Given a traumatic event such as the rollover, minute nerve stretching and/or compression may be an issue. You'll require a specialist. I might go on here with neurology and/or electromyography, but my point is this. Being young, you've all kinds of choices, Melissa, all but one. You should not and must not drum for the Mad March. Look at me, Miss Minch. It's over."

Throughout the office, heads found a shoulder to lean on.

"You can solicit additional medical opinions. They will look at pictures and underscore my findings. You can say 'to hell with it,' and keep on with the band. You can fight the pain with ever-increasing doses of pain pills, synthetics and steroids … and you will wind up, before you're thirty, with a withered arm, disabled, perhaps for the remainder of your life." March's voice rose. "Listen to me carefully. Treatment now will improve your long-term outcome. Don't become a mom who can't toss a ball with her kid. Heed me, Melissa, the rock 'n' roll drumming is over."

The doctor's office appeared to be posing for a still life painting, as if da Vinci himself had shouted, *"Non muoverti! Don't even breathe."* At long last, Melissa stood and walked directly to Sal, standing in the corner. Sobbing, she fell into his arms. "I'm sorry to let you down, Mr. Tuchinardi, I'm so sorry."

chapter sixty-one

September 2, Los Angeles: Roxy Theater

Henry tapped his microphone, checking the connection. A wisp of feedback melted into the crowd. The room quieted.

"I want to thank the good Captain and the Magic Band for allowing us the use of their keyboard. Thanks, too, to the Roxy for okaying this encore. We're the Mad March. We're closing the show tonight. We played on this very stage last night. That gig was supposed to end our summer tour. Turns out we had one more song to sing."

It was late, and a number of patrons had already drifted out into the mild California night. Taking a moment, Henry looked out on what was still a good crowd. "That's what so important in our lives, isn't it? That each and every one of us have one more song to sing. So, one more for the band with Gretchen on bass, Melissa on drums, Christine on lead and Henry here on the ivories; an old Neil Young tune, one we once played not so long ago."

Tyler stood at the back, an arm interlocked with Tony. "Tell me somebody is taping this."

"Somebody is taping this."

Henry sat at the piano and stared. He simply couldn't take

his eyes off her. She still wore the scruffy leather boots she'd found in that hip clothing boutique in New York City. She still slung the bass. But the dress—wow. Soft cotton, orange with white dots, sleeveless, generously v-necked front and back, wide shoulder straps and the sweeping skirt gathered at the waist with a sash tied at the side. Holy Bloomingdale's, Tarbeaux looked completely out of place and completely perfect.

Gretchen made for Henry and whispered, "Let me take the vocal, boss."

Henry gave a thumbs-up. "That would be awesome, just like the dress."

"Don't start, Hollins."

He did just that. Aware his live mike, Henry stood for attention, pointed, and said, "Could we get some Roxy feedback with regards to the bass player's ensemble this evening?"

Wolf whistles poured from the crowd.

Gretchen felt herself turning the dress color. Fist-shaking at Henry, she then stood center stage, bass slung to her side, hand on her hip and deadpanned a centerfold pose. The whistling and clapping grew. Henry thought, *Holy Cosmo, someone snap a picture. Five minutes ago—she's an unknown, now she's got the whole crowd in her pocket. Where have I seen this before? Oh yeah ... the whole freaking tour.*

Henry grinned back at Melissa and shouted, "Where's your cardboard box and wooden spoon?"

She grinned back, "Three ... two ... go."

They began with a short solo keyboard opening. The singer's plaintive, raspy, sexy contralto began, and the whole band kicked in. Henry played by rote, his eyes locked into Gretchen, then Melissa, then Christine, then back and forth; his thoughts flying back to a dayroom at a halfway house in Liberty, Iowa, as Gret sang:

Robert Espenscheid, Jr.

> When you were young and on your own,
> How did it feel to be alone?
> I was always thinking of games that I was
>   playing,
> Trying to make the best of my time ...

part three

Snapshots and Postcards

september 1973

Los Angeles, California
Melissa: "I can be replaced."
Henry: "No, you can't."

Chicago, Illinois
Celeste: "Gretchen just called, Mauri. She's in a state, blaming herself. The stolen pickup, the rollover ... all her fault."

Henry Ford Hospital, Detroit, Michigan
"White cell blood counts and chest X-rays have confirmed a cancer, Christine. I'm scheduling immediate treatment."

december 1973

Austin, Texas

"How ya doin', kid?"

"I'm fine, Sallie. A remission thing. Getting better every day."

"That's good, because I've got a duo down here, a couple of cowboys from Texas who've got everything but a lead guitarist."

"Are they cute?"

february 1974

Des Moines, Iowa

"… and I'm pregnant, Henry. Mark and I are over the moon."

"I'm truly happy for you, Esther. I'm honored you called."

"I've heard some. I wanted to say how sorry I am for everyone. I'm sure you're hurting. You stay in touch, okay?"

"You bet."

april 1974

Bon Secours Medical Center, Grosse Pointe, Michigan
"There are no one-all treatments for grief and broken hearts, Wes. I wish there were. I'm prescribing Marion a sedative. Keep a close eye."

Chicago
Celeste: "I told Gretchen on the phone. Come stay with us awhile."
Maurice: "Christine, the polite shy one, a little coy, right? The sweet smile. I'm thinking, she's much too good a person for this backstabbing, ego-inflating, drug-infested business. Then she's onstage, the red hair, the firecracker."

Liberty, Iowa
Tyler: "Where are the words to comfort? How do I explain to a heartbroken fourteen-year-old the unexplainable?"
Rigg: "Tony called. Pickford's a morgue."

june 1974

Anna Maria Island, Florida

Sal: "I was cold. I drove south. I walked a beach. I sat at a bar on the beach. Pretty soon, I worked at the bar on the beach."

Pickford

"Well sir, at long last. Henry, it's Helen Slade. The Steinway requires your attention. Where have you been? I've been calling."

"Did you ever have a dream so real, Helen, that you can no longer separate the real from the surreal? And if the dream was truly just a dream, that's a good thing, right? Because dreams aren't real, and Christine is still alive and well."

"Are you alright, Henry?"

july 1974

KCCI-TV, Des Moines Iowa

Hey, all you early risers ... happy Independence Day. Both the east and west mixmasters are reporting that incoming 235 city traffic is light. Let's get right to the weather. Sunrise is due this morning at 6:48 a.m. ...

august 1974

Grosse Pointe, Michigan
Wes: "Marion. Rise and shine. I've an idea."

march 1978

SST Records, Long Beach, California

"Hey Tony, Mike Zeybel from SST. We got the Mad March live tapes you sent. We're pumped. Come on out to see us. Bring whatever else you've got. Let's talk. Hey partner, don't forget your sun lotion."

june 1978

Wayne State University, Detroit, Michigan

"I'm privileged to stand here today to honor and confer the following graduates ... summa cum laude ... magna cum laude, Melissa Minch, bachelor of science in biochemistry."

Chicago, Illinois

Maurice: "When? And I don't get an invitation? What am I, the designated hitter, everybody hates me?"

Sal: "They meet up in a bar. She puts eight stitches in his head. Now happily ever after. Go figure."

Pickford

Melissa: "You open it. Sweaty fingers here."

Dorothy: "I'm an old heart, young lady, and let me find my glasses. Okay now, I'm set. Let's see ... On behalf of the president and trustees ... *Oh my* ... I am delighted to inform you of your admission to the University of Iowa's Carver College of Medicine, class of ..."

december 1979

Grosse Pointe, Michigan

"What are you showing me here?"

"The society section from today's *Free Press*, Wes. Pictures taken at the Holiday Formal. That's Marion, our sponsor no less ... wearing a T-shirt. 'Mad March' something. Gracious sakes. The *Formal,* Wes! Everyone else was dressed to the nines in gowns. Is she alright?"

Wes (looking closely): "She looks good."

april 1980

Liberty, Iowa

The Chronicle: Longtime resident Cecil Sidel passed in his sleep at age 85.

At the memorial service held at the RLDS church, following former Sheriff Marion Buckpool's tribute, Gretchen, accompanying herself on guitar, sings "Cecil's Beer Run" in a slow, bluesy, folky arrangement that leaves Melissa in tears and Henry in awe.

may 1980

Iowa City Press-Citizen

The mayor announced yesterday the launch of a new direction to assist the city's homeless to include adding experienced personnel and a new outreach van, commissioned to. ...

june 1981

Los Angeles Times
Punk Rock Celebrates 5 Chaotic Years
Not a soothing headline for a host of music lovers, but to the initiated, a tribute to the blasts of mayhem that began back in 1976-77 introducing The Ramones, The Sex Pistols, CBGBs, Patti Smith, The Clash and a long list of other notables to include LA's X, who's recently released "Wild Gift" has garnered rave reviews nationwide. For five years now, punk music has raged with one voice: *We got something to say, we're here to stay* ...

july 1982

Port Huron, New York

Huron's Community Art Festival headlines Arlo Guthrie with supporting bands: The Underhill Society, Zini, G2, and Crooked Creek. Performances for the all-ages show begin on the fairgrounds stage at 4 p.m.

chapter sixty-two
October 1982

"Parker, back off. What's got into you? Make way you old hound, let me at least get to the door."

"Hi."

Henry stood starstruck. "You still look sixteen."

"Stay right where you are, Hollins. I have something to say, and I need space."

"Yes, ma'am. Holding in place as ordered. What do you think, Park, do we need Dorothy's opinion? Maybe seventeen."

"How's Gunny?"

"Slowed, fine, and you should know. I read your letters."

Melissa bent low, greeting Parker. "And what are you, a hundred now? You look like an old T-Rex. Okay, let me deal with this guy first."

"He is a hundred, Mel. He's also overwhelmed, and he's not alone."

"No more greets. Important stuff, Hollins."

"Not a smidge over eighteen. All ears."

"I'm practically twenty=four hours on at the university hospital. Insane hours. Insane schedule. My residency. I was warned. I should be way blotto by now. I'm not. I've pretty much loved every minute. And you know what, Mr. Hollins?

"What, Miss Minch?"

"I'm good at it."

"If you can drum, you can …"

"The Bairds gifted me Christine's trust. Incredible. A chance to track down those fucking cancer sleeper cells that shot down a shooting star and ended the most beautiful life I've ever known. And I'm going to do the tracking. I'm obsessed. Years have passed, Henry. You won't recognize the girl in front of you."

"But I do."

"I accepted the gift. I filed you away and now … I'm here with a problem."

"Still holding."

"I'm also twenty-four hours off and I don't have a warm bed with a warm body to crawl into and next to."

"This is a situation, Minch, not a problem."

"Given my residency, I won't be around Pickford much, but my stint at Iowa City won't last forever."

"Not like us."

"The drummer in me won't let go, boss man. I can't believe I'm crying. What a wuss. And there will be lonesome nights. All you're going to dream about are pianos."

"All those keys."

Melissa laughed. With the sheepish look on his wonderful face, her reservations of time passed gave way to a growing warmth.

"Don't forget, we *do* have a chapter one, Miss Minch."

"What's that, Mr. Hollins?"

"The Sanity Soundcheck, our Vegas rehearsal."

Henry's grin proved infectious.

Melissa was a messy happy face. "And I'm holding a rain check—anytime, anyplace."

"I truly hope so, Mel."

They were acting both goofy and heartfelt—and the two fit so well together. Henry. This dream-laden knight errant from

King Arthur's Square Table who led them all on a quest that made little sense while somehow making all the sense in the world. Right from the start, she'd never let on to anyone, basically because it was *so cliché, so dumb*. But she was never able to shake the knowing. And now, there it was, right in front of her. Even with all the years gone past—being with Henry drummed a heartbeat within her like no other.

He laughed. The two of them giddy. "We'll make this work, Doctor."

Embraced, holding onto him with all her might, Parker snuggling in, she managed, "Don't forget … I'm obsessed."

"Oh, yeah."

interview (abridged) with lita ford

Creem Magazine: June 1983

By May Chen – contributing editor

May: Hi Lita. Creem says thanks for this.
 Lita: Crazy mag.
 May: Taking that as a compliment.
 Lita: Meant to be.
 May: Big-time solo artist now. The new album. Moving up the charts. Good for you.
 Lita: Woo, woo.
 May: Can we start with the Runaways?
 Lita: Most do.
 May: Prepping for our get-together, I read through troves of Runaway copy: commentary, reviews, newspaper and magazine articles. I found very few, if any, centered on Lita Ford.
 Lita: Lost in the woodwork.
 May: You were in that band, right?
 Lita: I still have the scars.
 May: You were the goddamn lead guitar player, Lita.
 Lita: Goddamn right, May.
 May: It's like Hollywood making a Runaways movie and you're not in it.

Lita: Hah! Left on the cutting-room floor. Maybe Joan does the film editing.

May: Ba-boom. Oh, this is going to be such catty fun.

Lita: I'm just teasing, May. And Hollywood calling? I'm too horsey-faced.

May: You are a gorgeous musician who began at the top. 1975. The Runaways hit the stage and bada-bing, you're a hot ticket in California, mobbed by thousands of fans in Japan.

Lita: All true.

May: Then "swoosh," the rug is pulled, the band quits and splits, and you're tossed into rock 'n' roll quicksand.

Lita: 1979, four years ago, and I don't have a bulge between my legs.

May: How did you cope?

Lita: Not very well. Depression's a bitch.

May: I'm sure, but the legacy, Lita—you mothered a sea of six-string sisters that followed.

Lita: You are way over the top, May, but I thank you for that and hey, you got time for a story where my own life-resolve first took root?

May: There is no cutting-room floor for the Queen of Metal at Creem Magazine.

Lita: I was fifteen, 1973, growing up in Long Beach, and me and my friend Robyn got a ride to LA to see Deep Purple. The band's lead guitar was such a fave. And we were so bad. Weather moved in, the stadium show is nowhere, and we ended up backdooring into the Roxy Theater. Robyn and I were so good at weaseling into clubs. What a rush. Inside, some band takes the stage. Three girls and a guy. I'm like, "holy shit." They played a killer set, and wow, my life was signed and sealed.

May: Details, amiga.

Lita: Christine Baird played lead. My eyes never left her. I was watching my future self. I've never felt a clearer path … like she was shouting at me, "You can do this."

And ... hearing and seeing the set wasn't enough. As the final group was setting up, Robyn held our place while I slipped backstage, a dressing room, and found Christine sitting, cooling down in a corner, by herself. A moment we all live for, right? And like with bull's balls, I just barged in, a total jabbering idiot, telling her about my Gibson, practicing every day, my dreams. I expected her to call security, "Get this fucking kid out of my face." But no, she finally gets a word in edgewise. Guess what she says.

May: Tell me.

Lita: Christine goes, "You up for a beer?"

May: My kind of babe.

Lita: We drank. We talked. I can't recall the specifics. I was so in awe, you know, that she would take the time. What I *do* recall is how serene she looked, like here was someone exactly where she was supposed to be and goddamn, I'm sitting there thinking someday I want to strap her guitar and capture her vibe. You dig?

May: Very cool.

Lita: There were lots of dark times after the Runaways flamed out. But, whenever the rock 'n' roll storms wash over me, I get back to that dressing room, that moment ... Christine's serenity. I calm. I'm where I want to be. I'm living my dream. I won't quit what I've fought for.

May: Name of Christine's band?

Lita: I was fifteen-years-old "stupid." We never crossed paths again. But, over the years, I'd recounted this magic-moment Roxy story to bandmates and close friends. Then around 1981, Joan called out of the blue and told me she'd recently played a gig at a motorcycle rally in the Dakotas and had read some promo that paid tribute to Christine Baird of the Mad March, the famous Dakota "Taps" girl, who had died of breast cancer years ago. Back then, May, I'd been struck dumb over my own non-existent career. Now Joan's on the line

Robert Espenscheid, Jr.

about Christine and I'm holding the phone, turning to jelly. I bawled my eyes out.

May: There are times that our lives get ripped, Lita.

Lita: Goddamn, May ... I've still got that beer can.

chapter sixty-three
November 1983

"What is this? A friendship? Celeste and I have been checking the Trib obits for months."

"Maurice, I've called."

"So does my tax lawyer. You with NASA now, on the moon all this time? Celeste, bring the glasses. Is it too early?"

"I've got a duo, Maurice."

"He never stops. My pills. Celeste?"

"What am I, Mauri, a candy striper?"

"I got a good feeling about these two. My ears. You know all about my twitchy ears, Maurice."

"That doesn't help my heart. Your new superstars got a name?"

"G2."

"Sounds like a mountain. Wait …"

Sal smiled. "You take a gnarly biker … add an unstable bass player … whaddaya got?"

"Attila's back? Celeste, pour a splash for all of us. What am I listening to here?"

"Quoting Gretchen: 'Take a noisy racket, add a little romance.' "

Maurice was pointing a finger first to Sal then himself.

"You let her know from me, I shoulda been best man. Celeste, when's Johnny returning? Where's the lineup?"

"Thirty years in show business, Mauri. When does 'organized' kick in? Stop looking, I got mine. What have we got? Let's see. Chicago's Crown Theater is proud to present John Prine in concert on Friday, November 12 at 8 p.m."

"We'll open." Sal was on his feet. "Give us twenty minutes."

acknowledgments

First and foremost, to Stoney Creek Publishing for their acceptance and support, especially Frank Smith for his editing excellence.

Second, to the musicians. So much fun interviewing everyone and drawing out all the backstage, onstage, on-the-road stories: Dan Keegan, guitar (Underhill Society), Dan Fisherman, drums (Mommyheads), Andy Espenscheid, guitar (Tan Mal), Emily Kaitz, guitar, bass (Crooked Creek), Rick Hoyt, guitar (The Cool Club).

Also to the Smithville Writers Club: Karen Derr, Sheri Godwin, Lissa Johnston, and Patty Reid, whose goodhearted biweekly critiques (not to mention the eye rolling) kept the manuscript in bounds on the playing field.

So many thanks to Emily Kaitz for the fun illustration and the early editing. Same to Ivy Espenscheid for the cool Band tee. Lastly to Adrienne Smith for the fantastic cover art.

about the author

At 79, I'm winding down, getting old. I've literally "rocked around the clock." Born in '45, I've been with rock 'n' roll from the very beginning. Lucky me—and I can still recall my intro back in 1956 hearing Guy Mitchell's "Singing the Blues" on the radio in the backseat of my mom's car (might have been her Studebaker Packard) ... and I'm glad I made the effort to write about the music I've dug my whole life. Writing *The Rise of the Mad March* was a labor of love. I hope readers feel the same.

Robert Espenscheid, Jr. The author makes his home in Smithville, Texas. Visit Rob and his books at www.firejacker.net

Looking for your next book?
We publish the stories you've been waiting to read!

Scan the QR code below to get 20% off your next Stoney Creek title!

For author book signings, speaking engagements, or other events, please contact us at info@stoneycreekpublishing.com

StoneyCreekPublishing.com